The Golden Butterfly

The Golden Butterfly

Walter Besant and James Rice

MINT EDITIONS

The Golden Butterfly was first published in 1876.

This edition published by Mint Editions 2021.

ISBN 9781513290959 | E-ISBN 9781513293806

Published by Mint Editions®

 MINT
EDITIONS

minteditionbooks.com

Publishing Director: Jennifer Newens
Design & Production: Rachel Lopez Metzger
Project Manager: Micaela Clark
Typesetting: Westchester Publishing Services

Contents

PREFACE

The Golden Butterfly, which gives a name to this novel, was seen by an English traveller, two years ago, preserved as a curiosity in a mining city near Sacramento, where it probably still remains. This curious freak of Nature is not therefore an invention of our own. To the same traveller—Mr. Edgar Besant—we are indebted for the description on which is based our account of Empire City.

The striking of oil in Canada in the manner described by Gilead P. Beck was accomplished—with the waste of millions of gallons of the oil, for want of casks and buckets to receive it, and with the result of a promise of almost boundless wealth—by a man named Shaw, some ten years ago. Shaw speculated, we believe; lost his money, and died in poverty.

Names of great living poets and writers have been used in this book in connection with a supposed literary banquet. A critic has expressed surprise that we have allowed Gilead Beck's failure to appreciate Browning to stand as if it were our own. Is a writer of fiction to stop the action of his story in order to explain that it is his character's opinion and not his own, that he states? And it surely is not asking too much to demand of a critic that he should consider first of all the consistency of a character's actions or speeches. Gilead Beck, a man of no education and little reading, but of considerable shrewdness, finds Browning unintelligible and harsh. What other verdict could be expected if the whole of Empire City in its palmiest days had been canvassed?

Moreover, we have never, even from that great writer's most ardent admirers, heard an opinion that he is either easy to read, or musical. The compliments which Mr. Beck paid to the guests who honoured his banquet are of course worded just as he delivered them.

Gilead Beck's experiences as an editor are taken—with a little dressing—from the actual experiences of a living Canadian journalist.

From their Virginian home Jack Dunquerque and Phillis his wife send greetings to those who have already followed their fortunes. She only wishes us to add that Mr. Abraham Dyson was right, and that the Coping Stone of every woman's education is Love. Most people know this, she says, from reading: but she never did read; and the real happiness is to find it out for yourself.

W. B.
J. R.

March, 1877

Prologue

I

"WHAT DO YOU THINK, CHIEF?"

The speaker, who was leading by a half a length, turned in his saddle and looked at his companion.

"Push on," growled the chief, who was a man of few words.

"If you were not so intolerably conceited about the value of your words—hang it, man, you are not the Poet Laureate!—you might give your reasons why we should not camp where we are. The sun will be down in two hours; the way is long, the wind is cold, or will be soon. This pilgrim has tightened his belt to stave off the gnawing at his stomach; here is running water, here is wood, here is everything calculated to charm the poetic mind even of Captain Ladds—"

"Road!" interrupted his fellow-traveller, pointing along the track marked more by deep old wheel-ruts, grown over with grass, than by any evidences of engineering skill. "Roads lead to places; places have beds; beds are warmer than grass—no rattlesnakes in beds; miners in hotels—amusing fellows, miners."

"If ever I go out again after buffaloes, or bear, or mountain-deer, or any other game whatever which this great continent offers, with a monosyllabic man, may I be condemned to another two months of buffalo steak without Worcester sauce, such as I have had already; may I be poisoned with bad Bourbon whisky; may I never again see the sweet shady side of Pall Mall; may I—"

Here he stopped suddenly, for want of imagination to complete the curse.

The first speaker was a young man of four and twenty—the age which is to my sex what eighteen is to the other, because at four and twenty youth and manhood meet. He of four and twenty is yet a youth, inasmuch as women are still angels; every dinner is a feast, every man of higher rank is a demigod, and every book is true. He is a man, inasmuch as he has the firm step of manhood, he has passed through his calf-love, he knows what claret means, and his heart is set upon the things for which boys care nothing. He is a youth, because he can still play a game of football and rejoice amazingly in a boat-race; he is a man, because he knows that these things belong to the past, and that to concern one's self seriously with athletics, when you can no longer be an athlete in the games, is to put yourself on the level of a rowing coach or the athletic critic of a sporting paper.

Being only four and twenty, the speaker was in high spirits. He was also hungry. He was always both. What has life better to offer than a continual flow of animal spirits and a perpetual appetite? He was a tall, slight, and perhaps rather a weedy youth, a little too long of leg, a little too narrow in the beam, a little spare about the shoulders; but a youth of a ruddy and a cheerful countenance. To say that the lines of his face were never set to gravity would be too much, because I defy any man to laugh when he is sleeping, eating, or drinking. At all other times this young man was ready to laugh without stopping. Not a foolish cackle of idiotic vacuity such as may be heard in Earlswood asylum or at a tea-party to meet the curate, but a cheerful bubble of mirth and good-humour, proof that the spirit within took everything joyously, seeing in every misadventure its humorous side, and in every privation its absurdity.

The other who rode beside him was some years older at least. A man of thirty-five, or perhaps more; a man with a hatchet-face—nose and forehead in one straight line; long chin and long upper lip in another; face red with health as well as bronzed with the sun—a good honest face, supernaturally grave, grave beyond all understanding; lips that were always tightly closed; eyes which sometimes sparkled in response to some genial thought, or bubbled over at some joke of his companion, but which, as a rule, were like gimlets for sternness, so that strangers, especially stranger servants—the nigger of Jamaica, the guileless Hindoo of his Indian station, and other members of the inferior human brotherhood—trembled exceedingly when they met those eyes. Captain Ladds was accordingly well served, as cold, reserved men generally are. Mankind takes everything unknown *pro terribili*, for something dreadful, and until we learn to know a man, and think we know him, he is to be treated with the respect due to a possible enemy. *Hostis* means a stranger, and it is for strangers that we keep our brickbats.

People who knew Ladds laughed at this reputation. They said the gallant captain was a humbug; they pretended that he was as gentle as a turtle-dove; beneath those keen eyes, they said, and behind that sharp hatchet-face, lurked the most amiable of dispositions. At any rate, Ladds was never known to thrash a native servant, or to swear more than is becoming and needful at a syce, while his hatchet-face had been more than once detected in the very act of looking as soft and tender as a young mother's over her first-born. The name of this cavalier was short and simple. It was Thomas Ladds. His intimate friends called him Tommy.

They were in California, and were not buffalo-hunting now, because there is not a buffalo within five hundred miles of Sacramento. Their buffalo-hunting was over, having been accompanied by such small hardships as have been already alluded to. They rode along a track which was as much like a road as Richmond Park is like the Forest of Arden. They were mounted on a pair of small nervous mustangs; their saddles were the Mexican saddles used in the country, in front of which was the never-failing horn. Round this was wound the horsehair lariat, which serves the Western Nimrod for lassoing by day, and for keeping off snakes at night, no snake having ever been known to cross this barrier of bristly horsehair. You might as well expect a burgling coolie, smeared with oil, and naked, to effect his escape by crawling through a hedge of prickly pear. Also, because they were in a foreign land, and wished to be in harmony with its institutions, they wore immense steel spurs, inlaid with silver filigree, and furnished with "lobs" attached to them, which jangled and danced to make melody, just as if they formed part of an illustration to a Christmas book. Boots of course, they wore, and the artistic instinct which, a year before, had converted the younger man into a thing of beauty and a joy for the whole Park in the afternoon, now impelled him to assume a *cummerbund* of scarlet silk, with white-tasselled fringes, the like of which, perhaps, had never before been seen on the back of a Californian mustang. His companion was less ornate in his personal appearance. Both men carried guns, and if a search had been made, a revolver would have been found either hidden in the belt of each or carried *perdu* in the trousers-pocket. In these days of Pacific Railways and scampering Globe Trotters, one does not want to parade the revolver; but there are dark places on the earth, from the traveller's as well as from the missionary's point of view, where it would be well to have both bowie and Derringer ready to hand. On the American continent the wandering lamb sometimes has to lie down with the leopard, the harmless gazelle to journey side by side with the cheetah, and the asp may here and there pretend to play innocently over the hole of the cockatrice.

Behind the leaders followed a little troop of three, consisting of one English servant and two "greasers." The latter were dressed in plain unpretending costume of flannel shirt, boots, and rough trousers. Behind each hung his rifle. The English servant was dressed like his master, but more so, his spurs being heavier, the pattern of his check-shirt being larger, his saddle bigger; only for the silk cummerbund he wore a leather strap, the last symbol of the honourable condition of dependence. He rode in advance of the greasers, whom he held in contempt, and some thirty yards behind the leaders. The Mexicans rode in silence; smoking cigarettes perpetually. Sometimes they looked to their guns, or they told a story, or one would sing a snatch of a song in a low voice; mostly they were grave and thoughtful, though what a greaser thinks about has never yet been ascertained.

The country was so far in the Far West that the Sierra Nevada lay to the east. It was a rich and beautiful country: there were park-like tracts—supposing the park to be of a primitive and early settlement-kind—stretching out to the left. These were dotted with white oaks. To the right rose the sloping sides of a hill, which were covered with the brush-wood called the chaparelle, in which grew the manzanita and the scrub-oak, with an occasional cedar pine, not in the least like the cedars of Lebanon and Clapham Common. Hanging about in the jungle or stretching its arms along the side of the dry water course which ran at the traveller's feet beside the road was the wild vine loaded with its small and pretty grapes now ripe. Nature, in inventing the wild grape, has been as generous as in her gift of the sloe. It is a fruit of which an American once observed that it was calculated to develop the generosity of a man's nature, "because," he explained, "you would rather give it to your neighbour than eat it yourself."

The travellers were low down on the western slopes of the Sierra; they were in the midst of dales and glades—cañons and gulches, of perfect loveliness, shut in by mountains which rose over and behind them like friendly giants guarding a troop of sleeping maidens. Pelion was piled on Ossa as peak after peak rose higher, all clad with pine and cedar, receding farther and farther, till peaks became points, and ridges became sharp edges.

It was autumn, and there were dry beds, which had in the spring been rivulets flowing full and clear from the snowy sides of the higher slopes; yet among them lingered the flowers of April upon the shrubs, and the colours of the fading leaves mingled with the hues of the autumn berries.

A sudden turn in the winding road brought the foremost riders upon a change in the appearance of the country. Below them to the left stretched a broad open space, where the ground had been not only cleared of whatever jungle once grew upon it, but also turned over. They looked upon the site of one of the earliest surface-mining grounds. The shingle and gravel stood about in heaps; the gullies and ditches formed by the miners ran up and down the face of the country like the wrinkles in the cheek of a baby monkey; old pits, not deep enough to kill, but warranted to maim and disable, lurked like man-traps in the open; the old wooden aqueducts, run up by the miners in the year '52, were still standing where they were abandoned by the "pioneers"; here and there lay about old washing-pans, rusty and broken, old cradles, and bits of rusty metal which had once belonged to shovels. These relics and signs of bygone gatherings of men were sufficiently dreary in themselves, but at intervals there stood the ruins of a log-house, or a heap which had once been a cottage built of mud. Palestine itself has no more striking picture of desolation and wreck than a deserted surface-mine.

They drew rein and looked in silence. Presently they became aware of the presence of life. Right in the foreground, about two hundred yards before them, there advanced a procession of two. The leader of the show, so to speak, was a man. He was running. He was running so hard, that anybody could see his primary object was speed. After him, with heavy stride, seeming to be in no kind of hurry, and yet covering the ground at a much greater rate than the man, there came a bear—a real old grisly. A bear who was "shadowing" the man and meant claws. A bear who had an insult to avenge, and was resolved to go on with the affair until he had avenged it. A bear, too, who had his enemy in the open, where there was nothing to stop him, and no refuge for his victim but the planks of a ruined log-house, could he find one.

Both men, without a word, got their rifles ready. The younger threw the reins of his horse to his companion and dismounted.

Then he stood still and watched.

The most exhilarating thing in the whole world is allowed to be a hunt. No greater pleasure in life than that of the Shekarry, especially if he be after big game. On this occasion the keenness of the sport was perhaps intensified to him who ran, by the reflection that the customary position of things was reversed. No longer did he hunt the bear; the bear hunted *him*. No longer did he warily follow up the game; the game boldly followed *him*. No joyous sound of horns cheered on the hunter: no shout, such as those which inspirit the fox and put fresh vigour into the hare—not even the short eager bark of the hounds, at the sound of which Reynard begins to think how many of his hundred turns are left. It was a silent chase. The bear, who represented in himself the field—men in scarlet, ladies, master, pack, and everything—set to work in a cold unsympathetic way, infinitely more distressing to a nervous creature than the cheerful ringing of a whole field. To hunt in silence would be hard for any man; to be hunted in silence is intolerable.

Grisly held his head down and wagged it from side to side, while his great silent paws rapidly cleared the ground and lessened the distance.

"Tommy," whispered the young fellow, "I can cover him now."

"Wait, Jack. Don't miss. Give Grisly two minutes more. Gad! how the fellow scuds!"

Tommy, you see, obeyed the instinct of nature. He loved the hunt: if not to hunt actively, to witness a hunt. It is the same feeling which crowds the benches at a bullfight in Spain. It was the same feeling which lit up the faces in the Coliseum when Hermann, formerly of the Danube, prisoner, taken red-handed in revolt, and therefore *moriturus*, performed with vigour, sympathy, and spirit the *rôle* of Actæon, ending, as we all know, in a splendid chase by bloodhounds; after which the poor Teuton, maddened by his long flight and exhausted by his desperate resistance, was torn to pieces, fighting to the end with a rage past all acting. It is our modern pleasure to read of pain and suffering. Those were the really pleasant days to the Roman ladies when they actually witnessed living agony.

"Give Grisly two minutes," said Captain Ladds.

By this time the rest of the party had come up, and were watching the movements of man and bear. In the plain stood the framework of a ruined wooden house. Man made for log-house. Bear, without any apparent effort, but just to show that he saw the dodge, and meant that it should not succeed, put on a spurt, and the distance between them lessened every moment. Fifty yards; forty yards. Man looked round over his shoulder. The log-house was a good two hundred yards ahead. He hesitated; seemed to stop for a moment. Bear diminished the space by a good dozen yards—and then man doubled.

"Getting pumped," said Ladds the critical. Then he too dismounted, and stood beside the younger man, giving the reins of both horses to one of the Mexicans. "Mustn't let Grisly claw the poor devil," he murmured.

"Let me bring him down, Tommy."

"Bring him down, young un."

The greasers looked on and laughed. It would have been to them a pleasant termination to the "play" had Bruin clawed the man. Neither hunter nor quarry saw the party clustered together on the rising ground on which the track ran. Man saw nothing but the ground over which he flew; bear saw nothing but man before him. The doubling manoeuvre was, however, the one thing needed to bring Grisly within easy reach. Faster flew the man, but it was the last flight of despair; had the others been near enough they would have seen the cold drops of agony standing on his forehead; they would have caught his panting breath, they would have heard his muttered prayer.

"Let him have it!" growled Ladds.

It was time. Grisly, swinging along with leisurely step, rolling his great head from side to side in time with the cadence of his footfall—one roll to every half-dozen strides, like a fat German over a *trois-temps* waltz, suddenly lifted his face, and roared. Then the man shrieked: then the bear stopped, and raised himself for a moment, pawing in the air; then he dropped again, and rushed with quickened step upon his foe; then—but then—ping! one shot. It has struck Grisly in the shoulder; he stops with a roar.

"Good, young un!" said Ladds, bringing piece to shoulder. This time Grisly roars no more. He rolls over. He is shot to the heart, and is dead.

The other participator in this *chasse* of two heard the crack of the rifles. His senses were growing dazed with fear; he did not stop, he ran on still, but with trembling knees and outstretched hands; and when he came to a heap of shingle and sand—one of those left over from the old surface-mines—he fell headlong on the pile with a cry, and could not rise. The two who shot the bear ran across the ground—he lay almost at their feet—to secure their prey. After them, at a leisurely pace, strode John, the servant. The greasers stayed behind and laughed.

"Grisly's dead," said Tommy, pulling out his knife. "Steak?"

"No; skin," cried the younger. "Let me take his skin. John, we will have the beast skinned. You can get some steaks cut. Where is the man?"

They found him lying on his face, unable to move.

"Now, old man," said the young fellow cheerfully, "might as well sit up, you know, if you can't stand. Bruin's gone to the happy hunting-grounds."

The man sat up, as desired, and tried to take a comprehensive view of the position.

Jack handed him a flask, from which he took a long pull. Then he got up, and somewhat ostentatiously began to smooth down the legs of his trousers.

He was a thin man, about five and forty years of age; he wore an irregular and patchy kind of beard, which flourished exceedingly on certain square half-inches of chin and cheek, and was as thin as grass at Aden on the intervening spaces. He had no boots; but a sort of moccasins, the lightness of which enabled him to show his heels to the bear for so long a time. His trousers might have been of a rough tweed, or they might have been black cloth, because grease, many drenchings, the buffeting of years, and the holes into which they were worn, had long deprived them of their original colour and brilliancy. Above the trousers he wore a tattered flannel shirt, the right arm of which, nearly torn to pieces, revealed a tattooed limb, which was strong although thin; the buttons had long ago vanished from the front of the garment; thorns picturesquely replaced them. He wore a red-cotton handkerchief round his neck, a round felt hat was on his head; this, like the trousers, had lost its pristine colour, and by dint of years and weather, its stiffness too. To prevent the hat from flapping in his eyes, its possessor had pinned it up with thorns in the front.

Necessity is the mother of invention: there is nothing morally wrong in the use of thorns where other men use studs, diamond pins, and such gauds; and the effect is picturesque. The stranger, in fact, was a law unto himself. He had no coat; the rifle of Californian civilisation was missing; there was no sign of knife or revolver; and the only encumbrance, if that was any, to the lightness of his flight was a small wooden box strapped round tightly, and hanging at his back by means of a steel chain, grown a little rusty where it did not rub against his neck and shoulders.

He sat up and winked involuntarily with both eyes. This was the effect of present bewilderment and late fear.

Then he looked round him, after, as before explained, a few moments of assiduous leg-smoothing, which, as stated above, looked ostentatious, but was really only nervous agitation. Then he rose, and saw Grisly lying in a heap a few yards off. He walked over with a grave face, and looked at him.

When Henri Balafré, Duc de Guise, saw Coligny lying dead at his feet, he is said—only it is a wicked lie—to have kicked the body of his murdered father's enemy. When Henri III of France, ten years later, saw Balafré dead at his feet, he did kick the lifeless body, with a wretched joke. The king was a cur. My American was not. He stood over Bruin with a look in his eyes which betokened respect for fallen greatness and sympathy with bad luck. Grisly would have been his victor, but for the chance which brought him within reach of a friendly rifle.

"A near thing," he said. "Since I've been in this doggoned country I've had one or two near things, but this was the nearest."

The greasers stood round the body of the bear, and the English servant was giving directions for skinning the beast.

"And which of you gentlemen," he went on with a nasal twang more pronounced than before—perhaps with more emphasis on the word "gentlemen" than was altogether required—"which of you gentlemen was good enough to shoot the critter?"

The English servant, who was, like his master, Captain Ladds, a man of few words, pointed to the young man, who stood close by with the other leader of the expedition.

The man snatched from the jaws of death took off his shaky thorn-beset felt, and solemnly held out his hand.

"Sir," he said, "I do not know your name, and you do not know mine. If you did you would not be much happier, because it is not a striking name. If you'll oblige me, sir, by touching that"—he meant his right hand—"we shall be brothers. All that's mine shall be yours. I do not ask you, sir, to reciprocate. All that's mine, sir, when I get anything, shall be yours. At present, sir, there is nothing; but I've Luck behind me. Shake hands, sir. Once a mouse helped a lion, sir. It's in a book. I am the mouse, sir, and you are the lion. Sir, my name is Gilead P. Beck."

The young man laughed and shook hands with him.

"I only fired the first shot," he explained. "My friend here—"

"No; first shot disabled—hunt finished then—Grisly out of the running. Glad you're not clawed—unpleasant to be clawed. Young un did it. No thanks. Tell us where we are."

Mr. Gilead P. Beck, catching the spirit of the situation, told them where they were, approximately. "This," he said, "is Patrick's Camp; at least, it was. The Pioneers of '49 could tell you a good deal about Patrick's Camp. It was here that Patrick kept his store. In those old days—they're gone now—if a man wanted to buy a blanket, that article, sir, was put into one scale, and weighed down with gold-dust in the other. Same with a pair of boots; same with a pound of raisins. Patrick might have died rich, sir, but he didn't—none of the pioneers did—so he died poor; and died in his boots, too, like most of the lot."

"Not much left of the camp."

"No, sir, not much. The mine gave out. Then they moved up the hills, where, I conclude, you gentlemen are on your way. Prospecting likely. The new town, called Empire City, ought to be an hour or so up the track. I was trying to find my way there when I met with old Grisly. Perhaps if I had let him alone he would have let me alone. But I blazed at him, and, sir, I missed him; then he shadowed me. And the old rifle's gone at last."

"How long did the chase last?"

"I should say, sir, forty days and forty nights, or near about. And you gentlemen air going to Empire City?"

"We are going anywhere. Perhaps, for the present, you had better join us."

II

MR. GILEAD P. BECK, PARTLY RECOVERED FROM the shock caused to his nerves by the revengeful spirit of the bear, and in no way discomfited by any sense of false shame as to his ragged appearance, marched beside the two Englishmen. It was characteristic of his nationality that he regarded the greasers with contempt, and that he joined the two gentlemen as if he belonged to their grade and social rank. An Englishman picked up in such rags and duds would have shrunk abashed to the rear, or he would have apologised for his tattered condition, or he would have begged for some garments—any garments—to replace his own. Mr. Beck had no such feeling. He strode along with a swinging slouch, which covered the ground as rapidly as the step of the horses. The wind blew his rags about his long and lean figure as picturesquely as if he were another Autolycus. He was as full of talk as that worthy, and as lightsome of spirit, despite the solemn gravity of his face. I once saw a poem—I think in the *Spectator*—on Artemus Ward, in which the bard apostrophised the light-hearted merriment of the Western American; a very fortunate thing to say, because the Western American is externally a most serious person, never merry, never witty, but always humorous. Mr. Beck was quite grave, though at the moment as happy as that other grave and thoughtful person who has made a name in the literature of humour—Panurge—when he escaped half-roasted from the Turk's Serai.

"I ought," he said, "to sit down and cry, like the girl on the prairie."

"Why ought you to cry?"

"I guess I ought to cry because I've lost my rifle and everything except my Luck"—here he pulled at the steel chain—"in that darned long stern chase."

"You can easily get a new rifle," said Jack.

"With dollars," interrupted Mr. Beck. "As for them, there's not a dollar left—nary a red cent; only my Luck."

"And what is your Luck?"

"That," said Mr. Beck, "I will tell you by-and-by. Perhaps it's your Luck, too, young boss," he added, thinking of a shot as fortunate to himself as William Tell's was to his son.

He pulled the box attached to the steel chain round to the front, and looked at it tenderly. It was safe, and he heaved a sigh.

The way wound up a valley—a road marked only, as has been said, by deep ruts along its course. Behind the travellers the evening sun was slowly sinking in the west; before them the peaks of the Sierra lifted their heads, coloured purple in the evening light; and on either hand rose the hill-sides, with their dark foliage in alternate "splashes" of golden light and deepest shade.

It wanted but a quarter of an hour to sunset when Mr. Gilead P. Beck pointed to a township which suddenly appeared, lying at their very feet.

"Empire City, I reckon."

A good-sized town of wooden houses. They were all alike and of the same build as that affected by the architects of doll's houses; that is to say, they were of one story only, had a door in the middle, and a window on either side. They were so small, also, that they looked veritable dolls' houses.

There were one or two among them of more pretentious appearance, and of several stories. These were the hotels, billiard-saloons, bars, and gambling-houses.

"It's a place bound to advance, sir," said Mr. Beck proudly. "Empire City, when I first saw it, which is two years ago, was only two years old. It is only in our country that a great city springs up in a day. Empire City will be the Chicago of the West."

"I see a city," said Captain Ladds; "can't see the people."

It was certainly curious. There was not a soul in the streets; there was no smoke from the chimneys; there was neither carts nor horses; there was not the least sign of occupation.

Mr. Gilead P. Beck whistled.

"All gone," he said. "Guess the city's busted up."

He pushed aside the brambles which grew over what had been a path leading to the place, and hurried down. The others followed him, and rode into the town.

It was deserted. The doors of the houses were open, and if you looked in you might see the rough furniture which the late occupants disdained to carry away with them. The two Englishmen dismounted, gave their reins to the servants, and began to look about them.

The descendants of Og, king of Bashan, have left their houses in black basalt, dotted about the lava-fields of the Hauran, to witness how they lived. In the outposts of desert stations of the East, the Roman soldiers have left their barracks and their baths, their jokes written on the wall, and their names, to show how they passed away the weary hours of garrison duty. So the miners who founded Empire City, and deserted it *en masse* when the gold gave out, left behind them marks by which future explorers of the ruins should know what manner of men once dwelt there. The billiard saloon stood open with swinging doors; the table was still there, the balls lay about on the table and the floor; the cues stood in the rack; the green cloth, mildewed, covered the table.

"Tommy," said the younger, "we will have a game tonight."

The largest building in the place had been an hotel. It had two stories, and was, like the rest of the houses, built of wood, with a verandah along the front. The upper story looked as if it had been recently inhabited; that is, the shutters were not dropping off the hinges, nor were they flapping to and fro in the breeze.

But the town was deserted; the evening breeze blew chilly up its vacant streets; life and sound had gone out of the place.

"I feel cold," said Jack, looking about him.

They went round to the back of the hotel. Old iron cog-wheels lay rusting on the ground with remains of pumps. In the heart of the town behind the hotel stretched an open space of ground covered with piles of shingle and intersected with ditches.

Mr. Beck sat down and adjusted one of the thorns which served as a temporary shirt-stud.

"Two years ago," he said, "there were ten thousand miners here; now there isn't one. I thought we should find a choice hotel, with a little monty or poker afterwards. Now no one left; nothing but a Chinaman or two."

"How do you know there are Chinamen?"

"See those stones?"

He pointed to some great boulders, from three to six feet in diameter. Some operation of a mystical kind had been performed upon them, for they were jagged and chipped as if they had been filed and cut into

WALTER BESANT AND JAMES RICE

shape by a sculptor who had been once a dentist and still loved the profession.

"The miners picked the bones of those rocks, but they never pick quite clean. Then the Chinamen come and finish off. Gentlemen, it's a special Providence that you picked me up. I don't altogether admire the way in which that special Providence was played up to in the matter of the bar; but a Christian without a revolver alone among twenty Chinamen—"

He stopped and shrugged his shoulders.

"They'd have got my Luck," he concluded.

"Chief, I don't like it"; said the younger man. "It's ghostly. It's a town of dead men. As soon as it is dark the ghosts will rise and walk about—play billiards, I expect. What shall we do?"

"Hotel," growled the chief. "Sleep on floor—sit on chairs—eat off a table."

They entered the hotel.

A most orderly bar: the glasses there; the bright-coloured bottles: two or three casks of Bourbon whisky; the counter; the very dice on the counter with which the bar-keeper used to "go" the miners for drinks. How things at once so necessary to civilised life and so portable as dice were left behind, it is impossible to explain.

Everything was there except the drink. The greasers tried the casks and examined the bottles. Emptiness. A miner may leave behind him the impedimenta, but the real necessaries of life—rifle, revolver, bowie, and cards—he takes with him. And as for the drink, he carries that away too for greater safety, inside himself.

The English servant looked round him and smiled superior.

"No tap for beer, as usual, sir," he said. "These poor Californians has much to learn."

Mr. Gilead P. Beck looked round mournfully.

"Everything gone but the fixin's," he sighed. "There used to be good beds, where there wasn't more'n two at once in them; and there used to be such a crowd around this bar as you would not find nearer'n St. Louis City."

"Hush!" said Jack, holding up his hand. There were steps.

Mr. Beck pricked up his ears.

"Chinamen, likely. If there's a row, gentlemen, give me something, if it's only a toothpick, to chime in with. But that's not a Chinese step; that's an Englishman's. He wears boots, but they are not miner's boots;

he walks firm and slow, like all Englishmen; he is not in a hurry, like our folk. And who but an Englishman would be found staying behind in the Empire City when it's gone to pot?"

The footsteps came down the stairs.

"Most unhandsome of a ghost," said the younger man, "to walk before midnight."

The producer of the footsteps appeared.

"Told you he was an Englishman!" cried Mr. Beck.

Indeed, there was no mistaking the nationality of the man, in spite of his dress, which was cosmopolitan. He wore boots, but not, as the quick ear of the American told him, the great boots of the miner; he had on a flannel shirt with a red silk belt; he wore a sort of blanket thrown back from his shoulders; and he had a broad felt hat. Of course he carried arms, but they were not visible.

He was a man of middle height, with clear blue eyes; the perfect complexion of an Englishman of good stock and in complete health; a brown beard, long and rather curly, streaked with here and there a grey hair; square and clear-cut nostrils; and a mouth which, though not much of it was visible, looked as if it would easily smile, might readily become tender, and would certainly find it difficult to be stern. He might be any age, from five and thirty to five and forty.

The greasers fell back and grouped about the door. The questions which might be raised had no interest for them. The two leaders stood together; and Mr. Gilead P. Beck, rolling an empty keg to their side, turned it up and sat down with the air of a judge, looking from one party to the other.

"Englishmen, I see," said the stranger.

"Ye-yes," said Ladds, not, as Mr. Beck expected, immediately holding out his hand for the stranger to grasp.

"You have probably lost your way?"

"Been hunting. Working round—San Francisco. Followed track; accident; got here. Your hotel, perhaps? Fine situation, but lonely."

"Not a ghost, then," murmured the other, with a look of temporary disappointment.

"If you will come upstairs to my quarters, I may be able to make you comfortable for the night. Your party will accommodate themselves without our help."

He referred to the greasers, who had already begun their preparations for spending a happy night. When he led the way up the stairs, he was followed, not only by the two gentlemen he had invited, but also by the ragamuffin hunter, miner, or adventurer, and by the valet, who conceived it his duty to follow his master.

He lived, this hermit, in one of the small bed-rooms of the hotel, which he had converted into a sitting-room. It contained a single rocking-chair and a table. There was also a shelf, which served for a sideboard, and a curtain under the shelf, which acted as a cupboard.

"You see my den," he said. "I came here a year or so ago by accident, like yourselves. I found the place deserted. I liked the solitude, the scenery, whatever you like, and I stayed here. You are the only visitors I have had in a year."

"Chinamen?" said Mr. Gilead P. Beck.

"Well, Chinamen, of course. But only two of them. They take turns, at forty dollars a month, to cook my dinners. And there is a half-caste, who does not mind running down to Sacramento when I want anything. And so, you see, I make out pretty well."

He opened the window, and blew a whistle.

In two minutes a Chinaman came tumbling up the stairs. His inscrutable face expressed all the conflicting passions of humanity at once—ambition, vanity, self respect, humour, satire, avarice, resignation, patience, revenge, meekness, long-suffering, remembrance, and a thousand others. No Aryan comes within a hundred miles of it.

"Dinner as soon as you can," said his master.

"Ayah! can do," replied the Celestial. "What time you wantchee?"

"As soon as you can. Half an hour."

"Can do. My no have got cully-powder. Have makee finish. Have got?"

"Look for some; make Achow help."

"How can? No, b'long his pidgin. He no helpee. B'long my pidgin makee cook chow-chow. Ayah! Achow have go makee cheat over Mexican man. Makee play cards all same euchre."

In fact, on looking out of the window, the other Celestial was clearly visible, manipulating a pack of cards and apparently inviting the Mexicans to a friendly game, in which there could be no deception.

Then Ladds' conscience smote him.

"Beg pardon. Should have seen. Make remark about hotel. Apologise."

"He means," said the other, "that he was a terrible great fool not to see that you are a gentleman."

Ladds nodded.

"Let me introduce our party," the speaker went on. "This is our esteemed friend Mr. Gilead P. Beck, whom we caught in a bear-hunt—"

"Bar behind," said Mr. Beck.

"This is Captain Ladds, of the 35th Dragoons."

"Ladds," said Ladds. "Nibs, cocoa-nibs—pure aroma—best breakfast-digester—blessing to mothers—perfect fragrance."

"His name is Ladds; and he wishes to communicate to you the fact that he is the son of the man who made an immense fortune—immense, Tommy?"

Ladds nodded.

"By a crafty compound known as 'Ladds' Patent Anti-Dyspeptic Cocoa.' This is Ladd's servant, John Boimer, the best servant who ever put his leg across pig-skin; and my name is Roland Dunquerque. People generally call me Jack; I don't know why, but they do."

Their host bowed to each, including the servant, who coloured with pleasure at Jack's description of him; but he shook hands with Ladds.

"One of ours," he said. "My name is Lawrence Colquhoun. I sold out before you joined. I came here as you see. And—now, gentlemen, I think I hear the first sounds of dinner. Boimer—you will allow me, Ladds?—you will find claret and champagne behind that curtain. Pardon a hermit's fare. I think they have laid out such a table as the wilderness can boast in the next room."

The dinner was not altogether what a man might order at the Junior United, but it was good. There was venison, there was a curry, there was some mountain quail, there was claret, and there was champagne—both good, especially the claret. Then there was coffee.

The Honourable Roland Dunquerque, whom we will call in future, what everybody always called him, Jack, ate and drank like Friar John. The keen mountain air multiplied his normal twist by ten. Mr. Gilead P. Beck, who sat down to dinner perfectly unabashed by his rags, was good as a trencherman, but many plates behind the young Englishman. Mr. Lawrence Colquhoun, their host, went on talking almost as if they were in London, only now and then he found himself behind the world. It was his ignorance of the last Derby, the allusion to an old and half-forgotten story, perhaps his use of little phrases—not slang phrases, but those delicately-shaded terms which imply knowledge of current things—which showed him to have been out of London and Paris for more than one season.

"Four years," he said, "since I left England."

"But you will come back to it again?"

"I think not."

"Better," said Jack, whose face was a little flushed with the wine. "Much better. Robinson Crusoe always wanted to get home again. So did Selkirk. So did Philip Quarles."

Then the host produced cigars. Later on, brandy-and-water.

The brandy and water made Mr. Gilead P. Beck, who found himself a good deal crowded out of the conversation, insist on having his share. He placed his square box on the table, and loosed the straps.

"Let me tell you," he said, "the story of my Luck. I was in Sonora City," he began, patting his box affectionately, "after the worst three months I ever had; and I went around trying to borrow a few dollars. I got no dollars, but I got free drinks—so many free drinks, that at last I lay down in the street and went to sleep. Wal, gentlemen, I suppose I walked in that slumber of mine, for when I woke up I was lying a mile outside the town.

"I also entertained angels unawares, for at my head there sat an Indian woman. She was as wrinkled an old squaw as ever shrieked at a buryin'. But she took an interest in me. She took that amount of interest in me that she told me she knew of gold. And then she led me by the hand, gentlemen, that aged and affectionate old squaw, to a place not far from the roadside; and there, lying between two rocks, and hidden in the chaparelle, glittering in the light, was this bauble." He tapped his box. "I did not want to be told to take it. I wrapped it in my handkerchief and carried it in my hand. Then she led me back to the road again. 'Bad luck you will have,' she said; 'but it will lead to good luck so long as that is not broken, sold, given away, or lost.' Then she left me, and here it is."

He opened the little box. There was nothing to be seen but a mass of white wool.

"Bad luck I *have* had. Look at me, gentlemen. Adam was not more destitute when the garden-gates were shut on him. But the good will come, somehow."

He removed the wool, and, behold, a miracle of nature! Two thin plates of gold delicately wrought in lines and curious chasing, like the pattern of a butterfly's wing, and of the exact shape, but twice as large. They were poised at the angle, always the same, at which the insect balances itself about a flower. They were set in a small piece of quaintly marked quartz, which represented the body.

"A golden butterfly!"

"A golden butterfly," said Mr. Beck. "No goldsmith made this butterfly. It came from Nature's workshop. It is my Luck."

> *"And If the butterfly fall and break,*
> *Farewell the Luck of Gilead Beck,"*

said Jack.

"Thank you, sir. That's very neat. I'll take that, sir, if you will allow me, for my motto, unless you want it for yourself."

"No," said Jack; "I have one already."

> *"If this golden butterfly fall and break,*
> *Farewell the Luck of Gilead P. Beck,"*

repeated the owner of the insect. "If you are going on, gentlemen, to San Francisco, I hope you will take me with you."

"Colquhoun," said Ladds, "you do not mean to stay by yourself? Much better come with us, unless, of course—"

Lying on the table was a piece of an old newspaper in which Jack had wrapped something. Ladds saw Colquhoun mechanically take up the paper, read it, and change color. Then he looked straight before him, seeing nothing, and Ladds stopped speaking. Then he smiled in a strange far-off way.

"I think I will go with you," he said.

"Hear, hear!" cried Jack. "Selkirk returns to the sound of the church-going bell."

Ladds refrained from looking at the paper in search of things which did not concern himself, but he perceived that Colquhoun had, like Hamlet, seen something. There *was*, in fact, an announcement in the fragment which greatly interested Lawrence Colquhoun:

"On April 3, by the Right Rev. the Lord Bishop of Turk's Island, at St. George's Hanover Square, Gabriel Cassilis, of etc., to Victoria, daughter of the Late Admiral Sir Benbow Pengelley, K.C.B."

In the morning they started, Mr. Beck being provided with a new rig-out of a rough and useful kind.

At the last moment one of the Chinamen, Leeching, the cook,

besought from his late master, as a parting favour and for the purpose of self-protection, the gift of a pistol, powder, and ball.

Mr. Colquhoun gave them to him, thinking it a small thing after two years of faithful service. Then Leeching, after loading his pistol, went to work with his comrade for an hour or so.

Presently, Achow being on his knees in the shingle, the perfidious Leeching suddenly cocked his pistol, and fired it into Achow's right ear, so that he fell dead.

By this lucky accident Leeching became sole possessor of the little pile of gold which he and the defunct Achow had scraped together and placed in a *cache*.

He proceeded to unearth this treasure, put together his little belongings, and started on the road to San Francisco with a smile of satisfaction.

There was a place in the windings of the road where there was a steep bank. By the worst luck in the world a stone slipped and fell as Leeching passed by. The stone by itself, would not have mattered much, as it did not fall on Leeching's head; but with it fell a rattlesnake, who was sleeping in the warmth of the sun.

Nothing annoys a rattlesnake more than to be disturbed in his sleep. With angry mind he awoke, looked around, and saw the Chinaman. Illogically connecting him with the fall of the stone, he made for him, and, before Leeching knew there was a rattlesnake anywhere near him, bit him in the calf.

Leeching sat down on the bank and realized the position. Being a fatalist, he did not murmur; having no conscience, he did not fear; having no faith, he did not hope; having very little time, he made no testamentary dispositions. In point of fact, he speedily curled up his legs and died.

Then the deserted Empire City was deserted indeed, for there was not even a Chinaman left in it.

I

Joseph and His Brethren

The largest and most solid of all the substantial houses in Carnarvon Square, Bloomsbury, is Number Fifteen, which, by reason of its corner position (Mulgrave Street intersecting it at right angles at this point), has been enabled to stretch itself out at the back. It is a house which a man who wanted to convey the idea of a solid income without ostentation or attempt at fashion would find the very thing to assist his purpose. The ladies of such a house would not desire to belong to the world farther west; they would respect the Church, law, and medicine; they would look on the City with favourable eyes when it was represented by a partner in an old firm; they would have sound notions of material comfort; they would read solid books, and would take their pleasure calmly. One always, somehow, in looking at a house wonders first of what sort its women are. There were, however, no women at Number Fifteen at all, except the maids. Its occupants consisted of three brothers, all unmarried. They were named respectively Cornelius, Humphrey, and Joseph Jagenal. Cornelius and Humphrey were twins. Joseph was their junior by ten years. Cornelius and Humphrey were fifty—Joseph was forty. People who did not know this thought that Joseph was fifty and his brethren forty.

When the Venerable the Archdeacon of Market Basing, the well-known author of *Sermons on the Duty of Tithe-Offerings*, the *Lesbia of Catullus*, and a *Treatise on the Right Use of the Anapæst in Greek Iambic Verse*, died, it was found that he had bequeathed his little savings, worth altogether about £500 a year, to his three sons in the following proportions: the twins, he said, possessed genius; they would make their mark in the world, but they must be protected. They received the yearly sum of £200 apiece, and it was placed in the hands of trustees to prevent their losing it; the younger was to have the rest, without trustees, because, his father said, "Joseph is a dull boy and will keep it." It was a wise distribution of the money. Cornelius, then nineteen, left Oxford immediately, and went to Heidelberg, where he called himself a poet, studied metaphysics, drank beer, and learned to fence. Humphrey, for his part, deserted Cambridge—their father having chosen that they should not be rivals—and announced his intention of devoting his life to Art. He took up his residence in Rome. Joseph stayed at school, having no other choice. When the boy was sixteen, his guardians articled him to a solicitor. Joseph was dull, but he was methodical, exact, and endowed with a retentive memory. He had also an excellent manner, and the "appearance of age," as port wine advertisers say, before he was out of his articles. At twenty-five, Joseph Jagenal was a partner; at thirty-five, he was the working partner; at forty, he was the senior partner in the great Lincoln's-Inn firm of Shaw, Fairlight, and Jagenal, the confidential advisers of as many respectable county people as any firm in London.

When he was twenty-five, and became a partner, the brethren returned to England simultaneously, and were good enough to live with him and upon him. They had their £200 a year each, and expensive tastes. Joseph, who had made a thousand for his share the first year of his admission to the firm, had no expensive tastes, and a profound respect for genius. He took in the twins joyfully, and they stayed with him. When his senior partner died, and Mr. Fairlight retired, so that Joseph's income was largely increased, they made him move from Torrington Square, where the houses are small, to Carnarvon Square, and regulated his household for him on the broadest and most liberal scale. Needless to say, no part of the little income, which barely served the twins with pocket-money and their *menus plaisirs*, went towards the housekeeping. Cornelius, poet and philosopher, superintended the dinner and daily interviewed the cook. Humphrey, the devotee of art, who furnished the rooms according to the latest designs of the most correct taste, was in command of the cellar. Cornelius took the best sitting-room for himself, provided it with books, easy-chairs, and an immense study-table with countless drawers. He called it carelessly his Workshop. The room on the first floor overlooking Mulgrave Street, and consequently with a north aspect, was appropriated by Humphrey. He called it his Studio, and furnished it in character, not forgetting the easy-chairs. Joseph had the back room behind the dining-room for himself; it was not called a study or a library, but Mr. Joseph's room. He sat in it alone every evening, at work. There was also a drawing-room, but it was never used. They dined together at half-past six: Cornelius sat at the head, and Humphrey at the foot, Joseph at one side. Art and Intellect, thus happily met together and housed under one roof, talked to each other. Joseph ate his dinner in silence. Art held his glass to the light, and flashed into enthusiasm over the matchless sparkle, the divine hues, the incomparable radiance, of the wine. Intellect, with a sigh, as one who regrets the loss of a sense, congratulated his brother on his vivid passion for colour, and, taking another glass, discoursed on the æsthetic aspects of a vintage wine. Joseph drank one glass of claret, after which he retired to his den, and left the brethren to finish the bottle. After dinner the twins sometimes went to the theatre, or they repaired arm-in-arm to their club—the Renaissance, now past its prime and a little fogyish; mostly they sat in the Studio or in the Workshop, in two arm-chairs, with a table between them, smoked pipes, and drank brandy and potash-water. They went to bed at anytime they felt sleepy—perhaps at twelve, and perhaps at three. Joseph went to bed at half-past ten. The brethren generally breakfasted at eleven, Joseph at eight. After breakfast, unless on rainy days, a uniform custom was observed. Cornelius, poet and philosopher, went to the window and looked out.

Humphrey, artist, and therefore a man of intuitive sympathies, followed him. Then he patted Cornelius on the shoulder, and shook his head.

"Brother, I know your thought. You want to drag me from my work; you think it has been too much for me lately. You are too anxious about me."

Cornelius smiled.

"Not on my own account too, Humphrey?"

"True—on your account. Let us go out at once, brother. Ah, why did you choose so vast a subject?"

Cornelius was engaged—had been engaged for twenty years—upon an epic poem, entitled the *Upheaving of Ælfred*. The school he belonged to would not, of course, demean themselves by speaking of Alfred. To them Edward was Eadward, Edgar was Eadgar, and old Canute was Knut. In the same way Cicero became Kikero, Virgil was Vergil, and Socrates was spelt, as by the illiterate bargee, with a *k*. So the French prigs of the ante-Boileau period sought to make their trumpery pedantries pass for current coin. So, too, Chapelain was in labour with the *Pucelle* for thirty years; and when it came—But Cornelius Jagenal could not be compared with Chapelain, because he had as yet brought forth nothing. He sat with what he and his called "English" books all round him; in other words, he had all the Anglo-Saxon literature on his shelves, and was amassing, as he said, material.

Humphrey, on the other hand, was engaged on a painting, the composition of which offered difficulties which, for nearly twenty years, had proved insuperable. He was painting, he said, the "Birth of the Renaissance." It was a subject which required a great outlay in properties, Venetian glass, Italian jewelry, mediæval furniture, copies of paintings—everything necessary to make this work a masterpiece—he bought at Joseph's expense. Up to the present no one had been allowed to see the first rough drawings.

"Where's Cæsar?" Humphrey would say, leading the way to the hall. "Cæsar! Why, here he is. Cæsar must actually have heard us proposing to go out."

Cornelius called the dog Kaysar, and he refused to answer to it; so that conversation between him and Cornelius was impossible.

There never was a pair more attached to each other than these twin brethren. They sallied forth each morning at twelve, arm-in-arm, with an open and undisguised admiration for each other which was touching. Before them marched Cæsar, who was of mastiff breed, leading the way. Cornelius, the poet, was dressed with as much care as if he were still a young man of five-and-twenty, in a semi-youthful and wholly-æsthetic costume, in which only the general air, and not the colour, revealed the man of delicate perceptions. Humphrey, the artist, greatly daring, affected a warm brown velvet with a crimson-purple ribbon. Both carried flowers. Cornelius had gloves; Humphrey a cigar. Cornelius was smooth-faced, save for a light fringe on the upper lip. Humphrey wore a heavy moustache and a full long silky beard of a delicately-shaded brown, inclining when the sun shone upon it to a suspicion of auburn. Both were of the same height, rather below the middle; they had features so much alike that, but for the hair on the face of one, it would have been difficult to distinguish between them. Both were thin, pale of face, and both had, by some fatality, the end of their delicately-carved noses slightly tipped with red. Perhaps this was due to the daily and nightly brandy-and-water. And in the airy careless carriage of the two men, their sunny faces and elastic tread, it was impossible to suppose that they were fifty and Joseph only forty.

To be sure, Joseph was a heavy man, stout of build, broad in frame, sturdy in the under-jaw; while his brothers were slight shadowy men. And, to be sure, Joseph had worked all his life, while his brothers never did a stroke. They were born to consume the fruits which Joseph was born to cultivate.

Outside the house the poet heaved a heavy sigh, as if the weight of the epic was for the moment off his mind. The artist looked round with a critical eye on the lights and shadows of the great commonplace square.

"Even in London," he murmured, "Nature is too strong for man. Did you ever, my dear Cornelius, catch a more brilliant effect of sunshine than that upon the lilac yonder?"

Time, end of April; season forward, lilacs on the point of bursting into flower; sky dotted with swift-flying clouds, alternate withdrawals and bursts of sunshine.

"I really must," said Humphrey, "try to fix that effect."

His brother took the arm of the artist and drew him gently away.

In front marched Cæsar.

Presently the poet looked round. They were out of the square by this time.

"Where is Kaysar?" he said, with an air of surprise. "Surely, brother Humphrey, the dog can't be in the Carnarvon Arms?"

"I'll go and see," said Humphrey, with alacrity.

He entered the bar of the tavern, and his brother waited outside. After two or three minutes, the poet, as if tired of waiting, followed the artist into the bar. He found him with a glass of brandy-and-water cold.

"I had," he explained, "a feeling of faintness. Perhaps this spring air is chilly. One cannot be too careful."

"Quite right," said the poet. "I almost think—yes, I really do feel—ah! Thank you, my dear."

The girl, as if anticipating his wants, set before him a "four" of brandy and the cold water. Perhaps she had seen the face before. As for the dog, he was lying down with his head on his paws. Perhaps he knew there would be no immediate necessity for moving.

They walked in the direction of the Park, arm-in-arm, affectionately.

It might have been a quarter of an hour after leaving the Carnarvon Arms when the poet stopped and gasped—

"Humphrey, my dear brother, advise me. What would you do if you had a sharp and sudden pain like a knife inside you?"

Humphrey replied promptly:

"If I had a sharp and sudden pain like a knife inside me, I should take a small glass of brandy neat. Mind, no spoiling the effect with water."

Cornelius looked at his brother with admiration.

"Such readiness of resource!" he murmured, pressing his arm.

"I think I see—ah, yes—Kaysar—he's gone in before us. The sagacity of that dog is more remarkable than anything I ever read." He took his small glass of brandy neat.

The artist, looking on, said he might as well have one at the same time. Not, he added, that he felt any immediate want of the stimulant, but he might; and at all times prevention is better than cure.

It was two o'clock when they returned to Carnarvon Square. They walked arm-in-arm, with perhaps even a greater show of confiding affection than had appeared at starting. There was the slightest possible lurch in their walk, and both looked solemn and heavy with thought.

In the hall the artist looked at his watch.

"Pa—pasht two. Corneliush, Work—"

He marched to the Studio with a resolute air, and, arrived there, drew an easy-chair before the fire, sat himself in it, and went fast asleep.

The poet sought the workshop. On the table lay the portfolio of papers, outside which was emblazoned on parchment, with dainty scroll-work by the hands of his brother the artist, the title of his poem:

The Upheaving of Ælfred:
AN EPIC IN TWENTY-FOUR CANTOS.
BY CORNELIUS JAGENAL.

He gazed at it fondly for a few minutes; vaguely took up a pen, as if he intended to finish the work on the spot; and then with a sigh, thought being to much for brain, he slipped into his arm-chair, put up his feet, and was asleep in two minutes. At half-past five, one of the maids—they kept no footman in Carnarvon Square—brought him tea.

"I have been dozing, have I, Jane?" he asked. "Very singular thing for me to do."

We are but the creatures of habit. The brethren took the same walk everyday, made the same remarks, with an occasional variation, and took the same morning drams; they spent the middle of the day in sleep, they woke up for the afternoon tea, and they never failed to call Jane's attention to the singularity of the fact that they had been asleep. This day Jane lingered instead of going away when the tea was finished.

"Did master tell you, sir," she asked, "that Miss Fleming was coming today?"

It was an irritating thing that, although Cornelius ordered the dinner and sat at the head of the table, although Humphrey was in sole command of the wine-cellar, the servants always called Joseph the master. Great is the authority of him who keeps the bag; the power of the penniless twins was a shadowy and visionary thing.

The master had told his brothers that Miss Fleming would probably have to come to the house, but no date was fixed.

"Miss Fleming came this afternoon, sir," said Jane, "with a French maid. She's in Mr. Joseph's room now."

"Oh, tell Mr. Humphrey, Jane, and we will dress for dinner. Tell Mr. Humphrey, also, that perhaps Miss Fleming would like a glass of champagne today."

Jane told the artist.

"Always thoughtful," said Humphrey, with enthusiasm. "Cornelius is forever thinking of others' comfort. To be sure Miss Fleming shall have a glass of champagne."

He brought up two bottles, such was his anxiety to give full expression to his brother's wishes.

When the dinner-bell rang, the brethren emerged simultaneously from their rooms, and descended the stairs together, arm-in-arm. Perhaps in expectation of dinner, perhaps in anticipation of the champagne, perhaps with pleasure at the prospect of meeting with Joseph's ward, the faces of both were lit with a sunny smile, and their eyes with a radiant light, which looked like the real and genuine enthusiasm of humanity. It was a pity that Humphrey wore a beard, or that Cornelius did not; otherwise it would have been difficult to distinguish between this pair so much alike—these youthful twins of fifty, who almost looked like five-and-twenty.

II

"Phillis is my only joy."

M y brothers, Miss Fleming!"

Joseph introduced the twins with a pride impossible to dissemble. They were so youthful-looking, so airy, so handsome, besides being so nobly endowed with genius, that his pride may be excused. Castor and Pollux the wrong side of forty, but slim still and well preserved—these Greek figures do not run tall—might have looked like Cornelius and Humphrey.

They parted company for a moment to welcome the young lady, large-eyed as Hêrê, who rose to greet them, and then took up a position on the hearthrug, one with his hand on the other's shoulder, like the Siamese twins, and smiled pleasantly, as if, being accustomed to admiration and even awe, they wished to reassure Miss Fleming and put her at ease.

Dinner being announced, Cornelius, the elder by a few moments, gave his arm to the young lady. Humphrey, the younger, hovered close behind, as if he too was taking his part in the chivalrous act. Joseph followed alone, of course, not counting in the little procession.

Phillis Fleming's arrival at No. 15 Carnarvon Square was in a manner legal. She belonged to the office, not to the shrine of intellect, poesy, and art created by the twin brethren. She was an orphan and a ward. She had two guardians: one of them, Mr. Lawrence Colquhoun, being away from England; and the other, Mr. Abraham Dyson, with whom she had lived since her sixth birthday, having finished his earthly career just before this history begins, that is to say, in the spring of last year. Shaw, Fairlight, and Jagenal were solicitors to both gentlemen. Therefore Joseph found himself obliged to act for this young lady when, Mr. Abraham Dyson buried and done with, it became a question what was to be done with her. There were offers from several disinterested persons on Miss Fleming's bereaved condition being known. Miss Skimpit, of the Highgate Collegiate Establishment for Young Ladies, proposed by letter to receive her as a parlour-boarder, and hinted at the advantages of a year's discipline, tempered by Christian kindness, for a young lady educated in so extraordinary and godless a manner. The clergyman of the new district church at Finchley called personally upon Mr. Jagenal. He said that he did not know the young lady except by name, but that, feeling the dreadful condition of a girl brought up without any of the gracious influences of Anglican Ritual and Dogma, he was impelled to offer her a home with his Sisterhood. Here she would receive clear dogmatic teaching and learn what the Church meant by submission, fasting, penance, and humiliation. Mr. Jagenal thought she might also learn how to bestow her fortune on Anglo Catholic objects when she came of age, and dismissed his reverence with scant courtesy. Two or three widows who had known better days offered their services, which were declined with thanks. Joseph even refused to let Miss Fleming stay with Mrs. Cassilis, the wife of Abraham Dyson's second cousin. He thought that perhaps this lady would not be unwilling to enliven her house by the attraction of an heiress and a *débutante*. And it occurred to him that, for a short time at least, she might, without offending a censorious world, and until her remaining guardian's wishes could be learned, take up her abode at the house of the three bachelors.

"I am old, Miss Fleming," he said, "Forty years old; a great age to you, and my brothers, Cornelius and Humphrey, who live with me, are older still. Cornelius is a great poet; he is engaged on a work—*The Upheaving of Ælfred*—which will immortalise his name. Humphrey is an artist; he is working at a group the mere conception of which, Cornelius says, would make even the brain of Michel Angelo stagger. You will be proud, I think, in after years, to have made the acquaintance of my brothers."

She came, having no choice or any other wish, accompanied by her French maid and the usual impedimenta of travel.

Phillis Fleming—her father called her Phillis because she was his only joy—was nineteen. She is twenty now, because the events of this story only happened last year. Her mother died in giving her birth; she had neither brothers nor sisters, nor many cousins, and those far away. When she was six her father died too—not of an interesting consumption or of a broken heart, or any ailment of that kind. He was a jovial fox-hunting ex-captain of cavalry, with a fair income and a carefully cultivated taste for enjoyment. He died from an accident in the field. By his will he left all his money to his one child and appointed as her trustees his father's old friend, Abraham Dyson of Twickenham and the City, and with him his own friend, Lawrence Colquhoun, a man some ten years younger than himself, with tastes and pursuits very much like his own. Of course, the child was taken to the elder guardian's house, and Colquhoun, going his way in the world, never gave his trust or its responsibilities a moment's thought.

Phillis Fleming had the advantage of a training quite different from that which is usually accorded to young ladies. She went to Mr. Abraham Dyson at a time when that old gentlemen, always full of crotchety ideas, was developing a plan of his own for female education. His theory of woman's training having just then grown in his mind to finished proportions, he welcomed the child as a subject sent quite providentially to his hand, and proceeded to put his views into practice upon little Phillis. That he did so showed a healthy belief in his own judgment. Some men would have hastened into print with a mere theory. Mr. Dyson intended to wait for twelve years or so, and to write his work on woman's education when Phillis's example might be the triumphant proof of his own soundness. The education conducted on Mr. Dyson's principles and rigidly carried out was approaching completion when it suddenly came to an abrupt termination. Few things in this world quite turn out as we hope and expect. It was on the cards that Abraham Dyson might die before the proof of his theory. This, in fact, happened; and his chief regret at leaving a world where he had been supremely comfortable, and able to enjoy his glass of port to his eightieth and last year, was that he was leaving the girl, the creation of his theory, in an unfinished state.

"Phillis," he said, on his deathbed, "the edifice is now complete,—all but the Coping-stone. Alas, that I could not live to put it on!"

And what the Coping-stone was no man could guess. Great would be the cleverness of him, who seeing a cathedral finished save for roof and upper courses, would undertake to put on these, with all the ornaments, spires, lanterns, gargoyles, pinnacles, flying buttresses, turrets, belfries, and crosses drawn in the dead designer's lost plans.

Abraham Dyson was a wealthy man. Therefore he was greatly respected by all his relations, in spite of certain eccentricities, notably those which forbade him to ask any of them to his house. If the nephews, nieces and cousins wept bitterly on learning their bereavement, deeper and more bitter were their lamentations when they found that Mr. Dyson had left none of them any money.

Not one penny; not a mourning ring; not a single sign or token of affection to one of them. It was a cruel throwing of cold water on the tenderest affections of the heart, and Mr. Dyson's relations were deeply pained. Some of them swore; others felt that in this case it was needless to give sorrow words, and bore their suffering in silence.

Nor did he leave any money to Phillis.

This obstinate old theorist left it all to found a college for girls, who were to be educated in the same manner as Phillis Fleming, and in accordance with the scheme stated to be fully drawn up and among his papers.

Up to the present, Joseph Jagenal had not succeeded in finding the scheme. There were several rolls of paper, forming portions of the great work, but none were finished, and all pointed to the last chapter, that entitled the "Coping-stone," in which, it was stated, would be found the whole scheme with complete fulness of detail. But this last chapter could not be found anywhere. If it never was found, what would become of the will? Then each one of Mr. Dyson's relations began to calculate what might fall to himself out of the inheritance. That was only natural, and perhaps it was not everyone who, like Mr. Gabriel Cassilis, openly lamented the number of Mr. Dyson's collateral heirs.

Not to be found. Joseph Jagenal's clerks now engaged in searching everywhere for it, and all the relations praying—all fervently and some with faith—that it might never turn up.

So that poor Phillis is sitting down to dinner with her education unfinished—where is that Coping-stone? Every young lady who has had a finishing year at Brighton may look down upon her. Perhaps, however, as her education has been of a kind quite unknown in polite circles, and she has never heard of a finishing year, she may be calm even in the presence of other young ladies.

What sort of a girl is she?

To begin with, she has fifty thousand pounds. Not the largest kind of fortune, but still something. More than most girls have, more than the average heiress has. Enough to make young Fortunio Hunter prick up his ears, smooth down his moustache, and begin to inquire about guardians; enough to purchase a roomy cottage where Love may be comfortable; enough to enable the neediest wooer, if he be successful, to hang up his hat on the peg behind the door and sit down for the rest of his years. Fifty thousand pounds is a sum which means possibilities. It was her mother's, and, very luckily for her, it was so tied up that Captain Fleming, her father, could not touch more than the interest, which, at three percent., amounts, as may be calculated, to fifteen hundred a year. Really, after explaining that a young lady has fifty thousand, what further praise is wanted, what additional description is necessary? By contemplation of fifty thousand pounds, ardent youth is inflamed as by a living likeness of Helen. Be she lovely or be she loathly, be she young or old, be she sweet or shrewish—she has fifty thousand pounds.

With her fifty thousand pounds the gods have given Phillis Fleming a tall figure, the lines of which are as delicately curved as those of any yacht in the Solent or of any statue from Greek studio. She is slight, perhaps too slight; she has hair of a common dark brown, but it is fine hair, there is a great wealth of it, it has a gleam and glimmer of its own as the sunlight falls upon it, as if there were a hidden colour lying somewhere in it waiting to be discovered; her eyes, like her hair, are brown—they are also large and lustrous; her lips are full; her features are not straight and regular, like those of women's beauties, for her chin is perhaps a little short, though square and determined; she has a forehead which is broad and rather low; she wears an expression in which good temper, intelligence, and activity are more marked than beauty. She is quick to mark the things that she sees, and she sees everything. Her hands are curious, because they are so small, so delicate, and so sympathetic; while her face is in repose you may watch a passing emotion by the quivering of her fingers, just as you may catch, if you have the luck, the laughter or tears of most girls first in the brightness or the clouding of their eyes.

There are girls who, when we meet them in the street, pass us like the passing of sunshine on an April day; who, if we spend the evening in a room where they are, make us understand something of the warmth which Nature intended to be universal, but has somehow only made special; whom it is a pleasure to serve, whom it is a duty to reverence, who can bring purity back to the brain of a rake, and make a young man's heart blossom like a rose in June.

Of such is Phillis Fleming.

III

PHILLIS'S EDUCATION

The dinner began without much conversation; partly because the twins were hungry, and partly because they were a little awed by the presence of an unwonted guest in white draperies.

Phillis noted that, so far as she had learned as yet, things of a domestic kind in the outer world were much like things at Mr. Dyson's, that is to say, the furniture of the dining-room was similar, and the dinner was the same. I do not know why she expected it, but she had some vague notion that she might be called upon to eat strange dishes.

"The Böllinger, brother Cornelius," said the artist.

"Thoughtful of you, brother Humphrey," the poet answered. "Miss Fleming, the Böllinger is in your honour."

Phillis looked puzzled. She did not understand where the honour came in. But she tasted her glass.

"It is a little too dry for me," she said with admirable candour. "If you have any Veuve Clicquot, Mr. Jagenal"—she addressed the younger brother—"I should prefer that."

All three perceptibly winced. Jane, the maid, presently returned with a bottle of the sweeter wine. Miss Fleming tasted it critically and pronounced in its favor.

"Mr. Dyson, my guardian," she said, "always used to say the ladies like their wine sweet. At least I do. So he used to drink Perier Jout très sec, and I had Veuve Clicquot."

The poet laid his forefinger upon his brow and looked meditatively at his glass. Then he filled it again. Then he drank it off helplessly. This was a remarkable young lady.

"You have lived a very quiet life," said Joseph, with a note of interrogation in his voice, "with your guardian at Highgate."

"Yes, very quiet. Only two or three gentlemen ever came to the house, and I never went out."

"A fair prisoner, indeed," murmured the poet. "Danae in her tower waiting for the shower of gold."

"Danae must have wished," said Phillis, "when she was put in the box and sent to sea, that the shower of gold had never come."

Cornelius began to regret his allusion to the mythological maid for his classical memory failed, and he could not at the moment recollect what box the young lady referred to. This no doubt came of much poring over Anglo-Saxon Chronicles. But he remembered other circumstances connected with Danae's history, and was silent.

"At least you went out," said Humphrey, "to see the Academy and the Water-colours."

She shook her head.

"I have never seen a picture-gallery at all. I have not once been outside Mr. Dyson's grounds until today, since I was six years old."

Humphrey supported his nervous system, like his brother, with another glass of the Böllinger.

"You found your pleasure in reading divine Poetry," said the Maker softly; "perhaps in writing Poetry yourself."

"Oh dear no!" said Phillis. "I have not yet learned to read. Mr. Dyson said that ladies ought not to learn reading till they are of an age when acquiring that mischievous art cannot hurt themselves or their fellow-creatures."

Phillis said this with an air of superior wisdom, as if there could be no disputing the axiom.

Humphrey looked oceans of sympathy at Cornelius, who took out his handkerchief as if to wipe away a tear, but as none was in readiness he only sighed.

"You were taught other things, however?" Joseph asked.

"Yes; I learned to play. My master came twice a week, and I can play pretty well; I play either by ear or by memory. You see," she added simply, "I never forget anything that I am told."

Compensation of civilised nature. We read, and memory suffers. Those who do not read remember. Before wandering minstrels learned to read and write, the whole Iliad was handed down on men's tongues; there are Brahmins who repeat all their Sacred Books word for word without slip or error, and have never learned to read; there are men at Oxford who can tell you the winners of Events for a fabulous period, and yet get plucked for Greats because, as they will tell you themselves, they really cannot read. Phillis did not know how to read. But she remembered—remembered everything; could repeat a poem dictated twice if it were a hundred lines long, and never forgot it; caught up an air and learned how to play it at a sitting.

She could not read. All the world of fiction was lost to her. All the fancies of poets were lost to her; all the records of folly and crime which we call history were unknown to her.

Try to think what, and of what sort, would be the mind of a person, otherwise cultivated, unable to read. In the first place, he would be clear and dogmatic in his views, not having the means of comparison; next, he would be dependent on oral teaching and rumor for his information; he would have to store everything as soon as learned, away in his mind to be lost altogether, unless he knew where to lay his hand upon it; he would hear little of the outer world, and very little would interest him beyond his own circle; he would be in the enjoyment of all the luxuries of civilisation without understanding how they got there; he would be like the Mohammedans when they came into possession of Byzantium, in the midst of things unintelligible, useful, and delightful.

"You will play to us after dinner, if you will be so kind," said Joseph.

"Can it be, Miss Fleming," asked Humphrey, "that you never went outside the house at all?"

"Oh no; I could ride in the paddock. It was a good large field and my pony was clever at jumping; so I got on pretty well."

"Would it be too much to ask you how you managed to get through the day?"

"Not at all," she replied; "it was very easy. I had a ride before breakfast; gave Mr. Dyson his tea at ten; talked with him till twelve; we always talked 'subjects,' you know, and had a regular course. When we had done talking, he asked me questions. Then I probably had another ride before luncheon. In the afternoon I played, looked after my dress, and drew."

"You are, then, an Artist!" cried Humphrey enthusiastically. "Cornelius, I saw from the first that Miss Fleming had the eye of an Artist."

"I do not know about that; I can draw people. I will show you some of my sketches, if you like, tomorrow. They are all heads and figures; I shall draw all of you tonight before going to bed."

"And in the evening?"

"Mr. Dyson dined at seven. Sometimes he had one or two gentlemen to dine with him; never any lady. When there was no one, we talked 'subjects' again."

WALTER BESANT AND JAMES RICE

Never any lady! Here was a young woman, rich, of good family, handsome, and in her way accomplished, who had never seen or talked with a lady, nor gone out of the house save into its gardens, since she was a child.

Yet, in spite of all these disadvantages and the strangeness of her position, she was perfectly self-possessed. When she left the table, the two elder brethren addressed themselves to the bottle of Château Mouton with more rapidity than was becoming the dignity of the wine. Joseph almost immediately joined his ward. When the twins left the dining-room with its empty decanters, and returned arm-in-arm to the drawing-room, they found their younger brother in animated conversation with the girl. Strange that Joseph should so far forget his usual habits as not to go straight to his own room. The two bosoms which heaved in a continual harmony with each other felt a simultaneous pang of jealousy for which there was no occasion. Joseph was only thinking of the Coping stone.

"Did I not feel it strange driving through the streets?" Phillis was saying. "It is all so strange that I am bewildered—so strange and so wonderful. I used to dream of what it was like; my maid told me something about it; but I never guessed the reality. There are a hundred things more than I can ever draw."

It was, as hinted above, the custom of this young person, as it was that of the Mexicans, to make drawings of everything which occurred. She was thus enabled to preserve a tolerably faithful record of her life.

"Show me," said Joseph—"show me the heads of my brothers and myself, that you promised to do, as soon as they are finished."

The brethren sat together on a sofa, the Poet in his favorite attitude of meditation, forefinger on brow; the Artist with his eyes fixed on the fire, catching the effects of colour. Their faces were just a little flushed with the wine they had taken.

One after the other crossed the room and spoke to their guest.

Said Cornelius:

"You are watching my brother Humphrey. Study him, Miss Fleming; it will repay you well to know that childlike and simple nature, innocent of the world, and aglow with the flame of genius."

"I think I can draw him now," said Phillis, looking at the Artist as hard as a turnkey taking Mr. Pickwick's portrait.

Then came Humphrey:

"I see your eyes turned upon my brother Cornelius. He is a great, a noble fellow, Miss Fleming. Cultivate him, talk to him, learn from him. You will be very glad some day to be able to boast that you have met my brother Cornelius. To know him is a Privilege; to converse with him is an Education."

"Come," said Joseph cheerfully, "where is the piano? This is a bachelor's house, but there is a piano somewhere. Have you got it, Cornelius?"

The Poet shook his head, with a soft sad smile.

"Nay," he said, "is a Workshop the place for music? Let us rather search for it in the Realms of Art."

In fact it was in Mr. Humphrey's Studio, whither they repaired. The girl sat down, and as she touched the keys her eyes lit up and her whole look changed. Joseph was the only one of the three who really cared for music. He stood by the fire and said nothing. The brethren on either side of the performer displayed wonders of enthusiastic admiration, each in his own way—the Poet sad and reflective, as if music softened his soul; the Artist with an effervescing gaiety delightful to behold. Joseph was thinking. "Can we"—had his thoughts taken form of speech—"can we reconstruct from the girl's own account the old man's scheme anew, provided the chapter on the Coping-stone be never found? Problem given. A girl brought up in seclusion, without intercourse with any of her sex except illiterate servants, yet bred to be a lady: not allowed even to learn reading, but taught orally, so as to hold her own in talk: required, to discover what the old man meant by it, and what was wanted to finish the structure. Could it be reading and writing? Could Abraham Dyson have intended to finish where all other people begin?"

This solution mightily commended itself to Joseph, and he went to bed in great good spirits at his own cleverness.

In the dead of night he awoke in fear and trembling.

"They will go into Chancery," he thought. "What if the Court refuses to take my view?"

At three in the morning the brethren, long left alone with their pipes, rose to go to bed.

Brandy-and-soda sometimes makes men truthful after the third tumbler, and beguiles them with illusory hopes after the fourth. The twins were at the end of their fourth.

"Cornelius," said the Artist, "she has £50,000."

"She has, brother Humphrey."

"It is a pity, Cornelius, that we, who have only £200 a year each, are already fifty years of age."

"Humphrey, what age do we feel?"

"Thirty. Not a month more," replied the Artist, striking out with both fists at an imaginary foe—probably old Time.

"Right. Not an hour above the thirty," said the Bard, smiting his chest gently. "As for Joseph, he is too old—"

"Very much too old—"

"To think of marrying such a young—"

"Fresh and innocent—"

"Engaging and clever girl as Miss Phillis Fleming."

Did they, then, both intend to marry the young lady?

IV

"To taste the freshness of the morning air."

Phillis retreated to her own room at her accustomed hour of ten. Her nerves were excited; her brain was troubled with the events of this day of emancipation. She was actually in the world, the great world of which her guardian had told her, the world where history was made, where wicked kings, as Mr. Dyson perpetually impressed upon her, made war their play and the people their playthings. She was in the world where all those things were done of which she had only heard as yet. She had seen the streets of London, or some of them—those streets along which had ridden the knights whose pictures she loved to draw, the princesses and queens whose stories Mr. Dyson had taught her; where the business of the world was carried on, and where there flowed up and down the ceaseless stream of those whom necessity spurs to action. As a matter of narrow fact, she had seen nothing but that part of London which lies between Highgate Hill and Carnarvon Square; but to her it seemed the City, the centre of all life, the heart of civilisation. She regretted only that she had not been able to discern the Tower of London. That might be, however, close to Mr. Jagenal's house, and she would look for it in the morning.

What a day! She sat before her fire and tried to picture it all over again. Horses, carriages, carts, and people rushing to and fro; shops filled with the most wonderful exhibition of precious things; eccentric people with pipes, who trundled carts piled with yellow oranges; gentlemen in blue with helmets, who lounged negligently along the streets; boys who ran and whistled; boys who ran and shouted; boys who ran and sold papers; always boys—where were all the girls? Where were they all going? and what were they all wishing to do?

In the evening the world appeared to narrow itself. It consisted of dinner with three elderly gentlemen; one of whom was thoughtful about herself, spoke kindly to her, and asked her about her past life; while the other two—and here she laughed—talked unintelligently about Art and themselves, and sometimes praised each other.

Then she opened her sketch-book and began to draw the portraits of her new friends. And first she produced a faithful *effigies* of the twins. This took her nearly an hour to draw, but when finished it made a pretty picture. The brethren stood with arms intertwined like two children, with eyes gazing fondly into each other's and heads thrown back, in the attitude of poetic and artistic meditation which they mostly affected. A clever sketch, and she was more than satisfied when she held it up to the light and looked at it, before placing it in her portfolio.

"Mr. Humphrey said I had the eye of an artist," she murmured. "I wonder what he will say when he sees this."

Then she drew the portrait of Joseph. This was easy. She drew him sitting a little forward, playing with his watch-chain, looking at her with deep grave eyes.

Then she closed her eyes and began to recall the endless moving panorama of the London streets. But this she could not draw. There came no image to her mind, only a series of blurred pictures running into each other.

Then she closed her sketch-book, put up her pencils, and went to bed. It was twelve o'clock. Joseph was still thinking over the terms of Mr. Dyson's will and the chapter on the Coping-stone. The twins were taking their third split soda—it was brotherly to divide a bottle, and the mixture was less likely to be unfairly diluted.

Phillis went to bed, but she could not sleep. The steps of the passers-by, the strange room, the excitement of the day kept her awake. She was like some fair yacht suddenly launched from the dock where she had grown slowly to her perfect shape, upon the waters of the harbour, which she takes for the waters of the great ocean.

She looked round her bedroom in Carnarvon Square, and because it was not Highgate, thought it must be the vast, shelterless and unpitying world of which she had so often heard, and at thought of which, brave as she was, she had so often shuddered.

It was nearly three when she fairly slept, and then she had a strange dream. She thought that she was part of the great procession which never ended all day long in the streets, only sometimes a little more crowded and sometimes a little thinner. She pushed and hastened with the rest. She would have liked to stay and examine the glittering things exhibited—the gold and jewelry, the dainty cakes and delicate fruits, the gorgeous dresses in the windows—but she could not. All pushed on, and she with them; there had been no beginning of the rush, and there seemed to be no end. Faces turned round and glared at her—faces which she marked for a moment—they were the same which she had seen in the morning; faces hard and faces hungry; faces cruel and faces forbidding; faces that were bent on doing something desperate—every kind of face except a sweet face. That is a rare thing for a stranger to find in a London street. The soft sweet faces belong to the country. She wondered why they all looked at her so curiously. Perhaps because she was a stranger.

Presently there was a sort of hue and cry and everybody began running, she with them. Oddly enough, they all ran after her. Why? Was that also because she was a stranger? Only the younger men ran, but the rest looked on. The twins, however were both running among the pursuers. The women pointed and flouted at her; the older men nodded, wagged their heads, and laughed. Faster they ran and faster she fled; they distanced, she and her pursuers the crowd behind; they passed beyond the streets and into country fields, where hedges took the place of the brilliant windows; they were somehow back in the old Highgate paddock which had been so long her only outer world. The pursuers were reduced to three or four, among them, by some odd chance, the twin brethren and as one, but who she could not tell, caught up with her and laid his hand upon hers, and she could run no longer and could resist no more, but fell, not with terror at all, but rather a sense of relief and gladness, into a clutch which was like an embrace of a lover for softness and strength, she saw in front of her dead old Abraham Dyson, who clapped his hands and cried, "Well run, well won! The Coping-stone, my Phillis, of your education!"

She woke with a start, and sat up looking round the room. Her dream was so vivid that she saw the group before her very eyes in the twilight—herself, with a figure, dim and undistinguishable in the twilight, leaning over her; and a little distance off old Abraham Dyson himself, standing, as she best remembered him, upright, and with his hands upon his stick. He laughed and wagged his head and nodded it as he said: "Well run, well won, my Phillis; it is the Coping-stone!"

This was a very remarkable dream for a young lady of nineteen. Had she told it to Joseph Jagenal it might have led his thoughts into a new channel.

She rubbed her eyes, and the vision disappeared. Then she laid her head again upon the pillow, just a little frightened at her ghosts, and presently dropped off to sleep.

This time she had no more dreams; but she awoke soon after it was daybreak, being still unquiet in her new surroundings.

And now she remembered everything with a rush. She had left Highgate; she was in Carnarvon Square; she was in Mr. Joseph Jagenal's house; she had been introduced to two gentlemen, one of whom was said to have a child-like nature all aglow with the flame of genius, while the other was described as a great, a noble fellow, to know whom was a Privilege and to converse with whom was an Education.

She laughed when she thought of the pair. Like Nebuchadnezzar, she had forgotten her dream. Unlike that king, she did not care to recall it.

The past was gone. A new life was about to begin. And the April sun was shining full upon her window-blinds.

Phillis sprang from her bed and tore open the curtains with eager hand. Perhaps facing her might be the Tower of London. Perhaps the Thames, the silver Thames, with London Bridge. Perhaps St. Paul's Cathedral, "which Christopher Wren built in place of the old one destroyed by the Great Fire." Phillis's facts in history were short and decisive like the above.

No Tower of London at all. No St. Paul's Cathedral. No silver Thames. Only a great square with houses all round. Carnarvon Square at dawn. Not, perhaps, a fairy piece, but wonderful in its novelty to this newly emancipated cloistered nun, with whom a vivid sense of the beautiful had grown up by degrees in her mind, fed only in the pictures supplied by the imagination. She knew the trees that grew in Lord Manfield's park, beyond the paddock; she could catch in fine days a glimpse of the vast city that stretches itself out from the feet of breezy Highgate; she knew the flowers of her own garden; and for the rest she imagined it. River, lake, mountain, forest, and field, she knew them only by talk with her guardian. And the mighty ocean she knew because her French maid had crossed it when she quitted fair Normandy, and told her again and again of the horrors encountered by those who go down to the sea in ships.

So that a second garden was a new revelation. Besides it was bright and pretty. There were the first flowers of spring, gay tulips and pretty things, whose name she did not know or could not make out from the window. The shrubs and trees were green with the first sweet chlorine foliage of April, clear and fresh from the broken buds which lay thick upon the ground, the tender leaflets as yet all unsullied by the London smoke.

The pavement was deserted, because it was as yet too early for anyone, even a milk-boy, to be out. The only living person to be seen was a gardener, already at work among the plants.

A great yearning came over her to be out in the open air and among the flowers. At Highgate she rose at all hours; worked in the garden; saddled and rode her pony in the field; and amused herself in a thousand ways before the household rose, subject to no restraint or law but one—that she was not to open the front-door, or venture herself in the outer world.

"Mr. Jagenal said I was to do as I liked," she said, hesitating. "It cannot be wrong to go out of the front-door now. Besides," reasoning here like a casuist, "perhaps it is the back-door which leads to that garden."

In a quarter of an hour she was ready. She was not one of those young ladies who, because no one is looking at them, neglect their personal appearance. On the contrary, she always dressed for herself; therefore, she always dressed well.

This morning she wore a morning costume, all one colour, and I think it was gray, but am not quite certain. It was in the graceful fashion of last year, lying in long curved lines, and fitting closely to her slender and tall figure. A black ribbon was tied round her neck, and in her hat— the hats of last year did not suit every kind of face, but they suited the face of Phillis Fleming—she wore one of those bright little birds whose destruction for the purposes of fashion we all deplore. In her hand she carried, as if she were still at Highgate and going to saddle her pony, a small riding-whip. And thus she opened the door, and slid down the stairs of the great silent house as stealthily and almost as fearfully as the Lady Godiva on a certain memorable day. It was a ghostly feeling which came over her when she ran across the broad hall, and listened to the pattering of her own feet upon the oilcloth. The broad daylight streamed through the *réverbère*; but yet the place seemed only half lit up. The closed doors on either hand looked as if dreadful things lurked behind them. With something like a shudder she let down the door-chain, unbarred the bolts, and opened the door. As she passed through she was aware of a great rush across the hall behind her. It was Cæsar, the mastiff. Awakened by a noise as of one burgling, he crept swiftly and silently up the kitchen-stairs, with intent to do a desperate deed of valour, and found to his rapturous joy that it was only the young lady, she who came the night before, and that she was going out for an early morning walk—a thing he, for his part, had not been permitted to do for many, many moons, not since he had been brought—a puppy yet, and innocent—to the heart of London.

No one out at all except themselves. What joy! Phillis shut the door very carefully behind her, looked up and down the street, and then running down the steps, seized the happy Cæsar by the paws and danced round and round with him upon the pavement. Then they both ran a race. She ran like Atalanta, but Cæsar led till the finish, when out of a courtesy more than Castilian, he allowed himself to be beaten, and Phillis won by a neck. This result pleased them both, and Phillis discovered that her race had brought her quite to the end of one side of the square. And then, looking about her, she perceived that a gate of the garden was open, and went in, followed by Cæsar, now in the seventh heaven. This was better, better, than leading a pair of twins who sometimes tied knots with their legs. The gate was left open by the under-gardener, who had arisen thus early in the morning with a view to carrying off some of the finer tulips for himself. They raced and chased each other up and down the gravel walks between the lilacs and laburnums bursting into blossom. Presently they came to the under-gardener himself, who was busy potting a selection of the tulips. He stared as if at a ghost. Half-past five in the morning, and a young lady, with a dog, looking at him!

He stiffened his upper lip, and put the spade before the flower-pots.

"Beg pardon, miss. No dogs allowed. On the rules, miss."

"William," she replied—for she was experienced in undergardeners, knew that they always answer to the name of William, also that they are exposed to peculiar temptations in the way of bulb—"William, for whom you are potting those tulips?"

Then, because the poor youth's face was suffused and his countenance was "unto himself for a betrayal," she whistled—actually whistled—to Cæsar, and ran on laughing.

"Here's a rum start," said William. "A young lady as knows my name, what I'm up to and all, coming here at five o'clock in the blessed morning when all young ladies as I ever heard of has got their noses in their pillowses—else 'tain't no good being a young lady. Ketches me a disposin' of the toolups. With a dawg, and whistles like a young nobleman."

He began putting back the flowers.

"No knowin' who she mayn't tell, nor what she mayn't say. It's dangerous, William."

By different roads, Montaigne wrote, we arrive at the same end. William's choice of the path of virtue was in this case due to Phillis's early visit.

V

"Te duce Cæsar."

Tired of running, the girl began to walk. It was an April morning, when the east wind for once had forgotten to blow. Walking, she whistled one of the ditties that she knew. She had a very superior mode of performing on that natural piccolo-flute, the human mouth; it was a way of her own, not at all like the full round whistle of the street-boy, with as much volume as in a bottle of '51 port, as full of unmeaning sound as a later poem of Robert Browning's, and as unmelodious as the instrument on which that poet has always played. Quite the contrary. Phillis's whistle was of a curious delicacy and of a bullfinch-like note, only more flexible. She trilled out an old English ditty, "When Love was young," first simply, and then with variations. Presently, forgetting that she was not in the old paddock, she began to sing it in her fresh young voice, William the under-gardener and Cæsar the dog her only audience. They were differently affected. William grew sad, thinking of his sins. The dog wagged his tail and rushed round and round the singer by way of appreciation. Music saddens the guilty, but maketh glad those who are clear of conscience.

It was half past six when she became aware that she was getting hungry. In the old times it was easy to descend to the kitchen and make what Indian people call a *chota hazri*, a little breakfast for herself. Now she was not certain whether, supposing the servants were about, her visit would be well received; or, supposing they were not yet up, she should know where to find the kettle, the tea, and the firewood.

She left the garden, followed by Cæsar, who was also growing hungry after his morning walk, and resolved on going straight home.

There were two objections to this.

First, she did not know one house from another, and they were all alike. Second, she did not know the number, and could not have read it had she known it.

Mr. Jagenal's door was painted a dark brown; so were they all. Mr. Jagenal's door had a knocker; so had they all. Could she go all round the square knocking at every door, and waking up the people to ask if Mr. Jagenal lived there? She knew little of the world, but it did occur to her that it would seem unconventional for a young lady to "knock in" at six in the morning. She did not, most unfortunately, think of asking William the under-gardener.

She turned to the dog.

"Now, Cæsar," she said, "take me home."

Cæsar wagged his tail, nodded his head, and started off before her at a smart walk, looking round now and then to see that his charge was following.

"Lucky," said Phillis, "that I thought of the dog."

Cæsar proceeded with great solemnity to cross the road, and began to march down the side of the square, Phillis expecting him to stop at every house. But he did not. Arrived at the corner where Carnarvon Street strikes off the square he turned aside, and looking round to see that his convoy was steering the same course, he trudged sturdily down that thoroughfare.

"This cannot be right," thought Phillis. But she was loath to leave the dog, for to lose him would be to lose everything, and she followed. Perhaps he knew of a back way. Perhaps he would take her for a little walk, and show her the Tower of London.

Cæsar, no longer running and bounding around her, walked on with the air of one who has an important business on hand, and means to carry it through. Carnarvon Street is long, and of the half-dismal, half-genteel order of Bloomsbury, Cæsar walked halfway down the street. Then he suddenly came to a dead stop. It was in front of a tavern, the Carnarvon Arms, the door of which, for it was an early house, was already open, and the potboy was taking down the shutters. The fact that the shutters were only half down made the dog at first suspect that there was something wrong. The house, as he knew it, always had the shutters down and the portals open. As, however, there seemed no unlawfulness of licensed hours to consider, the dog marched into the bar without so much as looking to see if Phillis was following, and immediately lay down with his head on his paws.

"Why does he go in there?" said Phillis. "And what is the place?"

She pushed the door, which, as usual in such establishments, hung half open by means of a leathern strap, and looked in. Nobody in the place but Cæsar. She entered, and tried to understand where she was. A smell of stale beer and stale tobacco hanging about the room smote her senses, and made her sick and faint. She saw the bottles and glasses, the taps and the counters, and she understood—she was in a drinking-place, one of the wicked dens of which her guardian sometimes spoke. She was in a tavern, that is, a place where workmen spend their earnings and leave their families to starve. She looked round her with curiosity and a little fear.

Presently she became aware of the early-risen potboy, who, having taken down the shutters, was proceeding about his usual work behind the bar, when his eyes fell upon the astonishing sight of a young lady, a real young lady, as he saw at once, standing in the Bottle and Jug department. He then observed the dog, and comprehended that she was come there after Cæsar, and not for purposes of refreshment.

"Why, miss," he said, "Cæsar thinks he's out with the two gentlemen. He brings them here regular, you see, every morning, and they takes their little glass, don't they, Cæsar?"

Probably—thought watchful Phillis, anxious to learn,—probably a custom of polite life which Mr. Dyson had neglected to teach her. And yet he always spoke with such bitterness of public-houses.

"Will you take a drop of somethink, miss?" asked the polite assistant, tapping the handles hospitably. "What shall it be?"

"I should like—" said Phillis.

"To be sure, it's full early," the man went on, "for a young lady and all. But Lor' bless your 'art, it's never none too early for most, when they've got the coin. Give it a name, miss, and there, the guvnor he isn't hup, and we won't chalk it down to you, nor never ask you for the money. On'y give it a name."

"Thank you very much," said Phillis. "I *should* like to have a cup of tea, if I could take it outside."

He shook his head, a gesture of disappointment.

"It can't be had here. Tea!"—as if he had thought better things of so much beauty—"Tea! Swipes! After all, miss, it's your way, and no doubt you don't know no better. There's a Early Caufy-'ouse a little way up the street. You must find it for yourself, because the dawg he don't know it; knows nothink about Tea, that dawg. You go out, miss, and Cæsar he'll go to."

Phillis thanked him again for his attention, and followed his advice. Cæsar instantly got up and sallied forth with her. Instead, however, of returning to the square, he went straight on down Carnarvon Street, still leading the way. Turning first to the right and then to the left, he conducted Phillis through what seemed a labyrinth of streets. These were mostly streets of private houses, not of the best, but rather of the seediest. It was now nearly seven o'clock, and the signs of life were apparent. The paper-boy was beginning, with the milk-man, his rounds; the postman's foot was preparing for the first turn on his daily treadmill of doorsteps and double knocks. The workmen, paid by time, were strolling to their hours of idleness with bags of tools; windows were thrown open here and there; and an early servant might be seen rejoicing to bang her mats at the street-door. Phillis tried to retain her faith in Cæsar, and followed obediently. It was easy to see that the dog knew where he was going, and had a distinct purpose in his mind. It was to be hoped, she thought, that his purpose included a return home as soon as possible, because she was getting a little tired.

Streets—always streets. Who were the people who lived in them all? Could there be in every house the family life of which Mr. Dyson used to tell her—the life she had never seen, but which he promised she should one day see—the sweet life where father and mother and children live together and share their joys and sorrows? She began to look into the windows as she walked along, in the hope of catching a hasty glance at so much of the family life as might be seen so early in the morning.

She passed one house where the family were distinctly visible gathered together in the front kitchen. She stopped and looked down through the iron railings. The children were seated at the table. The mother was engaged in some cooking operations at the fire. Were they about to sing a hymn and to have family prayers before their breakfast? Not at this house apparently, for the woman suddenly turned from her occupation at the fire and, without any adequate motive that Phillis could discern, began boxing the children's ears all round. Instantly there arose a mighty cry from those alike who had already been boxed and those who sat expectant of their turn. Evidently this was one of the houses where the family life was not a complete success. The scene jarred on Phillis, upsetting her pretty little Arcadian castle of domestic happiness. She felt disappointed, and hurried on after her conductor.

It is sad to relate that Cæsar presently entered another public-house. This time Phillis went in after him with no hesitation at all. She encountered the landlord in person, who greeted the dog, asked him what he was doing so early, and then explained to Miss Fleming that he was accustomed to call at the house everyday about noon, accompanied by two gentlemen, who had their little whack and then went away; and that she only had to go through the form of coming and departing in order to get Cæsar out too.

"Little whack," thought Phillis. "Little glass! What a lot of customs and expressions I have to learn!"

For those interested in the sagacity of dogs, or in comparative psychology, it may be noted as a remarkable thing that when Cæsar came out of that second public-house he hesitated, as one struck suddenly with a grievous doubt. Had he been doing right? He took a few steps in advance, then he looked round and stopped, then he looked up and down the street. Finally he came back to Phillis, and asked for instructions with a wistful gaze.

Phillis turned round and said, "Home, Cæsar." Then, after barking twice, Cæsar led the way back again with alacrity and renewed confidence.

He not only led the way home, but he chose a short cut known only to himself. Perhaps he thought his charge might be tired; perhaps he wished to show her some further varieties of English life.

In the districts surrounding Bloomsbury are courts which few know except the policeman; even that dauntless functionary is chary of venturing himself into them, except in couples, and then he would rather stay outside, if only out of respect to a playful custom, of old standing, prevalent among the inhabitants. They keep flower-pots on their first and second floors, and when a policeman passes through the court they drop them over. If no one is hurt, there is no need of an apology; if a constable receives the projectile on his head or shoulder, it is a deplorable accident which those who have caused it are the first to publicly lament. It was through a succession of these courts that the dog led Phillis.

Those of the men who had work to do were by this time gone to do it. Those who had none, together with those who felt strongly on the subject of Adam's curse and therefore wished for none, stayed at home and smoked pipes, leaning against the doorposts. The ideal heaven of these noble Englishmen is forever to lean against doorposts and forever to smoke pipes in a land where it is always balmy morning, and where there are "houses" handy into which they can slouch from time to time for a drink.

The ladies, their consorts, were mostly engaged in such household occupations as could be carried on out of doors and within conversation reach of each other. The court was therefore musical with sweet feminine voices.

The children played together—no officer of the London School Board having yet ventured to face those awful flower-pots—in a continuous stream along the central line of the courts. Phillis observed that the same game was universal, and that the players were apparently all of the same age.

She also remarked a few things which struck her as worth noting. The language of the men differed considerably from that used by Mr. Dyson, and their pronunciation seemed to her to lack delicacy. The difference most prominent at first was the employment of a single adjective to qualify everything—an observance so universal as to arrest at once the attention of a stranger. The women, it was also apparent, were all engaged in singing together a kind of chorus of lamentation, in irregular strophe and antistrophe, on the wicked ways of their men.

Rough as were the natives of this place, no one molested Phillis. The men stared at her and exchanged criticisms on her personal appearance. These were complimentary, although not poetically expressed. The women stared harder, but said nothing until she had passed by. Then they made remarks which would have been unpleasant had they been audible. The children alone took no notice of her. The immunity from insult which belongs to young ladies in English thoroughfares depends, I fear, more upon force of public opinion than upon individual chivalry. Una could trust herself alone with her lion: she can only trust herself among the roughs of London when they are congregated in numbers. Nor, I think, the spectacle of goodness and purity, combined with beauty, produce in their rude breasts, by comparison with themselves, those feelings of shame, opening up the way to repentance, which are expected by self-conscious maidens ministering in the paths of Dorcas.

Phillis walked along with steadfast eyes, watching everything and afraid of nothing, because she knew of no cause for fear. The dog, decreasing the distance between them, marched a few feet in advance, right through the middle of the children, who fell back and formed a lane for them to pass. Once Phillis stopped to look at a child—a great-eyed, soft-faced, curly-haired, beautiful boy. She spoke to him, asked him his name, held out her hand to him. The fathers and the mothers looked on and watched for the result, which would probably take the form of coin.

The boy prefaced his reply with an oath of great fulness and rich flavour. Phillis had never heard the phrase before, but it sounded unmusically on her ear. Then he held out his hand and demanded a copper. The watchful parents and guardians on the door-steps murmured approval, and all the children shouted together like the men of Ephesus.

At this juncture Cæsar looked round. He mastered the situation in a moment, surrounded and isolated his convoy by a rapid movement almost simultaneous in flank and rear; barked angrily at the children, who threatened to close in *en masse* and make short work of poor Phillis; and gave her clearly to understand once for all that she was to follow him with silent and unquestioning docility.

She obeyed, and they came out of the courts and into the squares. Phillis began to hope that the Tower of London would presently heave in sight, or at least the silver Thames with London Bridge; but they did not.

She was very tired by this time. It was nearly eight, and she had been up and out since five. Even her vigorous young limbs were beginning to feel dragged by her three hours' ramble. Quite suddenly Cæsar turned a corner, as it seemed, and she found herself once more in Carnarvon Square. The dog, feeling that he had done enough for reputation, walked soberly along the pavement, until he came to No. 15, when he ascended the steps and sat down.

The door was open, Jane the housemaid assiduously polishing the bell-handles.

"Lor' a mercy, miss!" she cried, "I thought you was a-bed and asleep. Wherever have you a-bin—with Cæsar too?"

"We went for a walk and lost ourselves," Phillis replied. "Jane, I am very hungry; what time is breakfast?"

"The master has his at eight, miss. But Mr. Cornelius he told me yesterday that you would breakfast with him and Mr. Humphrey—about eleven, he said. And Mr. Humphrey thought you'd like a little fresh fish and a prawn curry, perhaps."

"I shall breakfast with Mr. Joseph," said Phillis.

She went to her room in a little temper. It was too bad to be treated like a child wanting nice things for breakfast. A little more experience taught her that any culinary forethought on the part of the Twins was quite sure to be so directed as to secure their own favourite dishes.

She did breakfast with Joseph: made tea for him, told him all about her morning adventures, received his admonitions in good part, and sent him to his office half an hour later than usual. One of his letters bore an American stamp. This he opened, putting the rest in a leather pocket-book.

"This letter concerns you, Miss Fleming," he apologised, in an old-fashioned way; "that is why I opened it before you. It comes from your remaining guardian, Mr. Lawrence Colquhoun. Listen to what he says. He writes from New York; 'I am sorry to hear that my old friend Abraham Dyson is gone. I shall be ready to assume my new responsibilities in a fortnight after you receive this letter, as I hope to land in that time at Liverpool. Meantime give my kindest regards to my ward.' So—Lawrence Colquhoun home again!"

"Tell me about him: is he grave and old, like Mr. Dyson? Will he want me to go back to the old life and talk 'subjects'? Mr. Jagenal, much as I loved my dear old guardian, I *could* not consent to be shut up anymore."

"You will not be asked, my dear young lady. Mr. Colquhoun is a man under forty. He is neither old nor grave. He was in the army with your father. He sold out seven or eight years ago, spent a year or two about London, and then disappeared. I am his lawyer, and from time to time he used to send me his address and draw on me for money. That is all I can tell you of his travels. Lawrence Colquhoun, Miss Fleming, was a popular man. Everybody liked him; especially the—the fair sex."

"Was he very clever?"

"N-no; I should say *not* very clever. Not stupid. And, now one thinks of it, it is remarkable that he never was known to excel in anything, though he hunted, rode, shot, and did, I suppose, all the other things that young men in the army are fond of. He was fond of reading too, and had a considerable fund of information; but he never excelled in anything."

Phillis shook her head.

"Mr. Dyson used to say that the people we like best are the people who are in our own line and have acknowledged their own inferiority to ourselves. Perhaps the reason why Mr. Colquhoun was liked was that he did not compete with the men who wished to excel, but contentedly took a second place."

This was one of the bits of Dysonian philosophy with which Phillis occasionally graced her conversation, quoting it as reverently as if it had been a line from Shakespeare, sometimes with startling effect.

"I shall try to like him. I am past nineteen, and at twenty-one I shall be my own mistress. If I do not like him, I shall not live with him any longer after that."

"I think you will not, in any case, live at Mr. Colquhoun's residence," said Joseph; "but I am sure you will like him."

"A fortnight to wait."

"You must not be shy of him," Joseph went on; "you have nothing to be afraid of. Think highly of yourself, to begin with."

"I do," said Phillis; "Mr. Dyson always tried to make me think highly of myself. He told me my education was better than that of any girl he knew. Of course that was partly his kind way of encouraging me. Mr. Dyson said that shyness was a kind of cowardice, or else a kind of vanity. People who are afraid of other people, he said, either mistrust themselves or think they are not rated at their true value. But I think I am not at all afraid of strangers. Do I look like being afraid?" She drew herself up to her full height and smiled a conscious superiority. "Perhaps you will think that I rate myself too highly."

"That," said Joseph, with a compliment really creditable for a beginner,—"that would be difficult, Miss. Fleming."

When the Twins prepared to take their morning walk at twelve an unexpected event happened. Cæsar, for the first time on record, and for no reason apparent or assigned, refused to accompany them. They went out without him, feeling lonely, unhappy, and a little unprotected. They passed the Carnarvon Arms without a word. At the next halting-place they entered the bar in silence, glancing guiltily at each other. Could it be that the passion for drink, divested of its usual trappings of pretence, presented itself suddenly to the brethren in its horrid ugliness? They came out with shame-faced looks, and returned home earlier than usual. They were perfectly sober, and separated without the usual cheery allusions to Work. Perhaps the conscience was touched, for when Jane took up their tea she found the Poet in his Workshop sitting at the table, and the Artist in his Studio standing at his easel. Before the one was a blank sheet of paper; before the other was a blank canvas. Both were fractious, and both found fault with the tea. After dinner they took a bottle of port, which Humphrey said, they really felt to want.

VI

"I do not know
One of my sex; no woman's face remember
Save, from my glass, mine own."

In the afternoon Phillis, who was "writing up" her diary after the manner of the ancient Aztec, received a visitor. For the first time in her life the girl found herself face to face with—a lady. Men she knew—chiefly men of advanced age; they came to dine with Abraham Dyson. Women-servants she knew, for she had a French maid—imported too young to be mischievous; and there had been a cook at Highgate, with two or three maids. Not one of these virgins possessed the art of reading, or they would never have been engaged by Mr. Dyson. Nor was she encouraged by her guardian to talk with them. Also she knew that in the fulness of time she was to be somehow transferred from the exclusive society of men to that in which the leading part would be taken by ladies—women brought up delicately like herself, but not all, unhappily, on the same sound fundamental principle of oral teaching.

Among the loose odds and ends which remained in Mr. Dyson's portfolios, and where lay all that Joseph Jagenal could ever find to help in completing his great system of education, was the following scrap:—

"Women brought up with women are hindered in their perfect development. Let the girls be separated from the society of their sex, and be educated mostly among men. In this way the receptivity of the feminine mind may be turned to best account in the acquirement of robust masculine ideas. Every girl may become a mother; let her therefore sit among men and listen."

Perhaps this deprivation of the society of her own sex was a greater loss to Phillis than her ignorance of reading. Consider what it entailed. She grew up without the most rudimentary notions of the great art of flirtation; she had never even heard of looking out for an establishment; she had no idea of considering every young man as a possible husband; she had, indeed, no glimmerings, not the faintest streak of dawning twilight in the matter of love; while as for angling, hooking a big fish and landing him, she was no better than a heathen Hottentot. This was the most important loss, but there were others; she knew how to dress, partly by instinct, partly by looking at pictures; but she knew nothing about Making-up. Nature, which gave her the figure of Hebe, made this loss insignificant to her, though it is perhaps the opinion of Mr. Worth that there is no figure so good but Art can improve it. But not to *know* about Making-up is, for a woman, to lose a large part of useful sympathy for other women.

Again, she knew nothing of the way in which girls pour little confidences, all about trifles, into each other's ears; she had not cultivated that intelligence which girls can only learn from each other, and which enables them to communicate volumes with a half-lifted eyelid; she had a man's way of saying out what she thought, and even, so far as her dogmatic training permitted, of thinking for herself. She did not understand the mystery with which women enwrap themselves, partly working on the imagination of youth, and partly through their love of secluded talk—a remnant of barbaric times, and a proof of the subjection of the sex, the *frou-frou* of life was lost to her. And being without mystery, with the art of flirtation, with nothing to hide and no object to gain, Phillis was entirely free from the great vice into which women of the weaker nature are apt to fall—she was perfectly and wholly truthful.

And now she was about to make acquaintance for the first time with a lady—one of her own sex and of her own station.

I suppose Phillis must have preserved the characteristic instincts of her womanhood, despite her extraordinary training, because the first thing she observed was that her visitor was dressed in a style quite beyond her power of conception and imperfect taste. So she generalised from an individual case, and jumped at the notion that here was a very superior woman indeed.

The superiority was in the "young person" at Melton and Mowbray's, who designed the dress; but that Phillis did not know.

A more remarkable point with Mrs. Cassilis, Phillis's visitor, than her dress was her face. It was so regular as to be faultless. It might have been modelled, and so have served for a statue. It was also as cold as a face of marble. Men have prayed—men who have fallen into feminine traps—to be delivered from every species of woman except the cold woman; even King Solomon, who had great opportunities, including long life, of studying the sex, mentions her not; and yet I think that she is the worst of all. Lord, give us tender-hearted wives! When we carve our ideal woman in marble, we do not generally choose the wise Minerva nor the chaste Diana, but Venus, soft-eyed, lissom, tender—and generally true.

Mrs. Cassilis called. As she entered the room she saw a tall and beautiful girl, with eyes of a deep brown, who rose to greet her with a little timidity. She was taken by surprise. She expected to find a rough and rather vulgar young woman, of no style and unformed manners. She saw before her a girl whose attitude spoke unmistakably of delicacy and culture. Whatever else Miss Fleming might be, she was clearly a lady. That was immediately apparent, and Mrs. Cassilis was not likely to make a mistake on a point of such vital importance. A young lady of graceful figure, most attractive face, and, which was all the more astonishing, considering her education, perfectly dressed. Phillis, in fact, was attired in the same simple morning costume in which she had taken her early morning walk. On the table before her were her sketch-book and her pencils.

Mrs. Cassilis was dressed, for her part, in robes which it had taken the highest talent of Regent Street to produce. Her age was about thirty. Her cold face shone for a moment with the wintery light of a forced smile, but her eyes did not soften, as she took Phillis's hand.

Phillis's pulse beat a little faster, in spite of her courage.

Art face to face with Nature. The girl just as she left her nunnery, ignorant of mankind, before the perfect woman of the world. They looked curiously in each other's eyes. Now the first lesson taught by the world is the way to dissemble. Mrs. Cassilis said to herself, "Here is a splendid girl. She is not what I expected to see. This is a girl to cultivate and bring out—a girl to do one credit." But she said aloud—

"Miss Fleming? I am sure it is. You are *exactly* the sort of a girl I expected."

Then she sat down and looked at her comfortably.

"I am the wife of your late guardian's nephew—Mr. Gabriel Cassilis. You have never met him yet; but I hope you will very soon make his acquaintance."

"Thank you," said Phillis simply.

"We used to think, until Mr. Dyson died and his preposterous will was read, that his eccentric behaviour was partly your fault. But when we found that he had left you nothing, of course we felt that we had done you an involuntary wrong. And the will was made when you were a mere child, and could have no voice or wish in the matter."

"I had plenty of money," said Phillis; "why should poor Mr. Dyson want to leave me anymore?"

Quite untaught. As if anyone could have too much money!

"Forty thousand pounds a year! and all going to Female education. Not respectable Female education. If it had been left to Girton College, or even to finding bread-and-butter, with the Catechism and Contentment, for charity girls in poke bonnets, it would have been less dreadful. But to bring up young ladies as you were brought up, my poor Miss Fleming—"

"Am I not respectable?" asked Phillis, as humbly as a West Indian nigger before emancipation asking if he was not a man and a brother.

"My dear child, I hear you cannot even read and write."

"That is quite true."

"But everybody learns to read and write. All the Sunday school children even know how to read and write."

"Perhaps that is a misfortune for the Sunday school children," Phillis calmly observed; "it would very likely be better for the Sunday school children were they taught more useful things." Here Phillis was plagiarising—using Mr. Dyson's own words.

"At least everyone in society knows them. Miss Fleming, I am ten years older than you, and, if you will only trust me, I will give you such advice and assistance as I can."

"You are very kind," said Phillis, with a little distrust, of which she was ashamed. "I know that I must be very ignorant, because I have already seen so much, that I never suspected before. If you will only tell me of my deficiencies I will try to repair them. And I can learn reading and writing anytime, you know, if it is at all necessary."

"Then let us consider. My poor girl, I fear you have to learn the very rudiments of society. Of course you are quite ignorant of things that people talk about. Books are out of the question. Music and concerts; art and pictures; china—perhaps Mr. Dyson collected?"

"No."

"A pity. China would be a great help; the opera and theatres; balls and dancing; the rink—"

"What is the rink?" asked Phillis.

"The latest addition to the arts of flirtation and killing time. Perhaps you can fall back upon Church matters. Are you a Ritualist?"

"What is that?"

"My dear girl"—Mrs. Cassilis looked unutterable horror as a thought struck her—"did you actually never go to church?"

"No. Mr. Dyson used to read prayers everyday. Why should people go to church when they pray?"

"Why? why? Because people in society all go; because you must set

WALTER BESANT AND JAMES RICE

an example to the lower orders. Dear me! It is very shocking! and girls are all expected to take such an interest in religion. But the first thing is to learn reading."

She had been carrying a little box in her hands all this time, which she now placed on the table and opened. It contained small wooden squares, with gaudy pictures pasted on them.

"This is a Pictorial Alphabet: an introduction to all education. Let me show you how to use it. What is this?"

She held up one square.

"It is a very bad picture, abominably coloured, of a hatchet or a kitchen chopper."

"An axe, my dear—A, x, e. The initial letter A is below in its two forms. And this?"

"That is worse. I suppose it is meant for a cow. What a cow!"

"Bull, my dear—B, u, l, l, bull. The initial B is below."

"And is this," asked Phillis, with great contempt, "the way to learn reading? A kitchen chopper stands for A, and a cow with her legs out of drawing stands for B. Unless I can draw my cows for myself, Mrs. Cassilis, I shall not try to learn reading."

"You can draw, then?"

"I draw a little," said Phillis. "Not so well, of course, as girls brought up respectably."

"Pardon me, my dear Miss Fleming, if I say that sarcasm is not considered good style. It fails to attract."

Good style, thought Phillis, means talking so as to attract.

"Do let me draw you," said Phillis. Her temper was not faultless, and it was rising by degrees, so that she wanted the relief of silence. "Do let me draw you as you sit there."

She did not wait for permission, but sketched in a few moments a profile portrait of her visitor, in which somehow the face, perfectly rendered in its coldness and strength, was without the look which its owner always thought was there—the look which invites sympathy. The real unsympathetic nature, caught in a moment by some subtle artist's touch, was there instead. Mrs. Cassilis looked at it, and an angry flush crossed her face, which Phillis, wondering why, noted.

"You caricature extremely well. I congratulate you on that power, but it is a dangerous accomplishment—even more dangerous than the practice of sarcasm. The girl who indulges in the latter at most fails to attract; but the caricaturist repels."

"Oh!" said Phillis, innocent of any attempt to caricature, but trying to assimilate this strange dogmatic teaching.

"We must always remember that the most useful weapons in a girl's hands are those of submission, faith and reverence. Men hate—they hate and detest—women who think for themselves. They positively loathe the woman who dares turn them into ridicule."

She looked as if she could be one of the few who possess that daring.

"Fortunately," she went on, "such women are rare. Even among the strong-minded crew, the shrieking sisterhood, most of them are obliged to worship some man or other of their own school."

"I don't understand. Pardon me, Mrs. Cassilis, that I am so stupid. I say what I think, and you tell me I am sarcastic."

"Girls in society never say what they think. They assent, or at best ask a question timidly."

"And I make a little pencil sketch of you, and you tell me I am a caricaturist."

"Girls who can draw must draw in the conventional manner recognised by society. They do not draw likenesses; they copy flowers, and sometimes draw angels and crosses. To please men they draw soldiers and horses."

"But why cannot girls draw what they please? And why must they try to attract?"

Mrs. Cassilis looked at this most innocent of girls with misgiving. *Could* she be so ignorant as she seemed, or was she pretending.

"Why? Phillis Fleming, only ask me that question again in six months' time if you dare."

Phillis shook her head; she was clearly out of her depth.

"Have you any other accomplishments?"

"I am afraid not. I can play a little. Mr. Dyson liked my playing; but it is all from memory and from ear."

"Will you, if you do not mind, play something to me?"

Victoria Cassilis cared no more for music than the deaf adder which hath no understanding. By dint of much teaching, however, she had learned to execute creditably. The playing of Phillis, sweet, spontaneous, and full of feeling, had no power to touch her heart.

"Ye-yes," she said, "that is the sort of playing which some young men like: not those young men from Oxford who 'follow' Art, and pretend to understand good music. You may see them asleep at afternoon recitals. You must play at small parties only, Phillis. Can you sing?"

WALTER BESANT AND JAMES RICE

"I sing as I play," said Phillis, rising and shutting the piano. "That is only, I suppose, for small parties." The colour came into her cheeks, and her brown eyes brightened. She was accustomed to think that her playing gave pleasure. Then she reproached herself for ingratitude, and she asked pardon. "I am cross with myself for being so deficient. Pray forgive me, Mrs. Cassilis. It is very kind of you to take all this trouble."

"My dear, you are a hundred times better than I expected."

Phillis remembered what she had said ten minutes before, but was silent.

"A hundred times better. Can you dance, my dear?"

"No. Antoinette tells me how she used to dance with the villagers when she was a little girl at Yport."

"That can be easily learned. Do you ride?"

At any other time Phillis would have replied in the affirmative. Now she only asserted a certain power of sticking on, acquired on pony-back and in a paddock. Mrs. Cassilis sighed.

"After all, a few lessons will give you a becoming seat. Nothing so useful as clever horsemanship. But how shall we disguise the fact that you cannot read or write?"

"I shall not try to disguise it," Phillis cried, jealous of Mr. Dyson's good name.

"Well, my dear, we come now to the most important question of all. Where do you get your dresses?"

"O Mrs. Cassilis! do not say that my dresses are calculated to repel!" cried poor Phillis, her spirit quite broken by this time. "Antoinette and I made this one between us. Sometimes I ordered them at Highgate, but I like my own best."

Mrs. Cassilis put up a pair of double eye-glasses, because they were now arrived at a really critical stage of the catechism. There was something in the simple dress which forced her admiration. It was quite plain, and, compared with her own, as a daisy is to a dahlia.

"It is a very nice dress," she said critically. "Whether it is your figure, or your own taste, or material, I do not know; but you are dressed *perfectly*, Miss Fleming. No young lady could dress better."

Women meet on the common ground of dress. Phillis blushed with pleasure. At all events, she and her critic had something on which they could agree.

"I will come tomorrow morning, and we will examine your wardrobe together, if you will allow me; and then we will go to Melton &

Mowbray's. And I will write to Mr. Jagenal, asking him to bring you to dinner in the evening, if you will come."

"I should like it very much," said Phillis. "But you have made me a little afraid."

"You need not be afraid at all. And it will be a very small party. Two or three friends of my husband's, and two men who have just come home and published a book, which is said to be clever. One is a brother of Lord Isleworth, Mr. Ronald Dunquerque, and the other is a Captain Ladds. You have only to listen and look interested."

"Then I will come. And it is very kind of you, Mrs. Cassilis, especially since you do not like me."

That was quite true, but not a customary thing to be said. Phillis perceived dislike in the tones of her visitor's voice, in her eyes, in her manner. Did Mrs. Cassilis dislike her for her fresh and unsophisticated nature, or for her beauty, or for the attractiveness which breathed from every untaught look and gesture of the girl? Swedenborg taught that the lower nature cannot love the nobler; that the highest heavens are open to all who like to go there, but the atmosphere is found congenial to very few.

"Not like you!" Mrs. Cassilis, hardly conscious of any dislike, answered after her kind. "My dear, I hope we shall like each other very much. Do not let fancies get into your pretty head. I shall try to be your friend, if you will let me."

Again the wintry smile upon the lips, and the lifting of the cold eyes, which smiled not.

But Phillis was deceived by the warmth of the words. She took her visitor's hand and kissed it. The act was a homage to the woman of superior knowledge.

"Oh yes," she murmured, "if you only will."

"I shall call you Phillis. My name is Victoria."

"And you will tell me more about girls in society."

"I will show you girls in society, which is a great deal better for you," said Mrs. Cassilis.

"I looked at the girls I saw yesterday as we drove through the streets. Some of them were walking like this." She had been standing during most of this conversation, and now she began walking across the room in that ungraceful pose of the body which was more affected last year than at present. Ladies do occasionally have intervals of lunacy in the matter of taste, but if you give them time they come round again. Even crinolines went out at last, after the beauty of a whole generation had been spoiled by them. "Then there were others, who walked like this." She laid her head on one side, and affected a languid air, which I have myself remarked as being prevalent in the High Street of Islington. Now the way from Highgate to Carnarvon Square lies through that thoroughfare. "Then there were the boys. I never dreamed of such a lot of boys. And they were all whistling. This was the tune."

She threw her head back, and began to whistle the popular song of last spring. You know what it was. It came between the favourite air from the *Fille de Madame Angot* and that other sweet melody, "Tommy, make room for your Uncle," and was called "Hold the Fort." It refreshed the souls of Revivalists in Her Majesty's Theatre, and of all the street-boys in this great Babylon.

Mrs. Cassilis positively shrieked:

"My dear, *dear* DEAR girl," she cried, "you MUST not whistle!"

"Is it wrong to whistle?"

"Not morally wrong, I suppose. Girls never do anything morally wrong. But it is far worse, Phillis, far worse; it is unspeakably vulgar."

"Oh," said Phillis, "I am so sorry!"

"And, my dear, one thing more. Do not cultivate the power of mimicry, which you undoubtedly possess. Men are afraid of young ladies who can imitate them. For actresses, authors, artists, and common people of that sort, of course it does not matter. But for us it is different. And now, Phillis, I must leave you till tomorrow. I have great hopes of you. You have an excellent figure, a very pretty and attractive face, winning eyes, and a taste in dress which only wants cultivation. And that we will begin tomorrow at Melton and Mowbray's."

"Oh yes," said Phillis, clapping her hands, "that will be delightful! I have never seen a shop yet."

"She has—never—seen—a Shop!" cried Mrs. Cassilis. "Child, it is hard indeed to realise your Awful condition of mind. That a girl of nineteen should be able to say that she has never seen a Shop! My dear, your education has been absolutely unchristian. And poor Mr. Dyson, I fear, cut off suddenly in his sins, without the chance of repentance."

VII

"Bid me discourse, I will enchant thine ear."

Joseph Jagenal and his charge were the last arrivals at Mrs. Cassilis's dinner. It was not a large party. There were two ladies of the conventional type, well dressed, well looking, and not particularly interesting; with them their two husbands, young men of an almost preternatural solemnity—such solemnity as sometimes results from a too concentrated attention to the Money Market. They were there as friends of Mr. Cassilis, whom they regarded with the reverence justly due to success. They longed to speak to him privately on investments, but did not dare. There were also two lions, newly captured. Ladds, the "Dragoon" of the joint literary venture—"THE LITTLE SPHERE, by the Dragoon and the Younger Son"—is standing in that contemplative attitude by which hungry men, awaiting the announcement of dinner, veil an indecent eagerness to begin. The other, the "Younger Son," is talking to Mr. Cassilis.

Phillis remarked that the room was furnished in a manner quite beyond anything she knew. Where would be the dingy old chairs, sofas, and tables of Mr. Dyson's, or the solid splendour of Joseph Jagenal's drawing-room, compared with the glories of decorative art which Mrs. Cassilis had called to her aid? She had no time to make more than a general survey as she went to greet her hostess.

Mrs. Cassilis, for her part, observed that Phillis was dressed carefully, and was looking her best. She had on a simple white dress of that soft stuff called, I think, Indian muslin, which falls in graceful folds. A pale lavender sash relieved the monotony of the white, and set off her shapely figure. Her hair, done up in the simplest fashion, was adorned with a single white rose. Her cheeks were a little flushed with excitement, but her eyes were steady.

Phillis stole a glance at the other ladies. They were dressed, she was glad to observe, in the same style as herself, but not better. That naturally raised her spirits.

Then Mrs. Cassilis introduced her husband.

When Phillis next day attempted to reproduce her impressions of the evening, she had no difficulty in recording the likeness of Mr. Gabriel Cassilis with great fidelity. He was exactly like old Time.

The long lean limbs, the pronounced features, the stooping figure, the forelock which our enemy will *not* allow us to take, the head, bald save for that single ornamental curl and a fringe of gray hair over the ears—all the attributes of Time were there except the scythe. Perhaps he kept that at his office.

He was a very rich man. His house was in Kensington Palace Gardens, a fact which speaks volumes; its furnishing was a miracle of modern art; his paintings were undoubted; his portfolios of water-colours were worth many thousands; and his horses were perfect.

He was a director of many companies—but you cannot live in Kensington Palace Garden by directing companies and he had an office in the City which consisted of three rooms. In the first were four or five clerks, always writing; in the second was the secretary, always writing; in the third was Mr. Gabriel Cassilis himself, always giving audience.

He married at sixty-three, because he wanted an establishment in his old age. He was too old to expect love from a woman, and too young to fall in love with a girl. He did not marry in order to make a pet of his wife—indeed, he might as well have tried stroking a statue of Minerva as petting Victoria Pengelley; and he made no secret of his motive in proposing for the young lady. As delicately as possible he urged that, though her family was good, her income was small; that it is better to be rich and married than poor and single; and he offered, if she consented to become his wife, to give her all that she could wish for or ask on the material and artistic side of life.

Victoria Pengelley, on receipt of the offer, which was communicated by a third person, her cousin, behaved very strangely. She first refused absolutely; then she declared that she would have taken the man, but that it was now impossible; then she retracted the last statement, and, after a week of agitation, accepted the offer.

"And I must say, Victoria," said her cousin, "that you have made a strange fuss about accepting an offer from one of the richest men in London. He is elderly, it is true; but the difference between eight and twenty and sixty lies mostly in the imagination. I will write to Mr. Cassilis tonight."

Which she did, and they were married.

She trembled a great deal during the marriage ceremony. Mr. Cassilis was pleased at this appearance of emotion, which he attributed to causes quite remote from any thought in the lady's mind. "Calm to all outward seeming," he said to himself, "Victoria is capable of the deepest passion."

They had now been married between two and three years. They had one child—a boy.

It is only to be added that Mr. Cassilis settled the sum of fifteen thousand pounds upon the wedding-day on his wife, and that they lived together in that perfect happiness which is to be expected from well-bred people who marry without pretending to love each other.

Their dinners were beyond praise; the wine was incomparable; but their evenings were a little frigid. A sense of cold splendour filled the house—the child which belongs to new things and to new men.

The new man thirty years ago was loud, ostentatious, and vulgar. The new man now—there are a great many more of them—is very often quiet, unpretending, and well-bred. He understands art, and is a patron; he enjoys the advantages which his wealth affords him; he knows how to bear his riches with dignity and with reserve. The only objection to him is that he wants to go where other men, who were new in the last generation, go, and do what they do.

Mr. Cassilis welcomed Miss Fleming and Joseph Jagenal, and resumed his conversation with Jack Dunquerque. That young man looked much the same as when we saw him last on the slopes of the Sierra Nevada. His tall figure had not filled out, but his slight moustache had just a little increased in size. And now he looked a good deal bored.

"I have never, I confess," his host was saying, wielding a double eye-glass instead of his scythe,—"I have never been attracted by the manners and customs of uncivilised people. My sympathies cease, I fear, where Banks end."

"You are only interested in the country of Lombardy?"

"Yes; very good: precisely so."

"Outside the pale of Banks men certainly carry their money about with them—"

"Which prevents the accumulation of wealth, my dear sir. Civilisation was born when men learned to confide in each other. Modern history begins with the Fuggers, of whom you may have read."

"I assure you I never did," said Jack truthfully.

Then dinner was announced.

Phillis found herself on the right of Mr. Cassilis. Next to her sat Captain Ladds. Mr. Dunquerque was at the opposite corner of the table—he had given his arm to Mrs. Cassilis.

Mrs. Cassilis, Phillis saw, was watching her by occasional glances. The girl felt a little anxious, but she was not awkward. After all, she thought, the customs of society at a dinner-table cannot be very different from those observed and taught her by Mr. Dyson. Perhaps her manner of adjusting things was a little wanting in finish and delicacy—too downright. Also, Mrs. Cassilis observed she made no attempt to talk with Captain Ladds, her neighbour, but was, curiously enough, deeply interested in the conversation of Mr. Cassilis.

Ladds was too young for Phillis, despite his five and thirty years. Old men and greybeards she knew. Young men she did not know. She could form no guess what line of talk would be adopted by a young man—one who had a deep bass voice when he spoke, and attacked his dinner with a vigour past understanding. Phillis was interested in him, and a little afraid lest he should talk to her.

Others watched her too. Jack Dunquerque, his view a little intercepted by the épergne, lifted furtive glances at the bright and pretty girl at the other end of the table. Joseph Jagenal looked at her with honest pride in the beauty of his ward.

They talked politics, but not in the way to which she was accustomed. Mr. Dyson and his brother greybeards were like Cassandra, Elijah, Jeremiah, and a good many prophets of the present day, inasmuch as the more they discussed affairs the more they prophesied disaster. So that Phillis had learned from them to regard the dreadful future with terror. Everyday seemed to make these sages more dismal. Phillis had not yet learned that the older we get the wiser we grow, and the wiser we grow the more we tremble, that those are most light-hearted who know the least. At this table, politics were talked in a very different manner; they laughed where the sages wagged their heads and groaned; they even discussed, with a familiarity which seemed to drive out anxiety, the favorite bugbear of her old politicians, the continental supremacy of Germany.

The two young City men, who were as solemn as a pair of Home Secretaries, listened to their host with an eager interest and deference which the other two, who were not careful about investments, did not imitate. Phillis observed the difference, and wondered what it meant. Then Mr. Cassilis, as if he had communicated as many ideas about Russia as he thought desirable, turned the conversation upon travelling, in the interests of the Dragoon and the younger son.

"I suppose," he said, addressing Jack, "that in your travels among the islanders you practised the primitive mode of Barter."

"We did; and they cheated us when they could. Which shows that they have improved upon the primitive man. I suppose he was honest."

"I should think not," said the host. "The most honest classes in the world are the richest. People who want to get things always have a tendency to be dishonest. England is the most honest nation, because it is the richest. France is the next. Germany, you see, which is a poor country, yielded to the temptations of poverty and took Sleswick-Holstein, Alsace and Lorraine. I believe that men began with dishonesty."

"Adam, for example," said Ladds, "took what he ought not to have taken."

"O Captain Ladds!" this was one of two ladies, she who had read up the new book before coming to the dinner, and had so far an advantage over the other—"that is just like one of the wicked things, the delightfully wicked things, in the *Little Sphere*. Now we know which of the two did the wicked things."

"It was the other man," said Ladds.

"Is it fair to ask," the lady went on, "how you wrote the book?"

She was one of those who, could she get the chance, would ask Messieurs Erckmann and Chatrian themselves to furnish her with a list of the paragraphs and the ideas due to each in their last novel.

Ladds looked as if the question was beyond his comprehension.

At last he answered slowly—

"Steel pen. The other man had a gold pen."

"No—no; I mean did you write one chapter and your collaborateur the next, or how?"

"Let me think it over," replied Ladds, as if it were a conundrum.

Mrs. Cassilis came to the rescue.

"At all events," she said, "the great thing is that the book is a success. I have not read it, but I hear there are many clever and witty things in it. Also some wicked things. Of course, if you write wickedness you are sure of an audience. I don't think, Mr. Dunquerque," she added, with a smile, "that it is the business of gentlemen to attack existing institutions."

Jack shook his head.

"It was not my writing. It was the other man. I did what I could to tone him down."

"Have you read the immortal work?" Ladds asked his neighbour. He had not spoken to her yet, but he had eyes in his head, and he was gradually getting interested in the silent girl who sat beside him, and listened with such rapt interest to the conversation.

This great and manifest interest was the only sign to show that Phillis was not accustomed to dinners in society.

Ladds thought that she must be some shy maiden from the country—a little "rustical" perhaps. He noticed now that her eyes were large and bright, that her features were clear and delicate, that she was looking at himself with a curious pity, as if, which was indeed the case, she believed the statement about his having written the wicked things. And then he wondered how so bright a girl had been able to listen to the prosy dogmatics of Mr. Cassilis. Yet she had listened, and with pleasure.

Phillis was at that stage in her worldly education when she would have listened with pleasure to anybody—Mr. Moody, a lecture on astronomy, a penny-reading, an amateur dramatic performance, or an essay in the *Edinburgh*. For everything was new. She was like the blind man who received his sight and saw men, like trees, walking. Every new face was a new world; every fresh speaker was a new revelation. No one to her was stupid, was a bore, was insincere, was spiteful, was envious, or a humbug, because no one was known. To him who does not know, the inflated india-rubber toy is as solid as a cannon-ball.

"I never read anything," said Phillis, with a half blush. Not that she was ashamed of the fact, but she felt that it would have pleased Captain Ladds had she read his book. "You see, I have never learned to read."

"Oh!"

It was rather a facer to Ladds. Here was a young lady, not being a Spaniard, or a Sicilian, or a Levantine, or a Mexican, or a Paraguayan, or a Brazilian, or belonging to any country where such things are possible, who boldly confessed that she could not read. This in England; this in the year 1875; this in a country positively rendered unpleasant by reason of its multitudinous School Boards and the echoes of their wrangling!

Jack Dunquerque, in his place, heard the statement and looked up involuntarily as if to see what manner of young lady this could be—a gesture of surprise into which the incongruity of the thing startled him. He caught her full face as she leaned a little forward, and his glance rested for a moment on a cheek so fair that his spirits fell. Beauty disarms the youthful squire, and arms him who has won his spurs. I speak in an allegory.

Mrs. Cassilis heard it and was half amused, half angry.

Mr. Cassilis heard it, opened his mouth, as if to make some remark about Mr. Dyson's method of education, but thought better of it.

The two ladies heard it and glanced at her curiously. Then they looked at each other with the slightest uplifting of the eyebrow, which meant, "Who on earth can she be?"

Mrs. Cassilis noted that too, and rejoiced, because she was going to bring forward a girl who would make everybody jealous.

Ladds was the only one who spoke.

"That," he said feebly, "must be very jolly."

He began to wonder what could be the reason of this singular educational omission. Perhaps she had a crooked back; could not sit up to a desk, could not hold a book in her hand; but no, she was like Petruchio's Kate:

> "Like the hazel twig.
> As straight and slender."

Perhaps her eyes were weak; but no, her eyes were sparkling with the "right Promethean fire." Perhaps she was of weak intellect; but that was ridiculous.

Then the lady who had read the book began to ask more questions. I do not know anything more irritating than to be asked questions about your own book.

"Will you tell us, Mr. Dunquerque, if the story of the bear-hunt is a true one, or did you make it up?"

"We made up nothing. That story is perfectly true. And the man's name was Beck."

"Curious," said Mr. Cassilis. "An American named Beck, Mr. Gilead P. Beck, is in London now, and has been recommended to me. He is extremely rich. I think, my dear, that you invited him to dinner today?'

"Yes. He found he could not come at the last moment. He will be here in the evening."

"Then you will see the very man," said Jack, "unless there is more than one Gilead P. Beck, which is hardly likely."

"This man has practically an unlimited credit," said the host.

"And talks, I suppose, like, well, like the stage Americans, I suppose," said his wife.

"You know," Jack explained, "that the stage American is all nonsense. The educated American talks a great deal better than we do. He can string his sentences together; we can only bark."

"Perhaps our bark is better than their bite," Ladds remarked.

"A man who has unlimited credit may talk as he pleases," said Mr. Cassilis dogmatically.

WALTER BESANT AND JAMES RICE

The two solemn young men murmured assent.

"And he always did say that he was going to have luck. He carried about a Golden Butterfly in a box."

"How deeply interesting!" replied the lady who had read the book. "And is that other story true, that you found an English traveller living all alone in a deserted city?"

"Quite true."

"Really. And who was it? Anybody one has met?"

"I do not know whether you have ever met him. His name is Lawrence Colquhoun."

Mrs. Cassilis flushed suddenly, and then her pale face became paler.

"Lawrence Colquhoun, formerly of ours," said Ladds, looking at her.

Mrs. Cassilis read the look to ask what business it was of hers, and why she changed colour at his name.

"Colquhoun!" she said softly. Then she raised her voice and addressed her husband: "My dear, it is an old friend of mine of whom we are speaking, Mr. Lawrence Colquhoun."

"Yes!" he had forgotten the name. "What did he do? I think I remember—" He stopped, for he remembered to have heard his wife's name in connection with this man. He felt a sudden pang of jealousy, a quite new and rather curious sensation. It passed, but yet he rejoiced that the man was out of England.

"He is my guardian," Phillis said to Ladds. "And you actually know him? Will you tell me something about him presently?"

When the men followed, half an hour later, they found the four ladies sitting in a large semi-circle round the fire. The centre of the space so formed was occupied by a gentleman who held a cup of tea in one hand and declaimed with the other. That is to say, he was speaking in measured tones, and as if he were addressing a large room instead of four ladies: and his right hand and arm performed a pump-handle movement to assist and grace his delivery. He had a face so grave that it seemed as if smiles were impossible; he was apparently about forty years of age. Mrs. Cassilis was not listening much. She was considering, as she looked at her visitor, how far he might be useful to her evenings. Phillis was catching every word that fell from the stranger's lips. Here was an experience quite new and startling. She knew of America; Mr. Dyson, born not so very many years after the War of Independence, and while the memory of its humiliations was fresh in the mind of the nation, always thought and spoke of Americans as England's hereditary and implacable enemies. Yet here was one of the race talking amicably, and making no hostile demonstrations whatever. So that another of her collection of early impressions evidently needed reconsideration.

When he saw the group at the door, Mr. Gilead Beck—for it was he—strode hastily across the room, and putting aside Mr. Cassilis, seized Jack Dunquerque by the hand and wrung it for several moments.

"You have not forgotten me!" he said. "You remember that lucky shot? You still think of that Grisly?"

"Of course I do," said Jack; "I shall never forget him."

"Nor shall I, sir; never." And then he went through the friendly ceremony with Ladds.

"You are the other man, sir?"

"I always am the other man," said Ladds, for the second time that evening. "How are you, Mr. Beck, and how is the Golden Butterfly?"

"That Inseck, captain, is a special instrument working under Providence for my welfare. He slumbers at my hotel, the Langham, in a fire-proof safe."

Then he seized Jack Dunquerque's arm, and led him to the circle round the fire.

"Ladies, this young gentleman is my preserver. He saved my life. It is owing to Mr. Dunquerque that Gilead P. Beck has the pleasure of being in this drawing-room."

"O Mr. Dunquerque," said the lady who had read the book, "that is not in the volume!"

"Clawed I should have been, mauled I should have been, rubbed out I should have been, on that green and grassy spot, but for the crack of Mr. Dunquerque's rifle. You will not believe me, ladies, but I thought it was the crack of doom."

"It was a most charming, picturesque spot in which to be clawed," said Jack, laughing. "You could not have selected a more delightful place for the purpose."

"There air moments," said Mr. Beck, looking round the room solemnly, and letting his eyes rest on Phillis, who gazed at him with an excitement and interest she could hardly control—"there air moments when the soul is dead to poetry. One of those moments is when you feel the breath of a Grisly on your cheek. Even you, young lady, would, at such a moment, lose your interest in the beauty of Nature."

Phillis started when he addressed her.

"Did he save your life?" she asked, with flashing eyes.

Jack Dunquerque blushed as this fair creature turned to him with looks of such admiration and respect as the queen of the tournament bestowed upon the victor of the fight. So Desdemona gazed upon the Moor when he spake

> "Of most disastrous chances,
> Of moving accidents by flood and field."

Mrs. Cassilis affected a diversion by introducing her husband to Mr. Beck.

"Mr. Cassilis, sir," he said, "I have a letter for you from one of our most prominent bankers. And I called in the City this afternoon to give it you. But I was unfortunate. Sir, I hope that we shall become better acquainted. And I am proud, sir, I am proud of making the acquaintance of a man who has the privilege of life partnership with Mrs. Cassilis. That is a great privilege, sir, and I hope you value it."

"Hum—yes; thank you, Mr. Beck," replied Mr. Cassilis, in a tone which conveyed to the sharp-eared Phillis the idea that he thought considerable value ought to be attached to the fact of having a life partnership with *him*. "And how do you like our country?"

The worst of going to America, if you are an Englishman, or of crossing to England, if you are an American is that you can never escape that most searching and comprehensive question.

Said Mr. Gilead Beck:

"Well, sir, a dollar goes a long way in this country—especially in cigars and drinks."

"In drinks!" Phillis listened. The other ladies shot glances at each other.

"Phillis, my dear"—Mrs. Cassilis crossed the room and interrupted her rapt attention—"let me introduce Mr. Ronald Dunquerque. Do you think you could play something?"

She bowed to the young hero with sparkling eyes and rose to comply with the invitation. He followed her to the piano. She played in that sweet spontaneous manner which the women who have only been *taught* hear with despair; she touched the keys as if she loved them and as if they understood her; she played one or two of the "Songs without Words"; and then, starting a simple melody, she began to sing, without being asked, a simple old ballad. Her tone was low at first, because she did not know the room, not because she was afraid; but it gradually rose as she felt her power, till the room filled with the volumes of her rich contralto voice. Jack Dunquerque stood beside her. She looked up in his face with eyes that smiled a welcome while she went on singing.

"You told us you could not read," said the young man when she finished.

"It is quite true, Mr. Dunquerque. I cannot."

"How, then, can you play and sing?"

"Oh, I play by ear and by memory. That is nothing wonderful."

"Won't you go on playing?"

She obeyed, talking in low, measured tones, in time with the air.

"I think you know my guardian, Mr. Lawrence Colquhoun. Will you tell me all about him? I have never seen him yet."

This unprincipled young man saw his chance, and promptly seized the opportunity.

"I should like to very much, but one cannot talk here before all these people. If you will allow me to call tomorrow, I will gladly tell you all I know about him."

"You had better come at luncheon-time," she replied, "and then I shall be very glad to see you."

Mr. Abraham Dyson usually told his friends to come at luncheon-time, so she could not be wrong. Also, she knew by this time that the Twins were always asleep at two o'clock, so that she would be alone; and it was pleasant to think of a talk, *sola cum solo*, with this interesting specimen of newly-discovered humanity—a young man who had actually saved another man's life.

"Is she an outrageous flirt?" thought Jack, "or is she deliciously and wonderfully simple?"

On the way home he discussed the problem with Ladds.

"I don't care which it is," he concluded, "I must see her again. Ladds, old man, I believe I could fall in love with that girl. 'Ask me no more, for at a touch I yield.' Did you notice her, Tommy? Did you see her sweet eyes—I must say she has the sweetest eyes in all the world—looking with a pretty wonder at our quaint Yankee friend? Did you see her trying to take an interest in the twaddle of old Cassilis? Did you—"

"Have we eyes?" Ladds growled. "Is the heart at five and thirty a log?"

"And her figure, tall and slender, lissom and *gracieuse*. And her face, 'the silent war of lilies and of roses.' How I love the brunette faces! They are never insipid."

"Do you remember the half-caste Spanish girl in Manilla?"

"Ladds, don't dare to mention that girl beside this adorable angel of purity. I have found out her Christian name—it is Phillis—rhymes to lilies; and am going to call at her house tomorrow—Carnarvon Square."

"And I am going to have half an hour in the smoking-room," said Ladds, as they arrived at the portals of the club.

"So am I," said Jack. "You know what Othello says of Desdemona:

> *'O thou weed,*
> *Who art so lovely fair, and smell'st so sweet*
> *That the sense aches at thee!'"*

"I mean Phillis Fleming, of course, not your confounded tobacco."

VIII

"They say if money goes before, all ways do lie open."

I call this kind, boys," said Mr. Gilead P. Beck, welcoming his visitors, Captain Ladds and Jack Dunquerque; "I call this friendly. I asked myself last night, 'Will those boys come to see me, or will they let the ragged Yankee slide?' And here you are."

"Change," said Ladds the monosyllabic, looking round. "Gold looking up?"

There is a certain suite of rooms in the Langham Hotel—there may be a hundred such suites known to the travellers who have explored that mighty hostelry—originally designed for foreign princes, ambassadors, or those wandering kings whom our hospitality sends to an inn. The suite occupied by Mr. Beck consisted of a large reception-room, a smaller apartment occupied by himself, and a bedroom. The rooms were furnished in supposed accordance with the tastes of their princely occupants, that is to say, with solid magnificence. Mr. Beck had been in England no more than a week, and as he had not yet begun to buy anything, the rooms were without those splendid decorations of pictures, plate, and objects of art generally, with which he subsequently adorned them. They looked heavy and rather cheerless. A fire was burning on the hearth, and Mr. Beck was standing before it with an unlighted cigar in his lips. Apparently he had already presented some letters of introduction, for there were a few cards of invitation on the mantelshelf. He was dressed in a black frock-coat, as a gentleman should be, and he wore it buttoned up, so that his tall stature and thin figure were shown off to full advantage. He wore a plain black ribbon by way of necktie, and was modest in the way of studs. Jack Dunquerque noticed that he wore no jewelry of any kind, which he thought unusual in a man of unlimited credit, a new man whose fortune was not two years old. He was an unmistakable American. His chin was now close shaven, and without the traditional tuft; but he had the bright restless eye, the long spare form, the obstinately straight hair, the thin flexible mouth with mobile lips, the delicately shaped chin, and the long neck which seem points characteristic with our Transatlantic brethren. His grave face lit up with a smile of pleasure when he saw Jack Dunquerque. It was a thoughtful face; it had lines in it, such as might have been caused by the buffets of Fate; but his eyes were kindly. As for his speech, it preserved the nasal drawl of his New England birthplace; he spoke slowly, as if feeling for the right words, and his pronunciation was that of a man sprung from the ranks. Let us say at once that we do not attempt to reproduce by an affected spelling, save occasionally, the Doric of the New England speech. He was a typical man of the Eastern Estate—self-reliant, courageous, independent, somewhat prejudiced, roughly educated, ready for any employment and ashamed of none, and withal brave as an Elizabethan buccaneer, sensitive as a Victorian lady, sympathetic as—as Henry Longfellow.

"There is change, sir"—he addressed himself to Ladds—"in most things human. The high tides and the low tides keep us fresh. Else we should be as stagnant as a Connecticut gospel-grinder in his village location."

"This is high tide, I see," said Jack, laughing. "I hope that American high tides last longer than ours."

"I am hopeful, Mr. Dunquerque, that they air of a more abiding disposition. If you should be curious, gentlemen, to know my history since I left you in San Francisco, I will tell you it from the beginning. You remember that blessed inseck, the Golden Butterfly?"

"In the little box," said Ladds. "I asked you after his welfare last night."

Jack began to blush.

"Before you begin," he interposed, "we ought to tell you that since we came home we have written a book, we two, about our travels."

"Is that so?" asked Mr. Beck, with some natural reverence for the author of a book.

"And we have put you into it, with an account of Empire City."

"Me—as I was—in rags and without even a gun?"

"Yes; not a flattering likeness, but a true one."

"And the lucky shot, is that there too?"

"Some of it is there," said Ladds. "Jack would not have the whole story published. Looked ostentatious."

"Gentlemen, I shall buy that book. I shall take five hundred copies of that book for my people in the Dominion. Just as I was, you say—no boots but moccasins; not a dollar nor a cent; running for bare life before a Grisly. Gentlemen, that book will raise me in the estimation of my fellow-countrymen. And if you will allow me the privilege, I shall say it was written by two friends of mine."

Jack breathed freely. He was afraid Mr. Beck might have resented the intrusion of his ragged personality. An Englishman certainly would.

Mr. Beck seemed to think that the contrast between present broadcloth and past rags reflected the highest credit on himself.

This part of the work, indeed, which the critics declared to be wildly improbable, was the only portion read by Mr. Beck. And just as he persisted in giving Jack the sole credit of his rescue—perhaps because in his mental confusion he never even heard the second shot which finished the bear—so he steadfastly regarded Jack as the sole author of this stirring chapter, which was Ladd's masterpiece, and was grateful accordingly.

"And now," he went on, "I must show you the critter himself, the Golden Bug."

There was standing in a corner, where it would be least likely to receive any rude shocks or collisions, a small heavy iron safe. This he unlocked, and brought forth with great care a glass case which exactly fitted the safe. The frame of the case was made of golden rods; along the lower part of the front pane, in letters of gold, was the legend:

> *"If this Golden Butterfly fall and break,*
> *Farewell the Luck of Gilead P. Beck."*

"Your poetry, Mr. Dunquerque," said Mr. Beck, pointing to the distich with pride. "Your own composition, sir, and my motto."

Within the case was the Butterfly itself, but glorified. The bottom of the glass box was a thick sheet of pure gold, on which was fixed a rose, the leaves, flower, and stalk worked in dull gold. Not a fine work of art, perhaps, but a reasonably good rose, as good as that Papal rose they show in the Cluny Hotel. The Butterfly was poised upon the rose by means of thin gold wire, which passed round the strip of quartz which formed the body. The ends were firmly welded into the leaves of the flower, and when the case was moved the insect vibrated as if he was in reality alive.

"There! Look at it, gentlemen. That is the inseck which has made the fortune of Gilead P. Beck."

He addressed himself to both, but his eye rested on Jack with a look which showed that he regarded the young man with something more than friendliness. The man who fired that shot, the young fellow who saved him from a cruel death, was his David, the beloved of his soul.

Ladds looked at it curiously, as if expecting some manifestation of the supernatural.

"Is it a medium?" he asked. "Does it rap, or answer questions, or tell the card you are thinking of? Shall you exhibit the thing in the Egyptian Hall as a freak of Nature?"

"No, sir, I shall not. But I will tell you what I did, if you will let me replace him in his box, where he sits and works for Me. No harm will come to him there, unless an airthquake happens. Sit down, general, and you too, Mr. Dunquerque. Here is a box of cigars, which ought to be good, and you will call for your own drink."

It was but twelve o'clock, and therefore early for revivers of any sort. Finally, Mr. Beck ordered champagne.

"That drink," he said, "as you get it here, is a compound calculated to inspirit Job in the thick of his misfortunes. But if there is any other single thing you prefer, and it is to be had in this almighty city, name that thing and you shall have it."

Then he began:

"I went off, after I left you, by the Pacific Railway—not the first time I travelled up and down that line—and I landed in New York. Mr. Colquhoun gave me a rig out, and you, sir,"—he nodded to Jack— "you, sir, gave me the stamps to pay the ticket."

Jack, accused of this act of benevolence, naturally blushed a guilty acknowledgment.

Mr. Gilead P. Beck made no reference to the gift either then or at any subsequent period. Nor did he ever offer to repay it, even when he discovered the slenderness of Jack's resources. That showed that he was a sensitive and sympathetic man. To offer a small sum of money in repayment of a free gift from an extraordinarily rich man to a very poor one is not a delicate thing to do. Therefore this gentleman of the backwoods abstained from doing it.

"New York City," he continued, "is not the village I should recommend to a man without dollars in his pocket. London, where there is an institootion, or a charity, or a hospital, or a workhouse, or a hot-soup boiler in every street, is the city for that gentleman. Fiji, p'r'aps, for one who has a yearning after bananas and black civilisation. But not New York. No, gentlemen; if you go to New York, let it be when you've made your pile, and not before. Then you will find out that there air thirty theatres in the city, with lovely and accomplished actresses in each, and you can walk into Delmonico's as if the place belonged to you. But for men down on their luck, New York is a cruel place.

"I left that city, and I made my way North. I wanted to see the old folks I left behind long ago in Lexington; I found them dead, and I was sorry. Then I went farther North. P'r'aps I was driven by the yellow toy hanging at my back. Anyhow, it was only six weeks after I left you that I found myself in the city of Limerick on Lake Ontario."

"You do not know the city of Limerick, I dare say. It was not famous, nor was it pretty. In fact, gentlemen, it was the durndest misbegotten location built around a swamp that ever called itself a city. There were a few delooded farmers trying to persuade themselves that things would look up; there were a few down-hearted settlers wondering why they ever came there, and how they would get out again; and there were a few log-houses in a row which called themselves a street."

"I got there, and I stayed there. Their carpenter was dead, and I am a handy man; so I took his place. Then I made a few dollars doing chores around."

"What are chores?"

"All sorts. The clocks were out of repair; the handles were coming off the pails; the chairs were without legs; the pump-handle crank; the very bell-rope in the meetin' house was broken. You never saw such a helpless lot. I did not stay among them because I loved them, but because I saw things."

"Ghosts?" asked Ladds, with an eye to the supernatural.

"No, sir. That was what they thought I saw when I went prowling around by myself of an evening. They thought too that I was mad when I began to buy the land. You could buy it for nothing; a dollar an acre; half a dollar an acre; anything an acre. I've mended a cart-wheel for a five-acre lot of swamp. They laughed at me. The children used to cry out when I passed along, 'There goes mad Beck.' But I bought all I could, and my only regret was that I couldn't buy up the hull township—clear off men, women, and children, and start fresh. Some more champagne, Mr. Dunquerque."

"What was the Golden Butterfly doing all this time?" asked Ladds.

"That faithful inseck, sir, was hanging around my neck, as when you were first introduced to him. He was whisperin' and eggin' me on, because he was bound to fulfil the old squaw's prophecy. Without my knowing it, sir, that prodigy of the world, who is as alive as you are at this moment, will go on whisperin' till such time as the rope's played out and the smash comes. Then he'll be silent again."

He spoke with a solemn earnestness which impressed his hearers. They looked at the fire-proof safe with a feeling that at any moment the metallic insect might open the door, fly forth, and, after hovering round the room, light at Mr. Beck's ear, and begin to whisper words of counsel. Did not Mohammed have a pigeon? and did not Louis Napoleon at Boulogne have an eagle? Why should not Mr. Beck have a butterfly.

"The citizens of Limerick, gentlemen, in that dismal part of Canada where they bewail their miserable lives, air not a people who have eyes to see, ears to hear, or brains to understand. I saw that they were walking—no, sleeping—over fields of incalculable wealth, and they never suspected. They smoked their pipes and ate their pork. But they never saw and they never suspected. Between whiles they praised the Lord for sending them a fool like me, something to talk about, and somebody to laugh at. They wanted to know what was in the little box; they sent children to peep in at my window of an evening and report what I was doing. They reported that I was always doing the same thing; always with a map of Limerick City and its picturesque and interestin' suburbs, staking out the ground and reckoning up my acres. That's what I did at night. And in the morning I looked about me, and wondered where I should begin."

"What did you see when you looked about?"

"I saw, sir, a barren bog. If it had been a land as fertile as the land of Canaan, that would not have made my heart to bound as it did bound when I looked across that swamp; for I never was a tiller or a lover of the soil. A barren bog it was. The barrenest, boggiest part of it all was my claim; when the natives spoke of it they called it Beck's Farm, and then the poor critturs squirmed in their chairs and laughed. Yes, they laughed. Beck's Farm, they said. It was the only thing they had to laugh about. Wal, up and down the face of that almighty bog there ran creeks, and after rainy weather the water stood about on the morasses. Plenty of water, but a curious thing, none of it fit to drink. No living thing except man would set his lips to that brackish, bad-smelling water. And that wasn't all; sometimes a thick black slime rose to the surface of the marsh and lay there an inch thick; sometimes you came upon patches of 'gum-beds,' as they called them, where the ground was like tar, and smelt strong. That is what I saw when I looked around, sir. And to think that those poor mean pork raisers saw it all the same as I did and never suspected! Only cursed the gifts of the Lord when they weren't laughing at Beck's Farm."

"And you found—what? Gold?"

"No. I found what I expected. And that was better than gold. Mind, I say nothing against gold. Gold has made many a pretty little fortune—"

"Little!"

"Little, sir. There's no big fortunes made out of gold. Though many a pretty villa-location, with a tidy flower-garden up and down the States, is built out of the gold-mines. Diamonds again. One or two men likes the name of diamonds; but not many. There's the disadvantage about gold and diamonds that you have to dig for them, and to dig durned hard, and to dig by yourself mostly. Americans do not love digging. Like the young gentleman in the parable, they cannot dig, and to beg they air ashamed. It is the only occupation that they air ashamed of. Then there's iron, and there's coals; but you've got to dig for them. Lord! Lord! This great airth holds a hundred things covered up for them who know how to look and do not mind digging. But, gentlemen, the greatest gift the airth has to bestow she gave to me—abundant, spontaneous, etarnal, without bottom, and free."

"And that is—"

"It is ILE."

Mr. Beck paused a moment. His face was lit with a real and genuine enthusiasm, a pious appreciation of the choicer blessings of life; those, namely, which enable a man to sit down and enjoy the proceeds of other men's labour. No provision has been made in the prayer-book of any Church for the expression of this kind of thankfulness. Yet surely there ought to be somewhere a clause for the rich. No more blissful repose can fall upon the soul than, after long years of labour and failure, to sit down and enjoy the fruits of other men's labour. A Form of Thanksgiving for publishers, managers of theatres, owners of coal-mines, and such gentlemen as Mr. Gilead P. Beck, might surely be introduced into our Ritual with advantage. It would naturally be accompanied by incense.

"It is Ile, sir."

He opened another bottle of champagne and took a glass.

"Ile. Gold you have to dig, to pick, to wash. Gold means rheumatism and a bent back. Ile flows, and you become suddenly rich. You make all the loafers around fill your pails for you. And then your bankers tell you how many millions of dollars you are worth."

"Millions!" repeated Jack. "The word sounds very rich and luxurious."

"It is so, sir. There's nothing like it in the Old Country. England is a beautiful place, and London is a beautiful city. You've got many blessin's in this beautiful city. If you haven't got Joe Tweed, you've got—"

"Hush!" said Jack; "it's libellous to give names."

"And if you haven't got Erie stock and your whiskey-rings, you've got your foreign bonds to take your surplus cash. No, gentlemen; London is not, in some respects, much behind New York. But one thing this country has not got, and that is—Ile.

"It is nearly a year since I made up my mind to begin my well. I *knew* it was there, because I'd been in Pennsylvania and learned the signs; it was only the question whether I should strike it, and where. The neighbours thought I was digging for water, and figured around with their superior intellecks, because they were certain the water would be brackish. Then they got tired of watching, and I worked on. Boring a well is not quite the sort of work a man would select for a pleasant and variegated occupation. I reckon it's monotonous; but I worked on. I knew what was coming; I thought o' that Indian squaw, and I always had my Golden Butterfly tied in a box at my back. I bored and I bored. Day after day I bored. In that lonely miasmatic bog I bored all day and best part of the night. For nothing came, and sometimes qualms crossed my mind that perhaps there would never be anything. But always there was the gummy mud, smelling of what I knew was below, to lead me on.

"It was the ninth day, and noon. I had a shanty called the farmhouse, about a hundred yards from my well. And there I was taking my dinner. To you two young English aristocrats—"

"Ladds' Cocoa, the only perfect fragrance."

"Shut up, Ladds," growled Jack; "don't interrupt."

"I say, to you two young aristocrats a farmer's dinner in that township would not sound luxurious. Mine consisted, on that day and all days, of cold boiled pork and bread."

"Ah, yah!" said Jack Dunquerque, who had a proud stomach.

"Yes, sir, my own remark everyday when I sat down to that simple banquet. But when you are hungry you must eat, murmur though you will for Egyptian flesh-pots. Cold pork was my dinner, with bread. And the watter to wash it down with was brackish. In those days, gentlemen, I said no grace. It didn't seem to me that the most straight-walking Christian was expected to be more than tolerably thankful for cold pork. My gratitude was so moderate that it wasn't worth offering."

"And while you were eating the pork," said Ladds, "the Golden Butterfly flew down the shaft by himself, and struck oil of his own accord."

"No, sir; for once you are wrong. That most beautiful creation of Nature in her sweetest mood—she must have got up with the sun on a fine summer morning—was reposing in his box round my neck as usual. He did not go down the shaft at all. Nobody went down. But something came up—up like a fountain, up like the bubbling over of the airth's eternal teapot; a black muddy jet of stuff. Great sun! I think I see it now."

He paused and sighed.

"It was nearly all Ile, pure and unadulterated, from the world's workshop. Would you believe it, gentlemen? There were not enough bar'ls, not by hundreds, in the neighbourhood all round Limerick City, to catch that Ile. It flowed in a stream three feet down the creek; it was carried away into the lake and lost; it ran free and uninterrupted for three days and three nights. We saved what we could. The neighbours brought their pails, their buckets, their basins, their kettles; there was not a utensil of any kind that was not filled with Ile, from the pig's trough to the child's pap-bowl. Not one. It ran and it ran. When the first flow subsided we calculated that seven million bar'ls had been wasted and lost. Seven millions! I am a Christian man, and grateful to the Butterfly, but I sometimes repine when I think of that wasted Ile. Every bar'l worth nine dollars at least, and most likely ten. Sixty-three millions of dollars. Twelve millions of pounds sterling lost in three days for want of a few coopers. Did you ever think, Mr. Dunquerque, what you could do with twelve millions sterling?"

"I never did," said Jack. "My imagination never got beyond thousands."

"With twelve millions I might have bought up the daily press of England, and made you all republicans in a month. I might have made the Panama Canal; I might have bought Palesteen and sent the Jews back; I might have given America fifty ironclads; I might have put Don Carlos on the throne of Spain. But it warn't to be. Providence wants no rivals, meddling and messing. That was why the Ile ran away and was lost while I ate the cold boiled pork. Perhaps it's an interestin' fact that I never liked cold boiled pork before, and I have hated it ever since.

"The great spurt subsided, and we went to work in earnest. That well has continued to yield five hundred bar'ls daily. That is four thousand five hundred dollars in my pocket every four and twenty hours."

"Do you mean that your income is nine hundred pounds a day?" asked Jack.

"I do, sir. You go your pile on that. It is more, but I do not know how much more. Perhaps it's twice as much. There are wells of mine sunk all over the place; the swamp is covered with Gilead P. Beck's derricks. The township of Limerick has become the city of Rockoleaville—my name, that was—and a virtuous and industrious population are all engaged morning, noon, and night in fillin' my pails. There's twenty-five bars, I believe, at this moment. There are three meetin'-houses and two daily papers, and there air fifteen lawyers."

"It seems better than Cocoa Nibs," said Ladds.

"But the oil may run dry."

"It *has* run dry in Pennsylvania. That is so, and I do not deny it. But Ile will not run dry in Rockoleaville. I have been thinking over the geological problem, and I have solved it, all by myself."

"What is this world, gentlemen?"

"A round ball," said Jack, with the promptitude of a Board schoolboy and the profundity of a Woolwich cadet.

"Sir, it is like a great orange. It has its outer rind, what they call the crust. Get through that crust and what do you find?"

"More crust," replied Ladds, who was not a competition-wallah.

"Did you ever eat pumpkin pie, sir?" Mr. Beck replied, *more Socratico*, by asking another question. "And if you did, was your pie all crust? Inside that pie, sir, was pumpkin, apple, and juice. So inside the rind of the earth there may be all sorts of things: gold and iron, lava, diamonds, coals; but the juice, the pie-juice, is Ile. You tap the rind and you get the Ile. This Ile will run, I calculate, for five thousand and fifty-two years, if they don't sinfully waste it, at an annual consumption of eighteen million bar'ls. Now that's a low estimate when you consider the progress of civilisation. When it is all gone, perhaps before, this poor old airth will crack up like an empty egg."

This was an entirely new view of geology, and it required time for Mr. Beck's hearers to grasp the truth thus presented to their minds. They were silent.

"At Rockoleaville," he went on, "I've got the pipe straight into the middle of the pie, and right through the crust. There's no mistake about that main shaft. Other mines may give out, but my Ile will run forever."

"Then we may congratulate you," said Jack, "on the possession of a boundless fortune."

"You may, sir."

"And what do you intend to do?"

"For the present I shall stay in London. I like your great city. Here I get invited to dinner and dancin', because I am an American and rich. There they won't have a man who is not thoroughbred. Your friend Mrs. Cassilis asks me to her house—a first-rater. A New York lady turns up her pretty nose at a man who's struck Ile. 'Shoddy,' she says, and then she takes no more notice. Shoddy it may be. Rough my manners may be. But I don't pretend to anything, and the stamps air real."

"We always thought ourselves exclusive," said Jack.

"Did you, sir? Wall—" He stopped, as if he had intended to say something unpleasantly true. "I shall live in London for the present. I've got a big income, and I don't rightly know what to do with it. But I shall find out sometime.

"That was a lovely young thing with Mrs. Cassilis the other night," he went on meditatively. "A young thing that a man can worship for her beauty while she is young, and her goodness all her life. Not like an American gal. Ours are prettier, but they look as if they would blow away. And their voices are not so full. Miss Fleming is flesh and blood. Don't blush, Mr. Dunquerque, because it does you credit."

Jack did blush, and they took their departure.

"Mr. Dunquerque," whispered Gilead P. Beck when Ladds was through the door, "think of what I told you; what is mine is yours. Remember that. If I can do anything for you, let me know. And come to see me. It does me good to look at your face. Come here as often as you can."

Jack laughed and escaped.

IX

"By my modesty,
The jewel in my dower, I would not wish
Any companion in the world but you."

Jack Dunquerque was no more remarkable for shrinking modesty than any other British youth of his era; but he felt some little qualms as he walked towards Bloomsbury the day after Mrs. Cassilis's dinner to avail himself of Phillis's invitation.

Was it coquetry, or was it simplicity?

She said she would be glad to see him at luncheon. Who else would be there?

Probably a Mrs. Jagenal—doubtless the wife of the heavy man who brought Miss Fleming to the party; herself a solid person in black silk and a big gold chain; motherly with the illiterate Dryad.

"Houses mighty respectable," he thought, penetrating into Carnarvon Square. "Large incomes; comfortable quarters; admirable port, most likely, in most of them; claret certainly good, too—none of your Gladstone tap; sherry probably rather coarse. Must ask for Mrs. Jagenal, I suppose."

He did ask for Mrs. Jagenal, and was informed by Jane that there was no such person, and that, as she presently explained with warmth, no such person was desired by the household. Jack Dunquerque thereupon asked for Mr. Jagenal. The maid asked which Mr. Jagenal. Jack replied in the most irritating manner possible—the Socratic—by asking another question. The fact that Socrates went about perpetually asking questions is quite enough to account for the joy with which an exasperated mob witnessed his judicial murder. The Athenians bore for a good many years with his maddening questions—as to whether this way or that way or how—and finally lost patience. Hence the little bowl of drink.

Quoth Jack, "How many are there of them?"

Jane looked at the caller with suspicion. He seemed a gentleman, but appearances are deceptive. Suppose he came for what he could pick up? The twins' umbrellas were in the hall, and their great-coats. He laughed, and showed an honest front; but who can trust a London stranger? Jane remembered the silver spoons now on the luncheon-table, and began to think of shutting the door in his face.

"You can't be a friend of the family," she said, "else you'd know the three Mr. Jagenals by name, and not come here showing your ignorance by asking for Mrs. Jagenal. Mrs. Jagenal indeed! Perhaps you'd better call in the evening and see Mr. Joseph."

"I am not a friend of the family," he replied meekly. "I wish I was. But Miss Fleming expects me at this hour. Will you take in my card?"

He stepped into the hall, and felt as if the fortress was won. Phillis was waiting for him in the dining-room, where, he observed, luncheon was laid for two. Was he, then, about to be entertained by the young lady alone?

If she looked dainty in her white evening dress, she was far daintier in her half-mourning grey frock, which fitted so tightly to her slender figure, and was set off by the narrow black ribbon round her neck which was her only ornament; for she carried neither watch nor chain, and wore neither ear-rings nor finger-rings. This heiress was as innocent of jewelry as any little milliner girl of Bond Street, and far more happy, because she did not wish to wear any.

"I thought you would come about this time," she said, with the kindliest welcome in her eyes; "and I waited for you here. Let us sit down and take luncheon."

Mr. Abraham Dyson never had any visitors except for dinner or luncheon; so that Phillis naturally associated an early call with eating.

"I always have luncheon by myself," explained the young hostess; "so that it is delightful to have someone who can talk."

She sat at the head of the table, Jack taking his seat at the side. She looked fresh, bright, and animated. The sight of her beauty even affected Jack's appetite, although it was an excellent luncheon.

"This curried fowl," she went on. "It was made for Mr. Jagenal's brothers; but they came down late, and were rather cross. We could not persuade them to eat anything this morning."

"Are they home for the holidays?"

Phillis burst out laughing—such a fresh, bright, spontaneous laugh. Jack laughed too, and then wondered why he did it.

"Home for the holidays! They are always home, and it is always a holiday with them."

"Do you not allow them to lunch with you?"

She laughed again.

"They do not breakfast till ten or eleven."

Jack felt a little fogged, and waited for further information.

WALTER BESANT AND JAMES RICE

"Will you take beer or claret? No, thank you; no curry for me. Jane, Mr. Dunquerque will take a glass of beer. How beautiful!" she went on, looking steadily in the young man's face, to his confusion—"how beautiful it must be to meet a man whose life you have saved! I should like—once—just once—to do a single great action, and dream of it ever after."

"But mine was not a great action. I shot a bear which was following Mr. Beck and meant mischief; that is all."

"But you might have missed," said Phillis, with justice. "And then Mr. Beck would have been killed."

Might have missed! How many V.C. 's we should have but for that simple possibility! Might have missed! And then Gilead Beck would have been clawed, and the Golden Butterfly destroyed, and this history never have reached beyond its first chapter. Above all, Phillis might never have known Jack Dunquerque.

"And you are always alone in this great house?" he asked, to change the subject.

"Only in the day-time. Mr. Joseph and I breakfast at eight. Then I walk with him as far as his office in Lincoln's Inn-Fields, now that I know the way. At first he used to send one of his clerks back with me, for fear of my being lost. But I felt sorry for the poor young man having to walk all the way with a girl like me, and so I told him, after the second day, that I was sure he longed to be at his writing, and I would go home by myself."

"No doubt," said Jack, "he was rejoiced to go back to his pleasant and exciting work. All lawyers' clerks are so well paid, and so happy in their occupation, that they prefer it even to walking with a—a—a Dryad."

Phillis was dimly conscious that there was more in these words than a literal statement. She was as yet unacquainted with the figures of speech which consist of saying one thing and meaning another, and she made a mental note of the fact that lawyers' clerks are a happy and contented race. It adds something to one's happiness to know that others are also happy.

"And the boys—Mr. Jagenal's brothers?"

"They are always asleep from two to six. Then they come down to dinner, and talk of the work they have done. Don't you know them? Oh, they are not boys at all! One is Cornelius. He is a great poet. He is writing a long epic poem called the *Upheaving of Ælfred*. Humphrey, his brother, says it will be the greatest work of this century. But I do not think very much is done. Humphrey is a great artist, you know. He is engaged on a splendid picture—at least it will be splendid when it is finished. At present nothing is on the canvas. He says he is studying the groups. Cornelius says it will be the finest artistic achievement of the age. Will you have some more beer? Jane, give Mr. Dunquerque a glass of sherry. And now let us go into the drawing-room, and you shall tell me all about my guardian, Lawrence Colquhoun."

In the hall a thought struck the girl.

"Come with me," she said; "I will introduce you to the Poet and the Painter. You shall see them at work."

Her eyes danced with delight as she ran up the stairs, turning to see if her guest followed. She stopped at a door, the handle of which she turned with great care. Jack mounted the stairs after her.

It was a large and well-furnished room. Rows of books stood in order on the shelves. A bright fire burned on the hearth. A portfolio was on the table, with a clean inkstand and an unsullied blotting-pad. By the fire sat, in a deep and very comfortable easy-chair, the poet, sound asleep.

"There!" she whispered. "In the portfolio is the great poem. Look at it."

"We ought not to look at manuscripts, ought we?"

"Not if there is anything written. But there isn't. Of course, I may always turn over any pages, because I cannot read."

She turned them over. Nothing but blank sheets, white in virgin purity.

Cornelius sat with his head a little forward, breathing rather noisily.

"Isn't it hard work?" laughed the girl. "Poor fellow, isn't it exhaustive work? Let me introduce you. Mr. Cornelius Jagenal, Mr. Ronald Dunquerque." Jack bowed to the sleeping bard. "Now you know each other. That is what Mr. Dyson used always to say. Hush! we might wake him up and interrupt—the Work. Come away, and I will show you the Artist."

Another room equally well furnished, but in a different manner. There were "properties": drinking-glasses of a deep ruby red, luminous and splendid, standing on the shelves; flasks of a dull rich green; a model in armour; a lay figure, with a shawl thrown over the head and looped up under the arm; a few swords hanging upon the walls; curtains that caught the light and spread it over the room in softened colouring; and by the fire a couch, on which lay, sleeping, Humphrey with the wealth of silky beard.

There was an easel, and on it a canvas. This was as blank as Cornelius's sheets of paper.

"Permit me again," said the girl. "Mr. Humphrey Jagenal, Mr. Ronald Dunquerque. Now you know each other."

Jack bowed low to the genius.

Phillis, her eyes afloat with fun, beckoned the young man to the table. Pencil and paper lay there. She sat down and drew the sleeping painter in a dozen swift strokes. Then she looked up, laughing:

"Is that like him?"

Jack could hardly repress a cry of admiration.

"I am glad you think it good. Please write underneath, 'The Artist at work.' Thank you. Is that it? We will now pin it on the canvas. Think what he will say when he wakes up and sees it."

They stole out again as softly as a pair of burglars.

"Now you have seen the Twins. They are really very nice, but they drink too much wine, and sit up late. In the morning they are sometimes troublesome, when they won't take their breakfast; but in the evening, after dinner, they are quite tractable. And you see how they spend their day."

"Do they never do any work at all?"

"I will tell you what I think," she replied gravely. "Mr. Dyson used to tell me of men who are so vain that they are ashamed to give the world anything but what they know to be the best. And the best only comes by successive effort. So they wait and wait, till the time goes by, and they cannot even produce second-rate work. I think the Twins belong to that class of people."

By this time they were in the drawing-room.

"And now," said Phillis, "you are going to tell me all about my guardian."

"Tell me something more about yourself first," said Jack, not caring to bring Mr. Lawrence Colquhoun into the conversation just yet. "You said last night that you would show me your drawings."

"They are only pencil and pen-and-ink sketches." Phillis put a small portfolio on the table and opened it. "This morning Mr. Joseph took me to see an exhibition of paintings. Most of the artists in that exhibition cannot draw, but some can—and then—Oh!"

"They cannot draw better than you, Miss Fleming, I am quite sure."

She shook her head as Jack spoke, turning over the sketches.

"It seems so strange to be called Miss Fleming. Everybody used to call me Phillis."

"Was—was everybody young?" Jack asked, with an impertinence beyond his years.

"No; everybody was old. I suppose young people always call each other by their christian names. Yours seems to be rather stiff. Ronald, Ronald—I am afraid I do not like it very much."

"My brothers and sisters, uncles and aunts, cousins and kinsfolk—the people who pay my debts and therefore love me most—call me Ronald. But everybody else calls me Jack."

"Jack!" she murmured. "What a pretty name Jack is! May I call you Jack?"

"If you only would!" he cried, with a quick flushing of his cheek. "If you only would! Not when other people are present, but all to ourselves, when we are together like this. That is, if you do not mind."

Could the Serpent, when he cajoled Eve, have begun in a more subtle and artful manner? One is ashamed for Jack Dunquerque.

"I shall always call you Jack, then, unless when people like Mrs. Cassilis are present."

"And what am I to call you?"

"My name is Phillis, you know." But she knew, because her French maid had told her, that some girls have names of endearment, and she hesitated a little, in hope that Jack would find one for her.

He did. She looked him so frankly and freely in the face that he took courage, and said with a bold heart:

"Phillis is a very sweet name. You know the song, 'Phillis is my only joy?' I ought to call you Miranda, the Princess of the Enchanted Island. But it would be prettier to call you Phil."

"Phil!" Her lips parted in a smile of themselves as she shaped the name. It is a name which admits of expression. You may lengthen it out if you like; you may shorten it you like. "Phil! That is very pretty. No one ever called me Phil before."

"And we will be great friends, shall we not?"

"Yes, great friends. I have never had a friend at all."

"Let us shake hands over our promise. Phil, say, 'Jack Dunquerque, I will try to like you, and I will be your friend.'"

"Jack Dunquerque," she placed her hands, both of them, in his and began to repeat, looking in his face quite earnestly and solemnly, "I will try—that is nonsense, because I *do* like you very much already; and I will always be your friend, if you will be mine and will let me."

Then he, with a voice that shook a little, because he knew that this was very irregular and even wrong, but that the girl was altogether lovable, and a maiden to be desired, and a queen among girls, and too beautiful to be resisted, said his say:

"Phil, I think you are the most charming girl I have ever seen in all my life. Let me be your friend always, Phil. Let me"—here he stopped, with a guilty tremor in his voice—"I hope—I hope—that you will always go on liking me more and more."

He held both her pretty shapely hands in his own. She was standing a little back, with her face turned up to his, and a bright fearless smile upon her lips and in her eyes. Oh, the eyes that smile before the lips!

"Some people seal a bargain," he went on, hesitating and stammering, "after the manner of the—the—early Christians—with a kiss. Shall we, Phil?"

Before she caught the meaning of his words he stooped and drew her gently towards him. Then he suddenly released her. For all in a moment the woman within her, unknown till that instant, was roused into life, and she shrank back—without the kiss.

Jack hung his head in silence. Phil, in silence, too, stood opposite him, her eyes upon the ground.

She looked up stealthily and trembled.

Jack Dunquerque was troubled as he met her look.

"Forgive me, Phil," he said humbly. "It was wrong—I ought not. Only forgive me, and tell me we shall be friends all the same."

"Yes," she replied, not quite knowing what she said; "I forgive you. But, Jack, please don't do it again."

Then he returned to the drawings, sitting at the table, while she stood over him and told him what they were.

There was no diffidence or mock-modesty at all about her. The drawings were her life, and represented her inmost thoughts. She had never shown them all together to a single person, and now she was laying them all open before the young man whom yesterday she had met for the first time.

It seemed to him as if she were baring her very soul for him to read.

"I like to do them," she said, "because then I can recall everything that I have done or seen. Look! Here is the dear old house at Highgate, where I stayed for thirteen years without once going beyond its walls. Ah, how long ago it seems, and yet it is only a week since I came away! And everything is so different to me now."

"You were happy there, Phil?"

"Yes; but not so happy as I am now. I did not know you then, Jack."

He beat down the temptation to take her in his arms and kiss her a thousand times. He tried to sit calmly critical over the drawings. But his hand shook.

"Tell me about it all," he said softly.

"These are the sketches of my Highgate life. Stay; this one does not belong to this set. It is a likeness of you, which I drew last night when I came home."

"Did you really draw one of me? Let me have it. Do let me have it."

"It was meant for your face. But I could do a better one now. See, this is Mr. Beck, the American gentleman; and this is Captain Ladds. This is Mr. Cassilis."

They were the roughest unfinished things, but she had seized the likeness in everyone.

Jack kept his own portrait in his hand.

"Let me keep it."

"Please, no; I want that one for myself."

Once more, and for the last time in his life, a little distrust crossed Jack Dunquerque's mind. Could this girl, after all, be only the most accomplished of all coquettes? He looked up at her face as she stood beside him, and then abused himself for treachery to love.

"It is like me," he said, looking at the pencil portrait; "but you have made me too handsome."

She shook her head.

"You *are* very handsome, I think," she said gravely.

He was not, strictly speaking, handsome at all. He was rather an ugly youth, having no regularity of features. And it was a difficult face to draw, because he wore no beard—nothing but a light moustache to help it out.

"Phil, if you begin to flatter me you will spoil me; and I shall not be half so good a friend when I am spoiled. Won't you give this to me?"

"No; I keep my portfolio all to myself. But I will draw a better one, if you like, of you, and finish it up properly, like this."

She showed him a pencil-drawing of a face which Rembrandt himself would have loved to paint. It was the face of an old man, wrinkled and crows-footed.

"That is my guardian, Mr. Dyson. I will draw you in the same style. Poor dear guardian! I think he was very fond of me."

Another thought struck the young man.

"Phil, will you instead make me a drawing—of your own face?"

"But can you not do it for yourself?"

"I? Phil, I could not even draw a haystack."

"What a misfortune! It seems worse than not being able to read."

"Draw me a picture of yourself, Phil."

She considered.

"Nobody ever asked me to do that yet. And I never drew my own face. It would be nice, too, to think that you had a likeness of me, particularly as you cannot draw yourself. Jack, would you mind if it were not much like me?"

"I should prefer it like you. Please try. Give me yourself as you are now. Do not be afraid of making it too pretty."

"I will try to make it like. Here is Mrs. Cassilis. She did not think it was very good."

"Phil, you are a genius. Do you know that? I hold you to your promise. You will draw a portrait of yourself, and I will frame it and hang it up— no, I won't do that; I will keep it myself, and look at it when no one is with me."

"That seems very pleasant," said Phil, reflecting. "I should like to think that you are looking at me sometimes. Jack, I only met you yesterday, and we are old friends already."

"Yes; quite old familiar friends, are we not? Now tell all about yourself."

She obeyed. It was remarkable how readily she obeyed the orders of this new friend, and told him all about her life with Mr. Dyson—the garden and paddock, out of which she never went, even to church; the pony, the quiet house, and the quiet life with the old man who taught her by talking; her drawing and her music; and her simple wonder what life was like outside the gates.

"Did you never go to church, Phil?"

"No; we had prayers at home; and on Sunday evenings I sang hymns."

Clearly her religious education had been grossly neglected. "Never heard of a Ritualist," thought Jack, with a feeling of gladness. "Doesn't know anything about vestments; isn't learned in school feasts; and never attended a tea-meeting. This girl is a Phoenix." Why—why was he a Younger Son?

"And is Mr. Cassilis a relation of yours?"

"No; Mr. Cassilis is Mr. Dyson's nephew. All Mr. Dyson's fortune is left to found an institution for educating girls as I was educated—"

"Without reading or writing?"

"I suppose so. Only, you see, it is most unfortunate that my own education is incomplete, and they cannot carry out the testator's wishes, Mr. Jagenal tells me, because they have not been able to find the concluding chapters of his book. Mr. Dyson wrote a book on it, and the last chapter was called the 'Coping-stone.' I do not know what they will do about it. Mr. Cassilis wants to have the money divided among the relations, I know. Isn't it odd? And he has so much already."

"And I have got none."

"O Jack! take some of mine—do! I know I have such a lot somewhere; and I never spend anything."

"You are very good, Phil; but that will hardly be right. But do you know it is five o'clock? We have been talking for three hours. I must go—alas, I must go!"

"And you have told me nothing at all yet about Mr. Colquhoun."

"When I see you next I will tell you what I know of him. Goodbye, Phil."

"Jack, come and see me again soon."

"When may I come? Not tomorrow—that would be too soon. The day after. Phil, make me the likeness, and send it to me by post. I forgot you cannot write."

He wrote his address on a sheet of foolscap.

"Fold it in that, with this address outside, and post it to me. Come again, Phil? I should like to come everyday, and stay all day." He pressed her hand and was gone.

Phillis remained standing where he left her. What had happened to her? Why did she feel so oppressed? Why did the tears crowd her eyes? Five o'clock. It wanted an hour of dinner, when she would have to talk to the Twin brethren. She gathered up her drawings and retreated to her own room. As she passed Humphrey's door, she heard him saying to Jane:

"The tea, Jane? Have I really been asleep? A most extraordinary thing for me."

"Now he will see the drawing of the 'Artist at Work,'" thought Phillis. But she did not laugh at the idea, as she had done when she perpetrated the joke. She had suddenly grown graver.

She began her own likeness at once. But she could not satisfy herself. She tore up half a dozen beginnings. Then she changed her mind. She drew a little group of two. One was a young man, tall, shapely, gallant, with a queer attractive face, who held the hands of a girl in his, and was bending over her. Somehow a look of love, a strange and new expression, which she had never seen before in human eyes, lay in his. She blushed while she drew her own face looking up in that other, and yet she drew it faithfully, and was only half conscious how sweet a face she drew and how like it was to her own. Nor could she understand why she felt ashamed.

"Come again soon, Jack."

The words rang in the young man's ears, but they rang like bells of accusation and reproach. This girl, so sweet, so fresh, so unconventional, what would she think when she learned, as she must learn some day, how great was his sin against her? And what would Lawrence Colquhoun say! And what would the lawyer say? And what would the world say?

The worst was that his repentance would not take the proper course. He did not repent of taking her hands—he trembled and thrilled when he thought of it—he only repented of the swiftness with which the thing was done, and was afraid of the consequences.

"And I am only a Younger Son, Tommy"—he made his plaint to Ladds, who received a full confession of the whole—"only a Younger Son, with four hundred a year. And she's got fifty thousand. They will say I wanted her money. I wish she had nothing but the sweet grey dress—"

"Jack, don't blaspheme. Goodness sometimes palls; beauty always fades; grey dresses certainly wear out; figures alter for the worse; the funds remain. I am always thankful for the thought which inspired Ladds' Perfect Cocoa. The only true Fragrance. Aroma and Nutrition."

Humphrey did not discover the little sketch before dinner, so that his conversation was as animated and as artistic as usual. At two o'clock in the morning he discovered it. And at three o'clock the Twins, after discussing the picture with its scoffing legend in all its bearings, went to bed sorrowful.

X

"I have in these rough words shaped out a man
Whom this beneath world doth embrace and hug
With amplest entertainment."

Mr. Gabriel Cassilis, who, like Julius Cæsar and other illustrious men, was always spoken of by both his names, stepped from his carriage at the door of the Langham Hotel and slowly walked up the stairs to Mr. Beck's room. He looked older, longer, and thinner in the morning than in the evening. He carried his hands behind him and bore a look of pre-occupation and care. The man of unlimited credit was waiting for him, and, with his first cigar, pacing the room with his hands in his pockets.

"I got your letter," said Mr. Cassilis, "and telegraphed to you because I was anxious not to miss you. My time is valuable—not so valuable as yours, but still worth something."

He spread his hands palm downwards, and at right angles to the perpendicular line of his body, had that been erect. But it was curved, like the figure of the man with the forelock.

"Still worth something," he repeated. "But I am here, Mr. Beck, and ready to be of any service that I can."

"My time is worth nothing," said the American, "because my work is done for me. When I was paid by the hour, it was worth the hour's pay."

"But now," Mr. Cassilis interposed, "it is worth at the rate of your yearly income. And I observe that you have unlimited credit—un-lim-it-ed credit. That is what we should hardly give to a Rothschild."

He wanted to know what unlimited credit really meant. It was a thing hitherto beyond his experience.

"It is my Luck," said Mr. Beck. "Ile, as everybody knows, is not to be approached. You may grub for money like a Chinee, and you may scheme for it like a Boss in a whisky-ring. But for a steady certain flow there is nothing like Ile. And I, sir, have struck Ile as it never was struck before, because my well goes down to the almighty reservoir of this great world."

"I congratulate you, Mr. Beck."

"And I have ventured, sir, on the strength of that introductory letter, to ask you for advice. 'Mr. Cassilis,' I was told, 'has the biggest head in all London for knowledge of money.' And, as I am going to be the biggest man in all the States for income, I come to you."

"I am not a professional adviser, Mr. Beck. What I could do for you would not be a matter of business. It is true that, as a friend only, I might advise you as to investments. I could show you where to place money and how to use it."

"Sir, you double the obligation. In America we do nothing without an equivalent. Here men seem to work as hard without being paid as those who get wages. Why, sir, I hear that young barristers do the work of others and get nothing for it; doctors work for nothing in hospitals; and authors write for publishers and get nothing from them. This is a wonderful country."

Mr. Cassilis, at any rate, had never worked for nothing. Nor did he propose to begin now. But he did not say so.

He sat nursing his leg, looking up at the tall American who stood over him. They were two remarkable faces, that thus looked into each other. The American's was grave and even stern. But his eyes were soft. The Englishman's was grave also. But his eyes were hard. They were not stealthy, as of one contemplating a fraud, but they were curious and watchful, as of one who is about to strike and is looking for the fittest place—that is, the weakest.

"Will you take a drink, Mr. Cassilis?"

"A—a—a drink?" The invitation took him aback altogether, and disturbed the current of his thoughts. "Thank you, thank you. Nothing."

"In the silver-mines I've seen a man threatened with a bowie for refusing a drink. And I've known temperate men anxious for peace take drinks, when they were offered, till their back teeth were under whisky. But I know your English custom, Mr. Cassilis. When you don't feel thirsty you say so. Now let us go on, sir."

"Our New York friend tells me, Mr. Beck, that you would find it difficult to spend your income."

Mr. Beck brightened. He sat down and assumed a confidential manner.

"That's the hitch. That's what I am here for. In America you may chuck a handsome pile on yourself. But when you get out of yourself, unless you were to buy a park for the people in the centre of New York City, I guess you would find it difficult to get rid of your money."

"It depends mainly on the amount of that money."

"We'll come to figures, sir, and you shall judge as my friendly adviser. My bar'ls bring me in, out of my first well, 2,500 dollars, and that's

£500 a day, without counting Sundays. And there's a dozen wells of mine around, not so good, that are worth between them another £800 a day."

Mr. Cassilis gasped.

"Do you mean, Mr. Beck, do you actually mean that you are drawing a profit, a clear profit, of more than £1,300 a day from your rock-oil shafts?"

"That is it, sir—that is the lowest figure. Say £1,500 a day."

"And how long has this been going on?"

"Close upon ten months."

Mr. Cassilis produced a pencil and made a little calculation.

"Then you are worth at this moment, allowing for Sundays, at least a quarter of a million sterling."

"Wall, I think it is near that figure. We can telegraph to New York, if you like, to find out. I don't quite know within a hundred thousand."

"And a yearly income of £500,000, Mr. Beck!" said Mr. Cassilis, rising solemnly. "Let me—allow me to shake hands with you again. I had no idea, not the slightest idea, in asking you to my house the other day, that I was entertaining a man of so much weight and such enormous power."

He shook hands with a mixture of deference and friendship. Then he looked again, with a watchful glance, at the tall and wiry American with the stern face, the grave eyes, the mobile lips, and the muscular frame, and sat down and began to soliloquise.

"We are accustomed to think that nothing can compare with the great landholders of this country and Austria. There are two or three incomes perhaps in Europe, not counting crowned heads, which approach your own, Mr. Beck, but they are saddled. Their owners have great houses to keep up; armies of servants to maintain; estates to nurse; dilapidations to make good; farmers to satisfy; younger sons to provide for; poor people to help by hundreds; and local charities to assist. Why, I do not believe, when all has been provided for, that a great man, say the Duke of Berkshire, with coal-mines and quarries, Scotch, Irish, Welsh, and English estates, has more to put by at the end of the year than many a London merchant."

"That is quite right," said Mr. Beck; "a merchant must save, because he may crack up; but the land don't run away. When you want stability, you must go to the Airth. Outside there's the fields, the rivers, the hills. Inside there's the mines, and there's Ile for those who can strike it."

"What an income!" Mr. Cassilis went on. "Nothing to squander it on. No duties and no responsibilities. No tenants; no philanthropy; no frittering away of capital. You *can't* spend a tenth part of it on yourself. And the rest accumulates and grows—grows—spreads and grows." He spread out his hands, and a flush of envy came into his cheeks. "Mr. Beck, I congratulate you again."

"Thank you, sir."

"I see, Mr. Beck—you are yet an unmarried man, I believe, and without children—I foresee boundless possibilities. You may marry and found a great family; you may lay yourself out for making a fortune so great that it may prove a sensible influence on the course of events. You may bequeath to your race the tradition of good fortune and the habit of making money."

"My sons may take care of themselves," said Mr. Beck, "I want to spend money, not to save it."

It was remarkable that during all this generous outburst of vicarious enthusiasm Mr. Beck's face showed no interest whatever. He had his purpose, but it was not the purpose of Mr. Cassilis. To found a family, to become a Rothschild, to contract loans—what were these things to a man who felt strongly that he had but one life, that he wished to make the most of it, and that the world after him might get on as it could without his posthumous interference?

"Listen Mr. Beck, for one moment. Your income is £500,000 a year. You may spend on your own simple wants £5,000. Bah! a trifle—not a quarter of the interest. You save the whole; in ten years you have three millions. You are still under fifty?"

"Forty-five, sir."

"I wish I was forty-five. You may live and work for another quarter of a century. In that time you ought to be worth twelve millions at least. Twelve millions!"

"Nearly as much as ran away and was lost when the Ile was struck," said Mr. Beck. "Hardly worth while to work for five-and-twenty years in order to save what Nature spent in three days, is it?"

What, says the proverb, is easily got is lightly regarded. This man made money so easily that he despised the slow, gradual building up of an immense fortune.

"There is nothing beyond the reach of a man with twelve millions," Mr. Cassilis went on. "He may rule the world, so long as there are poor states with vast armies who want to borrow. Why, at the present moment a man with twelve millions at his command could undertake a loan with Russia, Austria, Turkey, Italy, or Egypt. He could absolutely govern the share market; he could rule the bank rate—"

Mr. Beck interrupted, quite unmoved by these visions of greatness:

"Wal, sir, I am not ambitious, and I leave Providence to manage the nations her own way. I might meddle and muss till I busted up the whole concern; play, after all, into the hands of the devil, and have the people praying to get back to their old original Providence."

"Or suppose," Mr. Cassilis went on, his imagination fired with the contemplation of possibilities so far beyond his own reach—"suppose you were to buy up land—to buy all that comes into the market. Suppose you were to hand down to your sons a traditional policy of buying land with the established principle of primogeniture. In twenty years you might have great estates in twenty counties—"

"I could have half a state," said Mr. Beck, "if I went out West."

"In your own lifetime you could control an election, make yourself President, carry your own principles, force your opinions on the country, and become the greatest man in it."

"The greatest country in the world is the United States of America— that is a fact," said Mr. Beck, laughing; "so the greatest man in it must be the greatest man in the world. I calculate that's a bitter reflection for Prince Bismarck when he goes to bed at night; also for the Emperor of all the Russias. And perhaps your Mr. Gladstone would like to feel himself on the same level with General Ulysses Grant."

"Mr. Beck," cried Mr. Cassilis, rising to his feet in an irrepressible burst of genuine enthusiasm, and working his right hand round exactly as if he was really Father Time, whom he so much resembled—"Mr. Beck, I consider you the most fortunate man in the world. We slowly amass money—for our sons to dissipate. Save when a title or an ancient name entails a conservative tradition which keeps the property together, the process in this country and in yours is always the same. The strong men climb, and the weak men fall. And even to great houses like the Grosvenors, which have been carried upwards by a steady tide of fortune, there will surely one day come a fool, and then the tide will turn. But for you and yours, Mr. Beck, Nature pours out her inexhaustible treasures—"

"She does, sir—in Ile."

"You may spend, but your income will always go on increasing."

"To a certain limit, sir—to five thousand and fifty-three years. I have had it reckoned by one of our most distinguished mathematicians,

Professor Hercules Willemott, of Cyprus University, Wisconsin. He made the calculations for me."

"Limit or not, Mr. Beck, you are now a most fortunate man. And I shall be entirely at your service. I believe," he added modestly, "that I have some little reputation in financial circles."

"That is so, sir. And now let me put my case." Mr. Beck became once more animated and interested. "Suppose, sir, I was to say to you, 'I have more than enough money. I will take the Luck of the Golden Butterfly and make it the Luck of other people.'"

"I do not understand," said Mr. Cassilis.

"Sir, what do you do with your own money? You do not spend it all on yourself?"

"I use it to make more."

"And when you have enough?"

"We look at things from a different point of view, Mr. Beck. *You* have enough; but I, whatever be my success, can never approach the fourth part of your income. However, let me understand what you want to do, and I will give such advice as I can offer."

"That's kind, sir, and what I expected of you. It is a foolish fancy, and perhaps you'll laugh; but I have heard day and night, ever since the Ile began to run, a voice which says to me always the same thing—I think it is the voice of my Golden Butterfly: 'What you can't spend, give.' 'What you can't spend, give.' That's my duty, Mr. Cassilis; that's the path marked out before me, plain and shinin' as the way to heaven. What I can't spend, I must give. I've given nothing as yet. And I am here in this country of giving to find out how to do it."

"We—I mean the—the—" Mr. Cassilis was on the point of saying "the Idiots," but refrained in time. "The people who give money send it to charities and institutions."

"I know that way, sir. It is like paying a priest to say your prayers for you."

"When the secretaries get the money they pay themselves their own salaries first; then they pay for the rent, the clerks, and the advertising. What remains goes to the charity."

"That is so, sir; and I do not like that method. I want to go right ahead; find out what to do, and then do it. But I must feel like giving, whatever I do."

"Your countryman, Mr. Peabody, gave his money in trust for the London poor. Would you like to do the same?"

"No, sir; I should not like to imitate that example. Mr. Peabody was a great man, and he meant well; but I want to work for myself. Let a man do all the good and evil he has to do in his lifetime, not leave his work dragging on after he is dead. 'They that go down into the pit cannot hope for the truth.' Do you remember that text, Mr. Cassilis? It means that you must not wait till you are dead to do what you have to do."

Mr. Cassilis altered his expression, which was before of a puzzled cheerfulness, as if he failed to see his way, into one of unnatural solemnity. It is the custom of certain Englishmen if the Bible is quoted. He knew no more than Adam what part of the Bible it came from. But he bowed, and pulled out his handkerchief as if he was at a funeral. In fact, this unexpected hurling of a text at his head floored him for the moment.

Mr. Beck was quite grave and in much earnestness.

"There is another thing. If I leave this money in trust, how do I know that my purpose will be carried out? In a hundred years things will get mixed. My bequests may be worth millions, or they may be worth nothing. The lawyers may fight over the letter of the will, and the spirit may be neglected."

"It is the Dead Hand that you dread."

"That may be so, sir. You air in the inside track, and you ought to know what to call it. But no Hand, dead or alive, shall ever get hold of my stamps."

"Your stamps?"

"My stamps, sir; my greenbacks, my dollars. For I've got them, and I mean to spend them. 'Spend what you can, and give what you cannot spend,' says the Voice to Gilead P. Beck."

"But, my dear sir, if you mean to give away a quarter of a million a year, you will have every improvident and extravagant rogue in the country about you. You will have to answer hundreds of letters a day. You will be deluged with prospectuses, forms, and appeals. You will be called names unless you give to this institution or to that—"

"I shall give nothing to any society."

"And what about the widows of clergymen, the daughters of officers, the nieces of Church dignitaries, the governess who is starving, the tradesman who wants a hundred pounds for a fortnight, and will repay you with blessings and 25 percent. after depositing in your hand as security all his pawn-tickets."

"Every boat wants steering, but I was not born last Sunday, and the ways of big cities, though they may be crooked, air pretty well known to me. There are not many lines of life in which Gilead P. Beck has not tried to walk."

"My dear sir, do you propose to act the part of Universal Philanthropist and Distributor at large?"

"No, sir, I do not. And that puzzles me too. I should like to be quiet over it. There was a man down to Lexington, when I was a boy, who said he liked his religion unostentatious. So he took a pipe on a Sunday morning and sat in the churchyard listening to the bummin' and the singin' within. Perhaps, sir, that man knew his own business. Perhaps thoughts came over his soul when they gave out the Psalm that he wouldn't have had if he'd gone inside, to sit with his back upright against a plank, his legs curled up below the seat, and his eyes wandering around among the gells. Maybe that is my case, too, Mr. Cassilis. I should like my giving to be unostentatious."

"Give what you cannot spend," said Mr. Cassilis. "There are at any rate plenty of ways of spending. Let us attend to them first."

"And there's another thing, sir," Mr. Beck went on, shifting his feet and looking uneasy and distressed. "It's on my mind since I met the young gentleman at your house. I want to do something big, something almighty big, for Mr. Ronald Dunquerque."

"Because he killed the bear?"

"Yes, sir, because he saved my life. Without that shot the Luck of Gilead P. Beck would have been locked up forever in that little box where the Golden Butterfly used to live. What can I do for him? Is the young gentleman rich?"

"On the contrary, I do not suppose—his brother is one of the poorest peers in the house—that the Honorable Mr. Ronald Dunquerque is worth £500 a year. Really, I should say that £300 would be nearer the mark."

"Then he is a gentleman, and I am—well, sir, I hope I am learning what a gentleman should do and think in such a position as the Golden Butterfly has brought me into. But the short of it is that I can't say to him: 'Mr. Dunquerque, I owe you a life, and here is a cheque for so many thousand dollars.' I can't do it, sir."

"I suppose not. But there are ways of helping a young man forward without giving him money. You can only give money to poets and clergymen."

"That is so, sir."

"Wait a little till your position is known and assured. You will then be able to assist Mr. Ronald Dunquerque, as much as you please." He rose and took up his gloves. "And now, Mr. Beck, I think I understand you. You wish to do something great with your money. Very good. Do not be in a hurry. I will think things over. Meantime, you are going to let it lie idle in the bank?"

"Wal, yes; I was thinking of that."

"It would be much better for me to place it for you in good shares, such as I could recommend to you. You would then be able to—to—give away"—he pronounced the words with manifest reluctance—"the interest as well as the principal. Why should the bankers have the use of it?"

"That seems reasonable," said Mr. Beck.

Mr. Cassilis straightened himself and looked him full in the face. He was about to strike his blow.

"You will place your money," he said quietly, as if there could be no doubt of Mr. Beck's immediate assent, "in my hands for investment. I shall recommend you safe things. For instance, as regards the shares of the George Washington Silver Mine—"

He opened his pocket-book.

"No, sir," said Mr. Beck with great decision.

"I was about to observe that I should not recommend such an investment. I think, however, I could place immediately £20,000 in the Isle of Man Internal Navigation Company."

"An English company?" said Mr. Beck.

"Certainly. I propose, Mr. Beck, to devote this morning to a consideration of investments for you. I shall advise you from day today. I have no philanthropic aims, and financing is my profession. But your affairs shall be treated together with mine, and I shall bring to bear upon them the same—may I say insight?—that has carried my own ventures to success. For this morning I shall only secure you the Isle of Man shares."

They presently parted, with many expressions of gratitude from Mr. Gilead Beck.

A country where men work for nothing? Perhaps, when men are young. Not a country where elderly men in the City work for nothing. Mr. Cassilis had no intention whatever of devoting his time and experience to the furtherance of Mr. Beck's affairs. Not at all: if the thoughts in his mind had been written down, they would have shown a joy almost boyish in the success of his morning's visit.

"The Isle of Man Company," we should have read, "is floated. That £20,000 was a lucky *coup*. I nearly missed my chances with the silver mine; I ought to have known that he was not likely to jump at such a bait. A quarter of a million of money to dispose of, and five hundred thousand pounds a year. And mine the handling of the whole. Never before was such a chance known in the City."

A thought struck him. He turned, and went back hastily to Gilead Beck's rooms.

"One word more. Mr. Beck, I need hardly say that I do not wish to be known as your adviser at all. Perhaps it would be well to keep our engagements a secret between ourselves."

That of course was readily promised.

"Half a million a year!" The words jangled in his brain like the chimes of St. Clement's. "Half a million a year! And mine the handling."

He spent the day locked up in his inner office. He saw no one, except the secretary, and he covered an acre or so of paper with calculations. His clerks went away at five; his secretary left him at six; at ten he was still at work, feverishly at work, making combinations and calculating results.

"What a chance!" he murmured prayerfully, putting down his pen at length. "What a blessed chance!"

Mr. Gilead Beck would have congratulated himself on the disinterested assistance of his unprofessional adviser had he known that the whole day was devoted to himself. He might have congratulated himself less had he known the thoughts that filled the financier's brains.

Disinterested? How could Mr. Cassilis regard anyone with money in his hand but as a subject for his skill. And here was a man coming to him, not with his little fortune of a few thousand pounds, not with the paltry savings of a lifetime, not for an investment for widows and orphans, but with a purse immeasurable and bottomless, a purse which he was going to place unreservedly in his hands.

"Mine the handling," he murmured as he got into bed. It was his evening hymn of praise and joy.

XI

"Higher she climbed, and far below her stretch'd
Hill beyond hill, with lightening slopes and glades,
And a world widening still."

Phillis's world widened daily, like a landscape, which stretches ever farther the higher you mount. Every morning brought her fresh delights, something more wonderful than she had seen the day before. Her portfolio of drawings swelled daily; but with riches came discontent, because the range of subjects grew too vast for her pencil to draw, and her groups became everyday more difficult and more complicated. Life was a joy beyond all that she had ever hoped for or expected. How should it be otherwise to her? She had no anxieties for the future; she had no past sins to repent; she had no knowledge of evil; she was young and in perfect health; the weight of her mortality was as yet unfelt.

During these early days of emancipation she was mostly silent, looking about and making observations. She sat alone and thought; she forgot to sing; if she played, it was as if she was communing confidentially with a friend, and seeking counsel. She had so much to think of: herself, and the new current of thoughts into which her mind had been suddenly diverted; the connection between the world of Mr. Dyson's teachings and the world of reality—this was a very hard thing; Mrs. Cassilis, with her hard, cold manner, her kind words, and her eternal teaching that the spring of feminine action is the desire to attract; finally, Jack Dunquerque. And of him she thought a good deal.

All the people she met were interesting. She tried to give each one his own individuality, rounded and complete. But she could not. Her experience was too small, and each figure in her mind was blurred. Now, if you listen to the conversation of people, as I do perpetually—in trains especially—you will find that they are always talking about other people. The reason of that I take to be the natural desire to have in your brain a clear idea of every man, what he is, and how he is likely to be acted upon. Those people are called interesting who are the most difficult to describe or imagine, and who, perpetually breaking out in new places, disturb the image which their friends have formed.

None of Phillis's new friends would photograph clear and distinct in her brain. She thought she missed the focus. It was not so, however;

it was the fault of the lens. But it troubled her, because if she tried to draw them there was always a sense of something wanting. Even Jack Dunquerque—and here her eyes brightened—had points about him which she could not understand. She was quiet, therefore, and watched.

It was pleasant only to watch and observe. She had made out clearly by this time that the Twins were as vain and self-conscious as the old peacock she used to feed at Highgate. She found herself bringing out their little vanities by leading questions. She knew that Joseph Jagenal, whom in their souls the Twins despised, was worth them both ten times over; and she found that Joseph rated himself far beneath his brothers. Then she gradually learned that their æsthetic talk was soon exhausted, but that they loved to enunciate the same old maxims over and over again, as children repeat a story. And it became one of her chief pleasures to listen to them at dinner, to mark their shallowness, and to amuse herself with their foibles. The Twins thought the young lady was fascinated by their personal excellences.

"Genius, brother Cornelius," said Humphrey, "always makes its way. I see Phillis Fleming every night waiting upon your words."

"I think the fascinations of Art are as great, brother Humphrey. At dinner Phillis Fleming watches your every gesture."

This was in the evening. In the morning every walk was a new delight in itself; every fresh street was different. Brought up for thirteen years within the same four walls, the keenest joy which the girl could imagine was variety. She loved to see something new, even a new disposition of London houses, even a minute difference in the aspect of a London square. But of all the pleasures which she had yet experienced—even a greater pleasure than the single picture-gallery which she had visited— was the one afternoon of shopping she had had with Mrs. Cassilis at Melton and Mowbray's in Regent Street.

Mrs. Cassilis took her there first on the morning of her dinner-party. It was her second drive through the streets of London, but an incomparable superior journey to the first. The thoroughfares were more crowded; the shops were grander; if there were fewer boys running and whistling, there were picturesque beggars, Punch-and-Judy shows, Italian noblemen with organs, and the other humours and diversions of the great main arteries of London. Phillis looked at all with the keenest delight, calling the attention of her companion to the common things which escape our notice because we see them everyday—the ragged broken down old man without a hat, who has long grey locks, who sells oranges from a basket, and betrays by his bibulous trembling lips the secret history of his downfall; the omnibus full inside and out; the tall Guardsman swaggering down the street; the ladies looking in at the windows; the endless rows of that great and wonderful exhibition which benevolent tradesmen show gratuitously to all; the shopman rubbing his hands at the door; the foreigners and pilgrims in a strange land—he with a cigarette in his mouth, lately from the Army of Don Carlos; he with a bad cigar, a blue-black shaven chin and cheek, and a seedy coat, who once adorned the ranks of Delescluze, Ferrè, Flourens & Company; he with the pale face and hard cynical smile, who hails from free and happy Prussia; the man, our brother, from Sierra Leone, coal-black of hue, with snowy linen and a conviction not to be shaken that all the world takes him for an Englishman; the booted Belgian, cross between the Dutchman and the Gaul; the young gentleman sent from Japan to study our country and its laws—he has a cigar in his mouth, and a young lady with yellow hair upon his arm; the Syrian, with a red cap and almond eyes; the Parsee, with lofty superstructure, a reminiscence of the Tower of Babel, which his ancestors were partly instrumental in building; Cretes, Arabians, men of Cappadocia and Pontus, with all the other mingled nationalities which make up the strollers along a London street,—Phillis marked them everyone, and only longed for a brief ten minutes with each in order to transfer his likeness to her portfolio.

"Phillis," said her companion, touching her hand, "can you practise looking at people without turning your head or seeming to notice?"

Phillis laughed, and tried to sit in the attitude of unobservant carelessness which was the custom in other carriages. Like all first attempts it was a failure. Then the great and crowded street reminded her of her dream. Should she presently—for it all seemed unreal together—begin to run, while the young men, among whom were the Twins, ran after her? And should she at the finish of the race see the form of dead old Abraham Dyson, clapping his hands and wagging his head, and crying, "Well run! well won! Phillis, it is the Coping-stone?"

"This is Melton & Mowbray's," said Mrs. Cassilis, as the carriage drew up in front of a shop which contained greater treasures then were ever collected for the harem of an Assyrian king.

She followed Mrs. Cassilis to some show rooms, in which lay about carelessly things more beautiful than she had ever conceived; hues more brilliant, textures more delicate then she ever knew.

Phillis's first shopping was an event to be remembered in all her after life. What she chose, what Mrs. Cassilis chose for her, what Joseph Jagenal thought when the bill came in, it boots not here to tell. Imagine only the delight of a girl of deep and artistic feeling, which has hitherto chiefly found vent in the study of form—such form as she could get from engravings and her own limited powers of observation—in being let loose suddenly in a wilderness of beautiful things. Every lady knows Messrs. Melton & Mowbray's great shop. Does anybody ever think what it would seem were they to enter it for the first time at the mature age of nineteen?

In one thing only did Phillis disgrace herself. There was a young person in attendance for the purpose of showing off all sorts of draperies upon her own back and shoulders. Phillis watched her for sometime. She had a singularly graceful figure and a patient face, which struck Phillis with pity. Mrs. Cassilis sat studying the effect through her double eye-glasses. The saleswoman put on and took off the things as if the girl were really a lay-figure, which she was, excepting that she turned herself about, a thing not yet achieved by any lay-figure. A patient face, but it looked pale and tired. The "Duchess"—living lay-figures receive that title, in addition to a whole pound a week which Messrs. Melton & Mowbray generously give them—stood about the rooms all day, and went to bed late at night. Some of the other girls envied her. This shows that there is no position in life which has not something beneath it.

Presently Phillis rose suddenly, and taking the opera-cloak which the Duchess was about to put on, said:

"You are tired. I will try it on myself. Pray sit down and rest."

And she actually placed a chair for the shop-girl.

Mrs. Cassilis gave a little jump of surprise. It had never occurred to her that a shopwoman could be entitled to any consideration at all. She belonged to the establishment; the shop and all that it contained were at the service of those who bought; the *personnel* was a matter for Messrs. Melton & Mowbray to manage.

But she recovered her presence of mind in a moment.

"Perhaps it will be as well," she said, "to see how it suits you by trying it on yourself."

When their purchases were completed and they were coming away, Phillis turned to the poor Duchess, and asked her if she was not very tired of trying on dresses, and whether she would not like to take a rest, and if she was happy, with one or two other questions; at which the saleswoman looked a little indignant and the Duchess a little inclined to cry.

And then they came away.

"It is not usual, Phillis," said Mrs. Cassilis, directly they were in the carriage, "for ladies to speak to shop-people."

"Is it not? The poor girl looked pale and tired."

"Very likely she was. She is paid to work, and work is fatiguing. But it was no concern of ours. You see, my dear, we cannot alter things; and if you once commence to pitying people and talking to them, there is an end of all distinctions of class."

"Mr. Dyson used to say that the difficulty of abolishing class distinctions was one of the most lamentable facts in human history. I did not understand then what he meant. But I think I do now. It is a dreadful thing, he meant, that one cannot speak or relieve a poor girl who is ready to drop with fatigue, because she is a shop-girl. How sad you must feel, Mrs. Cassilis, you, who have seen so much of shop-assistants, if they are all like that poor girl!"

Mrs. Cassilis had not felt sad, but Phillis's remark made her feel for the moment uncomfortable. Her complacency was disturbed. But how could she help herself? She was what her surroundings had made her. As riches increase, particularly the riches which are unaccompanied by territorial obligations, men and women separate themselves more and more; the lines of demarcation become deeper and broader; English castes are divided by ditches constantly widening; the circles into which outsiders may enter as guests, but not as members, become more numerous; poor people herd more together; rich people live more apart; the latter become more like gods in their seclusion, and they grow to hate more and more the sight and rumor of suffering. And the first step back to the unpitying cruelty of the old civilizations is the habit of looking on the unwashed as creatures of another world. If the gods of Olympus had known sympathy they might have lived till now.

This expedition occurred on the day of Phillis's first dinner-party, and on their way home a singular thing happened.

Mrs. Cassilis asked Phillis how long she was to stay with Mr. Jagenal.

"Until," said Phillis, "my guardian comes home; and that will be in a fortnight."

"Your guardian, child? But he is dead."

"I had two, you know. The other is Mr. Lawrence Colquhoun—What is the matter, Mrs. Cassilis?"

For she became suddenly pallid, and stared blankly before her, with no expression in her eyes, unless perhaps, a look of terror. It was the second time that Phillis had noted a change in this cold and passionless face. Before, the face had grown suddenly soft and tender at a recollection; now, it was white and rigid.

"Lawrence Colquhoun!" she turned to Phillis, and hardly seemed to know what she was saying. "Lawrence Colquhoun! He is coming home—and he promised me—no—he would not promise—and what will he say to me."

Then she recovered herself with an effort. The name, or the intelligence of Lawrence Colquhoun's return, gave her a great shock.

"Mr. Colquhoun your guardian! I did not know. And is he coming home?"

"You will come and see me when I am staying—if I am to stay—at his house?"

"I shall certainly," said Mrs. Cassilis, setting her lips together—"I shall certainly make a point of seeing Mr. Colquhoun on his return, whether you are staying with him or not. Here is Carnarvon Square. No, thank you, I will not get down, even to have a cup of tea with you. Goodbye, Phillis, till this evening. My dear, I think the white dress that you showed me will do admirably. Home at once."

A woman of steel? Rubbish! There is no man or woman of steel, save he who has brooded too long over his own perfections. A metallic statue, the enemies of Mrs. Cassilis called her. They knew nothing. A woman who had always perfect control over herself, said her husband. He knew nothing. A woman who turned pale at the mention of a name, and longed, yet feared, to meet a man, thought Phillis. And she knew something, because she knew the weak point in this woman's armour. Being neither curious, nor malignant, nor a disciple in the school for scandal, Phillis drew her little conclusion, kept it to herself, and thought no more about it.

As for the reasons which prompted Mrs. Cassilis to "take up" Phillis Fleming, they were multiplex, like all the springs of action which move us to act. She wanted to find out for her husband of what sort was this system of education which Joseph Jagenal could not discover anywhere. She was interested in, although not attracted by, the character of the girl, unlike any she had ever seen. And she wanted to use Phillis—an heiress, young, beautiful, piquante, strange—as an attraction to her house. For Mrs. Cassilis was ambitious. She wished to attract men to her evenings. She pictured herself—it is the dream of so many cultured women—as another Madame Récamier, Madame du Deffand, or Madame de Rambouillet. All the intellect in London was to be gathered in her *salon*. She caught lions; she got hold of young authors; she made beginnings with third-rate people who had written books. They were not amusing; they were not witty; they were devoured by envy and hatred. She let them drop, and now she wanted to begin again. An idle and a futile game. She had not the quick sympathies, the capacity for hero-worship, the lovableness of the Récamier. She had no tears for others. She did not know that the woman who aspires to lead men must first be able to be led.

There was another fatal objection, not fully understood by ladies who have "evenings" and sigh over their empty rooms. In these days of clubs, what man is going to get up after dinner and find his melancholy way from Pall Mall to Kensington Palace Gardens, in order to stand about a drawing-room for two hours and listen to "general" talk? It wants a Phillis, and a personal, if hopeless, devotion to a Phillis, to tear the freshest lion from his club, after dinner, even if it be to an altar of adulation. The evening begins properly with dinner: and where men dine they love to stay.

"Jack Dunquerque came to see me today," Phillis told Joseph. "You remember Mr. Dunquerque. He was at Mrs. Cassilis's last night. He came at two, to have luncheon and to tell me about Mr. Colquhoun; but he did not tell me anything about him. We talked about ourselves."

"Is Mr. Dunquerque a friend of yours?"

"Yes; Jack and I are friends," Phillis replied readily. There was not the least intention to deceive; but Joseph was deceived. He thought they had been old friends. Somehow, perhaps, Phillis did not like to talk very much about her friendship for Jack.

"I want you to ask him to dinner, if you will."

"Certainly, whenever you please. I shall be glad to make Mr. Dunquerque's acquaintance. He is the brother of Lord Isleworth," said Joseph, with a little satisfaction at seeing a live member of the aristocracy at his own table.

Jack came to dinner. He behaved extremely well; made no allusion to that previous occasion when he had been introduced to the Twins; listened to their conversation as if it interested him above all things; and not once called Phillis by her Christian name. This omission made her reflect; they were therefore, it was apparent, only Jack and Phil when they were alone. It was her first secret, and the possession of it became a joy.

She had not a single word with him all the evening. Only before he went he asked her if he might call the next day at luncheon-time. She said to him yes.

"After all these Bloomsbury people," said Cornelius, lighting his first pipe, "it does one good, brother Humphrey, to come across a gentleman. Mr. Ronald Dunquerque took the keenest interest in your Art criticisms at dinner."

"They were general principles only, Cornelius," said Humphrey. "He is really a superior young man. A little modest in your presence, brother. To be sure, it is not everyday that he finds himself dining with a Poet."

"And an Artist, Humphrey."

"Thank you, Cornelius. Miss Fleming had no charms for him, I think."

"Phillis Fleming, brother, is a girl who is drawn more towards, and more attracts, men of a maturer age—men no longer perhaps within the *première jeunesse*, but still capable of love."

"Men of our age, Cornelius. Shall we split this potash, or will you take some Apollinaris water?"

Jack called, and they took luncheon together as before. Phillis, brighter and happier, told him what things she had seen and what remarks she had made since last they met, a week ago. Then she told him of the things she most wished to see.

"Jack," she said, "I want to see the Tower of London and Westminster Abbey most."

"And then, Phil?"

"Then I should like to see a play."

"Would Mr. Jagenal allow me to take you to the Tower of London? Now, Phil—this afternoon?"

Phillis's worldly education was as yet so incomplete that she clapped her hands with delight.

"Shall we go now, Jack? How delightful! Of course Mr. Jagenal will allow me. I will be five minutes putting on my hat."

"Now, that's wrong too," said Jack to himself. "It is as wrong as calling her Phil. It's worse than wanting to kiss her, because the kiss never came off. I can't help it—it's pleasant. What will Colquhoun say when he comes home? Phil is sure to tell him everything. Jack Dunquerque, my boy, there will be a day of reckoning for you. Already, Phil? By Jove! how nice you look!"

"Do I, Jack? Do you like my hat? I bought it with Mrs. Cassilis the other day."

"Look at yourself in the glass, Phil. What do you see?"

She looked and laughed. It was not for her to say what she saw.

"There was a little maid of Arcadia once, Phil, and she grew up so beautiful that all the birds fell in love with her. There were no other creatures except birds to fall in love with her, because her sheep were too busy fattening themselves for the Corinthian cattle-market to pay any attention to her. They were conscientious sheep, you see, and wished to do credit to the Arcadian pastures." Jack Dunquerque began to feel great freedom in the allegorical method.

"Well, Jack?"

"Well Phil, the birds flew about in the woods, singing to each other how lovely she was, how prettily she played, and how sweetly she sang. Nobody understood what they said, but it pleased this little maid. Presently she grew a tall maid, like yourself, Phil. And then she came out into the world. She was just like you, Phil; she had the same bright eyes, and the same laugh, and the same identical sunlit face; and O Phil, she had your very same charming ways!"

"Jack, do you really mean it? Do you like my face, and are my ways really and truly not rough and awkward?"

Jack shook his head.

"Your face is entrancing, Phil; and your ways are more charming than I can tell you. Well, she came into the world and looked about her. It was a pleasant world, she thought. And then—I think I will tell you the rest of the story another time, Phil."

"Jack, did other people besides birds love your maid of Arcadia?"

"I'm afraid they did," he groaned. "A good many other people—confound them!"

Phil looked puzzled. Why did he groan? Why should not all the world love the Arcadian maid if they pleased?

Then they went out, Jack being rather silent.

"This is a great deal better than driving with Mrs. Cassilis, Jack," said the girl, as she made her first acquaintance with a hansom cab. "It is like sitting in a chair, while all the people move past. Look at the faces, Jack; how they stare straight before them! Is work so dear to them that they cannot find time to look at each other."

"Work is not dear to them at all, I think," said Jack. "If I were a clergyman I should talk nonsense and say that it is the race for gold. As a matter of fact, I believe it is a race for bread. Those hard faces have got wives and children at home, and life is difficult, that is all."

Phillis was silent again.

They drove through the crowded City, where the roll of the vehicles thundered on the girl's astonished ears, and the hard-faced crowd sped swiftly past her. Life was too multitudinous, too complex, for her brain to take it in. The shops did not interest her now, nor the press of business; it was the never-ending rush of the anxious crowd. She tried to realise, if ever so faintly, that everyone of their faces meant a distinct and important personality. It was too much for her, and, as it did to the Persian monarch, the multitudes brought tears into her eyes.

"Where are all the women?" she asked Jack at length.

"At home. These men are working for them. They are spending the money which their husbands and fathers fight for."

She was silent again.

The crowd diminished, but not much; the street grew narrower. Presently they came to an open space, and beyond—oh, joy of joys!— the Tower of London, which she knew from the pictures.

Only country people go to the Tower of London. It would almost seem a kindness to London readers were I to describe this national gaudy-show. But it is better, perhaps, that its splendours should remain unknown, like those of the National Gallery and the British Museum. The solitudes of London are not too many, and its convenient trysting places are few. The beef-eater who conducted the flock attached himself specially to Phillis, thereby showing that good taste has found a home among beef-eaters. Phillis asked him a thousand questions. She was eager to see everything. She begged him to take them slowly down the long line of armoured warriors; she did not care for the arms, except for such as she had heard about, as bows and arrows, pikes, battle-axes, and spears. She lingered in the room where Sir Walter Raleigh was confined; she studied the construction of the headsman's axe and the block; she glowed with delight at finding herself in the old chapel of the White Tower. Jack did not understand her enthusiasm. It was his own first visit also to the Tower, but he was unaffected by its historical associations. Nor did he greatly care for the arms and armour.

Think of Phillis. Her guardian's favourite lessons to her had been in history. He would read her passages at which her pulse would quicken and her eyes light up. Somehow these seemed all connected with the Tower. She constructed an imaginary Tower in her own mind, and peopled it with the ghosts of martyred lords and suffering ladies. But the palace of her soul was as nothing compared with the grim grey fortress that she saw. The knights of her imagination were poor creatures compared with these solid heroes of steel and iron on their wooden charges; the dungeon in which Raleigh pined was far more gloomy than any she had pictured; the ghosts of slain rebels and murdered princes gained in her imagination a place and surroundings worthy of their haunts. The first sight of London which an American visits is the Tower; the first place which the boy associates with the past, and longs to see, is that old pile beside the Thames.

Phillis came away at length, with a sigh of infinite satisfaction. On the way home she said nothing; but Jack saw, by her absorbed look, that the girl was happy. She was adjusting, bit by bit, her memories and her fancies with the reality. She was trying to fit the stories her guardian had read her so often with the chambers and the courts she had just seen.

Jack watched her stealthily. A great wave of passion roiled over the heart of this young man whenever he looked at this girl. He loved her: there was no longer any possible doubt of that: and she only liked him. What a difference! And to think that the French have only one word for both emotions! She liked to be with him, to talk to him, because he was young and she could talk to him. But love? Cold Dian was not more free from love.

"I can make most of it out," the girl said, turning to Jack. "All except Lady Jane Grey. I cannot understand at all about her. You must take me again. We will get that dear old beef-eater all by himself, and we will spend the whole day there, you and I together, shall we not?"

Then, after her wont, she put the Tower out of her mind and began to talk about what she saw. They passed a printseller's. She wanted to look at a picture in the window, and Jack stopped the cab and took her into the shop.

He observed, not without dismay, that she had not the most rudimentary ideas on the subject of purchase. She had only once been in a shop, and then, if I remember rightly, the bill was sent to Mr. Joseph Jagenal. Phillis turned over the engravings and photographs, and selected half a dozen.

Jack paid the bill next day. It was not much over fifteen pounds—a mere trifle to a Younger Son with four hundred a year. And then he had the pleasure of seeing the warm glow of pleasure in her eyes as she took the "Light of the World" from the portfolio. Pictures were her books, and she took them home to read.

At last, and all too soon, they came back to Carnarvon Square.

"Goodbye, Phil," said Jack, before he knocked at the door. "You have had a pleasant day?"

"Very pleasant, Jack; and all through you," she replied. "Oh, what a good thing for me that we became friends!"

He thought it might in the end be a bad thing for himself, but he did not say so. For every hour plunged the unhappy young man deeper in the ocean of love, and he grew more than ever conscious that the part he at present played would not be regarded with favour by her guardian.

"Jack," she said, while her hand rested in his, and her frank eyes looked straight in his face with an expression in which there was no love at all—he saw that clearly—but only free and childlike affection,—"Jack—why do you look at me so sadly?—Jack, if I were like—if I were meant for that maiden of Arcadia you told me of—"

"Yes, Phil?"

"If other people in the world loved me, you would love me a little, wouldn't you?"

XII

"Hearken what the Inner spirit sings,
'There is no joy but calm.'
Why should we only toil, the roof and crown of things?"

Lawrence Colquhoun was coming home. Phillis, counting the days, remembered, with a little prick of conscience, that Jack Dunquerque had never told her a single word concerning her second guardian. He was about forty years of age, as old as Joseph Jagenal. She pictured a grave heavy man, with massive forehead, thick black hair, and a responsible manner. She knew too that there was to be a change in her life, but of what kind she could not tell. The present mode of living was happiness enough for her: a drive with Mrs. Cassilis— odd that Phillis could never remove from herself the impression that Mrs. Cassilis disliked her; a walk with Joseph to his office and back in the morning; a day of occasional delight with her best friend, Jack the unscrupulous; her drawing for amusement and occupation; and a widely increased area, so to speak, of dress discussion with her maid.

Antoinette, once her fellow-prisoner, now emancipated like herself, informed her young mistress that should the new guardian insist on a return to captivity, she, Antoinette, would immediately resign. Her devotion to Phillis, she explained, was unalterable; but, contrary to the experience of the bard, stone walls, in her own case, did make a prison. Was Mademoiselle going to resign all these pleasures?— she pointed to the evening-dresses, the walking-dresses, the riding habits—was Mademoiselle about to give up taking walks when and where she pleased? was Mademoiselle ready to let the young gentleman, Monsieur Dunquerque, waste his life in regrets—and he so brave, so good? Antoinette, it may be observed, had, in the agreeable society of Jane the housemaid, Clarissa the cook, and Victoria Pamela, assistant in either department, already received enlightenment in the usages of London courtship. She herself, a little flirt with the Norman blue eyes and light-brown hair, was already the object of a devouring passion on the part of a young gentleman who cut other gentlemen's hair in a neighboring street. Further, did Mademoiselle reflect on the wickedness of burying herself and her beautiful eyes out of everybody's sight?

A change was inevitable. Phillis would willingly have stayed on at Carnarvon Square, where the Twins amused her, and the lawyer Joseph was kind to her. But Mrs. Cassilis explained that this was impossible; that steps would have to be taken with regard to her future; and that the wishes of her guardian must be consulted till she was of age.

"You are now nineteen, my dear. You have two years to wait. Then you will come into possession of your fortune, and you will be your own mistress, at liberty to live where and how you please."

Phillis listened, but made no reply. It was a new thought to her that in two years she would be personally responsible for the conduct and management of her own life, obliged to think and decide for herself, and undertaking all the responsibilities and consequences of her own actions. Then she remembered Abraham Dyson's warning and maxims. They once fell unheeded on her brain, which was under strict ward and tutelage, just like exhortations to avoid the sins of the world on the ears of convent girls. Now she remembered them.

"Life is made up of meeting bills drawn on the future by the improvidence of youth."

This was a very mysterious maxim, and one which had often puzzled her. Now she began to understand what was meant.

"The consequences of our own actions are what men call fate. They accompany us like our shadows."

Hitherto, she thought, she had had no chance of performing any action of her own at all. She forgot how she asked Jack Dunquerque to luncheon and went to the Tower with him.

"Every moment of a working life may be a decisive victory."

That would begin in two years' time.

"Brave men act; philosophers discuss; cowards run away. The brave are often killed: the talkers are always left behind; the cowards are caught and cashiered."

Better to act and be killed than to run away and be disgraced, thought Phillis. That was a thing to be remembered in two years' time.

"Women see things through the haze of a foolish education. They manage their affairs badly because they are unable to reason. You, Phillis, who have never learned to read, are the mistress of your own mind. Keep it clear. Get information and remember it. Learn by hearing and watching."

She was still learning—learning something new everyday.

"It is not in my power to complete your education, Phillis. That must be done by somebody else. When it is finished you will understand the whole. But do not be in a hurry."

When would the finisher of her education come? Was it Lawrence Colquhoun? And how would it be finished? Surely sometime in the next two years would complete the edifice, and she would step out into the world at twenty-one, her own mistress, responsible for her actions, equipped at all points to meet the chances and dangers of her life.

So she waited, argued with herself, and counted the days.

Meantime her conduct towards the Twins inspired these young men with mingled feelings of uncertainty and pleasure. She made their breakfast, was considerate in the morning, and did not ask them to talk. When the little dialogue mentioned in an early chapter was finished, she would herself pick out a flower—there were always flowers on the table, in deference to their artistic tastes—or their buttonholes, and despatch them with a smile.

That was very satisfactory.

At dinner, too, she would turn from one to the other while they discoursed sublimely on Art in its higher aspects. They took it for admiration. It was in reality curiosity to know what they meant.

After dinner she would too often confine her conversation to Joseph. On these occasions the brethren would moodily disappear, and retire to their own den, where they lit pipes and smoked in silence.

In point of fact they were as vain as a brace of peacocks, and as jealous as a domestic pet, if attention were shown by the young lady to any but themselves.

Cæsar, it may be observed, quickly learned to distinguish between the habits of Phillis and those of his masters. He never now offered to take the former into a public-house, while he ostentatiously, so to speak, paraded his knowledge of the adjacent bars when conveying the Twins.

One afternoon Phillis took it into her head to carry up tea to the Twins herself.

Cornelius was, as usual, sound asleep in an easy-chair, his head half resting upon one hand, and his pale cheek lit up with a sweet and childlike smile—he was dreaming of vintage wines. He looked sweetly poetical, and it was a thousand pities that his nose was so red. On the table lay his blotting-pad, and on it, clean and spotless, was the book destined to receive his epic poem.

Phillis touched the Divine Bard lightly on the shoulder.

He thought it was Jane; stretched, yawned, relapsed, and then awoke, fretful, like a child of five months.

"Give me the tea," he grumbled. "Too sweet again, I dare say, like yesterday."

"No sugar at all in it, Mr. Cornelius."

He sprang into consciousness at the voice.

"My dear Miss Fleming! Is it really you? You have condescended to visit the Workshop, and you find the Laborer asleep. I feel like a sentinel found slumbering at his post. Pray do not think—it is an accident quite novel to me—the exhaustion of continuous effort, I suppose."

She looked about the room.

"I see books; I see a table; I see a blotting-pad: and—" She actually, to the Poet's horror, turned over the leaves of the stitched book, with Humphrey's ornamental title page. "Not a word written. Where is your work, Mr. Cornelius?"

"I work at Poesy. That book, Miss Fleming, is for the reception of my great epic when it is completed. *Non omnis moriar.* There will be found in that blank book the structure of a lifetime. I shall live by a single work, like Homer."

"What is it all about?" asked Phillis. She set the tea on the table and sat down, looking up at the Poet, who rose from his easy chair and made answer, walking up and down the room:

"It is called the *Upheaving of Ælfred*. In the darkest moments of Ælfred's life, while he is hiding amid the Somersetshire morasses, comes the Spirit of his Career, and guides him in a vision, step by step, to his crowning triumphs. Episodes are introduced. That of the swineherd and the milkmaid is a delicate pastoral, which I hope will stand side by side with the Daphnis and Chloe. When it is finished, would you like me to read you a few cantos?"

"No thank you very much," said Phillis. "I think I know all that I want to know about Alfred. Disguised as a neatherd, he took refuge in Athelney, where one day, being set to bake some cakes by the woman of the cottage, he became so absorbed in his own meditations that— I never thought it a very interesting story."

"The loves of the swineherd and the milkmaid—" the Poet began.

"Yes," Phillis interrupted, unfeelingly. "But I hardly think I care much for swineherds. And if I had been Alfred I should have liked the stupid story about the cakes forgotten. Can't you write me some words for music, Mr. Cornelius? Do, and I will sing them to something or other. Or write some verses on subjects that people care to hear about, as Wordsworth did. My guardian used to read Wordsworth to me."

"Wordsworth could not write a real epic," said Cornelius.

"Could he not? Perhaps he preferred writing other things. Now I must carry Mr. Humphrey his tea. Goodbye, Mr. Cornelius; and do not go to sleep again."

Humphrey, too, was asleep on his sofa. Raffaelle himself could not have seemed a more ideal painter. The very lights of the afternoon harmonised with the purple hue of his velvet coat, the soft brown silkiness of his beard, and his high pale forehead. Like his brother, Humphrey spoiled the artistic effect by that unlucky redness of the nose.

The same awakening was performed.

"I have just found your brother," said Phillis, "at work on Poetry."

"Noble fellow, Cornelius!" murmured the Artist. "Always at it. Always with nose to the grindstone. He will overdo it some day."

"I hope not," said Phillis, with a gleam in her eye. "I sincerely hope not. Perhaps he is stronger than he looks. And what are you doing, Mr. Humphrey?"

"You found me asleep. The bow stretched too long must snap or be unbent."

"Yes," said Phillis; "you were exhausted with work."

"My great picture—no, it is not on the canvas," for Phillis was looking at the bare easel.

"Where is it, then? Do show it to me."

"When the groups are complete I will let you criticise them. It may be that I shall learn something from an artless and unconventional nature like your own."

"Thank you," said Phillis. "That is a compliment, I am sure. What is the subject of the picture?"

"It is the 'Birth of the Renaissance.' An allegorical picture. There will be two hundred and twenty-three figures in the composition."

"The 'Birth of the Renaissance,'" Phillis mused. "I think I know all about that. 'On the taking of Constantinople in the year 1433, the dispersed Greeks made their way to the kingdoms of the West, carrying with them Byzantine learning and culture. Italy became the chosen home of these exiles. The almost simultaneous invention of printing, coupled with an outburst of genius in painting and poetry, and a new-born thirst for classical knowledge, made up what is known by the name of the Renaissance.' That is what my guardian told me one night.

I think that I do not want to see any picture on that subject. Sit down now and draw me a girl's face."

He shook his head.

"Art cannot be forced," he replied.

"Mr. Humphrey,"—her eyes began to twinkle,—"when you have time—I should not like to force your Art, but when you have time—paint me a little group: yourself, Mr. Cornelius, and Cæsar, in the morning walk. You may choose for the moment of illustration either your going into or coming out of the Carnarvon Arms; when you intend to have or when you have had your little whack."

She laughed and ran away.

Humphrey sat upright, and gazed at the door through which she fled. Then he looked round helplessly for his brother, who was not there.

"Little whack!" he murmured. "Where did she learn the phrase? And how does she know that—Cæsar could not have told her."

He was very sad all the evening, and opened his heart to his brother when they sought the Studio at nine, an hour earlier than usual.

"I wish she had not come," he said; "she makes unpleasant remarks."

"She does; she laughed at my epic today." The Poet, who sat in a dressing-gown, drew the cord tighter round his waist, and tossed up his head with a gesture of indignation.

"And she laughed at my picture."

"She is dangerous, Humphrey."

"She watches people when they go for a morning walk, Cornelius, and makes allusion to the Carnarvon Arms and to afternoon naps."

"If, Humphrey, we have once or twice been obliged to go to the Carnarvon Arms—"

"Or have been surprised into an afternoon nap, Cornelius—"

"That is no reason why we should be ashamed to have the subjects mentioned. I should hope that this young lady would not speak of Us—of You, brother Humphrey, and of Myself—save with reverence."

"She has no reverence, brother Cornelius."

"Jane certainly tells me," said the Poet, "that a short time ago she brought Mr. Ronald Dunquerque, then a complete stranger, to my room, when I happened by the rarest accident to be asleep, and showed me to him."

"If one could hope that she was actuated only by respect! But no, I hardly dare to think that. Then, I suppose, she brought her visitor to the Studio."

"Brother Humphrey, we always do the same thing at the same time."

"*Mutatis mutandis*, my dear Cornelius. I design, you write; I group, you clothe your conceptions in undying words. Perhaps we both shall live. It was on the same day that she drew the sketch of me asleep." Humphrey's mind was still running on the want of respect. "Here it is."

"*Forsitan hoc nomen nostrum miscebitur illis*," resumed the Poet, looking at the sketch. "The child has a wonderful gift at catching a likeness. If it were not for the annoyance one might feel pleased. The girl is young and pretty. If our years are double what they should be, our hearts are half our years."

"They are. We cannot be angry with her."

"Impossible."

"Dear little Phillis!"—she was a good inch taller than either of the Twins, who, indeed, were exactly the same height, and it was five feet four—"she is charming in spite, perhaps on account, of her faults. Her property is in the Funds, you said Cornelius?"

"Three-percents. Fifty thousand pounds—fifteen hundred a year; which is about half what Joseph pays income tax upon. A pleasant income, brother Humphrey."

"Yes, I dare say." Humphrey tossed the question of money aside. "You and I, Cornelius, are among the few who care nothing about three-percents. What is money to us? what have we to do with incomes? Art, glorious Art, brother, is our mistress. She pays us, not in sordid gold, but in smiles, in gleams of a haven not to be reached by the common herd, in skies of a radiance visible only to the votary's eye."

Cornelius sighed response. It was thus that the brothers kept up the sacred flame of artistic enthusiasm. Pity that they were compelled to spend their working hours in subjection to sleep, instead of Art. Our actions and our principles are so often at variance that their case is not uncommon.

Then they had their first split soda; then they lit their pipes; for it was ten o'clock. Phillis was gone to bed; Joseph was in his own room; the fire was bright and the hearth clean. The Twins sat at opposite sides, with the "materials" on a chess-table between them, and prepared to make the usual night of it.

"Cornelius," said Humphrey, "Joseph is greatly changed since she came."

The Poet sat up and leaned forward, with a nod signifying concurrence.

"He is, Humphrey; now you mention it, he is. And you think—"

"I am afraid, Cornelius, that Joseph, a most thoughtful man in general, and quite awake to the responsibilities of his position—"

"It is not every younger son, brother Humphrey, who has thought of changing his condition in life."

Cornelius turned pale.

"He has her to breakfast with him; she walks to the office with him; she makes him talk at dinner; Joseph never used to talk with us. He sits in the drawing-room after dinner. He used to go straight to his own room."

"This is grave," said the Poet. "You must not, my dear Humphrey, have the gorgeous colouring and noble execution of your groups spoiled by the sordid cares of life. If Joseph marries, you and I would be thrown upon the streets, so to speak. What is two hundred a year?"

"Nor must you, my dear brother, have the delicate fancies of your brain shaken up and clouded by mean and petty anxieties."

"Humphrey," said the Poet, "come to me in half an hour in the Workshop. This is a time for action."

It was only half-past ten, and the night was but just begun. He buttoned his dressing-gown across his chest, tightened the cord, and strode solemnly out of the room. The Painter heard his foot descend the stairs.

"Excellent Cornelius," he murmured, lighting his second pipe; "he lives but for others."

Joseph was sitting as usual before a pile of papers. It was quite true that Phillis was brightening up the life of this hard-working lawyer. His early breakfast was a time of pleasure; his walk to the office was not a solitary one; he looked forward to dinner; and he found the evenings tolerable. Somehow, Joseph Jagenal had never known any of the little *agrèmens* of life. From bed to desk, from desk to bed, save when a dinner-party became a necessity, had been his life from the day his articles were signed.

"You, Cornelius!" He looked up from his work, and laid down his pen. "This is unexpected."

"I am glad to find you, as usual, at work, Joseph. We are a hard-working family. You with law-books; poor Humphrey, and I with—But never mind."

He sighed and sat down.

"Why poor Humphrey?"

"Joseph, we were happy before this young lady came."

"What has Phillis done? Why, we were then old fogies, with our bachelor ways; and she has roused us up a little. And again, why poor Humphrey?"

"We were settled down in a quiet stream of labour, thinking that there would be no change. I see a great change coming over us now."

"What change?"

"Joseph, if it were not for Humphrey I should rejoice. I should say, 'Take her; be happy in your own way.' For me, I only sing of love. I might perhaps sing as well in a garret and on a crust of bread, therefore it matters nothing. It is for Humphrey that I feel. How can that delicately-organised creature, to whom warmth, comfort and ease are as necessary as sunshine to the flower, face the outer world? For his sake, I ask you, Joseph, to reconsider your project, and pause before you commit yourself."

Joseph was accustomed to this kind of estimate which one Twin invariably made of the other, but the reason for making it staggered him. He actually blushed. Being forty years of age, a bachelor, and a lawyer—on all these grounds presumably acquainted with the world and with the sex—he blushed on being accused of nothing more than a mere tendency in the direction of marriage.

"This is the strangest whim!" he said. "Why, Cornelius, I am as likely to marry Phillis Fleming as I am to send Humphrey into the cold. Dismiss the thought at once, and let the matter be mentioned no more. Goodnight, Cornelius."

He turned to his papers again with the look of one who wishes to be alone. These Twins were a great pride to him, but he could not help sometimes feeling the slightest possible annoyance that they were not as other men. Still they were his charge, and in their future glory his own name would play an honourable part.

"Goodnight, Cornelius. It is good of you to think of Humphrey first. I shall not marry—either the child Phillis Fleming or any other woman."

"Goodnight, my dear Joseph. You have relieved my mind of a great anxiety. Goodnight."

Five minutes afterwards the door opened again.

Joseph looked around impatiently.

This time it was Humphrey. The light shone picturesquely on his great brown beard, so carefully trimmed and brushed; on the velvet jacket, in the pockets of which were his hands; and on his soft, large, limpid eyes, so full of unutterable artistic perception, such lustrous passion for colour and for form.

"Well, Humphrey!" Joseph exclaimed, with more sharpness than he was wont to display to his brothers. "Are you come here on the same wise errand as Cornelius?"

"Has Cornelius been with you?" asked the Painter artlessly. "What did Cornelius come to you for? Poor fellow! he is not ill, I trust, I thought he took very little dinner today."

"Tut, tut! Don't you know why he came here?"

"Certainly not, brother Joseph." This was of course strictly true, because Cornelius had not told him. Guesses are not evidence. "And it hardly matters, does it?" he asked, with a sweet smile. "For myself, I come because I have a thing to say."

"Well? Come, Humphrey, don't beat about the bush."

"It is about Miss—Fleming."

"Ah!"

"You guess already what I have to say, my dear Joseph. It is this: I have watched the birth and growth of your passion for this young lady. In some respects I am not surprised. She is certainly piquante as well as pretty. But, my dear brother Joseph, there is Cornelius."

Joseph beat the tattoo on his chair.

"Humphrey," he groaned, "I know all Cornelius's virtues."

"But not the fragile nature of his beautifully subtle brain. That, Joseph, I alone know. I tremble to think what would become of that—that *deliciæ musurum*, were he to be deprived of the little luxuries which are to him necessities. A poet's brain, Joseph, is not a thing to be lightly dealt with."

Joseph was touched at this appeal.

"You are really, Humphrey, the most tender-hearted pair of creatures I ever saw. Would that all the world were like you! Take my assurance, if that will comfort you, that I have no thought whatever of marrying Phillis Fleming."

"Joseph,"—Humphrey grasped his hand,—"this is, indeed, a sacrifice."

"Not at all," returned Joseph sharply. "Sacrifice? Nonsense. And please remember, Humphrey, that I am acting as the young lady's guardian; that she is an heiress; that she is intrusted to me; and that it would be an unworthy breach of trust if I were even to think of such a thing. Besides which, I have a letter from Mr. Lawrence Colquhoun, who is coming home immediately. It is not at all likely that the young lady will remain longer under my charge. Goodnight, Humphrey."

"I had a thing to say to Joseph," said Humphrey, going up to the Workshop, "and I said it."

"I too had a thing to say," said the Poet, "and I said it."

"Cornelius, you are the most unselfish creature in the world."

"Humphrey, you are—I have always maintained it—too thoughtful, much too thoughtful, for others. Joseph will not marry."

"I know it; and my mind is relieved. Brother, shall we split another soda? It is only eleven."

Joseph took up his paper. He neither smoked nor drank brandy-and-soda, finding in his work occupation which left him no time for either. Tonight, however, he could not bring his mind to bear upon the words before him.

He to marry? And to marry Phillis? The thought was new and startling. He put it from him; but it came back. And why not? he asked himself. Why should not he, as well as the rest of mankind, have his share of love and beauty? To be sure, it would be a breach of confidence as he told Humphrey. But Colquhoun was coming; he was a young man—his own age—only forty; he would not care to have a girl to look after; he would—again he thought behind him.

But all night long Joseph Jagenal dreamed a strange dream, in which soft voices whispered things in his ears, and he thrilled in his sleep at the rustle of a woman's dress. He could not see her face,—dreams are always so absurdly imperfect—but he recognised her figure, and it was that of Phillis Fleming.

XIII

"She never yet was foolish that was fair."

The days sped on; but each day, as it vanished, made Phillis's heart sadder, because it brought her guardian nearer, and the second great change in her life, she thought, was inevitable. Think of a girl, brought up a cloistered nun, finding her liberty for a few short weeks, and then ordered back to her whitewashed cell. Phillis's feelings as regards Lawrence Colquhoun's return were coloured by this fear. It seemed as if, argument and probability notwithstanding, she might be suddenly and peremptorily carried back to prison, without the consolations of a maid, because Antoinette, as we know, would refuse to accompany her, or the kindly society of the poor old Abraham Dyson, now lying in a synonymous bosom.

A short three weeks since her departure from Highgate; a short six weeks since Mr. Dyson's death; and the world was all so different. She looked back on herself, with her old ideas, contemptuously. "Poor Phillis!" she thought, "she knew so little." And as happens to everyone of us, in every successive stage of life, she seemed to herself now to know everything. Life without the sublime conceit of being uplifted, by reason of superior inward light and greater outward experience, above other men, would be but a poor thing. Phillis thought she had the Key to Universal Knowledge, and that she was on the high-road to make that part of her life which should begin in two years' time easy, happy, and clear of pitfalls. From the Archbishop of Canterbury to Joe the crossing-sweeper, we all think in exactly the same way. And when the ages bring experience, and experience does not blot out memory, we recall our old selves with a kind of shame—wonder that we did not drop into the snare, and perish miserably; and presently fall to thanking God that we are rid of a Fool.

A fortnight. Phillis counted the days, and drew a historical record of everyone. Jack came three times: once after Mrs. Cassilis's dinner; once when he took her to the Tower of London; and once—I have been obliged to omit this third visit—when he sat for his portrait, and Phillis drew him full length, leaning against the mantelshelf, with his hands in his pockets—not a graceful attitude, but an easy one, and new to Phillis, who thought it characteristic. She caught Jack's cheerful spirit too, and fixed it by a touch in the gleam of his eye. Mrs. Cassilis came four times, and on each occasion took the girl for a drive, bought something for her, and sent the bill to Joseph Jagenal. On each occasion, also, she asked particularly for Lawrence Colquhoun. There were the little events with the Twins which we have recorded; and there were walks with Cæsar about the square. Once Joseph Jagenal took her to a picture-gallery, where she wanted to stay and copy everything; it was her first introduction to the higher Art, and she was half delighted, half confused. If Art critics were not such humbugs, and did not pretend to feel what they do not, they might help the world to a better understanding of the glories of painters. As it is, they are the only people, except preachers, to whom unreal gush is allowed by gods and men. After all, as no Art critic of the modern unintelligible gush-and-conceit school can paint or draw, perhaps if they were not to gush and pile up Alpine heaps of words they would be found out for shallow-bags. The ideal critic in Art is the great Master who sits above the fear of rivalry or the imputation of envy; in Literature it is the great writer from whom praise is honoured and dispraise the admonition of a teacher; in the Drama, a man who himself has moved the House with his words, and can afford to look on a new rising playwright with kindliness.

Phillis in the Art Gallery was the next best critic to the calm and impartial Master. She was herself artist enough to understand the difficulties of art; she had that intense and real feeling for form and colour which Humphrey Jagenal affected; and her taste in Art was good enough to overmaster her sympathy with the subject. Some people are ready to weep at a tragical subject, however coarse the daub, just as they weep at the fustian of an Adelphi melodrama; Phillis was ready to weep when the treatment and the subject together were worthy of her tears. It seems as if she must have had her nature chilled; but it is not so.

Time, which ought to be represented as a locomotive engine, moved on, and brought Lawrence Colquhoun at length to London. He went first to Joseph Jagenal's office, and heard that his ward was in safe-keeping with that very safe solicitor.

"It was difficult," Joseph explained, "to know what to do. After the funeral of Mr. Dyson she was left alone in the place, with no more responsible person than a house-keeper. So, as soon as the arrangement could be made, I brought her to my own house. Three old bachelors might safely, I thought, be trusted with the protection of a young lady."

"I am much obliged to you," said Colquhoun. "You have removed a great weight off my mind. What sort of a girl is she?"

Joseph began to describe her. As he proceeded he warmed with his subject, and delineated a young lady of such passing charms of person and mind that Colquhoun was terrified.

"My dear Jagenal, if you were not such a steady old file I should think you were in love with her."

"My love days are over," said the man of conveyances. "That is, I never had any. But you will find Phillis Fleming everything that you can desire. Except, of course," he added, "in respect to her education. It certainly *is* awkward that she does not know how to read."

"Not know how to read?"

"And so, you see," said the lawyer, completing the story we know already, "Mr. Dyson's property will go into Chancery, because Phillis Fleming has never learnt to read, and because we cannot find that chapter on the Coping-stone."

"Hang the Coping-stone!" exclaimed Colquhoun. "I think I will go and see her at once. Will you let me dine with you tonight? And will you add to my obligations by letting her stay on with you till I can arrange something for her?"

"What do you think of doing!"

"I hardly know. I thought on the voyage, that I would do something in the very-superior-lady-companion way for her. To tell the truth, I thought it was a considerable bore—the whole thing. But she seems very different from what I expected, and perhaps I could ask my cousin, Mrs. L'Estrange, to take her into her own house for a time. Poor old Dyson! It is twelve years ago since I saw him last, soon after he took over the child. I remember her then, a solemn little thing, with big eyes, who behaved prettily. She held up her mouth to be kissed when she went to bed, but I suppose she won't do that now."

"You can hardly expect it, I think," said Joseph.

"Abraham Dyson talked all the evening about his grand principles of Female education. I was not interested, except that I felt sorry for the poor child who was to be an experiment. Perhaps I ought to have interfered as one of her trustees. I left the whole thing to him, you see, and did not even inquire after her welfare."

"You two were, by some curious error of judgment, as I take it, left discretionary trustees. As he is dead, you have now the care of Miss Fleming's fifty thousand pounds. Mr. Dyson left it in the funds, where he found it. As your legal adviser, Mr. Colquhoun, I strongly recommend you to do the same. She will be entitled to the control and management of it on coming of age, but it is to be settled on herself when she marries. There is no stipulation as to trustees' consent. So that you only have the responsibility of the young lady and her fortune for two years."

It was twelve o'clock in the day. Colquhoun left the office, and made his way in the direction of Carnarvon Square.

As he ascended the steps of Number Fifteen, the door opened and two young men appeared. One was dressed in a short frock, with a flower in his buttonhole: the other had on a velvet coat, and also had a flower; one was shaven; the other wore a long and silky beard. Both had pale faces and red noses. As they looked at the stranger and passed him down the steps, Colquhoun saw that they were not so young and beautiful as they seemed to be: there were crowsfeet round the eyes, and their step had lost a little of its youthful buoyancy. He wondered who they were, and sent in his card to Miss Fleming.

He was come, then, this new guardian. Phillis could not read the card, but Jane, the maid, told her his name.

He was come; and the second revolution was about to begin.

Instinctively Phillis's first thought was that there would be no more walks with Jack Dunquerque. Why she felt so it would be hard to explain, but she did.

She stood up to welcome him.

She saw a handsome young-looking man, with blue eyes, clear red and white complexion, regular features, a brown beard, and a curious look of laziness in his eyes. They were eyes which showed a repressed power of animation. They lit up at sight of his ward, but not much.

He saw a girl of nineteen, tall, slight, shapely; a girl of fine physique; a girl whose eyes, like her hair, were brown; the former were large and full, but not with the fulness of short-sight; the latter was abundant, and was tossed up in the simplest fashion, which is also the most graceful. Lawrence the lazy felt his pulse quicken a little as this fair creature advanced, with perfect grace and self-possession, to greet him. He noticed that her dress was perfect, that her hands were small and delicate, and that her head was shaped, save for the forehead, which was low and broad, like that of some Greek statue. The Greeks knew the perfect shape of the head, but they made the forehead too narrow. If you think of it, you will find that the Venus of Milo would have been more divine still had her brows been but a little broader.

"My ward?" he said. "Let us make acquaintance, and try to like each other. I am your new guardian."

Phillis looked at him frankly and curiously, letting her hand rest in his.

"When I saw you last—it was twelve years ago—you were a little maid of seven. Do you remember?"

"I think I do; but I am not quite sure. Are you really my guardian?"

"I am indeed. Do I not look like one? To be sure, it is my first appearance in the character."

She shook her head.

"Mr. Dyson was so old," she said, "that I suppose I grew to think all guardians old men."

"I am only getting old," he sighed. "It is not nice to feel yourself going to get old. Wait twenty years, and you will begin to feel the same perhaps. But though I am thirty years younger than Mr. Dyson, I will try to treat you exactly as he did."

Phillis's face fell, and she drew away her hand sharply.

"Oh!" she cried. "But I am afraid that will not do anymore."

"Why, Phillis—I may call you Phillis since I am your guardian, may I not?—did he treat you badly? Why did you not write to me?"

"I did not write, Mr. Colquhoun—if you call me Phillis, I ought to call you Lawrence, ought I not, because you are not old?—I did not write, because dear old Mr. Dyson treated me very kindly, and because you were away and never came to see me, and because I—I never learned to write."

By this time Phillis had learned to feel a little shame at not being able to write.

"Besides," she went on, "he was a dear old man, and I loved him. But you see, Lawrence, he had his views—Jagenal calls them crotchets— and he never let me go outside the house. Now I am free I do not like to think of being a prisoner again. If you try to lock me up, I am afraid I shall break the bars and run away."

"You shall not be a prisoner, Phillis. That is quite certain. We shall find something better than that for you. But it cannot be very lively, in this big house, all by yourself."

"Not very lively; but I am quite happy here."

"Most young ladies read novels to pass away the time."

"I know, poor things." Phillis looked with unutterable sympathy. "Mr. Dyson used to say that the sympathies which could not be quickened by history were so dull that fiction was thrown away upon them."

"Did you never—I mean, did he never read you novels?"

She shook her head.

"He said that my imagination was quite powerful enough to be a good servant, and he did not wish it to become my master. And then there was something else, about wanting the experience of life necessary to appreciate fiction."

"Abraham Dyson was a wise man, Phillis. But what do you do all day?"

"I draw; I talk to my maid, Antoinette; I give the Twins their breakfast—"

"Those were the Twins—Mr. Jagenal's elder brothers—whom I met on the steps, I suppose? I have heard of them. *Après*, Phillis?"

"I play and sing to myself; I go out for a walk in the garden of the square; I go to Mr. Jagenal's office, and walk home with him; and I look after my wardrobe. Then I sit and think of what I have seen and heard—put it all away in my memory, or I repeat to myself over again some of the poetry which I learned at Highgate."

"And you know no young ladies?"

"No; I wish I did. I am curious to talk to young ladies—quite young ladies, you know, of my own age. I want to compare myself with them, and find out my faults. You will tell me my faults, Lawrence, will you?"

"I don't quite think I can promise that, Phillis. You see, you might retaliate; and if you once begin telling me my faults, there would be no end."

"Oh, I am sorry!" Phillis looked curiously at her guardian for some outward sign or token of the old Adam. But she saw none. "Perhaps I shall find them out sometime, and then I will tell you."

"Heaven forbid!" he said, laughing. "Now, Phillis, I have been asked to dine here, and I am going to be at your service all day. It is only one o'clock. What shall we do, and where shall we go?"

"Anywhere," she replied, "anywhere. Take me into the crowded streets, and let me look at the people and the shops. I like that best of anything. But stay and have luncheon here first."

They had luncheon. Colquhoun confessed to himself that this was a young lady calculated to do him the greatest credit. She acted hostess with a certain dignity which sat curiously on so young a girl, and which she had learned from presiding at many a luncheon in Mr. Dyson's old age among his old friends, when her guardian had become too infirm to take the head of his own table. There was, it is true, something wanting. Colquhoun's practised eye detected that at once. Phillis was easy, graceful, and natural. But she had not—the man of the world noticed what Jack Dunquerque failed to observe—she had not the unmistakable stamp of social tone which can only come by practice and time. The elements, however, were there before him; his ward was a diamond which wanted but a little polish to make her a gem of the first water.

After luncheon they talked again; this time with a little more freedom. Colquhoun told her all he knew of the father who was but a dim and distant memory to her. "You have his eyes," he said, "and you have his mouth. I should know you for his daughter." He told her how fond this straight rider, this Nimrod of the hunting-field, had been of his little Phillis! how one evening after mess he told Colquhoun that he had made a will, and appointed him, Lawrence, with Abraham Dyson, the trustees of his little girl.

"I have been a poor trustee, Phillis," Lawrence concluded. "But I was certain you were in good hands, and I let things alone. Now that I have to act in earnest, you must regard me as your friend and adviser."

They had such a long talk that it was past four when they went out for their walk. Phillis was thoughtful and serious, thinking of the father, whom she lost so early. Somehow she had forgotten, at Highgate, that she once had a father. And the word mother had no meaning for her.

Outside the house Lawrence looked at his companion critically.

"Am I poorly dressed?" she asked, with a smile, because she knew that she was perfectly dressed.

At all events, Lawrence thought he would have no occasion to be ashamed of his companion.

"Let me look again, Phillis. I should like to give you a little better brooch than the one you have put on."

"My poor old brooch! I cannot give up my old friend, Lawrence."

She dropped quite easily into his Christian name, and hesitated no more over it than she did with Jack Dunquerque.

He took her into a jeweler's shop and bought her a few trinkets.

"There, Phillis, you can add those to your jewel-box."

"I have no jewels."

"No jewels! Where are your mother's?"

"I believe they are all in the Bank, locked up. Perhaps they are with my money."

Phillis's idea of her fifty thousand pounds was that the money was all in sovereigns, packed away in a box and put into a bank.

"Well, I think you ought to have your jewels out, at any rate. Did Mr. Dyson give you any money to spend?"

"No; and if he had I could not spend it, because I never went outside the house. Lawrence, give me some money, and let me buy something all by myself."

He bought her a purse, and filled it with two or three sovereigns and a handful of silver.

"Now you are rich, Phillis. What will you buy?"

"Pictures, I think."

In all this great exhibition of glorious and beautiful objects there was only one thing which Phillis wished to buy—pictures.

"Well, let us buy some photographs."

They were walking down Oxford Street, and presently they came to a photograph shop. Proud of her newly-acquired wealth, Phillis selected about twenty of the largest and most expensive. Colquhoun observed that her taste was good, and that she chose the best subjects. When she had all that she liked, together with one or two which she bought for Jack, with a secret joy surpassing that of buying for herself, she opened her purse and began to wonder how she was to pay.

"Do you think your slender purse will buy all these views?" Colquhoun asked. "Put it up, Phillis, and keep it for another time. Let me give you these photographs."

"But you said I should buy something." Her words and action were so childish that Lawrence felt a sort of pity for her. Not to know how to spend money seemed to lazy Lawrence, who had done nothing else all his life, a state of mind really deplorable. It would mean in his own case absolute deprivation of the power of procuring pleasure, either for himself or for anyone else.

"Poor little nun! Not to know even the value of money."

"But I do. A sovereign is twenty shillings, and a shilling is twelve pence."

"That is certainly true. Now you shall know the value of money. There is a beggar. He is going to tell us that he is hungry; he will probably add that he has a wife and twelve children, all under the age of three, in his humble home, and that none of them have tasted food for a week. What will you give him?"

Phillis paused. How should she relieve so much distress? By this time they were close to the beggar. He was a picturesque rogue in rags and tatters and bare feet. Though it was a warm day he shivered. In his hand he held a single box of lights. But the fellow was young, well fed, and lusty. Lawrence Colquhoun halted on the pavement, and looked at him attentively.

"This man," he explained to Phillis, "can get for a penny a small loaf; twopence will buy him a glass of ale; sixpence a dinner; for ten shillings he could get a suit of working clothes—which he does not want because he has no intention of doing any work at all; a sovereign would lodge and feed him for a fortnight, if he did not drink."

"I should give him a sovereign," said Phillis. "Then he would be happy for a week."

"Bless your ladyship," murmured the beggar. "I would get work, Gawd knows, if I could."

"I remember this fellow," said Colquhoun, "for six years. He is a sturdy rogue. Best give nothing to him at all. Come on Phillis. We must look for a more promising subject."

"Poor fellow!" said Phillis, closing her purse.

They passed on, and the beggar-man cursed audibly. I believe it is Mr. Tupper, in his *Proverbial Philosophy*, who explains that what a beggar most wants, to make him feel happier, is sympathy. Now that was just what Phillis gave, and the beggar-man only swore.

Colquhoun laughed.

"You may keep your pity, Phillis, for someone who deserves it better. Now let us take a cab and go to the Park. It is four years since I saw the Park."

It was five o'clock. The Park was fuller than when he saw it last. It grows more crowded year after year, as the upward pressure of an enriched multitude makes itself felt more and more. There was the usual throng about the gates, of those who come to look for great people, and like to tell whom they recognised, and who were pointed out to them. There were the pedestrians on either side the road; civilians after office hours; bankers and brokers from the City; men up from Aldershot; busy men hastening home; loungers leaning on the rails; curious colonials gazing at the carriages; Frenchmen trying to think that Hyde Park cannot compare with the Bois de Boulogne; Germans mindful of their mighty army, their great sprawling Berlin, the gap of a century between English prosperity and Teutonic militarism, and as envious as philosophy permits; Americans owning that New York, though its women are lovelier, has nothing to show beside the Park at five on a spring afternoon,—all the bright familiar scene which Colquhoun remembered so well.

"Four years since I saw it last," he repeated to the girl. "I suppose there will be none of the faces that I used to know."

He was wrong. The first man who greeted him was his old Colonel. Then he came across a man he had known in India. Then one whom he had last seen, a war correspondent, inside Metz. He shook hands with one, nodded to another, and made appointments with all at his club. And as each passed, he told something about him to his ward.

"That is my old Colonel—your father's brother officer. The most gallant fellow who ever commanded a regiment. As soon as you are settled, I should like to bring him to see you. That is Macnamara of the *London Herald*—a man you can't get except in England. That is Lord Blandish; we were together up-country in India. He wrote a book about his adventures in Cashmere. I did not."

It was a new world to Phillis. All these carriages? these people: this crowd—who were they?

"They are not like the faces I see in the streets," she said.

"No. Those are faces of men who work for bread. These are mostly of men who work not at all, or they work for honour. There are two or three classes of mankind, you know, Phillis."

"Servants and masters?"

"Not quite. You belong to the class of those who need not work—this class. Your father knew all these people. It is a happy world in its way— in its way," he repeated, thinking of certain shipwrecks he had known. "Perhaps it is better to *have* to work. I do not know. Phillis, who—" He was going to ask her who was bowing to her, when he turned pale, and stopped suddenly. In the carriage which was passing within a foot of where they stood was a lady whom he knew—Mrs. Cassilis. He took off his hat, and Mrs. Cassilis stopped the carriage and held out her hand.

"How do you do, Phillis dear? Mr. Colquhoun, I am glad to see you back again. Come as soon as you can and see me. If you can spare an afternoon as soon as you are settled, give it to me—for auld lang syne."

The last words were whispered. Her lips trembled, and her hand shook as she spoke. And Lawrence's face was hard. He took off his hat and drew back, Phillis did not hear what he said. But Mrs. Cassilis drove on, and left the Park immediately.

"Mrs. Cassilis trembled when she spoke to you, Lawrence." It was exactly what a girl of six would have said.

"Did she, Phillis? She was cold perhaps. Or perhaps she was pleased to see old friends again. So you know her?"

"Yes. I have dined at her house; and I have been shopping with her. She does not like me, I know; but she is kind. She has spoken to me about you."

"So you know Mrs. Cassilis?" he repeated. "She does not look as if she had any trouble on her mind, does she? The smooth brow of a clear conscience—Phillis, if you have had enough of the Park, I think it is almost time to drive you home."

Lawrence Colquhoun dined at Carnarvon Square. The Twins dined at their club; so that they had the evening to themselves and could talk.

"I have made up my mind," Lawrence said, "to ask my cousin to take charge of you, Phillis. Agatha L'Estrange is the kindest creature in the world. Will you try to like her if she consents!"

"Yes, I will try. But suppose she does not like me?"

"Everybody likes you, Miss Fleming," said Joseph.

"She is sure to like you," said Lawrence. "And I will come over often and see you; we will ride together, if you like. And if you would like to have any masters or lessons in anything—"

"I think I should like to learn reading," Phillis remarked meditatively. "Mr. Abraham Dyson used to say"—she held up her finger, and imitated the manner and fidgety dogmatism of an old man—"'Reading breeds a restless curiosity, and engenders an irreverent spirit of carping criticism. Any jackanapes who can read thinks himself qualified to judge the affairs of the nation. Reading, indeed!' But I think I *should* like, after all, to do what everybody else can do."

XIV

"You bear a gentle mind, and heavenly blessings
Follow such creatures."

Half a mile or so above Teddington Lock—where you are quite above the low tides, which leave the mud-banks in long stretches and spoil the beauty of the splendid river; where the stream flows on evenly between its banks, only sometimes swifter and stronger, sometimes slower and more sluggish; where you may lie and listen a whole summer's day to the murmurous wash of the current among the lilies and the reeds,—there stands a house, noticeable among other houses by reason of its warm red brick, its many gables, and its wealth of creepers. Its gardens and lawns slope gently down to the river's edge; the willows hang over it, letting their long leaves, like maidens' fingers, lie lightly on the cool surface of the water; there is a boat-house, where a boat used to lie, but it is empty now—ivy covers it over, dark ivy that contrasts with the lighter greens of the sweet May foliage; the lilacs and laburnums are exulting in the transient glory of foliage and flower; the wisteria hangs its purple clusters like grapes upon the wall; there are greenhouses and vineries; there are flower-beds bright with the glories of modern gardening; and there are old-fashioned round plots of ground innocent of bedding-out, where flourish the good old-fashioned flowers, stocks, pansies, boy's-love, sweet-william, and the rest, which used to be cultivated for their perfume and colour long before bedding-out was thought of; an old brick wall runs down to the river's edge as a boundary on either side, thick and warm, with peaches, plums, and apricots trained in formal lines, and crowned with wall-flowers and long grasses, like the walls of some old castle. Behind are rooms which open upon the lawn; round the windows clamber the roses waiting for the suns of June; and if you step into the house from the garden, you will enter a dainty drawing-room, light and sunny, adorned with all manner of feminine things, and you will find, besides, boudoirs, studies, all sorts of pretty rooms into which the occupants of the house may retire, the time they feel disposed to taste the joys of solitude.

The house of a lady. Does anyone ever consider what thousands of these dainty homes exist in England? All about the country they stand—houses where women live away their innocent and restful lives, lapped from birth to death in an atmosphere of peace and warmth. Such luxury as they desire is theirs, for they are wealthy enough to purchase all they wish. Chiefly they love the luxury of Art, and fill their portfolios with water-colours. But their passions even for Art are apt to be languid, and they mostly desire to continue in the warm air, perfumed like the wind that cometh from the sweet south, which they have created round themselves. The echoes of the outer world fall upon their ears like the breaking of the rough sea upon a shore so far off that the wild dragging of the shingle, with its long-drawn cry, sounds like a distant song. These ladies know nothing of the fiercer joys of life, and nothing of its pains. The miseries of the world they understand not, save that they have been made picturesque in novels. They have no ambition, and take no part in any battles. They have not spent their strength in action, and therefore feel no weariness. Society is understood to mean a few dinners, with an occasional visit to the wilder dissipations of town; and their most loved entertainments are those gatherings known as garden parties. Duty means following up in a steady but purposeless way some line of study which will never be mastered. Good works mean subscription to societies. Many a kind lady thinks in her heart of hearts that the annual guinea to a missionary society will be of far more avail to her future welfare than a life of purity and innocence. The Christian virtues naturally find their home in such a house. They grow of their own accord, like the daisies, the buttercups, and the field convolvulus: Love, Joy, Peace, Gentleness, Goodness, Faith, Meekness, Temperance, all the things against which there is no law—which of them is not to be seen abundantly blossoming and luxuriant in the cottages and homes of these English ladies?

In this house by the river lived Mrs. L'Estrange. Her name was Agatha, and everybody who knew her called her Agatha L'Estrange. When a woman is always called by her Christian name, it is a sign that she is loved and lovable. If a man, on the other hand, gets to be known, without any reason for the distinction, by *his* Christian name, it is generally a sure sign that he is sympathetic, but blind to his own interests. She was a widow, and childless. She had been a widow so long, her husband had been so much older than herself, her married life had been so short, and the current of her life so little disturbed by it, that she had almost forgotten that she was once a wife. She had an ample income; she lived in the way that she loved; she gathered her friends about her; she sometimes, but at rare intervals, revisited society; mostly she preferred her quiet life in the country. Girls came from London to stay with her, and wondered how Agatha managed to exist. When the season was over, leaving its regrets and its fatigues, with the usual share of hollowness and Dead-Sea fruit they came again, and envied her tranquil home.

She was first cousin to Lawrence Colquhoun, whom she still, from force of habit, regarded as a boy. He was very nearly the same age as herself, and they had been brought up together. There was nothing about his life that she did not know, except one thing—the reason of his abrupt disappearance four years before. She was his confidante: as a boy he told her all his dreams of greatness; as a young man all his dreams of love and pleasure. She knew the soft and generous nature, out of which great men cannot be formed, which was his. She saw the lofty dreams die away; and she hoped for him that he would keep something of the young ideal. He did. Lawrence Colquhoun was a man about town; but he retained his good-nature. It is not usual among the young gentlemen who pursue pleasure as a profession; it is not expected of them, after a few years of idleness, gambling, and the rest, to have any good-nature surviving, or any thought left at all, except for themselves; therefore Lawrence Colquhoun's case was unusual, and popularity proportional. He tired of garrison life; he sold out; he remained about town; the years ran on, and he neither married nor talked of marrying. But he used to go down to his cousin once a week, and talk to her about his idle life. There came a day when he left off coming, or if he came at all, his manner to his cousin was altered. He became gloomy; and one day she heard, in a brief and unsatisfactory letter, that he was going to travel for a lengthened period. The letter came from Scotland, and was as brief as a dinner invitation.

He went; he was away for four years; during that time he never once wrote to her; she heard nothing of him or from him.

One day, without any notice, he appeared again.

He was very much the same as when he left England—men alter little between thirty and fifty—only a little graver; his beard a little touched with the grey hairs which belong to the eighth lustrum; his eyes a little crows-footed; his form a little filled out. The gloom was gone, however; he was again the kindly Lawrence, the genial Lawrence, Lawrence the sympathetic, Lawrence the lazy.

He walked in as if he had been away a week. Agatha heard a step upon the gravel-walk, and knew it. Her heart beat a little—although

WALTER BESANT AND JAMES RICE

a woman may be past forty she may have a heart still—and her eyes sparkled. She was sitting at work—some little useless prettiness. On the work-table lay a novel, which she read in the intervals of stitching; the morning was bright and sunny, with only a suspicion of east wind, and her windows were open; flowers stood upon her table; flowers in pots and vases stood in her windows; such flowers as bloom in May were bright in her garden, and the glass doors of her conservatory showed a wealth of flowers within. A house full of flowers, and herself a flower too—call her a rose fully blown, or call her a glory of early autumn—a handsome woman still, sweet and to be loved, with the softness of her tranquil life in every line of her face, and her warmth of heart in every passing expression.

She started when she heard his step, because she recognised it. Then she sat up and smiled to herself. She knew how her cousin would come back.

In fact he walked in at her open window, and held out his hand without saying a word. Then he sat down, and took a single glance at his cousin first and the room afterwards.

"I have not seen you lately, Lawrence," said Agatha, as if he had been away for a month or so.

"No; I have been in America."

"Really! You like America?" She waited for him to tell her what he would.

"Yes. I came back yesterday. You are looking well, Agatha."

"I am very well."

"And you have got a new picture on the wall. Where did you buy this?"

"At Agnew's, three years ago. It was in the Exhibition. Now I think of it, you have been away for four years, Lawrence."

"I like it. Have you anything to tell me, Agatha?"

"Nothing that will interest you. The house is the same. We have had several dreadful winters, and I have been in constant fear that my shrubs would be killed. Some of them were. My dog Pheenie is dead, and I never intend to have another. The cat that you used to tease is well. My aviary has increased; my horses are the same you knew four years ago; my servants are the same; and my habits, I am thankful to say, have not deteriorated to my knowledge, although I am four years older."

"And your young ladies—the traps you used to set for me when I was four years younger, Agatha—where are they?"

"Married, Lawrence, all of them. What a pity that you could not fix yourself! But it is never too late to mend. At one time I feared you would be attracted by Victoria Pengelley."

Lawrence Colquhoun visibly changed colour, but Agatha was not looking at him.

"That would have been a mistake. I thought so then, and I know it now. She is a cold and bloodless woman, Lawrence. Besides, she is married, thank goodness. We must find you someone else."

"My love days are over," he said, with a harsh and grating voice. "I buried them before I went abroad."

"You will tell me all about that some day, when you feel communicative. Meantime, stay to dinner, and enliven me with all your adventures. You may have some tea if you like, but I do not invite you, because you will want to go away again directly afterwards. Lawrence, what do you intend to do, now you are home again? Are you going to take up the old aimless life, or shall you be serious?"

"I think the aimless life suits me best. And it certainly is the slowest. Don't you think, Agatha, that as we have got to get old and presently to die, we may as well go in for making the time go slow? That is the reason why I have never done anything."

"I never do anything myself, except listen to what other people tell me. But I find the days slip away all too quickly."

"Agatha, I am in a difficulty. That is one of the reasons why I have come to see you today."

"Poor Lawrence! You always are in a difficulty."

"This time it is not my fault; but it is serious. Agatha, I have got—a—"

I do not know why he hesitated, but his cousin caught him up with a little cry.

"Not a wife, Lawrence; not a wife without telling me!"

"No, Agatha," he flushed crimson, "not a wife. That would have been a great deal worse. What I have got is a ward."

"A ward?"

"Do you remember Dick Fleming, who was killed in the hunting-field about fifteen years ago?"

"Yes, perfectly. He was one of my swains ever so long ago, before I married my poor dear husband."

Agatha had used the formula of her "poor dear husband" for more than twenty years; so long, in fact, that it was become a mere collocation of words, and had no longer any meaning, certainly no sadness.

"He left a daughter, then a child of four or five. And he made me one of that child's guardians. The other was a Mr. Dyson, who took her and brought her up. He is dead, and the young lady, now nineteen years of age, comes to me."

"But, Lawrence, what on earth are you going to do with a girl of nineteen?"

"I don't know, Agatha. I cannot have her with me in the Albany, can I?"

"Not very well, I think."

"I cannot take a small house in Chester Square, and give evening-parties for my ward and myself, can I?"

"Not very well, Lawrence."

"She is staying with my lawyer, Jagenal; a capital fellow, but his house is hardly the right place for a young lady."

"Lawrence, what will you do? This is a very serious responsibility."

"Very."

"What sort of a girl is she?"

"Phillis Fleming is what you would call, I think, a beautiful girl. She is tall, and has a good figure. Her eyes are brown, and her hair is brown, with lots of it. Her features are small, and not too regular. She has got a very sweet smile, and I should say a good temper, so long as she has her own way."

"No, doubt," said Agatha. "Pray, go on; you seem to have studied her appearance with a really fatherly care."

"She has a very agreeable voice; a naïveté in manner that you should like; she is clever and well informed."

"Is she strong-minded, Lawrence?"

"No," said Lawrence, with emphasis, "she is not. She has excellent ideas on the subject of her sex."

"Always in extremes, of course, though I am not certain what."

"She wants, so far as I can see, nothing but the society of some amiable accomplished gentlewoman—"

"Lawrence, you are exactly the same as you always were. You begin by flattery. Now I know what you came here for."

"An amiable accomplished gentlewoman, who would exercise a gradual and steady influence upon her."

"You want her to stay with me, Lawrence. And you are keeping something back. Tell me instantly. You say she is beautiful. It must be something else. Are her manners in anyway unusual? Does she drop *h*'s, and eat with her knife?"

"No, her manners are, I should say, perfect.'

"Temper good, you say; manner perfect; appearance graceful. What can be the reserved objection? My dear cousin, you pique my curiosity. She is sometimes, probably insane?"

"No, Agatha, not that I know of. It is only that her guardian brought her up in entire seclusion from the world, and would not have her taught to read and write."

"How very remarkable!"

"On the other hand, she can draw. She draws everything and everybody. She has got a book full of drawings which she calls her diary. They are the record of her life. She will show them to you, and tell you all her story. You will take her for a little while, Agatha, will you?"

Of course she said "Yes." She had never refused Lawrence Colquhoun anything in her life. Had he been a needy man he would have been dangerous. But Lawrence Colquhoun wanted nothing for himself.

"My dear Agatha, it is very good of you. You will find the most splendid material to work upon, better than you ever had. The girl is different from any other girl you have ever known. She talks and thinks like a boy. She is as strong and active as a young athlete. I believe she would outrun Atalanta; and yet I think she is a thorough woman at heart."

"I should not at all wonder at her being a thorough woman at heart. Most of us are. But, Lawrence, you must not fall in love with your own ward."

He laughed a little uneasily.

"I am too old for a girl of nineteen," he replied.

"At any rate, you have excited my curiosity. Let her come, Lawrence, as soon as you please. I want to see this paragon of girls, who is more ignorant than a charity school girl."

"On the contrary, Agatha, she is better informed than most girls of her age. If she is not well read she is well told."

"But really, Lawrence, think. She cannot read, even."

"Not if you gave her a basketful of tracts. But that is rather a distinction now. At least she will never want to go in for what they call the Higher Education, will she?"

"She must learn to read; but will she ever master Spelling?"

"Very few people do; they only pretend. I am weak myself in spelling. Phillis does not want to be a certificated Mistress, Agatha."

"And Arithmetic, too."

"Well, my cousin, of course the Rule of Three is as necessary to life as the Use of the Globes, over which the schoolmistresses used to keep such a coil. And it has been about as accessible to poor Phillis as an easy seat to a tombstone cherub. But she can count and multiply and add, and tell you how much things ought to come to; and really when you think of it, a woman does not want much more, does she?"

"It is the mental training, Lawrence. Think of the loss of mental training."

"I feel that, too," he said, with a smile of sympathy. "Think of growing up without the discipline of Vulgar Fractions or Genteel Decimals. One is appalled at imagining what our young ladies would be without it. But you shall teach her what you like, Agatha."

"I am half afraid of her, Lawrence."

"Nonsense, my cousin; she is sweetness itself. Let me bring her tomorrow."

"Yes; she can have the room next to mine." Agatha sighed a little. "Suppose we don't get on together after all. It would be such a disappointment, and such a pain to part."

"Get on, Agatha?—and with you? Well, all the world gets on with you. Was there ever a girl in the world that you did not get on with?"

"Yes, there was. I never got on with Victoria Pengelley—Mrs. Cassilis. Shall you call upon her, Lawrence?"

"No—yes—I don't know, Agatha," he replied, hurriedly; and went away with scant leave-taking. He neither took any tea nor stayed to dinner.

Then Agatha remembered.

"Of course," she said. "How stupid of me! They used to talk about Lawrence and Victoria. Can he think of her still? Why, the woman is as cold as ice and as hard as steel, besides being married. A man who would fall in love with Victoria Pengelley would be capable of falling in love with a marble statue."

"My cousin, Lawrence Colquhoun," she told her friends in her letters—Agatha spent as much time letter-writing as Madame du Deffand—"has come back from his travels. He is not at all changed, except that he has a few grey hairs in his beard. He laughs in the same pleasant way; has the same soft voice; thinks as little seriously about life; and is as perfectly charming as he has always been. He has a ward, a young lady, daughter of an old friend of mine. She is named Phillis Fleming. I am going to have her with me for a while, and I hope you will come and make her acquaintance, but not just yet, not until we are used to each other. I hear nothing but good of her."

Thus did this artful woman gloss over the drawbacks of poor Phillis's education. Her friends were to keep away till such time as Phillis had been drilled, inspected, reviewed, manoeuvred, and taught the social tone. No word, you see, of the little deficiencies which time alone could be expected to fill up. Agatha L'Estrange, in her way, was a woman of the world. She expected, in spite of her cousin's favourable report, to find an awkward, rather pretty, wholly unpresentable hoyden. And she half repented that she had so easily acceded to Lawrence Colquhoun's request.

It was nearly six next day when Phillis arrived. Her guardian drove her out in a dog-cart, her maid following behind with the luggage. This mode of conveyance being rapid, open, and especially adapted for purposes of observation, pleased Phillis mightily; she even preferred it to a hansom cab. She said little on the road, being too busy in the contemplation of men and manners. Also she was yet hardly at home with her new guardian. He was pleasant; he was thoughtful of her; but she had not yet found out how to talk with him. Now, with Jack Dunquerque—and then she began to think how Jack would look driving a dog-cart, and how she should look beside him.

Lawrence Colquhoun looked at his charge with eyes of admiration. Many a prettier girl, he thought, might be seen in a London ballroom or in the Park, but not one brighter or fresher. Where did it come from, this piquant way?

Phillis asked no more questions about Mrs. L'Estrange. Having once made up her mind that she should rebel and return to Mr. Jagenal in case she did not approve of Mr. Colquhoun's cousin, she rested tranquil. To be sure she was perfectly prepared to like her, being still in the stage of credulous curiosity in which every fresh acquaintance seemed to possess all possible virtues. Up to the present she had made one exception; I am sorry to say it was that of the only woman she knew—Mrs. Cassilis. Phillis could not help feeling as if life with Mrs. Cassilis would after a time become tedious. Rather, she thought, life with the Twins.

They arrived at the house by the river. Agatha was in the garden. She looked at her visitor with a little curiosity, and welcomed her with both hands and a kiss. Mrs. Cassilis did not kiss Phillis. In fact, nobody ever had kissed her at all since the day when she entered Abraham

Dyson's house. Jack, she remembered, had proposed to commence their friendship with an imitation of the early Christians, but the proposal, somehow, came to nothing. So when Agatha drew her gently towards herself and kissed her softly on the forehead, poor Phillis changed colour and was confused. Agatha thought it was shyness, but Phillis was never shy.

"You are in good time, Lawrence. We shall have time for talk before dinner. You may lie about in the garden, if you please, till we come to look for you. Come, my dear, and I will show you your room."

At Highgate Phillis's room was furnished with a massive four post bedstead and adorned with dusky hangings. Solidity, comfort, and that touch of gloom which our grandfathers always lent to their bedrooms, marked the Highgate apartment. At Carnarvon Square she had the "spare room," and it was furnished in much the same manner, only that it was larger, and the curtains were of lighter colour.

She saw now a small room, still with the afternoon sun upon it, with a little iron bedstead in green and gold, and white curtains. There was a sofa, an easy-chair, a table at one of the windows, and one in the centre of the room; there were bookshelves; and there were pictures.

Phillis turned her bright face with a grateful cry of surprise.

"Oh, what a beautiful room!"

"I am glad you like it, my dear. I hope you will be comfortable in it."

Phillis began to look at the pictures on the wall.

She was critical about pictures, and these did not seem very good.

"Do you like the pictures?"

"This one is out of drawing," she said, standing before a water-colour. "I like this better," moving on to the next; "but the painting is not clear."

Agatha remembered what she had paid for these pictures, and hoped the fair critic was wrong. But she was not; she was right.

And then, in her journey round the room, Phillis came to the open window, and cried aloud with surprise and astonishment.

"O Mrs. L'Estrange! is it—it—" she asked, in an awestruck voice, turning grave eyes upon her hostess, as if imploring that no mistake should be made on a matter of such importance. "Is it—really—the Thames?"

"Why, my dear, of course it is."

"I have never seen a river. I have so longed to see a river, and especially the Thames. Do you know—

"Sweet Thames, run softly till I end my song!'

"And again—Oh, there are swans!

> *"With that I saw two swans of goodly hue*
> *Come softly swimming down along the lee;*
> *Two fairer birds I never yet did see.*'"

"I am glad you read poetry, my dear."

"But I do not. I cannot read; I only remember. Mrs. L'Estrange, can we get close to it, quite close to the water? I want to see it flowing."

They went back into the garden, where Lawrence was lying in the shade, doing nothing. Phillis looked not at the flowers or the spring blossoms; she hurried Agatha across the lawn, and stood at the edge, gazing at the water.

"I should like," she murmured presently, after a silence—"I should like to be in a boat and drift slowly down between the banks, seeing everything as we passed, until we came to the place where all the ships come up. Jack said he would take me to see the great ships sailing home laden with their precious things. Perhaps he will. But, O Mrs. L'Estrange, how sweet it is! There is the reflection of the tree; see how the swans sail up and down; there are the water-lilies; and look, there are the light and shade chasing each other up the river before the wind."

Agatha let her stay a little longer, and then led her away to show her the flowers and hothouses. Phillis knew all about these and discoursed learnedly. But her thoughts were with the river.

Lawrence went away soon after dinner. It was a full moon, and the night was warm. Agatha and Phillis went into the garden again when Lawrence left them. It was still and silent, and as they stood upon the walk, the girl heard the low murmurous wash of the current singing an invitation among the grasses and reeds of the bank.

"Let us go and look at the river again," she said.

If it was beautiful in the day, with the evening sun upon it, it was ten times as beautiful by night, when the shadows made great blacknesses, and the bright moon silvered all the outlines and threw a long way of light upon the rippling water.

Presently they came in and went to bed.

Agatha, half an hour later, heard Phillis's window open. The girl was looking at the river again in the moonlight. She saw the water glimmer in the moonlight; she heard the whisper of the waves. Her

WALTER BESANT AND JAMES RICE

thoughts—they were the long thoughts of a child—went up the stream, and wondered through what meadows and by what hills the stream had flowed; then she followed the current down, and had to picture it among the ships before it was lost in the mighty ocean.

As she looked there passed a boat full of people. They were probably rough and common people, but among them was a woman, and she was singing. Phillis wondered who they were. The woman had a sweet voice. As they rowed by the house one of the men lit a lantern, and the light fell upon their faces, making them clear and distinct for a moment, and then was reflected in the black water below. Two of them were rowing, and the boat sped swiftly on its way down the stream. Phillis longed to be with them on the river.

When they were gone there was silence for a space, and then the night became suddenly musical.

"Jug, jug, jug!" It was the nightingale; but Phillis's brain was excited, and to her it was a song with words. "Come, come, come!" sang the bird. "Stay with us here and rest—and rest. This is better than the town. Here are sweetness and peace; this is the home of love and gentleness; here you shall find the Coping-stone."

XV

"But if ye saw that which no eyes can see,
The inward beauty of her lively spright
Garnished with heavenly gifts of high degree,
Much more, then, would you wonder at the sight."

I like her, my dear Lawrence," Agatha wrote, a fortnight after Phillis's arrival. "I like her not only a great deal better than I expected, but more than any girl I have ever learned to know. She is innocent, but then innocence is very easily lost; she is fresh, but freshness is very often a kind of electro-plating, which rubs off and shows the base metal beneath. Still Phillis's nature is pure gold; of that I am quite certain; and with sincere people one always feels at ease.

"We were a little awkward at first, though perhaps the awkwardness was chiefly mine, because I hardly knew what to talk about. It seemed as if, between myself and a girl who cannot read or write, there must be such a great gulf that there would be nothing in common. How conceited we are over our education! Lawrence, she is quite the best-informed girl that I know; she has a perfectly wonderful memory; repeats pages of verse which her guardian taught her by reading it to her; talks French very well, because she has always had a French maid; plays and sings by ear; and draws like a Royal Academician. The curious thing, however, is the effect which her knowledge has had upon her mind. She knows what she has been told, and nothing more. Consequently her mind is all light and shade, like a moonlight landscape. She wants *atmosphere*; there is no haze about her. I did not at all understand, until I knew Phillis, what a very important part haze plays in our everyday life. I thought we were all governed by clear and definite views of duty, religion, and politics. My poor Lawrence, we are all in a fog. It is only Phillis who lives in the cloudless realms of pure conviction. In politics she is a Tory, with distinct ideas on the necessity of hanging all Radicals. As for her religion— But that does not concern you, my cousin. Or, perhaps, like most of your class, you never think about religion at all, in which case you would not be interested in Phillis's doctrines.

"I took her to church on Sunday. Before the service I read her the hymns which we were to sing, and after she had criticised the words in a manner peculiarly her own, I read them again, and she knew those

WALTER BESANT AND JAMES RICE

hymns. I also told her to do exactly as I did in the matter of uprising and downsitting.

"One or two things I forgot, and in other one or two she made little mistakes. It is usual, Lawrence, as you may remember, for worshippers to pray in silence before sitting down. Phillis was looking about the church, and therefore did not notice my performance of this duty. Also I had forgotten to tell her that loud speech is forbidden by custom within the walls of a church. Therefore it came upon me with a shock when Phillis, after looking round in her quick eager way, turned to me and said quite aloud, 'This is a curious place! Some of it is pretty, but some is hideous.'

"It was very true, because the church has a half-a-dozen styles, but the speech caused a little consternation in the place. I think the beadle would have turned us out had he recovered his presence of mind in time. This he did not, fortunately, and the service began.

"No one could have behaved better during prayers than Phillis. She knelt, listening to every word. I could have wished that her intensity of attitude had not betrayed a perfect absence of familiarity with church customs. During the psalms she began by listening with a little pleasure in her face. Then she looked a little bored; and presently she whispered to me, 'Dear Agatha, I really must go out if this tune is not changed.' Fortunately the psalms were not long.

"She liked the hymns, and made no remark upon them, except that one of the choir-boys was singing false, and that she should like to take him out of the choir herself, there and then. It was quite true, and I really feared that her sense of duty might actually impel her to take the child by the ear and lead him solemnly out of the church.

"During the sermon, I regret to say that she burst out laughing. You know Phillis's laugh—a pretty rippling laugh, without any malice in it. Oh, how rare a sweet laugh is! The curate, who was in the pulpit—a very nice young man, and a gentleman, but not, I must own, intellectual; and I hear he was plucked repeatedly for his degree—stopped, puzzled and indignant, and then went on with his discourse. I looked, I suppose, so horrified that Phillis saw she had done wrong, and blushed. There were no more *contretemps* in the church.

"'My dear Agatha,' she explained, when we came out, 'I suppose I ought not to have laughed. But I really could not help it. Did you notice the young gentleman in the box? He was trying to act, but he spoke the words so badly, just as if he did not understand them. And I laughed without thinking. I am afraid it was very rude of me.'

"I tried to explain things to her, but it is difficult, because sometimes you do not quite know her point of view.

"Next day the curate called. To my vexation Phillis apologised. Without any blushes she went straight to the point.

"'Forgive me,' she said. 'I laughed at you yesterday in church; I am very sorry for it.'

"He was covered with confusion, and stammered something about the sacred building.

"'But I never was in a church before,' she went on.

"'That is very dreadful!' he replied. 'Mrs. L'Estrange, do you not think it is a very dreadful state for a young lady?'

"Then she laughed again, but without apologising.

"'Mr. Dyson used to say,' she explained to me, 'that everybody's church is in his own heart. He never went to church, and he did not consider himself in a dreadful state at all, poor dear old man.'

"If she can fall back on an axiom of Mr. Abraham Dyson's, there is no further argument possible.

"The curate went away. He has been here several times since, and I am sure that I am not the attraction. We have had one or two little afternoons on the lawn, and it is pretty to see Phillis trying to take an interest in this young man. She listens to his remarks, but they fail to strike her; she answers his questions, but they seem to bore her. In fact, he is much too feeble for her; she has no respect for the cloth at all; and I very much fear that what is sport to her is going to be death to him. Of course, Lawrence, you may quite sure that I shall not allow Phillis to be compromised by the attentions of any young man—yet. Later on we shall ask your views.

"Her guardian must have been a man of great culture. He has taught her very well, and everything. She astonished the curate yesterday by giving him a little historical essay on his favourite Laud. He understood very little of it, but he went away sorrowful. I could read in his face a determination to get up the whole subject, come back, and have it out with Phillis. But she shall not be dragged into an argument, if I can prevent it, with any young man. Nothing more easily leads to entanglements, and we must be ambitious for our Phillis.

"'It is a beautiful thing!' she said the other day, after I had been talking about the theory of public worship—'a beautiful thing for the people to come together every week and pray. And the hymns are sweet, though I cannot understand why they keep on singing the same tune, and that such a simple thing of a few notes.'

"The next Sunday I had a headache, and Phillis refused to go to church without me. She spent the day drawing on the bank of the river.

"Mrs. Cassilis has been to call upon us. Victoria was never a great friend of mine when she was young, and I really like her less now. She was kind to Phillis, and proposed all sorts of hospitalities, which we escaped for the present. I quite think that Phillis should be kept out of the social whirl for a few months longer.

"Victoria looked pale and anxious. She asked after you in her iciest manner; wished to know where you were; said that you were once one of her friends; and hoped to see you before long. She is cold by nature, but her coldness was assumed here, because she suddenly lost it. I am quite sure, Lawrence, that Victoria Pengelley was once touched, and by you. There must have been something in the rumours about you two, four years ago. Lazy Lawrence! It is a good thing for you that there was nothing more than rumour.

"We were talking of other things—important things, such as Phillis's wardrobe, which wants a great many additions—when Victoria *a propos* of nothing, asked me if you were changed at all. I said no, except that you were more confirmed in laziness. Then Phillis opened her portfolio, where she keeps her diary after her own fashion, and showed the pencil sketch she has made of your countenance. It is a good deal better than any photograph, because it has caught your disgraceful indolence, and you stand confessed for what you are. How the girl contrives to put the *real* person into her portraits, I cannot tell. Victoria took it, and her face suddenly softened. I have seen the look on many a woman's face. I look for it when I suspect that one of my young friends has dropped head over ears in love; it comes into her eyes when young Orlando enters the room, and then I know and act accordingly. Poor Victoria! I ought not to have told you, Lawrence, but you will forget what I said. She glanced at the portrait and changed colour. Then she asked Phillis to give it to her. 'You can easily make another,' she said, 'and I will keep this, as a specimen of your skill and a likeness of an old friend.'

"She kept it, and carried it away with her.

"I have heard all about the Coping-stone. What a curious story it is! Phillis talks quite gravely of the irreparable injury to the science of Female Education involved in the loss of that precious chapter. Mr. Jagenal is of opinion that without it the Will cannot be carried out, in which case Mr. Cassilis will get the money. I sincerely hope he will. I am one of those who dislike, above all things, notoriety for women, and

I should not like our Phillis's education and its results made the subject of lawyers' wit and rhetoric in the Court of Chancery. Do you know Mr. Gabriel Cassilis? He is said to be the cleverest man in London, and has made an immense fortune. I hope Victoria is happy with him. She has a child, but does not talk much about it.

"I have been trying to teach Phillis to read. It is a slow process, but the poor girl is very patient. How we ever managed to 'worry through,' as the Americans say, with such a troublesome acquirement, I cannot understand. We spend two hours a day over the task, and are still in words of one syllable. Needless to tell you that the lesson-book—'First Steps in Reading'—is regarded with the most profound contempt, and is already covered with innumerable drawings in pencil.

"Notes in music are easier. Phillis can already read a little, but the difficulty here is, that if she learns the air from the notes, she knows it once for all, and further reading is superfluous. Now, little girls have as much difficulty in playing notes as in spelling them out, so that they have to be perpetually practising the art of reading. I now understand why people who teach are so immeasurably conceited. I am already so proud of my superiority to Phillis in being able to read, that I feel my moral nature deteriorating. At least, I can sympathise with all school-masters, from the young man who holds his certificated nose high in the air, to Dr. Butler of Harrow, who sews up the pockets of his young gentlemen's trousers.

"Are you tired of my long letter? Only a few words more.

"I have got a music and a singing master for Phillis. They are both delighted with her taste and musical powers. Her voice is very sweet, though not strong. She will never be tempted to rival professional people, and will always be sure to please when she sings.

"I have also got an artist to give her a few lessons in the management of her colours. He is an elderly artist, with a wife and bairns of his own, not one of the young gentlemen who wear velvet coats and want to smoke all day.

"You must yourself get a horse for her, and then you can come over and ride with her. At present she is happy in the contemplation of the river, which exercises an extraordinary power over her imagination. She is now, while I write, sitting in the shade, singing to herself in solitude. Beside her is the sketch-book, but she is full of thought and happy to be alone. Lawrence, she is a great responsibility, and it is sad to think that the Lesson she most requires to learn is the Lesson of distrust. She trusts everybody, and when anything is done or said which would arouse distrust in ourselves, she only gets puzzled and thinks of her own ignorance. Why cannot we leave her in the Paradise of the Innocent, and never let her learn that every stranger is a possible villain? Alas, that I must teach her this lesson; and yet one would not leave her to find it out by painful experience! My dear Lawrence, I once read that it was the custom in savage times to salute the stranger with clubs and stones, because he was sure to be an enemy. How far have we advanced in all these years? You sent Phillis to me for teaching, but it is I who learned from her. I am a worldly woman, cousin Lawrence, and my life is full of hollow shams. Sometimes I think that the world would be more tolerable were all the women as illiterate as dear Phillis.

"Do not come to see her for a few days yet, and you will find her changed in those few things which wanted change."

SITTING IN SOLITUDE? GAZING ON the river? Singing to herself? Phillis was quite otherwise occupied, and much more pleasantly.

She had been doing all these things, with much contentment of soul, while Agatha was writing her letters. She sat under the trees upon the grass, a little straw hat upon her head, letting the beauty of the season fill her soul with happiness. The sunlit river rippled at her feet; on its broad surface the white swans lazily floated! the soft air of early summer fanned her cheek: the birds darted across the water as if in ecstasy of joy at the return of the sun—as a matter of fact they had their mouths wide open and were catching flies; a lark was singing in the sky; there were a blackbird and a thrush somewhere in the wood across the river: away up the stream there was a fat old gentleman sitting in a punt; he held an umbrella over his head, because the sun was hot, and he supported a fishing-rod in his other hand. Presently he had a nibble, and in his anxiety he stood up the better to manoeuvre his float; it was only a nibble, and he sat down again. Unfortunately he miscalculated the position of the chair, and sat upon space, so that he fell backwards all along the punt. Phillis heard the bump against the bottom of the boat, and saw a pair of fat little legs sticking up in the most comical manner; she laughed, and resolved upon drawing the fat old gentleman's accident as soon as she could find time.

The afternoon was very still; the blackbird carolled in the trees, and the "wise thrush" repeated his cheerful philosophy; the river ran with soft whispers along the bank; and Phillis began to look before her with eyes that saw not, and from eyelids that, in a little, would close in sleep.

Then something else happened.

A boat came suddenly up the river, close to her own bank. She saw the bows first, naturally; and then she saw the back of the man in it. Then the boat revealed itself in full, and Phillis saw that the crew consisted of Jack Dunquerque. Her heart gave a great leap, and she started from the Sleepy Hollow of her thoughts into life.

Jack Dunquerque was not an ideal oar, such as one dreams of and reads about. He did not "grasp his sculls with the precision of a machine, and row with a grand long sweep which made the boat spring under his arms like a thing of life"—I quote from an author whose name I have forgotten. Quite the contrary; Jack was rather unskilful than otherwise; the ship in which he was embarked was one of those crank craft consisting of a cedar lath with crossbars of iron; it was a boat without outriggers, and he had hired it at Richmond. He was not so straight in the back as an Oxford stroke! and he bucketed about a good deal, but he got along.

Just as he was nearing Phillis he fell into difficulties, in consequence of one oar catching tight in the weeds. The effect of this was, as may be imagined, to bring her bows on straight into the bank. In fact, Jack ran the ship ashore, and sat with the bows high on the grass just a few inches off Phillis's feet. Then he drew himself upright, tried to disentangle the oar, and began to think what he should do next.

"I wish I hadn't come," he said aloud.

Phillis laughed silently.

Then she noticed the painter in the bows though she did not know it by that name. Painters in London boats are sometimes longish ropes, for convenience of mooring. Phillis noiselessly lifted the cord and tied it fast round the trunk of a small elder-tree beside her. Then she sat down again and waited. This was much better fun than watching an elderly gentleman tumbling backwards in a punt.

Jack, having extricated the scull and rested a little, looked at his palms, which were blistering under the rough exercise of rowing, and muttered something inaudible. Then he seized the oars again and began to back out vigorously.

The boat's bows descended a few inches, and then, the painter being taut, moved no more.

Phillis leaned forward, watching Jack with a look of rapturous delight.

"Damn the ship!" said Jack softly, after three or four minutes' strenuous backing.

"Don't swear at the boat, Jack," Phillis broke in, with her low laugh and musical voice.

Jack looked round. There was his goddess standing on the bank, clapping her hands with delight. He gave a vigorous pull, which drove the boat half-way up to shore and sprang out.

"Jack, you must not use words that sound bad. Oh, how glad I am to see you! I think you look best in flannels, Jack."

"You here, Phil? I thought it was a mile higher up."

"Did you know where I was gone to?"

"Yes, I found out. I asked Colquhoun, and he told me. But he did not offer to introduce me to Mrs. L'Estrange; and so I thought I would—I thought that perhaps if I rowed up the river, you know, I might perhaps see you."

"O Jack," she replied, touched by this act of friendship, "did you really row up in the hope of seeing me? I am so glad. Will you come in and be introduced to Agatha,—that is, Mrs. L'Estrange? I have not yet told her about you, because we had so many things to say."

"Let us sit down and talk a little first. Phil, you look even better than when you were at Carnarvon Square. Tell me what you are doing."

"I am learning to read for one thing; and, Jack, a much more important thing, I am taking lessons in water-colour drawing. I have learned a great deal already, quite enough to show me how ignorant I have been. But, Jack, Mr. Stencil cannot draw so well as I can, and I am glad to think so."

"When shall we be able to go out again for another visit somewhere, Phil?"

"Ah, I do not know. We shall stay here all the summer, I am sure; and Agatha talks of going to the seaside in the autumn. I do not think I shall like the sea so much as I like the river, but I want to see it. Jack, how is Mr. Gilead Beck? have you seen him lately?"

"Yes, I very often see him. We are great friends. But never mind him, Phil; go on telling me about yourself. It is a whole fortnight since I saw you."

"Is it really? O Jack! and we two promised to be friends. There is pretty friendship for you! I am very happy, Jack. Agatha L'Estrange is so kind that I cannot tell you how I love her. Lawrence Colquhoun is her first cousin. I like my guardian, too, very much; but I have not yet found out how to talk to him. I am to have a horse as soon as he can find me one; and then we shall be able to ride together, Jack, if it is not too far for you to come out here."

"Too far, Phil?"

"Agatha is writing letters. Certainly it must be pleasant to talk to your friends when they are away from you. I shall learn to write as fast as I can, and then we will send letters to each other. I wonder if she would mind being disturbed. Perhaps I had better not take you in just yet."

"Will you come for a row with me, Phil?"

"In the boat, Jack? on the river? Oh, if you will only take me!"

Jack untied the painter, pulled the ship's head round, and laid her alongside the bank.

"You will promise to sit perfectly still, and not move?"

"Yes, I will not move. Are you afraid for me Jack?"

"A little, Phil. You see, if we were to upset, perhaps you would not trust yourself entirely to me."

"Yes, I would, Jack. I am sure you would bring me safe to the bank."

"But we must not upset. Now, Phil."

He rowed her upstream. She sat in the stern, and enjoyed the situation. As in every fresh experience, she was silent, drinking in the details. She watched the transparent water beneath her, and saw the yellow-green weeds sloping gently downwards with the current; she noticed the swans, which looked so tranquil from the bank, and which now followed the boat, gobbling angrily. They passed the old gentleman in the punt. He had recovered his chair by this time, and was sitting in it, still fishing. But Phillis could not see that he had caught many fish. He looked from under his umbrella and saw them. "Youth and beauty!" he sighed.

"I like to *feel* the river," said Phillis, softly. "It is pleasant on the bank, but it is so much sweeter here. Can there be anything in the world," she murmured half to herself, "more pleasant than to be rowed along the river on such a day as this?"

There was no one on the river except themselves and the old angler. Jack rowed up stream for half a mile or so, and then turned her head and let her drift gently down with the current, occasionally dipping the oars to keep way on. But he left the girl to her own thoughts.

"It is all like a dream to me, this river," said Phillis, in a low voice. "It comes from some unknown place, and goes to some unknown place."

"It is like life, Phil."

"Yes; we come like the river, trailing long glories behind us—you know what Wordsworth says—but we do not go to be swallowed up in the ocean, and we are not alone. We have those that love us to be with us, and prevent us from getting sad with thought. I have you, Jack."

"Yes, Phil." He could not meet her face, which was so full of unselfish and passionless affection, because his own eyes were brimming over with passion.

"Take me in, Jack," she said, when they reached Agatha's lawn. "It is enough for one day."

She led him to the morning-room, cool and sheltered, where Agatha was writing the letter we have already read. And she introduced him as Jack Dunquerque, her friend.

Jack explained that he was rowing up the river, that he saw Miss Fleming by accident, that he had taken her for a row up the stream, and so on—all in due form.

"Jack and I are old friends," said Phillis.

Agatha did not ask how old, which was fortunate. But she put aside her letters and sent for tea into the garden. Jack became more amiable and more sympathetic than any young man Mrs. L'Estrange had ever known. So much did he win upon her that, having ascertained that he was a friend of Lawrence Colquhoun, she asked him to dinner.

Jack's voyage homeward was a joyful one. Many is the journey begun in joy that ends in sorrow; few are those which begin, as Jack's bucketing up the river, in uncertainty, and end in unexpected happiness.

XVI

"Souvent femme varie,
Bien foi qui s'y fie."

Lawrence Colquhoun was not, in point of fact, devoting much time to his ward at this time. She was pretty; she was fresh; she was unconventional; but then he was forty. For twenty years he had been moving through a panorama of pretty girls. It was hardly to be expected that a girl whom he had seen but once or twice should move a tough old heart of forty. Phillis pleased him, but lazy Lawrence wanted girls, if that could be managed, to come to him, and she necessarily stayed at Twickenham. Anyhow, she was in good and safe hands. It was enough to know that Agatha had her in safe charge and custody, and when he could find time he would go down and see her again. As he had been thirteen years trying to find time to visit Phillis at Highgate, it was possible that he might be in the same way prevented by adverse circumstances from going to Twickenham.

He was troubled also by other and graver matters.

Victoria Cassilis asked him in the Park to call upon her—for auld lang syne. What he replied is not on record, because, if anybody heard, it could only have been the lady. But he did not call upon her. After a day or two there came a letter from her. Of this he took no notice. It is not usual for a man to ignore the receipt from a lady, but Lawrence Colquhoun did do so. Then there came another. This also he tore in small pieces. And then another. "Hang the woman," said Lawrence; "I believe she wants to have a row. I begin to be sorry I came home at all."

His chambers were on the second floor in the Albany, and anyone who knows Lawrence Colquhoun will understand that they were furnished in considerable comfort, and even luxury. He did not pretend to a knowledge of Art, but his pictures were good; nor was he a dilettante about furniture, but his was in good style. China he abhorred, like many other persons of sound and healthy taste. Let us leave a loophole of escape; there may be some occult reason, unknown to the uninitiated, for finding beauty, loveliness, and desirability in hideous china monsters and porcelain. After all we are but a flock, and follow the leader. Why should we not go mad for china? It is as sensible as going mad over rinking. Why should we not buy water-colours at fabulous prices? At least these can be sold again for something, whereas books—an extinct form of madness—cannot; and besides, present their backs in a mute appeal to be read.

The rooms of a man with whom comfort is the first thing aimed at. The chairs are low, deep, and comfortable; there are brackets, tiny tables, and all sorts of appliances for saving trouble and exertion; the curtains are of the right shade for softening the light; the pictures are of subjects which soothe the mind; the books, if you look at them, are books of travel and novels. The place is exactly such a home as lazy Lawrence would choose.

And yet when we saw his laziness in the Prologue, he was living alone in a deserted city, among the bare wooden walls of a half-ruined hotel. But Lawrence was not then at home. He took what comfort he could get, even there; and while he indulged his whim for solitude, impressed into his own service for his own comfort the two Chinamen who constituted with him the population of Empire City.

But at Empire City he was all day shooting. That makes a difference to the laziest of men. And he would not have stayed there so long had he not been too lazy to go away. If a man does not mind lonely evenings, the air on the lower slope of the Sierra Nevada is pleasant and the game is abundant. Now, however, he was back in London, where the laziest men live beside the busiest. The sun streamed in at his windows, which were bright with flowers; and he sat in the shade doing nothing. Restless men take cigars; men who find their own thoughts insufficient for the passing hour take books; men who cannot sit still walk about, Lawrence Colquhoun simply lay back in an easy-chair, watching the sunlight upon the flowers with lazy eyes. He had the gift of passive and happy idleness.

To him there came a visitor—a woman whom he did not know.

She was a woman about thirty years of age, a hard-featured, sallow-faced woman. She looked in Lawrence's face with a grim curiosity as she walked across the room and handed him a letter.

"From Mrs. Cassilis, sir."

"Oh!" said Lawrence. "And you are—"

"I am her maid, sir."

"Where is Janet, then?"

"Janet is dead. She died three years ago, before Mrs. Cassilis married."

"Oh, Janet is dead, is she? Ah, that accounts—I mean, where did Janet die?"

"In lodgings at Ventnor, sir. Mrs. Cassilis—Miss Pengelley she was then, as you know, sir,"—Lawrence looked up sharply, but there was no change in the woman's impassive face as she spoke,—"Miss Pengelley sent me with her, and Janet died in my arms, sir, of consumption."

"Ah, I am sorry! And so Mrs. Cassilis has sent you to me with this letter, has she?" He did not open it. "Will you tell Mrs. Cassilis that I will send an answer by post, if there is any answer required?"

"I beg your pardon, sir; but Mrs. Cassilis told me expressly that if you were in town I was to wait for an answer, if I had to wait all day."

"In that case I suppose I had better read the letter."

He opened it, and it seemed as if the contents were not pleasant, because he rose from his chair and began to walk about. The sallow-faced woman watched him all the time, as one who has fired a shot, and wishes to know whether it has struck, and where.

He held the letter in his left hand, and with his right moved and altered the position of things on the mantel-shelf, a sign of mental agitation. Then he turned round brusquely and said:

"Tell your mistress that I will call upon her in the afternoon."

"Will you write that, sir?"

"No, I will not," he replied fiercely. "Take your answer and begone."

She went without a word.

"There will be trouble," she said to herself. "Janet said it would all come up again some day. He's a handsome chap, and missus is a fool. She's worse than a fool; she's a hard-hearted creature, with no more blood than a stone statue. If there's to be trouble, it won't fall on *his* head, but on hern. And if I was him, I'd go away again quiet, and then maybe no one wouldn't find it out. As for her, she'll blow on it herself."

Lawrence's thoughts assumed a form something like the following:

"Three notes from her in rapid succession, each one more vehement than the first. She must see me; she insists on my calling on her; she will see me; she has something important to tell me. It's a marvellous thing, and great proof of the absence of the inventive faculty in all of them, that when they want to see you they invariably pretend that they have something important to tell you. From the duchess to the nursemaid, by Jove, they are all alike! And now she is coming here unless I call upon her today.

"It won't do to let her come here. I might go down to the seaside, go into the country, go anywhere, back to America; but what would be the good of that? Besides, I have not done anything to be afraid of or ashamed of, unless a knowledge of a thing is guilt. I have nothing to fear for myself. Remains the question, Ought I not to screen her?

"But screen her from whom? No one knows except Janet, and Janet is dead. Perhaps that woman with a face like a horse knows; that would be awkward for Victoria if she were to offend her, for a more damned unforgiving countenance I never set eyes upon. But Janet was faithful; I am sure Janet would not split even when she was dying. And then there was very little to split about when she died. Victoria hadn't married Mr. Cassilis.

"What the deuce does she want to rake up old things for? Why can't she let things be? It's the way of women. They can't forget; and hang me if I don't think she can't forgive me because she has done me a wrong! Why did I come back from Empire City! There, at all events, one could be safe from annoyance.

"On a day like this, too, the first really fine day of the season, and it's spoiled. I might have dined with cousin Agatha and talked to Phillis—the pretty little Phillis! I might have mooned away the afternoon in the Park and dined at the Club. I might have gone to half-a-dozen places in the evening. I might have gone to Greenwich and renewed my youth at the Ship. I might have gone to Richmond with old Evergreen and his party. But Phillis for choice. But now I must have it out with Victoria Cassilis. There's a fate in it: We can't be allowed to rest and be happy. Like the schoolboy's scrag-end of the rolly-polly pudding, it is helped, and must be eaten."

Philosophy brings resignation, but it does not bring ease of mind. Those unfortunate gentlemen who used to be laid upon the wheel and have their limbs broken might have contemplated the approach of inevitable suffering with resignation, but never with happiness. In Colquhoun's mind, Victoria Cassilis was associated with a disagreeable and painful chapter in his life. He saw her marriage in the fragment of Ladds's paper, and thought the chapter closed. He came home and found her waiting for him ready to open it again.

"I *did* think," he said, turning over her letter in his fingers, "that for her own sake, she would have let things be forgotten. It's ruin for her if the truth comes out, and not pleasant for me, A pretty fool I should look explaining matters in a witness-box. But I must see her, if only to bring her to reason. Reason? When was a woman reasonable?"

"I am here," he said, standing before Mrs. Cassilis at her own house a few hours later. "I am here."

Athos, Parthos, Arimis, and D'Artagnan would have said exactly the same thing.

"*Me voici!*"

And they would have folded their arms and thrown back their heads with a preliminary tap at the sword-hilt, to make sure that the trusty blade was loose in the scabbard and easy to draw, in case M. le Mari—whom the old French allegorists called *Danger*—should suddenly appear.

But Lawrence Colquhoun said it quite meekly, to a woman who neither held out her hand nor rose to meet him, nor looked him in the face, but sat in her chair with bowed head and weeping eyes.

A woman of steel? There are no women of steel.

It was in Mrs. Cassilis's morning-room, an apartment sacred to herself; she used it for letter-writing, for interviews with dressmakers, for tea with ladies, for all sorts of things. And now she received her old friend in it. But why was she crying, and why did she not look up?

"I *did* want to see you, Lawrence," she murmured. "Can you not understand why?"

"My name is Colquhoun, Mrs. Cassilis. And I cannot understand why—"

"My name, Lawrence, is Victoria. Have you forgotten that?"

"I have forgotten everything, Mrs. Cassilis. It is best to forget everything."

"But if you cannot! O Lawrence!" she looked up in his face—"O Lawrence, if you cannot!"

Her weeping eyes, her tear-clouded face, her piteous gesture, moved the man not one whit. The power which she might once have had over him was gone.

"This is mere foolishness, Mrs. Cassilis. As a stranger, a perfect stranger, may I ask why you call me by my Christian name, and why these tears?"

"Strangers! it is ridiculous!" she cried, starting up and standing before him. "It is ridiculous, when all the world knows that we were once friends, and half the world thought that we were going to be something—nearer."

"Nearer—and dearer, Mrs. Cassilis? What a foolish world it was! Suppose we had become nearer, and therefore very much less dear."

"Be kind to me, Lawrence."

"I will be whatever you like, Mrs. Cassilis—except what I was—provided you do not call me Lawrence anymore. Come, let us be reasonable. The past is gone; in deference to your wishes I removed myself from the scene; I went abroad; I transported myself for four years; then I saw the announcement of your marriage in the paper by accident. And I came home again, because of your own free will and accord you had given me my release. Is this true?"

"Yes," she replied.

"Then, in the name of Heaven, why seek to revive the past? Believe me, I have forgotten the few days of madness and repentance. They are gone. Some ghosts of the past come to me, but they do not take the shape of Victoria Pengelley."

"Suppose we cannot forget?"

"Then we *must* forget. Victoria—Mrs. Cassilis, rouse yourself. Think of what you are—what you have made yourself."

"I do think. I think everyday."

"You have a husband and a child; you have your position in the world. Mrs. Cassilis, you have your honour."

"My honour!" she echoed. "What honour? And if all were known! Lawrence, don't you even pity me?"

"What is the good of pity?" he asked rudely. "Pity cannot alter things. Pity cannot make things which are as if they are not. You seem to me to have done what you have done knowing well what you were doing, and knowing what you were going to get by it. You have got one of the very best houses in London; you have got a rich husband; you have got an excellent position; and you have got—Mrs. Cassilis, you have got a child, whose future happiness depends upon your reticence."

"I will tell you what I have besides," she burst in, with passion. "I have the most intolerable husband, the most maddening and exasperating man in all the world!"

"Is he cruel to you?"

"No; he is kind to me. If he were cruel I should know how to treat him. But he is kind."

"Heroics, Mrs. Cassilis. Most women could very well endure a kind husband. Are you not overdoing it? You almost make me remember a scene—call it a dream—which took place in a certain Glasgow hotel about four years and a half ago."

"In the City he is the greatest financier living, I am told. In the house he is the King of Littleness."

"I think there was—or is—a bishop," said Lawrence meditatively, "who gave his gigantic intellect to a Treatise on the Sinfulness of Little

Sins. Perhaps you had better buy that work and study it. Or present it to your husband."

"Very well, Lawrence. I suppose you think you have a right to laugh at me?"

"Right! Good God, Mrs. Cassilis," he cried, in the greatest alarm, "do you think I claim any right—the smallest—over you? If I ever had a right it is gone now—gone, by your own act, and my silence."

"Yes, Lawrence," she repeated, with a hard smile on her lips, "your silence."

He understood what she meant. He turned from her and leaned against the window, looking into the shrubs and laurels. She had dealt him a blow which took effect.

"My silence!" he murmured; "my silence! What have I to do with your life since that day—that day which even you would find it difficult to forget? Do what you like, marry if you like, be as happy as you like, or as miserable—what does it matter to me? My silence! Am I, then, going to proclaim to the world my folly and your shame?"

"Let us not quarrel," she went on, pleased with the effect of her words. There are women who would rather stab a man in the heart, and so make some impression on him, than to see him cold and callous to what they say or think. "It is foolish to quarrel after four years and more of absence."

"Absence makes the heart grow fonder," said Lawrence. "Yes, Mrs. Cassilis, it is foolish to quarrel. Still I suppose it is old habit. And besides—"

"When a man has nothing else to say, he sneers."

"When a woman has nothing else to say, she makes a general statement."

"At all events, Lawrence, you are unchanged since I left you at that hotel to which you refer so often. Are its memories pleasing to you?"

"No; they are not. Are they to you? Come, Mrs. Cassilis, this is foolish. You told me you had something to say to me. What is it?"

"I wanted to say this. When we parted—"

"Oh, hang it!" cried the man, "why go back to that?"

"When we two parted"—she set her thin lips together as if she was determined to let him off no single word—"you used bitter words. You told me that I was heartless, cold, and bad-tempered. Those were the words you used."

"By Gad, I believe they were!" said Lawrence. "We had a blazing row; and Janet stood by with her calm Scotch face, and, 'Eh, sir! Eh, madam!' I remember."

"I might retaliate on you."

"You did then, Mrs. Cassilis. You let me have it in a very superior style. No need to retaliate anymore."

"I might tell you now that you are heartless and cold. I might tell you—"

"It seems that you are telling me all this without any use of the potential mood."

"That if you have any lingering kindness for me, even if you have any resentment for my conduct, you would pity the lonely and companionless life I lead."

"Your son is nearly a year old, I believe?"

"What is a baby?"

Lawrence thought the remark wanting in maternal feeling; but he said nothing.

"Come, Mrs. Cassilis, it is all no use. I cannot help you. I would not if I could. Hang it! it would be too ridiculous for me to interfere. Think of the situation. Here we are, we three; I first, you in the middle, and Mr. Cassilis third. You and I know, and he does not suspect. On the stage, the man who does not suspect always looks a fool. No French novel comes anywhere near this position of things. Make yourself miserable if you like, and make me uncomfortable; but for Heaven's sake, don't make us all ridiculous! As things are, so you made them. Tell me—what did you do it for?"

"Speak to me kindly, Lawrence, and I will tell you all. After that dreadful day I went back to the old life. Janet and I made up something—never mind what. Janet was as secret as the grave. The old life—Oh, how stupid and dull it was! Two years passed away. You were gone, never to return, as you said. Janet died. And Mr. Cassilis came."

"Well?"

"Well, I was poor. With my little income I had to live with friends, and be polite to people I detested. I saw a chance for freedom; Mr. Cassilis offered me that, at least. And I accepted him. Say you forgive me, Lawrence."

"Forgive! What a thing to ask or to say!"

"It was a grievous mistake. I wanted a man who could feel with me and appreciate me."

"Yes," he said. "I know. Appreciation—appreciation. Perhaps you got it, and at a truer estimate than you thought. I have sometimes found, Mrs. Cassilis, in the course of my travels, people who make themselves miserable because others do not understand their own ideals. If these people could only label themselves with a few simple descriptive sentences,—such as 'I am good; I am great; I am full of lofty thoughts; I am noble; I am wise; I am too holy for this world;' and so on,—a good deal of unhappiness might be saved. Perhaps you might even now try on this method with Mr. Cassilis."

"Cold and sneering," she said to herself, folding her hands, and laying her arms straight out before her in her lap. If you think of it, this is a most effective attitude, provided that the head be held well back and a little to the side.

"What astonishes me," he said, taking no notice of her remark, "is that you do not at all seem to realise the Thing you have done. Do you?"

"It is no use realising what cannot be found out. Janet is in her grave. Lawrence Colquhoun, the most selfish and heartless of men, is quite certain to hold his tongue."

He laughed good-naturedly.

"Very well, Mrs. Cassilis, very well. If you are satisfied, of course no one has the right to say a word. After all, no one has any cause to fear except yourself. For me, I certainly hold my tongue. It would be all so beautifully explained by Serjeant Smoothtongue: 'Six years ago, gentlemen of the jury, a man no longer in the bloom of early youth was angled for and hooked by a lady who employed a kind of tackle comparatively rare in English society. She was a *femme incomprise*. She despised the little ways of women; she was full of infinite possibilities; she was going to lead the world if only she could get the chance. And then, gentlemen of the jury'—"

Here the door opened, and Mr. Gabriel Cassilis appeared. His wife was sitting in the window, cold, calm, and impassive. Some four or five feet from her stood Lawrence Colquhoun; he was performing his imaginary speech with great rhetorical power, but stopped short at sight of M. le Mari, whom he knew instinctively. This would have been a little awkward, had not Mrs. Cassilis proved herself equal to the occasion.

"My dear!" She rose and greeted her husband with the tips of her fingers. "You are early today. Let me introduce Mr. Colquhoun, a very old friend of mine."

"I am very glad, Mr. Colquhoun, to know you. I have heard of you."

"Pray sit down, Mr. Colquhoun, unless you will go on with your description. Mr. Colquhoun, who has just arrived from America, my dear, was giving me a vivid account of some American trial-scene which he witnessed."

Her manner was perfectly cold, clear, and calm. She was an admirable actress, and there was not a trace left of the weeping, shamefaced woman who received Lawrence Colquhoun.

Gabriel Cassilis looked at his visitor with a little pang of jealousy. This, then, was the man with whom his wife's name had been coupled. To be sure, it was a censorious world; but then he was a handsome fellow, and a quarter of a century younger than himself. However, he put away the thought, and tapped his knuckles with his double glasses while he talked.

Today, whether from fatigue or from care, he was not quite himself; not the self-possessed man of clear business mind that he wished to appear. Perhaps something had gone wrong.

Lawrence and Mrs. Cassilis, or rather the latter, began talking about days of very long ago, so that her husband found himself out of the conversation. This made him uneasy, and less useful when the talk came within his reach. But his wife was considerate—made allowances, so to speak, for age and fatigue; and Lawrence noted that he was fond and proud of her.

He came away in a melancholy mood.

"I can't help it," he said. "I wish I couldn't feel anything about it, one way or the other. Victoria has gone off, and I wonder how in the world—And now she has made a fool of herself. It is not my fault. Some day it will all come out. And I am an accessory after the fact. If it were not for that Phillis girl—I must see after her—and she is pretty enough to keep any man in town—I would go back to America again, if it were to Empire City."

XVII

"Now you set your foot on shore
In Novo Orbe; here's the rich Peru;
And there, within, sir, are the golden mines,
Great Solomon's Ophir."

Unlimited credit! Wealth without bound! Power to gratify any desire—all desires! That was the luck of the Golden Butterfly. No wish within the reach of man that Gilead Beck could not gratify. No project or plan within limits far, far beyond what are generally supposed reasonable, that he could not carry out. Take your own case, brother of mine, struggling to realise the modest ambitions common to cultured humanity, and to force them within the bounds of a slender income. Think of the thousand and one things you want; think of the conditions of your life you would wished changed; think of the generous aspirations you would gratify: think of the revenges, malices, envies, hatreds, which you would be able to satiate—*had you the wealth which gives the power*. Then suppose yourself suddenly possessed of that wealth, and think what you would do with it.

Your brain is feeble; it falters at a few thousands; a hundred thousand a year is too much for it—it was as much, if I remember rightly, as even the imagination of the elder Dumas attained to. Beyond a paltry twenty thousand or so, one feels oppressed in imagination with a weight of income. Let us suppose you stick at twenty thousand. What would you do with it? What could you not do with it? Your ideal Society—the one thing wanting, only rich men cannot be brought to see it, to regenerate the world—that could instantly be put on a sound footing. Your works— those works which you keep locked up in a desk at home—you could publish, and at once step into your right position as a leader of thought, an ἄναξ ἀνδρῶν. Your projects, educational, moral, theatrical, literary, musical, could all together, for they are modest, be launched upon the ocean of public opinion. You could gratify your taste for travel. Like Charles Kingsley, you could stand in the shadow of a tropical forest (it would not be one quarter so beautiful as a hundred glades ten miles from Southampton) and exclaim, "At last!" You are an archæologist, and have as yet seen little. You could make that long-desired trip to Naples and see Pompeii; you could visit the cities of the Midi, and explore the

WALTER BESANT AND JAMES RICE

Roman remains you have as yet only read of; you could take that journey to Asia Minor, your dream of twenty years, and sketch the temples still standing, roofed and perfect, unvisited since the last stragglers of the last crusading army died of famine on the steps, scoffing with their latest breath at the desecrated altar. Their bones lay mouldering in front of the marble columns—silent monuments of a wasted enthusiasm—while the fleshless fingers pointed as if in scorn in the direction of Jerusalem. They have been dust this many a year. Dust blown about the fields; manure for the crops which the peasant raises in luxuriance by scratching the soil. But the temples stand still, sacred yet to the memory of Mother Earth, the many-breasted goddess of the Ephesians. Why, if you had that £20,000 a year, you would go there, sketch, photograph, and dig.

What could not one do if one had money? And then one takes to thinking what is done by those who actually have it. Well, they subscribe—they give to hospitals and institutions—and they save the rest. Happy for this country that Honduras, Turkey, and a few other places exist to plunder the British capitalists, or we should indeed perish of wealth-plethora. Thousands of things all round us wait to be done; things which must be done by rich men, and cannot be done by trading men, because they would not pay.

Exempli gratia; here are a few out of the many.

1. They are always talking of endowment of research; all the men who think they ought to be endowed are clamouring for it. But think of the luxury of giving a man a thousand a year, and telling him to work for the rest of his days with no necessity for doing pot-boilers. Yet no rich man does it. There was a man in Scotland, the other day, gave half a million to the Kirk. For all the luxury to be got out of that impersonal gift, one might just as well drop a threepenny-bit into the crimson bag.

2. This is a country in which the dramatic instinct is so strong as to be second only to that of France. We want a National Theatre, where such a thing as a 300 nights' run would be possible, and which should be a school for dramatists as well as actors. A paltry £10,000 a year would pay the annual deficit in such a theatre. Perhaps, taking year with year, less than half that sum would do. No rich man has yet proposed to found, endow, or subsidise such a theatre.

3. In this City of London thousands of boys run about the streets ragged and hungry. Presently they become habitual criminals. Then they cost the country huge sums in goals, policemen, and the like. Philanthropic people catch a few of these boys and send them to places

where they are made excellent sailors. Yet the number does not diminish. A small £15 a year pays for a single boy. A rich man might support a thousand of them. Yet no rich man does.

4. In this country millions of women have to work for their living. Everybody who employs those women under-pays them and cheats them. Women cannot form trade-unions—they are without the organ of government; therefore they are downtrodden in the race. They do men's work at a quarter of men's wages. No trade so flourishing as that which is worked by women—witness the prosperity of dress-making masters. The workwomen have longer hours, as well as lower pay, than the men. At the best, they get enough to keep body and soul together; not enough for self-respect; not enough, if they are young and good-looking, to keep them out of mischief. To give them a central office and a central protecting power might cost a thousand pounds a year No rich man, so far as I know, has yet come forward with any such scheme for the improvement of women's labour.

5. This is a country where people read a great deal. More books are printed in England than in any other country in the world. Reading forms the amusement of half our hours, the delight of our leisure time. For the whole of its reading Society agrees to pay Mundie & Smith from three to ten guineas a house. Here is a sum in arithmetic: house-bills, £1,500 a year; wine-bill, £300; horses, £500; rent, £400; travelling, £400; dress—Lord knows what; reading—say £5; also, spent at Smith's stalls in two-shilling novels, say thirty shillings. That is the patronage of Literature. Successful authors make a few hundreds a year—successful grocers make a few thousands—and people say, "How well is Literature rewarded!"

Mr. Gilead Beck once told me of a party gathered together in Virginia City to mourn the decease of a dear friend cut off prematurely. The gentleman intrusted with the conduct of the evening's entertainment had one-and-forty dollars put into his hands to be laid out to the best advantage. He expended it as follows:—

Whisky	Forty dollars,	(40$)
Bread	One dollar,	(1$)
Total	Forty-one dollars.	(41$)

"What, in thunder," asked the chairman, "made you waste all that money in bread?"

Note.—He had never read *Henry IV*.

The modern patronage of Literature is exactly like the proportion of bread observed by the gentleman of Virginia City.

Five pounds a year for the mental food of all the household.

Enough; social reform is a troublesome and an expensive thing. Let it be done by the societies; there are plenty of people anxious to be seen on platforms, and plenty of men who are rejoiced to take the salary of secretary.

Think again of Mr. Gilead Beck's Luck and what it meant. The wildest flights of your fancy never reach to a fourth part of his income. The yearly revenues of a Grosvenor fall far short of this amazing good fortune, Out of the bowels of the earth was flowing for him a continuous stream of wealth that seemed inexhaustible. Not one well, but fifty, were his, and all yielding. When he told Jack Dunquerque that his income was a thousand pounds a day, he was far within the limit. In these weeks he was clearing fifteen hundred pounds in every twenty-four hours. That makes forty-five thousand pounds a month; five hundred and forty thousand pounds a year. Can a Grosvenor or a Dudley reach to that?

The first well was still the best, and it showed no signs of giving out; and as Mr. Beck attributed its finding to the direct personal instigation of the Golden Butterfly, he firmly believed that it never would give out. Other shafts had been sunk round it, but with varying success; the ground covered with derricks and machinery erected for boring fresh wells and working the old, an army of men were engaged in these operations; a new town had sprung up in the place of Limerick City; and Gilead P. Beck, its King, was in London, trying to learn how his money might best be spent.

It weighed heavily upon his mind; the fact that he was by no effort of his own, through no merit of his own, earning a small fortune every week made him thoughtful. In his rough way he took the wealth as so much trust-money. He was entitled, he thought, to live upon it according to his inclination; he was to have what his soul craved for he was to use it first for his own purposes; but he was to devote what he could not spend—that is, the great bulk of it—somehow to the general good. Such was the will of the Golden Butterfly.

I do not know how the idea came into Gilead Beck's head that he was to regard himself a trustee. The man's antecedents would seem against such a conception of Fortune and her responsibilities. Born in a New

England village, educated till the age of twelve in a village school, he had been turned upon the world to make his livelihood in it as best he could. He was everything by turns; there was hardly a trade that he did not attempt, not a calling which he did not for a while follow. Ill luck attended him for thirty years; yet his courage did not flag. Every fresh attempt to escape from poverty only seemed to throw him back deeper in the slough. Yet he never despaired. His time would surely come. He preserved his independence of soul, and he preserved his hope.

But all the time he longed for wealth. The desire for riches is an instinct with the Englishman, a despairing dream with the German, a stimulus for hoarding with the Frenchman, but it is a consuming fire with the American. Gilead P. Beck breathed an atmosphere charged with the contagion of restless ambition. How many great men—presidents, vice-presidents, judges, orators, merchants—have sprung from the obscure villages of the older States? Gilead Beck started on his career with a vague idea that he was going to be something great. As the years went on he retained the belief, but it ceased to take a concrete form. He did not see himself in the chair of Ulysses Grant; he did not dream of becoming a statesman or an orator But he was going to be a man of mark. Somehow he was bound to be great.

And then came the Golden Butterfly.

See Mr. Beck now. It is ten in the morning. He has left the pile of letters, most of them begging letters, unopened opened at his elbow. He has got the case of glass and gold containing the Butterfly on the table. The sunlight pouring in at the opened window strikes upon the yellow metal, and lights up the delicately chased wings of this freak of Nature. Poised on the wire, the Golden Butterfly seems to hover of its own accord upon the petals of the rose. It is alive. As its owner sits before it, the creature seems endowed with life and motion. This is nonsense, but Mr. Beck thinks so at the moment.

On the table is a map of his Canadian oil-fields.

He sits like this nearly every morning, the gilded box before him. It is his way of consulting the oracle. After his interview with the Butterfly he rises refreshed and clear of vision. This morning, if his thoughts could be written down, they might take this form:

"I am rich beyond the dreams of avarice. I have more than I can spend upon the indulgence of every whim that ever entered the head of sane man. When I have bought all the luxuries that the world has to sell, there still remains to be saved more than any other living man has to spend.

"What am I to do with it?

"Shall I lay it up in the Bank? The Bank might break. That is possible. Or the well might stop. No; that is impossible. Other wells have stopped, but no well has run like mine, or will again; for I have struck through the crust of the earth into the almighty reservoir.

"How to work out this trust? Who will help me to spend the money aright? How is such a mighty pile to be spent?

"Even if the Butterfly were to fall and break, who can deprive me of my wealth?"

His servant threw open the door: "Mr. Cassilis, sir."

XVIII

"Doubtfully it stood,
As two spent swimmers that do cling together
And choke their art."

One of Gilead Beck's difficulties—perhaps his greatest—was his want of an adviser. People in England who have large incomes pay private secretaries to advise them. The post is onerous, but carries with it considerable influence. To be a Great Man's whisperer is a position coveted by many. At present the only confidential adviser of the American Croesus was Jack Dunquerque, and he was unsalaried and therefore careless. Ladds and Colquhoun were less ready to listen, and Gabriel Cassilis showed a want of sympathy with Mr. Beck's Trusteeship which was disheartening. As for Jack, he treated the sacred Voice, which was to Gilead Beck what his demon was to Socrates, with profound contempt. But he enjoyed the prospect of boundless spending in which he was likely to have a disinterested share. Next to unlimited "chucking" of his own money, the youthful Englishman would like—what he never gets—the unlimited chucking of other people's. So Jack brought ideas, and communicated them as they occurred.

"Here is one," he said. "It will get rid of thousands; it will be a Blessing and a Boon for you; it will make a real hole in the Pile; and it's Philanthropy itself. Start a new daily."

Mr. Beck was looking straight before him with his hands in his pockets. His face was clouded with the anxiety of his wealth. Who would wish to be a rich man?

"I have been already thinking of it, Mr. Dunquerque," he said. "Let us talk it over."

He sat down in his largest easy-chair, and chewed the end of an unlighted cigar.

"I have thought of it," he went on. "I want a paper that shall have no advertisements and no leading articles. If a man can't say what he wants to say in half a column, that man may go to someother paper. I shall get only live men to write for me. I will have no long reports of speeches, and the bunkum of life shall be cut out of the paper."

"Then it will be a very little paper."

WALTER BESANT AND JAMES RICE

"No, sir. There is a great deal to say, once you get the right man to say it. I've been an editor myself, and I know."

"You will not expect the paper to pay you?"

"No, sir; I shall pay for that paper. And there shall be no cutting up of bad books to show smart writing. I shall teach some of your reviews good manners."

"But we pride ourselves on the tone of our reviews."

"Perhaps you do, sir. I have remarked, that Englishmen pride themselves on a good many things. I will back a first-class British subject for bubbling around against all humanity. See, Mr. Dunquerque, last week I read one of your high-toned reviews. There was an article in it on a novel. The novel was a young lady's novel. When I was editing the *Clearville Roarer* I couldn't have laid it on in finer style for the rough back of a Ward Politician. And a young lady!"

"People like it, I suppose," said Jack.

"I dare say they do, sir. They used to like to see a woman flogged at the cart-tail. I am not much of a company man, Mr. Dunquerque, but I believe that when a young lady sings out of tune it is not considered good manners to get up and say so. And it isn't thought polite to snigger and grin. And in my country, if a man was to invite the company to make game of that young lady he would perhaps be requested to take a header through the window. Let things alone, and presently that young lady discovers that she is not likely to get cracked up as a vocaller. I shall conduct my paper on the same polite principles. If a man thinks he can sing and can't sing, let him be for a bit. Perhaps he will find out his mistake. If he doesn't, tell him gently. And if that won't do, get your liveliest writer to lay it on once for all. But to go sneakin' and pryin' around, pickin' out the poor trash, and cutting it up to make the people grin—it's mean, Mr. Dunquerque, it's mean. The cart-tail and the cat-o'-nine was no worse than this exhibition. I'm told it's done regularly, and paid for handsomely."

"Shall you be your own editor?"

"I don't know, sir. Perhaps if I stay long enough in this city to get to the core of things, I shall scatter my own observations around. But that's uncertain."

He rose slowly—it took him a long time to rise—and extended his long arms, bringing them together in a comprehensive way, as if he was embracing the universe.

"I shall have central offices in New York and London. But I shall drive the English team first. I shall have correspondents all over the world, and I shall have information of every dodge goin,' from an emperor's ambition to a tin-pot company bubble."

He brought his fingers together with a clasp. Jack noticed how strong and bony those fingers were, with hands whose muscles seemed of steel.

The countenance of the man was earnest and solemn. Suddenly it changed expression, and that curious smile of his, unlike the smile of any other man, crossed his face.

"Did I ever tell you my press experiences?" he asked. "Let us have some champagne, and you shall hear them."

The champagne having been brought he told his story, walking slowly up and down with his hands in his pockets, and jerking out the sentences as if he was feeling for the most telling way of putting them.

Mr. Gilead Beck had two distinct styles of conversation. Generally, but for his American tone, the length of his sentences, and a certain florid wealth of illustration, you might take him for an Englishman of eccentric habits of thought. When he went back to his old experiences he employed the vernacular—rich, metaphoric, and full—which belongs to the Western States in the rougher period of their development. And this he used now.

"I was in Chicago. Fifteen years ago. I wanted employment. Nobody wanted me. I spent most of the dollars, and thought I had better dig out for a new location, when I met one day an old schoolfellow named Rayner. He told me he was part proprietor of a morning paper. I asked him to take me on. He said he was only publisher, but he would take me to see the Editor, Mr. John B. Van Cott, and perhaps he would set me grinding at the locals. We found the Editor. He was a short active man of fifty, and he looked as cute as he was. Because, you see, Mr. Dunquerque, unless you are pretty sharp on a Western paper, you won't earn your mush. He was keeled back, I remember, in a strong chair, with his feet on the front of the table, and a clip full of paper on his knee. And in this position he used to write his leading articles. Squelchers, some of them; made gentlemen of opposite politics cry, and drove rival editors to polishing shooting-irons. The floor was covered with exchanges. And there was nothing else in the place but a cracked stove, half a dozen chairs standing around loose, and a spittoon.

"I mention these facts, Mr. Dunquerque, to show that there was good standing-room for a free fight of not more than two.

"Mr. Van Cott shook hands, and passed me the tobacco pouch, while Rayner chanted my praises. When he wound up and went away, the Editor began.

"'Wal, sir,' he said, 'you look as if you knew enough to go indoors when it rains, and Rayner seems powerful anxious to get you on the paper. A good fellow is Rayner; as white a man as I ever knew; and he has as many old friends as would make a good-sized city. He brings them all here, Mr. Beck, and wants to put everyone on the paper. To hear him hold forth would make a camp-meeting exhorter feel small. But he's disinterested, is Rayner. It's all pure goodness.'

"I tried to feel as if I wasn't down-hearted. But I was.

"'Anyway,' I said, 'if I can't get on here, I must dig out for a place nearer sundown. Once let me get a fair chance on a paper, and I can keep my end of the stick.'

"The Editor went on to tell me what I knew already, that they wanted live men on the paper, fellows that would do a murder right up to the handle. Then he came to business; offered me a triple execution just to show my style; and got up to introduce me to the other boys.

"Just then there was a knock at the door.

"'That's Poulter, our local Editor,' he said. 'Come in, Poulter. He will take you down for me.'

"The door opened, but it wasn't Poulter. I knew that by instinct. It was a rough-looking customer, with a black-dyed moustache, a diamond pin in his shirt front, and a great gold chain across his vest; and he carried a heavy stick in his hand.

"'Which is the one of you two that runs this machine?' he asked, looking from one to the other.

"'I am the Editor,' said Mr. Van Cott, 'if you mean that.'

"'Then you air the Rooster I'm after,' he went on. 'I am John Halkett of Tenth Ward. I want to know what in thunder you mean by printing infernal lies about me and my party in your miserable one-hoss paper.'

"He drew a copy of the paper from his pocket, and held it before the Editor's eyes.

"'You know your remedy, sir,' said Mr. Van Cott, quietly edging in the direction of the table, where there was a drawer.

"'That's what I do know. That's what I'm here for. There's two remedies. One is that you retract all the lies you have printed, the other'—

"'You need not tell me what the other is, Mr. Halkett.' As he spoke he drew open the drawer; but he hadn't time to take the pistol from it when the ward politician sprang upon him, and in a flash of lightning they were rolling over each other among the exchanges on the floor.

"If they had been evenly matched, I should have stood around to see fair. But it wasn't equal. Van Cott, you could see at first snap, was grit all through, and as full of fight as a game-rooster. But it was bulldog and terrier. So I hitched on to the stranger, and pulled him off by main force.

"'You will allow me, Mr. Van Cott,' I said, 'to take this contract off your hands. Choose a back seat sir, and see fair.'

"'Sail in,' cried Mr. Halkett, as cheerful as a coot, 'and send for the coroner, because he'll be wanted. I don't care which it is.'

"That was the toughest job I ever had. The strength of ward politicians' opinions lies in their powers of bruising, and John Halkett, as I learned afterwards, could light his weight in wild cats. Fortunately I was no slouch in those days.

"He met my advances halfway. In ten minutes you couldn't tell Halkett from me, nor me from Halkett. The furniture moved around cheerfully, and there was a lovely racket. The sub-editors, printers, and reporters came running in. It was a new scene for them, poor fellows, and they enjoyed it accordingly. The Editor they had often watched in a fight before, but here were two strangers worrying each other on the floor, with Mr. Van Cott out of it himself, dodging around cheering us on. That gave novelty.

"The sharpest of the reporters had his flimsy up in a minute, and took notes of the proceedings.

"We fought that worry through. It lasted fifteen minutes. We fought out of the office; we fought down the stairs; and we fought on the pavement.

"When it was over, I found myself arrayed in the tattered remnants of my grey coat, and nothing else. John Halkett hadn't so much as that. He was bruised and bleeding, and he was deeply moved. Tears stood in his eyes as he grasped me by the hand.

"'Stranger,' he said, 'will you tell me where you hail from?'

"'Air you satisfied, Mr. Halkett,' I replied, 'with the editorial management of this newspaper?'

"'I am,' he answered. 'You bet. This is the very best edited paper that ever ran. Good morning, sir. You have took the starch out of John Halkett in a way that no starch ever was took out of that man before. And if ever you get into a tight place, you come to me.'

"They put him in a cab, and sent him home for repairs. I went back to the Editor's room. He was going on again with his usual occupation of manufacturing squelchers. The fragments of the chairs lay around him, but he wrote on unmoved.

"'Consider yourself permanently engaged,' he said. 'The firm will pay for a new suit of clothes. Why couldn't you say at once that you were fond of fighting? I never saw a visitor tackled in a more lovable style. Why, you must have been brought up to it. And just to think that one might never have discovered your points if it hadn't been for the fortunate accident of John Halkett's call!'

"I said I was too modest to mention my tastes.

"'Most fortunate it is. Blevins, who used to do our fighting—a whole team he was at it—was killed three months ago on this very floor; there's the mark of his fluid still on the wall. We gave Blevins a first-class funeral, and ordered a two-hundred-dollar monument to commemorate his virtues. We were not ungrateful to Blevins.

"'Birkett came next,' he went on, making corrections with a pencil stump. 'But he was licked like a cur three times in a fortnight. People used to step in on purpose to wallop Birkett, it was such an easy amusement. The paper was falling into disgrace, so we shunted him. He drives a cab now, which suits him better, because he was always gentlemanly in his ways.

"'Carter, who followed, was very good in some respects, but he wanted judgment. He's in hospital with a bullet in the shoulder, which comes of his own carelessness. We can't take him on again anymore, even if he was our style, which he never was.'

"'And who does the work now?' I ventured to ask.

"'We have had no regular man since Carter was carried off on a shutter. Each one does a little, just as it happens to turn up. But I don't like the irregular system. It's quite unprofessional.'

"I asked if there was much of that sort of thing.

"'Depends on the time of year. It is the dull season just now, but we are lively enough when the fall elections come on. We sometimes have a couple a day then. You won't find yourself rusting. And if you want work, we can stir up a few editors by judicious writing. I'm powerful glad we made your acquaintance, Mr. Beck.'

"That, Mr. Dunquerque, is how I became connected with the press."

"And did you like the position?"

"It had its good points. It was a situation of great responsibility. People were continually turning up who disliked our method of depicting character, and so the credit of the paper mainly rested on my shoulders. No, sir; I got to like it, except when I had to go into hospital for repairs. And even that had its charms, for I went there so often that it became a sort of home, and the surgeons and nurses were like brothers and sisters."

"But you gave up the post?" said Jack.

"Well, sir, I did. The occupation, after all, wasn't healthy, and was a little too lively. The staff took a pride in me too, and delighted to promote freedom of discussion. If things grew dull for a week or two, they would scarify some ward ruffian just to bring on a fight. They would hang around there to see that ward ruffian approach the office, and they would struggle who should be the man to point me out as the gentleman he wished to interview. They were fond of me to such an extent that they could not bear to see a week pass without a fight. And I will say this of them, that they were as level a lot of boys as ever destroyed a man's character.

"Most of the business was easy. They came to see Mr. Van Cott, and they were shown up to me. What there is of me, takes up a good deal of the room. And when they'd put their case I used to open the door and point. 'Git,' I would say. 'You bet,' was the general reply; and they would go away quite satisfied with the Editorial reception. But one a week or so there would be a put-up thing, and I knew by the look of my men which would take their persuasion fighting.

"It gradually became clear to me that if I remained much longer there would be a first class funeral, with me taking a prominent part in the procesh; and I began to think of digging out while I still had my hair on.

"One morning I read an advertisement of a paper to be sold. It was in the city of Clearville, Illinois, and it seemed to suit. I resolved to go and look at it, and apprised Mr. Van Cott of my intention.

"'I'm powerful sorry,' he said; 'but of course we can't keep you if you will go. You've hoed your row like a square man ever since you came, and I had hoped to have your valuable services till the end.'

"I attempted to thank him, but he held up his hand, and went on thoughtfully.

"'There's room in our plat at Rose Hill Cemetery for one or two more; and I had made up my mind to let you have one side of the monument all to yourself. The sunny side, too—quite the nicest nest in the plat. And we'd have given you eight lines of poetry—Blevins only got four, and none of the other fellows any. I assure you, Beck, though you may not think it, I have often turned this over in my mind when you have been in hospital, and I got to look on it as a settled thing. And now this is how it ends. Life is made up of disappointments.'

"I said it was very good of him to take such an interest in my funeral, but that I had no yearning at present for Rose Hill Cemetery, and I thought it would be a pity to disturb Blevins. As I had never known him and the other boys, they mightn't be pleased if a total stranger were sent to join their little circle.

"Mr. Van Cott was good enough to say that they wouldn't mind it for the sake of the paper: but I had my prejudices, and I resigned.

"I don't know whether you visited Illinois when you were in America, Mr. Dunquerque; but if you did, perhaps you went to Clearville. It is in that part of the State which goes by the name of Egypt, and is so named on account of the benighted condition of the natives. It wasn't a lively place to go to, but still—

"The *Clearville Roarer* was the property of a Mrs. Scrimmager, widow of the lately defunct editor. She was a fresh buxom widow of thirty-five, with a flow of language that would down a town council or a vestry. I inferred from this that the late Mr. Scrimmager was not probably very sorry when the time came for him to pass in his checks.

"She occupied the upper flats of a large square building, in the lower part of which were the offices of the paper. I inspected the premises, and having found that the books and plant were pretty well what the advertisement pretended, I closed the bargain at once, and entered into possession.

"The first evening I took tea with Mrs. Scrimmager.

"'It must be more than a mite lonely for you,' she said, as we sat over her dough-nuts and flipflaps, 'up at the tavern. But you'll soon get to know all the leading people. They're a two-cent lot, the best of them. Scrimmy (we always called him Scrimmy for short) never cottoned to them. He used to say they were too low and common, mean enough to shoot a man without giving him a chance—a thing which Scrimmy, who was honourable from his boots up, would have scorned to do.'

"I asked if it was long since her husband had taken his departure.

"'He started,' she said, 'for kingdom come two months ago, if that's what you mean.'

"'Long ill?'

"'Ill?' she replied, as if surprised at the question. 'Scrimmy never was ill in his life. He was quite the wrong man for that. Scrimmy was killed.'

"'Was he,' I asked. 'Railway accident, I suppose?'

"Mrs. Scrimmager looked at me resentfully, as if she thought I really ought to have known better. Then she curved her upper lip in disdain.

"'Railway accident! Not much. Scrimmy was shot.'

"'Terrible!' I exclaimed, with a nervous sensation, because I guessed what was coming.

"'Well, it was rough on him,' she said. 'Scrimmy and Huggins of the *Scalper*—do you know Huggins? Well, you'll meet him soon enough for your health. They hadn't been friends for a long while, and each man was waiting to draw a bead on the other. How they did go for one another! As an ink-slinger, Huggins wasn't a patch on my husband; but Huggins was a trifle handier with his irons. In fact, Huggins has shot enough men to make a small graveyard of his own; and his special weakness is editors of your paper.'

"I began to think that Clearville was not altogether the place for peace and rest. But it was too late now.

"The lady went on:

"'Finally, Scrimmy wrote something that riled Huggins awful. So he sent him a civil note, saying that he'd bore a hole in him first chance. I've got the note in my desk there. That was gentlemanlike, so far; but he spoiled it all by the mean sneaking way he carried it through. Scrimmy, who was wonderful careless and never would take my advice, was writing in his office when Huggins crept in quiet, and dropped a bullet through his neck before he had time to turn. Scrimmy knew it was all up; but he was game to the last, and finished his article, giving the *Scalper* thunder. When he'd done it he came upstairs and died.'

"'And Mr. Huggins?'

"'They tried him; but, Lord, the jury were all his friends, and they brought it in justifiable homicide. After the funeral Huggins behaved handsome; he put the *Scalper* into deep mourning, and wrote a beautiful send-off notice, saying what a loss the community had suffered in Scrimmy's untimely end. I've got the article in my desk, and I'll show it to you; but somehow I never could bring myself to be friends with Huggins after it.'

"'Mr. Scrimmager was perhaps not the only editor who has fallen a victim in Clearville.'

"'The only one? Not by a long chalk,' she replied. 'The *Roarer* has had six editors in five years; they've all been shot except one, and he died of consumption. His was a very sad case. A deputation of leading citizens called to interview him one evening; he took refuge on the roof of the office, and they kept him there all night in a storm. He died in two months after it. But he was a poor nervous critter, quite unfit for his position.'

"'And this,' I thought, 'this is the place I have chosen for a quiet life.'

"I debated that night with myself whether it would be better to blow the roof off my head at once, instead of waiting for Huggins or someother citizen to do it for me. But I resolved on waiting a little.

"Next day I examined the files of the *Roarer*, and found that it had been edited with great vigor and force; there was gunpowder in every article, fire and brimstone in every paragraph. No wonder, I thought, that the men who wrote those things were chopped up into sausage-meat. I read more, and it seemed as if they might as well have set themselves up as targets at once. I determined on changing the tone of the paper; I would no longer call people midnight assassins and highway robbers, nor would I hint that political opponents were all related to suspended criminals. I would make the *Roarer* something pure, noble, and good; I would take Washington Irving for my model; it should be my mission to elevate the people.

"Wal, sir, I begun. I wrote for my first number articles as elevating as Kentucky whisky. Every sentence was richly turned; every paragraph was as gentle as if from the pen of Goldsmith. There was a mutiny among the compositors; they were unaccustomed to such language, and it made them feel small. One man, after swearing till the atmosphere was blue, laid down his stick in despair and went and got drunk. And the two apprentices fought over the meaning of a sentence in the backyard. One of those boys is now a cripple for life.

"It would have been better for me, a thousand times better, if I had stuck to the old lines of writing. The people were accustomed to that. They looked for it, and they didn't want any elevating. If you think of it, Mr. Dunquerque, people never do. The Clearville roughs liked to be abused, too, because it gave them prominence and importance. But my pure style didn't suit them, and as it turned out, didn't suit me either.

"The City Marshal was the earliest visitor after the issue of my first number. He came to say that, as the chief executive officer of the town, he would not be responsible for the public peace if I persevered in that inflammatory style. I told him I wouldn't change it for him or anybody else. Then he said it would cause a riot, and he washed his hands of it, and he'd done his duty.

"Next came the Mayor with two town-councillors.

"'What in thunder, do you think you mean, young man,' his honour began, pointing to my last editorial, 'by bringing everlasting disgrace on our town with such mush as that?'

"He called it mush.

"I asked him what was wrong in it.

"'Wrong? It is all wrong. Of all the mean and miserable twaddle'—

"He called it miserable twaddle.

"'Hold on, Mr. Mayor,' I said; 'we must discuss this article in a different way. Which member of your august body does the heavy business?'

"'We all take a hand when it's serious,' he replied; 'but in ordinary cases it's generally understood that I do the municipal fighting myself.'

"'We'll consider this an ordinary case, Mr. Mayor,' I said; and I went for that chief magistrate. He presently passed through the window— the fight had no details of interest—and then the town-councillors shook hands with me, congratulated me on my editorial, and walked out quiet through the door.

"Nearly a dozen Egyptians dropped in during the afternoon to remonstrate. I disposed of them in as gentlemanlike a manner as possible. Towards evening I was growing a little tired, and thinking of shutting up for the day, when my foreman, whom the day's proceedings had made young again—such is the effect of joy—informed me that Mr. Huggins of the *Scalper* was coming down the street. A moment later Mr. Huggins entered. He was a medium-sized man, with sharp, piercing eyes and a well-bronzed face, active as a terrier and tough as a hickory knot. I was sitting in the wreck of the office-desk, but I rose as he came in.

"'Don't stir,' he said pleasantly. 'My name is Huggins; but I am not going to kill you today.'

"I said I was much obliged to him.

"'I see you've been receiving visitors,' he went on, looking at the fragments of the chairs. 'Ours, Mr. Beck, is an active and a responsible profession.'

"I said I thought it was.

"'These people have been pressing their arguments home with unseemly haste,' he said. 'It is unkind to treat a stranger thus. Now as for me, I wouldn't draw on you for your first article, not to be made Governor of Illinois. It would be most unprofessional. Give a man a fair show, I say.'

"'Very good, Mr. Huggins.'

"'At the same time, Mr. Beck, I *do* think you've laid yourself open. You are reckless, not to say insulting. Take my case. You never saw me before, and you've had the weakness to speak of me as the gentlemanly editor of the *Scalper*.'

"'I'm sure, Mr. Huggins, if the term is offensive'—

"'Offensive? Of course it is offensive. But as this is our first interview, I must not let my dander rise.'

"'Let it rise by all means, and stay as high as it likes. We may find a way of bringing it down again.'

"'No, no,' he answered, smiling; 'it would be unprofessional. Still, I must say that your sneaking, snivelling city way of speaking will not go down, and I have looked in to tell you that it must not be repeated.'

"'It shall not be repeated, Mr. Huggins. I shall never again make the mistake of calling you a gentleman.'

"He started up like a flash, and moved his hand to his breast-pocket.

"'What do mean by that?'

"I was just in time, as I sprang upon and seized him by both arms before he could draw his pistol.

"'I mean this,' I said; 'you've waked up the wrong passenger this time, Mr. Huggins. You needn't wriggle. I've been chucking people through the window all day, and you shall end the lot. But first I want that shooting-iron; it might go off by accident and hurt someone badly.'

"It was a long and mighty heavy contract, for he was as supple as an eel and as wicked as a cat. But I got the best holt at last, relieved him of his pistol, and tossed him through the window.

"'Jim,' I said to the foreman, as I stretched myself in a corner, panting and bleeding, 'You can shut up. We shan't do anymore business today.'

"I issued two more numbers of the *Roarer* on the same refined and gentlemanly principle, and I fought half the county. But all to no purpose. Neither fighting nor writing could reform those Egyptians.

"Huggins shot me through the arm one evening as I was going home from the office. I shall carry his mark to the grave. Three nights later I was waited on by about thirty leading citizens, headed by the Mayor. They said they thought Clearville wasn't agreeing with me, and they were come to remove me. I was removed on a plank, escorted by a torch-light procesh of the local fire brigade. On the platform of the railway station the Mayor delivered a short address. He said, with tears, that the interests of party were above those of individuals, and that a change of residence was necessary for me. Then he put into my hands a purse of two hundred dollars, and we parted with every expression of mutual esteem.

"That is how I came out of the land of Egypt, Mr. Dunquerque; and that is the whole history of my connection with the press."

XIX

"We do not know
How she may soften at the sight o' the child."

I f life was pleasant at Carnarvon Square, it was far more pleasant by the banks of the river. Phillis expanded like a rose in June under the sweet and gracious influences with which Agatha L'Estrange surrounded her. Her straightforward way of speaking remained—the way that reminded one of a very superior schoolboy who had *not* been made a prig at Rugby—but it was rounded off by something more of what we call maidenly reserve. It should not be called reserve at all; it is an atmosphere with which women have learned to surround themselves, so that they show to the outward world like unto the haloed moon. Its presence was manifested in a hundred little ways—she did not answer quite so readily; she did not look into the face of a stranger quite so frankly; she seemed to be putting herself more upon her guard—strange that the chief charm of women should be a relic of barbarous times, when the stronger sex were to be feared for their strength and the way in which they often used it. Only with Jack Dunquerque there was no change. With him she was still the frank, free-hearted girl, the friend who opened all her heart, the maiden who, alone of womankind, knew not the meaning of love.

Phillis was perfectly at home with Agatha L'Estrange. She carolled about the house like a bird; she played and sang at her sweet will; she made sketches by thousands; and she worked hard at the elements of all knowledge. Heavens, by what arid and thirsty slopes do we climb the hills of Learning! Other young ladies had made the house by the river their temporary home, but none so clever, none so bright, none so entirely lovable as this emancipated cloister-child. She was not subdued, as most young women somehow contrive to become; she dared to have an opinion and to assert it; she did not tremble and hesitate about acting before it had been ascertained that action was correct; she had not the least fear of compromising herself; she hardly knew the meaning of proper and improper; and she who had been a close prisoner all her life was suddenly transformed into a girl as free as any of Diana's nymphs. Her freedom was the result of her ignorance; her courage was the result of her special training, which had not taught her the subjection of the sex; her liberty was not license, because she did not, and could not, use it for those purposes which schoolgirls learn in religious boarding-houses. She could walk with a curate, and often did, without flirting with the holy young man; she could make Jack Dunquerque take her for a row upon the river, and think of nothing but the beauty of the scene, her own exceeding pleasure, and the amiable qualities of her companion.

Of course, Agatha's friends called upon her. Among them were several specimens of the British young lady. Phillis watched them with much curiosity, but she could not get on with them. They seemed mostly to be suffering from feeble circulation of the pulse; they spoke as if they enjoyed nothing; those who were very young kindled into enthusiasm in talking over things which Phillis knew nothing about, such as dancing—Phillis was learning to dance, but did not yet comprehend its fiercer joys—and sports in which the other sex took an equal part. Their interest was small in painting; they cared for nothing very strongly; their minds seemed for the most part as languid as their bodies. This life at low ebb seemed to the girl whose blood coursed freely, and tingled in her veins as it ran, a poor thing; and she mentally rejoiced that her own education was not such as theirs. On the other hand, there were points in which these ladies were clearly in advance of herself. Phillis felt the cold ease of their manner; that was beyond her efforts; a formal and mannered calm was all she could assume to veil the intensity of her interest in things and persons.

"But what do they like, Agatha?" she asked one day, after the departure of two young ladies of the highest type.

"Well, dear, I hardly know. I should say that they have no strong likings in any direction. After all, Phillis dear, those who have the fewest desires enjoy the greatest happiness."

"No, Agatha, I cannot think that. Those who want most things can enjoy the most. Oh, that level line! What can shake them off it?"

"They are happier as they are, dear. You have been brought up so differently that you cannot understand. Some day they will marry. Then the equable temperament in which they have been educated will stand them in good stead with their husbands and their sons."

Phillis was silent, but she was not defeated.

Of course the young ladies did not like her at all.

They were unequal to the exertion of talking to a girl who thought differently from all other girls. Phil to them, as to all people who are weak in the imaginative faculty, was *impossible*.

But bit by bit the social education was being filled in, and Phillis was rapidly becoming ready for the *début* to which Agatha looked forward with so much interest and pride.

There remained another kind of education.

Brought up alone, with only her maid of her own age, and only an old man on whom to pour out her wealth of affection, this girl would, but for her generous nature, have grown up cold and unsympathetic. She did not. The first touch of womanly love which met her in her escape from prison was the kiss which Agatha L'Estrange dropped unthinkingly upon her cheek. It was the first of many kisses, not formal and unmeaning, which were interchanged between these two. It is difficult to explain the great and rapid change the simple caresses of another woman worked in Phillis's mind. She became softer, more careful of what she said, more thoughtful of others. She tried harder to understand people; she wanted to be to them all what Agatha L'Estrange was to her.

One day, Agatha, returning from early church, whither Phillis would not accompany her, heard her voice in the kitchen. She was singing and laughing. Agatha opened the door and looked in.

Phillis was standing in the middle of a group. Her eyes were bright with a sort of rapture; her lips were parted; her long hair was tossing behind her; she was singing, talking, and laughing, all in a breath.

In her arms she held the most wonderful thing to a woman which can be seen on this earth.

A BABY.

The child of the butter-woman. The mother stood before Phillis, her pleased red face beaming with an honest pride. Phillis's maid, Antoinette, and Agatha's three servants, surrounded these two, the principal figures. In the corner, grinning, stood the coachman. And the baby crowed and laughed.

"Oh, the pretty thing! Oh, the pretty thing!" cried Phillis, tossing the little one-year-old, who kicked and laughed and pulled at her hair. "Was there ever such a lovely child? Agatha, come and see, come and see! He talks, he laughs, he dances!"

"Ah, madame!" said Antoinette, wiping away a sympathetic tear. "Dire que ma'amsell n'en a jamais vu? Mais non, mais non—pas memes des poupees!"

XX

"Go seek your fortune farther than at home."

Lawrence Colquhoun returned home to find himself famous. Do you remember a certain book of travels written four or five years ago by Lord Milton and Dr. Cheadle, in which frequent mention was made of *un nomme* Harris, an inquiring and doubting Christian, who wore a pair of one-eyed spectacles and carried a volume of Paley? If that Harris, thus made illustrious, had suddenly presented himself in a London drawing-room while the book was enjoying his first run, he would have met with much the same success which awaited Lawrence Colquhoun. Harris let his opportunity go, and never showed up; perhaps he is still wandering in the Rocky Mountains and pondering over Paley. But Colquhoun appeared while the work of the Dragoon and the Younger Son was still in the mouths of men and women. The liveliest thing in that book is the account of Empire City and its Solitary. Everybody whose memory can carry him back to last year's reading will remember so much. And everybody who knew Colquhoun knew also that he was the Solitary.

The Hermit; the man with the Golden Butterfly, now a millionaire; the Golden Butterfly, now in a golden cage—all these actually present, so to speak, in the flesh, and ready to witness if the authors lied. Why, each was an advertisement of the book, and if the two Chinamen had been added, probably people might be reading the work still. But they, poor fellows, were defunct.

It annoyed Lawrence at first to find himself, like Cambuscan, with his tale half told; and it was monotonous to be always asked whether it was really true, and if he was the original Hermit. But everything wears off; people in a week or two began to talk of something else, and when Colquhoun met a man for the first time after his return he would startle and confuse that man by anticipating his question. He knew the outward signs of its approach. He would watch for the smile, the look of curiosity, and the parting of the lips before they framed the usual words:

"By the way, Colquhoun, is it actually true that you are the Hermit in Jack Dunquerque's book?"

And while the questioner was forming the sentence, thinking it a perfectly original one, never asked before, Lawrence would answer it for him.

"It is perfectly true that I was the Hermit. Now talk of something else."

For the rest he dropped into his old place. Time, matrimony, good and evil hap, had made havoc among his set; but there was still some left. Club-men come and club-men go; but the club goes on forever.

Colquhoun had the character of being at once the laziest and the most good-natured of men. A dangerous reputation, because gratitude is a heavy burden to bear. If you do a man a good turn he generally finds it too irksome to be grateful, and so becomes your enemy. But Colquhoun cared little about his reputation.

When he disappeared, his friends for a day or two wondered where he was. Then they ceased to talk of him. Now he was come back they were glad to have him among them again. He was a pleasant addition. He was not altered in the least—his eyes as clear from crows-feet, his beard as silky, and his face as cheerful as ever. Some men's faces have got no sun in them; they only light up with secret joy at a friend's misfortunes; but this is an artificial fire, so to speak; it burns with a baleful and lurid light. There are others whose faces are like the weather in May, being uncertain and generally disagreeable. But Lawrence Colquhoun's face always had a cheerful brightness. It came from an easy temper, a good digestion, a comfortable income, and a kindly heart.

Of course he made haste to find Gilead P. Beck. Jack Dunquerque, who forgot at the time to make any mention of Phillis Fleming, informed him of the Golden Butterfly's wonderful Luck. And they all dined together—the Hermit, the Miner, the Dragoon, and the Younger Son.

They ran the Bear Hunt over again; they talked of Empire City, and speculated on the two Chinamen; had they known the fate of the two, their speculations might have taken a wider range.

"It was rough on me that time," said Gilead. "It had never been so rough before, since I began bumming around."

They waited for more, and presently he began to tell them more. It was the way of the man. He never intruded his personal experiences, being for the most part a humble and even a retiring man; but when he was among men he knew, he delighted in his recollections.

"Thirty-three years ago since I began. Twelve years old; the youngest of the lot. And I wonder where the rest are. Hiram, I know, sat down beside a rattle one morning. He remembered he had an appointment somewhere else, and got up in a hurry. But too late, and his constitution broke up suddenly. But for the rest I never did know what became of them. When I go back with that almighty Pile of mine, they will find me out, I dare say. Then they will bring along all their friends and the rest of the poor relations. The poorer the relations in our country, the more affectionate and self-denying they are."

"What did you do first?" asked Ladds.

"Ran messages; swept out stores; picked up trades; went handy boy to a railway engineer; read what I could and when I could. When I was twenty I kept a village school at a dollar a day. That was in Ohio. I've been many things in my pilgrimage and tried to like them all, but that was most too much for me. Boys *was* gells, Captain Ladds. Boys themselves are bad; but boys and gells mixed, they air—wal, it's a curious and interestin' thing that, ever since that time, when I see the gells snoopin' around with their eyes as soft as velvet, and their sweet cheeks the colour of peach, I say to myself, 'Shoddy. It is shoddy. I've seen you at school, and I know you better than you think.' As the poet says, 'Let gells delight to bark and bite, for 'tis their nature to.' You believe, Mr. Dunquerque, because you are young and inexperienced, that gells air soft. Air they? Soft as the shell of a clam. And tender? Tender as hickory-nut. Air they gentle, unselfish, and yieldin'? As rattlesnakes. The child is mother to the woman, as the poet says; and school-gells grow up mostly into women. They're sweet to look at; but when you've tended school, you feel to know them. And then you don't yearn after them so much.

"There was once a boy I liked. He was eighteen, stood six foot high in his stocking-boots, and his name was Pete Conkling. The lessons that boy taught me were useful in my after life. We began it every morning at five minutes past nine. Any little thing set us off. He might heave a desk, or a row of books, or the slates of the whole class at my head. I might go for him first. It was uncertain how it began, but the fight was bound to be fought. The boys expected it, and it pleased the gells. Sometimes it took me half an hour, and sometimes the whole morning, to wallop that boy. When it was done, Pete would take his place among the little gells, for he never could learn anything, and school would begin. To see him after it was over sitting alongside of little Hepzibah and Keziah, as meek as if he'd never heard of a black eye, and never seen the human fist, was one of my few joys. I was fond of Pete, and he was fond of me. Ways like his, gentlemen, kinder creep round the heart of the lonely teacher. Very fond of him I grew. But I got restless and dug out for another place; it was when I went on the boards and became an actor, I think; and it was close on fifteen years afterwards that I met him. Then he was lying on the slopes of Gettysburg—it was after the last battle—and his eyes were turned up to the sky; one of them, I noticed, was black; so that he had kept up his fighting to the end. For he was stark dead, with a Confed. bullet in his heart. Poor Pete!"

"You fought for the North?" asked one of his audience.

"I *was* a Northerner," he replied simply. How could he help taking his part in maintaining undivided that fair realm of America, which everyone of his countrymen love as Queen Elizabeth's yeoman loved the realm of England? We have no yeomen now, which is perhaps one of the reasons why we could not understand the cause of the North.

"I worried through that war without a scratch. We got wary towards the end, and let the bullets drop into trunks of trees for choice. And when it was over, I was five and-thirty, and had to begin the world again. But I was used to it."

"And you enjoyed a wandering life?"

"Yes, I believe I did enjoy barking up a new tree. There's a breed of Americans who can't keep still. I belong to that breed. We do not like to sit by a river and watch the water flow; we get tired livin' in the village lookin' in each other's faces while the seasons come round like the hands of a clock. There's a mixture among us of Dutch and German and English to sit quiet and till the ground. They get their heels well grounded in the clay, and there they stick."

"Where do you get it from, the wandering blood?" asked Colquhoun.

Gilead P. Beck became solemn.

"There air folk among us," he whispered, "Who hold that we are descended from the Ten Tribes. I don't say those folk are right, but I do say that it sometimes looks powerful like as if they were. Descended from the Ten Tribes, they say, and miraculously kept separate from the English among whom they lived. Lost their own language—which, if it was Hebrew, I take it was rather a good thing to be quit of—and speakin' English, like the rest. What were the tribes? Wanderers, mostly. Father Abraham went drivin' his cows and his camels up and down the country. Isaac went around on the rove, and Jacob couldn't sit still. Very well, then. Didn't their children walk about, tryin' one location after another, for forty years, and always feelin' after a bit as if there must be a softer plank farther on? And when they'd be settled down for a few hundred years, didn't they get up and disappear altogether? Mark you, they *didn't want* to settle. And where are the Ten Tribes now? For they never went back; you may look Palesteen through and through, and nary a tribe."

He looked round asking the question generally, but no one ventured to answer it.

"Our folk, who have mostly gut religion, point to themselves. They say; 'Look at us; we air the real original Wanderers.' Look at us all over the world. What are the hotels full of? Full of Americans. We are everywhere. We eat up the milk and the honey, and we tramp off on ramble again. But there's more points of gen'ral resemblance. We like bounce and bunkum; so did those people down in Syria; we like to pile up the dollars; so did the Jews; they liked to set up their kings and pull them down again; we pursue the same generous and confiding policy with our presidents; and if they were stiff-necked and backsliding, we are as stiff-necked and backsliding as any generation among all the lot."

"A very good case, indeed," said Colquhoun.

"I did not think so, sir, till lately. But it's been borne in upon me with the weight and force that can't be resisted, and I believe it now. The lost Ten Tribes, gentlemen, air now located in the United States. I am certain of it from my own case. Do any of you think—I put it to you seriously—that such an inseck as the Golden Butterfly would have been thrown away upon an outsider? It is likely that such all-fired Luck as mine would have been wasted on a man who didn't belong to the Chosen People? No, sir; I am of the children of Israel; and I freeze to that."

XXI

"Animum pictura pascit inani."

When Panurge was in that dreadful difficulty of his about marrying he took counsel of all his friends. Pantagruel, as we know, advised him alternately for and against, according to the view taken at the moment by his versatile dependent. Gilead Beck was so far in Panurge's position that he asked advice of all his friends. Mr. Cassilis recommended him to wait and look about him; meantime, he took his money for investment; and, as practice makes perfect, and twice or thrice makes a habit, he found now no difficulty in making Mr. Beck give him cheques without asking their amount or their object, while the American Fortunatus easily fell into the habit of signing them without question. He was a Fool? No doubt. The race is a common one; especially common is that kind of Fool which is suspicious from long experience, but which, having found, as he thinks, a fellow-creature worthy of trust, places entire and perfect trust in him, and so, like a ship riding at anchor with a single stout cable, laughs at danger even while the wind is blowing, beam on, to a lee shore. Perfect faith is so beautiful a thing that neither religionists who love to contemplate it, nor sharpers who profit by it, would willingly let it die out.

Lawrence Colquhoun recommended pictures.

"You may as well spend your money on Artists as on any other people. They are on the whole a pampered folk, and get much too well paid. But a good picture is generally a good investment. And then you will become a patron and form a gallery of your own, the Beck collection, to hand down to posterity."

"I can't say, Colonel—not with truth—that I know a good picture from a bad one. I once tried sign painting. But the figures didn't come out right, somehow. Looked easy to do, too. Seems I didn't know about Perspective, and besides, the colours got mixed. Sign-painting is not a walk in life that I should recommend from personal experience."

But the idea took root in his brain.

Jack Dunquerque encouraged it.

"You see, Beck," he said, "you may as well form a gallery of paintings as anything else. Buy modern pictures; don't buy Old Masters, because you will be cheated. The modern pictures will be old in a hundred years, and then your collection will be famous."

"I want to do my work in my own lifetime," said the millionaire. He was a man of many ideas but few convictions, the strongest being that man ought to do what he has to do in his own lifetime, and not to devise and bequeath for posthumous reputation.

"Why, and so you would. You buy the pictures while you are living; when you go off, the pictures remain."

A patron of Art. The very name flattered his vanity, being a thing he had read of, and his imagination leaped up to the possibilities of the thing. Why should he not collect for his own country? He saw himself, like Stewart, returning to New York with a shipload of precious Art treasures bought in London; he saw his agent ransacking the studios and shops of Florence, Naples, Rome, Dresden—wherever painters congregate and pictures are sold; he imagined rich argosies coming to him across the ocean—the American looks across the ocean for the luxuries and graces of life, his wines, his Art, and his literature. Then he saw a great building, grander than the Capitol at Washington, erected by a grateful nation for the reception of the Gilead P. Beck Collection of Ancient and Modern Paintings.

Now one of the earliest callers upon Mr. Beck was a certain picture-dealer named Burls. Mr. Burls and his fraternity regard rich Americans with peculiar favour. It is said to have been Bartholomew Burls who invented especially for American use the now well-known "multiplication" dodge. The method is this. You buy a work by a rising artist, one whose pictures may be at some future time, but are not yet, sufficiently known to make their early wanderings matter of notoriety. One of your young men—he must be a safe hand and a secret—make two, three, or four copies, the number depending on the area, rather than the number, of your *clientele*. You keep the Artist's receipt, a proof of the genuineness of the picture. The copies, name and all, are so well done that even the painter himself would be puzzled to know his own. You then proceed to place your pictures at good distances from each other, representing each as genuine. It is a simple, beautiful, and lucrative method. Not so profitable, perhaps, as cleaning oil-paintings, which takes half an hour apiece and is charged from ten shillings to ten pounds, according to the dealer's belief in your power to pay. Nor is it more profitable than the manufacture of a Correggio or a Cuyp for a guileless cotton manufacturer, and there is certainly a glow of pride to

WALTER BESANT AND JAMES RICE

be obtained by the successful conversion of a new into an old picture by the aid of mastic varnish, mixed with red and yellow lake to tone it down, and the simple shaking of a door-mat over it. But then people have grown wary, and it is difficult to catch a purchaser of a Correggio, for which a large sum has to be asked. The multiplication dodge is the simpler and the safer.

Mr. Beck, as has been already shown, was by no means deficient in a certain kind of culture. He had read such books as fell in his way during his wandering and adventurous life. His reading was thus miscellaneous. He had been for a short time an actor, and thus acquired a little information concerning dramatic literature. He had been on a newspaper, one of the rank and file as well as an editor. He knew a good deal about many things, arts, customs, and trades. But of one thing he was profoundly ignorant, and that was of painting.

He looked at Burls' card, however—"Bartholomew Burls and Co., Church Street, City, Inventors of the only safe and perfect Method of Cleaning Oil Paintings"—and, accompanied by Jack Dunquerque, who knew about as much of pictures as himself, hunted up the shop, and entered it with the meekness of a pigeon about to be plucked.

They stood amid a mass of pictures, the like of which Gilead Beck had never before conceived. They were hanging on the walls; they were piled on the floor; they were stretched across the ceiling; they climbed the stairs; they were hiding away in dark corners; a gaping doorway lit with gas showed a cellar below where they were stacked in hundreds. Pictures of all kinds. The shop was rather dark, though the sun of May was pouring a flood of light even upon the narrow City streets. But you could make out something. There were portraits in hundreds. The effigies of dead men and women stared at you from every second frame. Your ancestor—Mr. Burls was very particular in ascertaining beyond a doubt that it was your own ancestor, and nobody else's—frowned at you in bright steel armour with a Vandyke beard; or he presented a shaven face with full cheeks and a Ramillies wig; or he smirked upon you from a voluminous white scarf and a coat-collar which rose to the top of his head. The ladies of your family—Mr. Burls was very particular, before selling you one, in ascertaining beyond a doubt that she belonged to your own branch of the house, and none other—smiled upon you with half-closed lids, like the consort of Potiphar, the Egyptian, or they frisked as shepherdesses in airy robes, conscious of their charms; or they brandished full-blown petticoats, compared with which crinolines were graceful, or they blushed in robes which fell tightly about the figure, and left the waist beneath the arms. Name any knight, or mayor, or court beauty, or famous toast among your ancestry whose portrait is wanting to your gallery, and Burls, the great genealogical collector, will find you before many weeks that missing link in the family history. Besides the portraits, there were landscapes, nymphs bathing, Venuses asleep, Venuses with a looking-glass, Venuses of all sorts; scenes from *Don Quixote*; Actæons surprising Dianas; battle-pieces, sea-pieces, river-pieces; "bits" of Hampstead Heath, and boats on the Thames.

Mr. Beck looked round him, stroked his chin, and addressed the guardian of this treasure-house:

"I am going to buy pictures," he began comprehensively. "You air the Boss?"

"This gentleman means," Jack explained, "that he wants to look at your pictures with a view to buying some if he approves of them."

The man in the shop was used to people who would buy one picture after a whole mornings haggling, but he was not accustomed to people who wanted to buy pictures generally. He looked astonished, and then, with a circular sweep of his right hand, indicated that here were pictures, and all Mr. Beck had to do was to go in and buy them.

"Look round you, gentlemen," he said; "pray look round you; and the more you buy, the better we shall like it."

Then he became aware that the elder speaker was an American, and he suddenly changed his front.

"Our chicer pictures," he explained, "are up stairs. I should like you to look at them first. Will you step up, gentlemen?"

On the stairs, more pictures. On the landing, more pictures. On the stairs mounting higher, more pictures. But they stopped on the first floor. Mr. Burls and his assistants never invited any visitors to the second and third floors, because these rooms were sacred to the manufacture of old pictures, the multiplication of new, and the sacred processes of cleaning, lining, and restoring. In the first-floor rooms were fewer pictures but more light.

One large composition immediately caught Mr. Beck's eye. A noble picture; a grand picture; a picture whose greatness of conception was equalled by its boldness of treatment. It occupied the whole of one side of the wall, and might have measured twenty feet in length by fourteen in height. The subject was scriptural—the slaying of Sisera by Jael, Heber the Kenite's wife. The defeated general lay stretched on the couch, occupying a good ten feet of the available space. Beside him stood the woman, a majestic figure, with a tent-peg and a mallet, about to commit that famous breach of hospitality. The handle of the mallet was rendered most conscientiously, and had evidently been copied from a model. Through the open hangings of the tent were visible portions of the army chasing the fugitives and lopping off their heads.

"That seems a striking picture," said Mr. Beck. "I take that picture, sir, to represent George Washington after the news of the surrender at Saratoga, or General Jackson after the battle of New Orleans."

"Grant after Gettysburg," suggested Jack.

"No, sir. I was at Gettysburg myself; and the hero asleep on the bed, making every allowance for his fancy dress, which I take to be allegorical, is not at all like General Ulysses Grant, nor is he like General Sherman. The young female, I s'pose, is Liberty, with a hammer in one hand, and a dagger in the other. Too much limb for an American gell, and the flesh is redder than one could wish. But on the hull a striking picture. What may be the value of this composition, mister?"

"I beg your pardon, sir. Not Washington, sir, nor General Jackson, though we can procure you in a very short time fine portraits of both these 'eroes. This, gentlemen, is a biblical subject. Cicero, overtaken, by sleep while in jail, about to be slain by 'Eber the wife of the Kenite. That is 'Eber, with the 'eavy 'ammer in 'er 'and. The Kenite belonged, as I have always understood—for I don't remember the incident myself—to the opposite faction. That splendid masterpiece, gentlemen, has been valued at five 'undred. For a town'all, or for an altar-piece, it would be priceless. To let it go at anything under five 'undred would be a sin and a shame, besides a-throwing away of money. Look at the light and shade. Look at 'Eber's arm and Cicero's leg. That leg alone has been judged by connisseers worth all the money."

Mr. Beck was greatly disappointed in the subject and in the price; even had it been the allegorical picture which he thought, he was not yet sufficiently educated in the prices of pictures to offer five hundred for it; and when Mr. Burls's assistant spoke of pounds, Mr. Beck thought dollars. So he replied:

"Five hundred dollars? I will give you five-and-twenty."

"That," interposed Jack Dunquerque, "is a five-pound note."

"Then, by gad, sir," said the man, with alacrity, "it's yours! It's been hangin' there for ten years, and never an offer yet. It's yours!"

This splendid painting, thus purchased at the rate of rather more than threepence a square foot, was the acquisition made by Mr. Beck towards his great Gallery of Ancient and Modern Masters.

He paid for it on the spot calling Jack to witness the transaction.

"We will send it up to the hotel tomorrow," said the man.

"I shall have it fixed right away along the side of my room," said Mr. Beck. "Should it be framed?"

"I should certainly have it framed," said Jack.

"Yes, sir; we shall be happy to frame it for you."

"I dare say you would," Jack went on. "This is a job for a house-carpenter, Mr. Beck. You will have to build the frame for this gigantic picture. Have it sent over, and consider the frame afterwards."

This course was approved; but, for reasons which will subsequently appear, the picture never was framed.

The dealer proceeded to show other pictures.

"A beautiful Nicolas Pushing—'Nymphs and Satyrs in a Bacchanalian Dance'—a genuine thing."

"I don't think much of that, Mr. Dunquerque; do you? The Nymphs haven't finished dressing; and the gentlemen with the goats' legs may be satires on human nature, but they are not pretty. Let us go on to the next show in the caravan, mister."

"This is Hetty. In the master's best style. 'Graces surprised while Bathing in the River.' Much admired by connisseers."

"No, sir; not at all," said Mr. Beck severely. "*My* gallery is going to elevate the morals of our gells and boys. It's a pretty thing, too, Mr. Dunquerque, and I sometimes think it's a pity morality was ever invented. Now, Boss."

"Quite so, sir. Hetty is, as you say—rayther—What do you think of this, now—a lovely Grooze?"

"Grooze," said Mr. Beck, "is French, I suppose, for gell. Yes, now that's a real pretty picture; I call that a picture you ain't ashamed to admire; there's lips you can kiss; there's a chin you can chuck—"

"How about the morals?" asked Jack.

"Wal, Mr. Dunquerque, we'll buy the picture first, and we'll see how it rhymes with morals afterwards. There's eyes to look into a man's. Anymore heads of pretty Groozes, mister? I'll buy the lot."

"This is a Courage-oh!" the exhibitor went on, after expressing his sorrow that he had no more Groozes, and bringing out a Madonna. "Thought to be genuine by the best judges. History of the picture unknown redooces the value."

"I can't go fooling around with copies in *my* gallery," said Mr. Beck. "I must have genuine pictures, or none."

"Then we will not offer you that Madonna, sir. I think I have something here to suit you. Come this way. A Teniers, gentlemen—a real undoubted gem of Teniers. This is a picture now for any gentleman's collection. It came from the gallery of a nobleman lately deceased, and was bought at the sale by Mr. Burls himself, who knows a picture when he sees one. Mr. Bartholomew Burls, our senior partner, gentlemen. 'The Bagpipe-player.'"

It was an excellent imitation, but of a well-known picture, and it required consummate impudence to pretend that it was original.

"Oh," said Jack, "but I have seen this somewhere else. In the Louvre, I believe."

"Very likely, sir," replied the unabashed vendor. "Teniers painted one hundred pictures. There was a good many 'Bagpipe-players' among them. One is in the Louvre. This is another."

On the advice of Jack Dunquerque Mr. Beck refrained from buying, and contented himself with selecting, with the option of purchase. When they left the shop, some twenty pictures were thus selected.

The seller, who had a small interest or commission on sales, as soon as their steps were fairly out of the shop, executed a short dance indicative of joy. Then he called up the stairs, and a man came slowly down.

A red-nosed bibulous person, by name Critchett. He was manufacturer of old masters in ordinary to Bartholomew Burls and Co.; cleaned and restored pictures when other orders were slack, and was excellent at "multiplication." He had worked for Burls for a quarter of a century, save for a few weeks, when one Frank Melliship, a young gentleman then down on his luck, worked in his stead. A trustworthy and faithful creature, though given to drink; he could lie like an echo; was as incapable of blushing as the rock on which the echo plays; and bore cross-examination like a Claimant.

"Come down, Critchett—come down. We've sold 'Cicero and 'Eber.'"

"'Sisera and Jael.'"

"Well, it don't matter—and I said 'Cicero in Jail.' They've gone for five pounds. The governor he always said I could take whatever was offered, and keep it for myself. Five pounds in my pocket! Your last Teniers—that old bagpipe-party—I tried him, but it was no go. But I've sold the only one left of your Groozes, and you had better make a few more, out of hand. Look here, Critchett: it isn't right to drink in hours, and the guv'nor out and all; but this is an occasion. This ain't a common day, because I've sold the Cicero. I won't ask you to torse, nor yet to pay; but I says, 'Critchett, come across the way, my boy, and put your lips to what you like best.' Lord, Lord! on'y give me an American, and give him to me green! Never mind your hat, Critchett. 'It's limp in the brim and it's gone in the rim,' as the poet says; and you look more respectable without it, Critchett."

"That's a good beginning," Beck observed, after luncheon. They were in Jack Dunquerque's club, in the smoking room. "That's a first-rate beginning. How many pictures go to a gallery?"

"It depends on the size of it. About five hundred for a moderate sized one."

Mr. Beck whistled.

"Never mind. The Ile pays for all. A Patron of Art. Yes, sir, that seems the right end of the stick for a rich man to keep up. But I've been thinking it over. It isn't enough to go to shops and buy pictures. We must go in for sculpting too, and a Patron ought to get hold of a struggling artist, and lend him a helping hand; he should advance unknown talent. That's my idea."

"I think I can help you there," said Jack, his eyes twinkling. "I know just such a man; an artist unknown, without friends, with slender means, of great genius, who has long languished in obscurity."

"Bring him to me, Mr. Dunquerque. Bring that young man to me. Let me be the means of pushing the young gentleman. Holy thunder! What is money if it isn't used. Tell me his name."

"I think I ought to have spoken to him first," said Jack, in some confusion, and a little taken aback by Mr. Beck's determination. "But, however, you can only try. His name is Humphrey Jagenal. I will, if you please, go and see him today. And I will ask him to call upon you tomorrow morning."

"I would rather call upon *him*," said Mr. Beck. "It might look like the pride of patronage asking him to call at the Langham. I don't want him to start with a feeling of shame."

"Not at all; at least, of course, it will be patronage, and I believe he will prefer it. There is no shame in taking a commission to execute a picture."

"Mr. Dunquerque, everyday you confer fresh obligations upon me. And I can do nothing for you—nothing at all."

At this time it was Gilead Beck's worst misfortune that he was not taken seriously by anyone except Gabriel Cassilis, who literally

WALTER BESANT AND JAMES RICE

and liberally interpreted his permission to receive all his money for safe investment. But as for his schemes, vague and shadowy as they were, for using his vast income for some practically philanthropic and benevolent objects, none of his friends sympathised with him, because none of them understood him. Yet the man was deeply in earnest. He meant what he said, and more, when he told Gabriel Cassilis that a voice urged him by day and by night not to save his money, but to use for others what he could not use himself. He had been two months in England on purpose to learn a way, but saw no way yet. And every way seemed barred. He would not give money to societies, because they were societies; he wanted to strike out something new for himself. Nor would he elaborate a scheme to be carried out after his death. Let every man, he repeated everyday, do what he has to do in his lifetime. How was he to spend his great revenues? A Patron of Art? It was the first tangible method that he had struck upon. He would be that to begin with. Art has the great advantage, too, of swallowing up any conceivable quantity of money.

And on the way from the Burls's Depot of Real and Genuine Art, he hit upon the idea of advancing artists as well as Art. He was in thorough earnest when he raised his grave and now solemn eyes to Jack Dunquerque, and thanked him for his kindness. And Jack's conscience smote him.

"I must tell you," Jack explained, "that I have never seen any of Mr. Humphrey Jagenal's pictures. Miss Fleming, the young lady whom you met at Mrs. Cassilis's, told me once that he was a great artist."

"Bring him to me, bring him to me, and we will talk. I hope that I may be able to speak clearly to him without hurting his feelin's. If I brag about my Pile, Mr. Dunquerque, you just whisper 'Shoddy,' and I'll sing small."

"There will be no hurting of feelings. When you come to a question of buying and selling, an artist is about the same as everybody else. Give him a big commission; let him have time to work it out; and send him a cheque in advance. I believe that would be the method employed by patrons whom artists love. At least, I should love such a patron.

"Beck," he went on after a pause: both were seated in the long deep easy-chairs of the club smoking-room, with the chairs pretty close together, so that they could talk in low tones,—"Beck, if you talk about artists, there's Phil—I mean Miss Fleming. By Jove! she only wants a little training to knock the heads off half the R.A.s. Come out with me and call upon her. She will show us her sketches."

"I remember her," said Gilead Beck slowly; "a tall young lady; a lovely Grooze, as the man who grinds that picture-mill would say; she had large brown eyes that looked as if they could be nothing but tender and true, and a rosebud mouth all sweetness and smiles, and lips that trembled when she thought. I remember her—a head like a queen's piled up with her own brown hair and flowers, an' a figure like—like a Mexican half-caste at fourteen."

"You talk of her as if you were in love with her," said Jack jealously.

"No, Mr. Dunquerque; no, sir. That is, I may be. But it won't come between you and her, what I feel. You air a most fortunate man. Go down on your knees when you get home, and say so. For or'nary blessin's you may use the plan of Joshua Mixer, the man who had the biggest claim in Empire City before it busted up. He got his Petitions and his Thanksgivin's printed out neat on a card together, and then he hung that card over his bed. 'My sentiments,' he used to say, jerkin' his thumb to the card when he got in at night. Never omitted his prayers; never forgot that jerk, drunk or sober. Joshua Mixer was the most religious man in all that camp. But for special Providences; for Ile; for a lucky shot; for a sweet, pure, heavenly, gracious creature like Miss Fleming,—I say, go on your knees and own to it, as a man should. Well, Mr. Dunquerque," he continued, "I wish you success; and if there's anything I can do to promote your success, let me know. Now there's another thing. What I want to do is to unlock the door which keeps me from the society of men of genius. I can get into good houses; they all seem open to me because I've got money. London is the most hospitable city in this wide world for those who have the stamps. Republican? Republican ain't the word for it. Do they ask who a man is? Not they. They ask about his dollars, and they welcome him with smiles. It's a beautiful thing to look at, and it makes an Amer'can sigh when he thinks of his own country, where they inquire into a stranger's antecedents. But there's exceptions, and artists and authors I cannot get to. And I want to meet your great men. Not to interview them, sir. Not at all. They may talk a donkey's hind leg off, and I wouldn't send a single line to the New York papers to tell them what was said nor what they wore. But I should like, just for one evening, to meet and talk with the great writers whom we respect across the water."

Again Jack Dunquerque's eyes began to twinkle. He *could* not enter into the earnestness of this man. And an idea occurred to him at which his face lit up with smiles.

"It requires thinking over. Suppose I was to be able to get half-a-dozen or so of our greatest writers, how should we manage to entertain them?"

"I should like, if they would only come—I should like to give them a dinner at the Langham. A square meal; the very best dinner that the hotel can serve. I should like to make them feel like being at the Guildhall."

"I will think about it," said Jack, "and let you know in a day or two what I can do for you."

XXII

"Ambition should be made of sterner stuff."

A patron at last, Cornelius," said Humphrey Jagenal, partly recovering from the shock of Jack Dunquerque's communication. "A Patron. Patronage is, after all, the breath of life in Art. Let others pander to the vitiated public taste and cater for a gaping crowd round the walls of the Royal Academy. I would paint for a Lorenzo only, and so work for the highest interests of Art. We will call, brother, upon this Mr. Beck tomorrow."

"We will!" said Cornelius, with enthusiasm.

It was in the Studio. Both brothers, simultaneously fired with ardour, started to their feet and threw back their heads with a gesture of confidence and determination. The light of high resolve flashed from their eyes, which were exactly alike. The half-opened lips expressed their delight in the contemplation of immortal fame. Their chance had arrived; their youth was come back to them.

True, that Gilead Beck at present only proposed to become a Patron to the Artist; but while it did not enter into Humphrey's head for one moment that he could make that visit unsupported by his brother, so the thought lay in either's brain that a Poet wanted patronage as much as an Artist.

They were both excited. To Humphrey it was clear that the contemplation of his great work, in which he had basked so many years, was to be changed for days of active labour. No longer could he resolve to carry it into execution the "day after tomorrow," as the Arabs say. This was difficult to realise, but as yet the thought was like the first shock of ice-cold water, for it set his veins tingling and braced his nerves. He felt within him once more the strength felt by every young man at first, which is the strength of Michael Angelo. He saw in imagination his great work, the first of many great works, finished, a glorious canvas glowing with the realization of a painter's dream of colour, crowded with graceful figures, warm with the thought of genius, and rich with the fancy of an Artist-scholar—a work for all time. And he gasped. But for his beard he might have been a boy waiting for the morrow, when he should receive the highest prize in the school; or an undergraduate, the favourite of his year, after the examination, looking confidently to the Senior Wranglership.

In the morning they took no walk, but retired silently each to his own room. In the Studio the Artist opened his portfolios, and spread out the drawings made years ago when he was studying in Rome. They were good drawings; there was feeling in every line; but they were copies. There was not one scrap of original work, and his Conscience began to whisper—only he refused at first to listen—that the skill of hand and touch was gone. Then Conscience, which gets angry if disregarded, took to whispering more loudly, and presently he heard. He took crayon and paper, and began, feverishly and in haste, to copy one of his old drawings. He worked for a quarter of an hour, and then, looking at the thing he had once done beside the thing he was then doing, he dashed the pencil from him, and tore up the miserable replica in disgust. His spirit, which had flown so high, sank dull and heavy as lead; he threw himself back in his chair and began to think, gazing hopelessly into space.

It was the opportunity of Conscience, who presently began to sing as loudly as any skylark, but not so cheerfully. "You are fifty," said that voice which seldom lies, "you have wasted the last twenty years of your life; you have become a wind-bag and a shallow humbug; you cannot now paint or draw at all; what little power was in you has departed. Your brother, the Poet, has been steadily working while you have slept"—and it will be perceived that Conscience spoke from imperfect information. "He will produce a great book, and live. You will die. The grave will close over you, and you will be forgotten."

It was a hard saying, and the Artist groaned as he listened to it.

In the workshop, Cornelius also, startled into action, spread out upon the table a bundle of papers which had been lying undisturbed in his desk for a dozen years or more. They were poems he had written in his youth, unpublished verses, thoughts in rhyme such as an imaginative young man easily pours forth, reproducing the fashion of the time and the thoughts of others. He began to read these over again with mingled pleasure and pain. For the thoughts seemed strange to him. He felt that they were good and lofty thoughts, but the conviction forced itself upon him that the brain which had produced them was changed. No more of such good matter was left within it. The lines of thought were changed. The poetic faculty, a delicate plant, which droops unless it is watered and carefully tended, was dead within him.

And the whole of the Epic to be written.

Not a line done, not a single episode on paper, though to Phillis he claimed to have done so much.

He seized a pen, and with trembling fingers and agitated brain forced himself to write.

In half an hour he tore the paper into shreds, and, with a groan, threw down the pen. The result was too feeble.

Then he too began to meditate, like his brother in the Studio. Presently his guardian angel, who very seldom got such a chance, began to admonish him, even as the dean admonishes an erring undergraduate.

"You are fifty," said the invisible Censor. "What have you done with yourself for twenty years and more. Your best thoughts have passed away; the poetical eye is dim; you will write no more. Your brother, the Artist, is busy with pencil and brain. He will produce a great work, and live forever. You will do nothing; you will go down into the pit and be forgotten."

It was too much for the Poet. His lips trembled, his hand shook. He could no more rest in his chair.

He walked backwards and forwards, the voice pursuing him.

"Wasted years; wasted energies; wasted gifts; your chance is gone. You cannot write now."

Poets are more susceptible than artists. That is the reason why Cornelius rushed out of the Workshop to escape this torture and sought his brother Humphrey.

Humphrey started like a guilty person. His face was pale, his eye was restless.

"Cornelius?"

"Do not me disturb you, my dear brother. You are happy; you are at work; your soul is at peace."

"And you, Cornelius?"

"I am not at peace. I am restless this morning. I am nervous and agitated."

"So am I, Cornelius. I cannot work. My pencil refuses to obey my brain."

"My own case. My pen will not write what I wish. The link between the brain and the nerves is for the moment severed."

"Let us go out, brother. It is now three. We will walk slowly in the direction of the Langham Hotel."

As they put on their hats Cornelius stopped, and said reflectively—

"The nervous system is a little shaken with both of us. Can you suggest anything, brother Humphrey?"

"The best thing for a shaken nervous system," replied Humphrey promptly, "is a glass of champagne. I will get some champagne for you, brother Cornelius."

He returned presently with a modest pint bottle, which they drank together, Humphrey remarking (in italics) that in such a case it is not a question of what a man *wants*, so much as of what he *needs*.

A pint of champagne is not much between two men, but it produced an excellent effect upon the Twins. Before it they were downcast; they looked around with the furtive eyes of conscious imposture; their hands trembled. After it they raised their heads, laughed, and looked boldly in each other's eyes, assumed a gay and confident air, and presently marched off arm-in-arm to call upon the Patron.

Gilead Beck, unprepared to see both brethren, welcomed them with a respect almost overwhelming. It was his first interview with Genius

They introduced each other.

"Mr. Beck," said Cornelius, "allow me to introduce my brother, Humphrey Jagenal. In his case the world is satisfied with the Christian name alone, without the ceremonial prefix. He is, as you know, the Artist."

If his brother had been Titian or Correggio he could not have said more.

"Sir," said Mr. Beck, shaking Humphrey's hand warmly, "I am proud indeed to make your acquaintance. I am but a rough man myself, sir, but I respect genius."

"Then," said Humphrey, with admirable presence of mind, "allow me to introduce my brother. Cornelius Jagenal, as you doubtless know, Mr. Beck, is the Poet."

Mr. Beck did not know it, and said so. But he shook hands with Cornelius none the less cordially.

"Sir, I have been knocking about the world, and have not read any poetry since I was a boy. Then I read Alexander Pope. You know Pope, Mr. Jagenal?"

Cornelius smiled, as if he might allow some merit to Pope, though small in comparison with his own.

"I have never met with your poem, Mr. Cornelius Jagenal or your pictures, Mr. Humphrey, but I hope you will now enable me to do so."

"My brother is engaged"—said Cornelius.

"My brother is engaged"—began Humphrey. "Pardon, brother."

"Sit down, gentlemen. Will you take anything? In California, up country, we always begin with a drink. Call for what you please, gentlemen. Sail in, as we say."

They took champagne, for the second time that day, and then their eyes began to glisten.

Mr. Beck observed that they were both alike—small and fragile-looking men, with bright eyes and delicate features; he made a mental note to the effect that they would never advance their own fortunes. He also concluded from their red noses, and from the way in which they straightened their backs after placing themselves outside the champagne, that they loved the goblet, and habitually handled it too often.

"Now, gentlemen," he began, after making these observations, "may I be allowed to talk business?"

They both bowed.

"Genius, gentlemen, is apt to be careless of the main chance. It don't care for the almighty dollar; it lets fellows like me heap up the stamps. What can we do but ask Genius to dig into our Pile?"

Humphrey poured out another glass of champagne for his brother, and one for himself. Then he turned to Cornelius and nodded gravely.

"Cornelius, so far as I understand him, Mr. Beck speaks the strongest common sense."

"We agree with you so far, Mr. Beck," said Cornelius critically, because he was there to give moral support to his brother.

"Why should I have any delicacy in saying to a young man, or a man of any age," he added doubtfully, for the years of the Twins seemed uncertain, "'You, sir, are an Artist and a Genius. Take a cheque, and carry out your ideas'?"

"What reason indeed?" asked Cornelius. "The offer does honour to both."

"Or to another man, 'You, sir, are a Poet. Why should the cares of the world interfere with your thoughts? Take a cheque, and make the world rejoice'!"

Humphrey clapped his hands.

"The world lies in travail for such a patron of poetry," he said.

"Why, then, we are agreed," said Mr. Beck. "Gentlemen, I say to you both, collectively, let me usher into the world those works of genius which you are bound to produce. You, sir, are painting a picture. When can you finish me that picture?"

"In six months," said Humphrey, his brain suffused with a rosy warmth of colour which made him see things in an impossibly favourable light.

WALTER BESANT AND JAMES RICE

"I buy that picture, sir, at your own price," said the patron. "I shall exhibit it in London, and it shall then go to New York with me. And you, Mr. Cornelius Jagenal, are engaged upon poems. When would you wish to publish your verses?"

"My Epic, the *Upheaval of Ælfred*, will be ready for publication about the end of November," said Cornelius.

Humphrey felt a passing pang of jealousy as he perceived that his brother would be before the world a month in advance of himself. But what is a month compared with immortality?

"I charge myself, sir, if you will allow me," said the American, "with the production of that work. It shall be printed in the best style possible, on the thickest paper made, and illustrated by the best artist that can be found—you, perhaps, Mr. Humphrey Jagenal. It shall be bound in Russian leather; its exterior shall be worthy of its contents. And as for business arrangements, gentlemen, you will please consider them at your leisure, and let me know what you think. We shall be sure to agree, because, if you will not think it shoddy in me to say so, I have my Pile to dig into. And I shall send you, if you will allow me, gentlemen, a small cheque each in advance."

They murmured assent and rose to go.

"If you would favor me further, gentlemen, by dining with me—say this day week—I should take it as a great distinction. I hope, with the assistance of Mr. Dunquerque, to have a few prominent men of letters to meet you. I want to have my table full of genius."

"Can we, brother Humphrey, accept Mr. Beck's invitation?"

Cornelius asked as if they were weeks deep in engagements. As it was, nobody ever asked them anywhere, and they had no engagements at all.

Humphrey consulted a pocket-book with grave face.

"We can, Mr. Beck."

"And if you know anyone else, gentlemen, any men of Literature and Art who will come too, bring them along with you, and I shall feel it an honour."

They knew no one connected with Literature and Art, not even a printer's devil, but they did not say so.

At twelve o'clock, toward the close of this fatiguing day, Cornelius asked Humphrey, with a little hesitation, if he really thought he should have finished his great work in six months.

"Art cannot be forced, Cornelius," said the Painter airily. "If I am not ready, I shall not hesitate to consider the pledge conditional. My work must be perfect ere it leaves my hands."

"And mine, too," said the Poet. "I will never consent to let a poem of mine go forth unfinished to the world. The work must be polished *ad unguem*."

"This is a memorable day, brother. The tumblers are empty. Allow me. And, Cornelius, I really do think that, considering the way in which we have been treated by Phillis Fleming, and her remarks about afternoon work, we ought to call and let her understand the reality of our reputation."

"We will, Humphrey. But it is not enough to recover lost ground; we must advance farther. The fortress shall be made to surrender."

"Let us drink to your success, brother, and couple with the toast the name of Phillis—Phillis—Phillis Jagenal, brother?"

They drank that toast, smiling unutterable things.

XXIII

"Call me not fool till Heaven hath sent me fortune."

W hen Jack Dunquerque communicated to Lawrence Colquhoun the fact of having made the acquaintance of Miss Fleming, and subsequently that of Mrs. L'Estrange, Lawrence expressed no surprise and felt no suspicions. Probably, had he felt any, they would have been at once set aside, because Colquhoun was not a man given to calculate the future chances, and to disquiet himself about possible events. Also at this time he was taking little interest in Phillis. A pretty piquante girl; he devoted a whole day to her; drove her to Twickenham, and placed her in perfect safety under the charge of his cousin. What more was wanted? Agatha wrote to him twice a week or so, and when he had time he read the letters. They were all about Phillis, and most of them contained the assurance that he had no entanglements to fear.

"Entanglements!" he murmured impatiently. "As if a man cannot dine with a girl without falling in love with her. Women are always thinking that men want to be married."

He was forgetting, after the fashion of men who have gone through the battle, how hot is the fight for those who are just beginning it. Jack Dunquerque was four-and-twenty; he was therefore, so to speak, in the thick of it. Phillis's eyes were like two quivers filled with darts, and when she turned them innocently upon her friend the enemy, the darts flew straight at him, and transfixed him as if he were another Sebastian. Colquhoun's time was past; he was clothed in the armour of indifference which comes with the years, and he was forgetting the past.

Still, had he known of the visit to the Tower of London, the rowing on the river, the luncheons in Carnarvon Square, it is possible that even he might have seen the propriety of requesting Jack Dunquerque to keep out of danger for the future.

He had no plans for Phillis, except of the simplest kind. She was to remain in charge of Agatha for a year, and then she would come out. He hoped that she would marry well, because her father, had he lived, would have wished it. And that was all he hoped about her.

He had his private worries at this time—those already indicated—connected with Victoria Cassilis. The ice once broken, that lady allowed him no rest. She wrote to him on some pretence nearly everyday; she sent her maid, the unlovely one, with three-cornered notes all about nothing; she made him meet her in society, she made him dine with her; it seemed as if she was spreading a sort of net about him, through the meshes of which he could not escape.

With the knowledge of what had been, it was an unrighteous thing for Colquhoun to go to the house of Gabriel Cassilis; he ought not to be there, he felt, it was the one house in all London in which he had no business. And yet—how to avoid it?

And Gabriel Cassilis seemed to like him; evidently liked to talk to him; singled him out, this great financier, and talked with him as if Colquhoun too was interested in stock; called upon him at his chambers, and told him, in a dry but convincing way, something of his successes and his projects.

It was after many talks of this kind that Lawrence Colquhoun, forgetful of the past, and not remembering that of all men in the world Gabriel Cassilis was the last who should have charge of his money, put it all in his hands, with power-of-attorney to sell out and reinvest for him. But that was nothing. Colquhoun was not the man to trouble about money. He was safe in the hands of this great and successful capitalist: he gave no thought to any risk; he congratulated himself on his cleverness in persuading the financier to take the money for him; and he continued to see Victoria Cassilis nearly everyday.

They quarrelled when they did meet; there was not a conversation between them in which she did not say something bitter, and he something savage. And yet he did not have the courage to refuse the invitations which were almost commands. Nor could she resign the sweet joys of making him feel her power.

A secret, you see, has a fatal fascination about it. Schoolgirls, I am told, are given to invent little secrets which mean nothing, and to whisper them in the ears of their dearest friends to the exclusion of the rest. The possession of this unknown and invaluable fact brings them together, whispering and conspiring, at every possible moment. Freemasons again—how are they kept together; except by the possession of secrets which are said to have been published over and over again? And when two people have a secret which means—all that the secret between Colquhoun and Mrs. Cassilis meant, they can no more help being drawn together than the waters can cease to find their own level. To be together, to feel that the only other person in the world who knows that secret is with you, is a kind of safety. Yet what did it matter to Colquhoun? Simply nothing. The secret was his as well as hers, but the reasons for keeping it a secret were not his at all, but hers entirely.

So Phillis was neglected by her guardian and left to Agatha and Jack Dunquerque, with such results as we shall see.

So Lawrence Colquhoun fell into the power of this man of stocks, about the mouth of whose City den the footsteps pointed all one way. He congratulated himself; he found out Gilead Beck, and they congratulated each other.

"I don't see," said Colquhoun, who had already enough for four bachelors, "why one's income should not be doubled."

"With Mr. Cassilis," said Gilead Beck, "you sign cheques, and he gives you dividends. It's like Ile, because you can go on pumping."

"He understands more than any other living man," said Lawrence.

"He is in the inner track, sir," said Mr. Beck.

"And a man," said Lawrence, "ready to take in his friends with himself."

"A high-toned and a whole-souled man," said Gilead Beck, with enthusiasm. "That man, sir, I do believe would take in the hull world."

XXIV

"I had rather hear a brazen candlestick turn'd,
Or a dry wheel grate on an axle-tree;
And that would set my teeth nothing on edge.
Nothing so much as mincing poetry."

Jack Dunquerque repaired to the Langham, the day after the call on the Twins, with a face in which cheerful anticipation and anxiety were curiously blended. He was serious with his lips, but he laughed with his eyes. And he spoke with a little hesitation not often observed in him.

"I think your dinner will come off next Wednesday," he said. "And I have been getting together your party for you."

"That is so, Mr. Dunquerque?" asked Gilead Beck, with a solemnity which hardly disguised his pride and joy. "That is so? And those great men, your friends, are actually coming?"

"I have seen them all, personally. And I put the case before each of them. I said, 'Here is an American gentleman most anxious to make your acquaintance; he has no letters of introduction to you, but he is a sincere admirer of your genius; he appreciates you better than any other living man.'"

"Heap it up, Mr. Dunquerque," said the Man of Oil. "Heap it up. Tell them I am Death on appreciation."

"That is in substance what I did tell them. Then I explained that you deputed me, or gave me permission to ask them to dinner. 'The honour,' I said, 'is mutual. On the one hand, my friend, Mr. Gilead P. Beck'—I ventured to say, 'my friend, Mr. Gilead P. Beck'—"

"If you hadn't said that you should have been scalped and gouged. Go on, Mr. Dunquerque; go on, sir."

"'On the one hand, my friend, Mr. Gilead P. Beck'—"

"That is so—that is so."

"'Will feel himself honoured by your company; on the other hand, it will be a genuine source of pleasure for you to know that you are as well known and as thoroughly appreciated on the other side of the water as you are here.' I am not much of a speechmaker, and I assure you that little effort cost me a good deal of thought. However, the end of it is all you care about. Most of the writing swells will come, either on Wednesday next or on any other day you please."

"Mr. Dunquerque, not a day passes but you load me with obligations. Tell me, if you please, who they are."

"Well, you will say I have done pretty well, I think." Jack pulled out a paper. "And you will know most of the names. First of all, you would like to see the old Philosopher of Cheyne Walk, Thomas Carlyle, as your guest?"

"Carlyle, sir, is a name to conjure with in the States. When I was Editor of the *Clearville Roarer* I had an odd volume of Carlyle, and I used to quote him as long as the book lasted. It perished in a fight. And to think that I shall meet the man who wrote that work! An account of the dinner must be written for the *Rockoleaville Gazette*. We'll have a special reporter, Mr. Dunquerque. We'll get a man who'll do it up to the handle."

Jack looked at his list again.

"What do you say of Professor Huxley and Mr. Darwin?"

Mr. Beck shook his head. These two writers began to flourish— that is, to be read—in the States after his editorial days, and he knew them not.

"I should say they were prominent citizens, likely, if I knew what they'd written. Is Professor Huxley a professing Christian? There was a Professor Habukkuk Huckster once down Empire City way in the Moody and Sankey business, with an interest in the organs and a percentage on the hymn-books; but they're not relations, I suppose? Not probable. And the other genius—what is his name—Darwin? Grinds novels perhaps?"

"Historical works of fiction. Great in genealogy is Darwin."

"Never mind my ignorance, Mr. Dunquerque. And go on, sir. I'm powerful interested."

"Ruskin is coming; and I had thought of Robert Browning, the poet, but I am afraid he may not be able to be present. You see, Browning is so much sought after by the younger men of the day. They used to play polo and billiards and other frivolous things till he came into fashion with his light and graceful verse, so simple that all may understand it. His last poem, I believe, is now sung about the streets. However, there are Tennyson and Swinburne—they are both coming. Buchanan I would ask, if I knew him, but I don't. George Eliot, of course, I could not invite to a stag party. Trollope we might get, perhaps—"

"Give me Charles Reade, sir," said Gilead Beck. "He is the novelist they like on our side."

"I am afraid I could not persuade him to come; though he might be pleased to see you if you would call at his house, perhaps. However, Beck, the great thing is"—he folded up his list and placed it in his pocket-book—"that you shall have a dinner of authors as good as any that sat down to the Lord Mayor's spread last year. Authors of all sorts, and the very best. None of your unknown little hungry anonymous beggars who write novels in instalments for weekly papers. Big men, sir, with big names. Men you'll be proud to know. And they shall be asked for next Wednesday."

"That gives only four days. It's terrible sudden," said Gilead Beck. He shook his head with as much gravity as if he was going to be hanged in four days. Then he sat down and began to write the names of his guests.

"Professor Huxley," he said, looking up. "I suppose I can buy that clergyman's sermons? And the Universal Genius who reels out the historical romances, Mr. Darwin? I shall get his works, too. And there's Mr. Ruskin, Mr. Robert Browning—"

"What are you going to do?"

"Well, Mr. Dunquerque, I am going to devote the next four days, from morning till night, to solid preparation for that evening. I shall go out right away, and I shall buy every darned book those great men have written; and if I sit up every night over the job, I'm bound to read every word."

"Oh!" said Jack. "Then I advise you to begin with Robert Browning."

"The light and graceful verse that everybody can understand? I will," said Gilead Beck. "They shall not find me unacquainted with their poems. Mr. Dunquerque, for the Lord's sake don't tell them it was all crammed up in four days."

"Not I. But—I say—you know, authors don't like to talk about their own books."

"That's the modesty of real genius," said the American, with admiration.

It will be perceived that Jack spoke with a certain rashness. Most authors I have myself known do love very much to talk about their own books.

"That is their modesty. But they will talk about each other's books. And it is as well to be prepared. What I'm bound to make them feel, somehow, is that they have a man before them who has gone in for the hull lot and survived. A tough contract, Mr. Dunquerque, but you trust me."

"Very well," said Jack, putting on his hat, "only don't ask them questions. Authors don't like being questioned. Why, I shouldn't wonder

WALTER BESANT AND JAMES RICE

if next Wednesday some of them pretended not to know the names of their own books. Don't you know that Shakespeare, when he went down to Stratford, to live like a retired grocer at Leytonstone, used to pretend not to know what a play meant? And when a strolling company came round, and the manager asked permission to play *Hamlet*, he was the first to sign a petition to the mayor not to allow immoral exhibitions in the borough."

"Is that so, sir?"

"It may be so," said Jack, "because I never heard it contradicted."

As soon he was gone, Gilead Beck sought the nearest bookseller's shop and gave an extensive order. He requested to be furnished with all the works of Carlyle, Ruskin, Tennyson, Swinburne, Browning, Buchanan, Huxley, Darwin, and a few more. Then he returned to the Langham, gave orders that he was at home to no one except Mr Dunquerque, took off his coat, lit a cigar, ordered more champagne, and began the first of the three most awful days he ever spent in all his life.

The books presently came in a great box, and he spread them on the table with a heart that sank at the mere contemplation of their numbers. About three hundred volumes in all. And only four days to get through them. Seventy-five volumes a day, say, at the rate of fifteen hours' daily work; five an hour, one every twelve minutes. He laid his watch upon the table, took the first volume of Robert Browning that was uppermost, sat down in his long chair with his feet up, and began.

The book was *Fifine at the Fair*. Gilead Beck read cheerfully and with great ease the first eight or ten pages. Then he discovered with a little annoyance that he understood nothing whatever of the author's meaning. "That comes of too rapid reading," he said. So he turned back to the beginning and began with more deliberation. Ten minutes clean wasted, and not even half a volume got through. When he had got to tenth page for the second time, he questioned himself once more, and found that he understood less than ever. Were things right? Could it be Browning, or some impostor? Yes, the name of Robert Browning was on the title-page; also, it was English. And the words held together, and were not sprinkled out of a pepper-pot. He began a third time. Same result. He threw away his cigar and wiped his brow, on which the cold dews of trouble were gathering thickly.

"This is the beginning of the end, Gilead P. Beck," he murmured. "The Lord, to try you, sent His blessed Ile, and you've received it with a proud stomach. Now you air going off your head. Plain English, and you can't take in a single sentence."

It was in grievous distress of mind that he sprang to his feet and began to walk about the room.

"There was no softenin' yesterday," he murmured, trying to reassure himself. "Why should there be today? Softenin' comes by degrees. Let us try again. Great Jehoshaphat!"

He stood up to his work, leaning against a window-post, and took two pages first, which he read very slowly. And then he dropped the volume in dismay, because he understood less than nothing.

It was the most disheartening thing he had ever attempted.

"I'd rather fight John Halkett over again," he said. "I'd rather sit with my finger on a trigger for a week, expecting Mr. Huggins to call upon me."

Then he began to construe it line by line, thinking every now and then that he saw daylight.

It is considered rather a mark of distinction, a separating seal upon the brow, by that poet's admirers, to reverence his later works. Their creed is that because a poem is rough, harsh, ungrammatical, and dark, it must have a meaning as deep as its black obscurity.

"It's like the texts of a copybook," said Gilead. "Pretty things, all of them, separate. Put them together and where are they? I guess this book would read better upsy down."

He poured cold water on his head for a quarter of an hour or so, and then tried reading it aloud.

This was worse than any previous method, because he comprehended no more of the poet's meaning, and the rough hard words made his front teeth crack and fly about the room in splinters.

"Cæsar's ghost!" he exclaimed, thinking what he should do if Robert Browning talked as he wrote. "The human jaw isn't built that could stand it."

Two hours were gone. There ought to have been ten volumes got through, and not ten pages finished of a single one.

He hurled *Fifine* to the other end of the room, and took another work by the same poet. It was *Red Cotton Nightcap Country*, and the title looked promising. No doubt a light and pretty fairy story. Also the beginning reeled itself off with a fatal facility which allured the reader onwards.

WHEN THE CLOCK STRUCK SIX he was sitting among the volumes on the table, with *Red Cotton Nightcap Country* still in his hand. His eyes were bloodshot, his hair was pushed in disorder about his head, his cheeks were flushed, his hands were trembling, the nerves in his face were twitching.

He looked about him wildly, and tried to collect his faculties. Then he arose and cursed Robert Browning. He cursed him eating, drinking, and sleeping. And then he took all his volumes, and disposing them carefully in the fire-place, he set light to them.

"I wish," he said, "that I could put the Poet there, too." I think he would have done it, this mild and gentle-hearted stranger, so strongly was his spirit moved to wrath.

He could not stay any longer in the room. It seemed to be haunted with ghosts of unintelligible sentences; things in familiar garb, which floated before his eyes and presented faces of inscrutable mystery. He seized his hat and fled.

He went straight to Jack Dunquerque's club, and found that hero in the reading-room.

"I have a favour to ask you," he began in a hurried and nervous manner. "If you have not yet asked Mr. Robert Browning to the little spread next week, don't."

"Certainly not, if you wish it. Why?"

"Because, sir, I have spent eight hours over his works."

Jack laughed.

"And you think you have gone off your head? I'll tell you a secret. Everybody does at first; and then we all fall into the dodge, and go about pretending to understand him."

"But the meaning, Mr. Dunquerque, the meaning?"

"Hush! he *hasn't got any*. Only no one dares to say so, and it's intellectual to admire him."

"Well, Mr. Dunquerque, I guess I don't want to see that writer at my dinner, anyhow."

"Very well, then. He shall not be asked."

"Another day like this, and you may bury me with my boots on. Come with me somewhere, and have dinner as far away from those volumes of Mr. Browning as we can get in the time."

They dined at Greenwich. In the course of the next three days Gilead Beck read diligently. He did not master the three hundred volumes, but he got through some of the works of every writer, taking them in turn.

The result was a glorious and inextricable mess. Carlyle, Swinburne, Huxley, Darwin, Tennyson, and all of them, were hopelessly jumbled in his brains. He mixed up the *Sartor Resartus* with the *Missing Link*, confounded the history of *Frederick the Great* with that of *Queen Elizabeth*, and thought that *Maud* and *Atalanta in Calydon* were written by the same poet. But time went on, and the Wednesday evening, to which he looked forward with so much anxiety and pride, rapidly drew near.

XXV

"Why, she is cold to all the world."

A nd while Gilead Beck was setting himself to repair in a week the defects of his early education, Jack Dunquerque was spending his days hovering round the light of Phillis's eyes. The infatuated youth frequented the house as if it was his own. He liked it, Mrs. L'Estrange liked it, and Phillis liked it. Agatha looked with matronly suspicion for indications and proofs of love in her ward's face. She saw none, because Phillis was not in love at all. Jack to her was the first friend she made on coming out of her shell. Very far, indeed, from being in love. Jack looked too for any of those signs of mental agitation which accompany, or are supposed to accompany, the birth of love. There were none. Her face lit up when she saw him; she treated him with the frankness of a girl who tells her brother everything; but she did not blush when she saw him, nor was she ever otherwise than the sweetest and lightest-hearted of sisters. He knew it, and he groaned to think of it. The slightest sign would have encouraged him to speak; the smallest indication that Phillis felt something for him of what he felt for her would have been to him a command to tell what was in his heart. But she made no sign. It was Jack's experience, perhaps, which taught him that he is a fool who gives his happiness to a woman before he has learned to divine her heart. Those ever make the most foolish marriages who are most ignorant of the sex. Hooker, the Judicious is a case in point, and many a ghostly man could, from his country parsonage, tell the same tale.

Jack was not like the Judicious Divine; he was wary, though susceptible; he had his share of craft and subtlety; and yet he was in love, in spite of all that craft, with a girl who only liked him in return.

Had he possessed greater power of imagination he would have understood that he was expecting what was impossible. You cannot get wine out of an empty bottle, nor reap corn without first sowing the seed; and he forgot that Phillis, who was unable to read novels, knew nothing, positively nothing, of that great passion of Love which makes its victims half divine. It was always necessary, in thinking of this girl, to remember her thirteen years of captivity. Jack, more than any other person, not excepting Agatha L'Estrange, knew what she would say and think on most things. Only in this matter of love he was at fault. Here he did not know because here he was selfish. To all the world except Jack and Agatha she was an *impossible* girl; she said things that no other girl would have said; she thought as no one else thought. To all those who live in a tight little island of their own, fortified by triple batteries of dogma, she was impossible. But to those who accepted and comprehended the conditions of Phillis's education she was possible, real, charming, and full of interest.

Jack continually thought what Phillis would say and what she would think. For her sake he noticed the little things around him, the things among which we grow up unobservant. We see so little for the most part. Things to eat and drink interest us; things that please the eye; fair women and rare wine. We are like cattle grazing on the slopes of the Alps. Around us rise the mountains, with their ever-changing marvels of light and colour; the sunlight flashes from their peaks; the snow-slopes stretch away and upwards to the deep blues beyond in curves as graceful as the line of woman's beauty; at our feet is the belt of pines perfumed and warmed by the summer air; the mountain stream leaps, bubbles, and laughs, rushing from the prison of its glacier cave; high overhead soars the Alpine eagle; the shepherds yodel in the valleys; the rapid echoes roll the song up into the immeasurable silence of the hills,—and amid all this we browse and feed, eyes downward turned.

So this young man, awakened by the quick sympathies of the girl he loved, lifted his head, taught by her, and tried to catch, he too, something of the childlike wonder, the appreciative admiration, the curious enthusiasm, with which she saw everything. Most men's thoughts are bound by the limits of their club at night, and their chambers or their offices by day; the suns rise and set, and the outward world is unregarded. Jack learned from Phillis to look at these unregarded things. Such simple pleasures as a sunset, the light upon the river, the wild flowers on the bank, he actually tasted with delight, provided that she was beside him. And after a day of such Arcadian joys he would return to town, and find the club a thirsty desert.

If Phillis had known anything about love, she would have fallen in love with Jack long before; but she did not. Yet he made headway with her, because he became almost necessary to her life. She looked for his coming; he brought her things he had collected in his "globe trotting"; he told her stories of adventure; he ruined himself in pictures; and then he looked for the love softening of her eyes, and it came not at all.

Yet Jack was a lovable sort of young man in maidens' eyes. Everybody liked him to begin with. He was, like David, a youth of a cheerful, if not of a ruddy countenance. Agatha L'Estrange remarked of him that it did her good to meet cheerful young men—they were so scarce. "I know quantities of young men, Phillis my dear; and I assure you that most of them are enough to break a woman's heart even to think of. There is the athletic young man—he is dreadful indeed, only his time soon goes by; and there is the young man who talks about getting more brain power. To be sure, he generally looks as if he wants it. There is the young man who ought to turn red and hot when the word Prig is used. There is the bad young man who keeps betting-books; and the miserable young man who grovels and flops in a Ritualist church. I know young men who are envious and backbite their friends; and young men who aspire to be somebody else; and young men who pose as infidels, and would rather be held up to execration in a paper than not to be mentioned at all. But, my dear, I don't know anybody who is so cheerful and contented as Jack. He isn't clever and learned, but he doesn't want to be; he isn't sharp, and will never make money, but he is better without it; and he is true, I am sure."

Agatha unconsciously used the word in the sense which most women mean when they speak of a man's truth. Phillis understood it to mean that Jack Dunquerque did not habitually tell fibs, and thought the remark superfluous, But it will be observed that Agatha was fighting Jack's battle for him.

After all, Jack might have taken heart had he thought that all these visits and all this interest in himself were but the laying of the seed, which might grow into a goodly tree.

"If only she would look as if she cared for me, Tommy," he bemoaned to Ladds.

"Hang it! can't expect a girl to begin making eyes at you."

"Eyes! Phillis make eyes! Tommy, as you grow older you grow coarser. It's a great pity. That comes of this club life. Always smoking and playing cards."

Tommy grinned. Virtue was as yet a flower new to Jack Dunquerque's buttonhole, and he wore it with a pride difficult to dissemble.

"Better go and have it out with Colquhoun," Tommy advised. "He won't care. He's taken up with his old flame, Mrs. Cassilis, again. Always dangling at her heels, I'm told. Got no time to think of Miss Fleming. Great fool, Colquhoun. Always was a fool, I believe. Might have gone after flesh and blood instead of a marble statue. Wonder how Cassilis likes it."

"There you go," cried Jack impatiently. "Men are worse than women. At Twickenham one never hears this foolish sort of gossip."

"Suppose not. Flowers and music, muffins, tea, and spoons. Well, the girl's worth it, Jack; the more flowers and music you get the better it will be for you. But go on and square it with Colquhoun."

XXVI

"A right royal banquet."

At seven o'clock on the great Wednesday Gilead Beck was pacing restlessly in his inner room, the small apartment which formed his sanctum, waiting to receive his guests. All the preparations were complete: a quartette of singers was in readiness, with a piano, to discourse sweet music after the dinner; the noblest bouquet ever ordered at the Langham was timed for a quarter to eight punctually; the wine was in ice; the waiters were adding the last touches to the artistic decorations of a table which, laid for thirteen only, might have been prepared for the Prince of Wales. In fact, when the bill came up a few days later, even Gilead Beck, man of millions, qualled for a moment before its total. Think of the biggest bill you ever had at Véfour's—for francs read pounds, and then multiply by ten; think of the famous Lord Warden bill for the Emperor Napoleon when he landed in all his glory, and then consider that the management of the Langham is in no way behind that of the Dover hostelry. But this was to come, and when it did come, was received lightly.

Gilead Beck took a last look at the dinner-table. The few special injunctions he had given were carried out; they were not many, only that the shutters should be partly closed and the curtains drawn, so that they might dine by artificial light; that the table and the room should be entirely illuminated by wax-candles, save for one central light, in which should be burning, like the sacred flame of Vesta, his own rock-oil. He also stipulated that the flowers on the table should be disposed in shallow vessels, so as to lie low, and not interfere with the freedom of the eyes across the table. Thus there was no central tower of flowers and fruit. To compensate for this he allowed a whole bower of exotics to be erected round the room.

The long wall opposite the window was decorated with his famous piece by an unknown master, bought of Bartholomew Burls, known as "Sisera and Jael." As the frame had not yet been made it was wreathed about for its whole length and breadth with flowers. The other pictures, also wreathed with flowers, were genuine originals, bought of the same famous collector. For the end of the room Gilead Beck had himself designed, and partly erected with his own hands, an allegorical trophy.

From a pile of books neatly worked in cork, there sprang a jet of water illuminated on either side by a hidden lamp burning rock-oil. He had wished to have the fountain itself of oil, but was overruled by Jack Dunquerque. Above, by an invisible wire, hovered a golden butterfly in gilded paper. And on either side hung a flag—that on the right displaying the Stars and Stripes, that on the left the equally illustrious Union Jack.

At every man's place lay a copy of the *menu*, in green and gold, elaborately decorated, a masterpiece of illumination. Gilead Beck, after making quite sure that nothing was neglected, took his own, and, retiring to the inner room, read it for the fiftieth time with a pleasure as intense as that of the young author who reads his first proof-sheet. It consisted of a large double card. On the top of the left-hand side was painted in colours and gold a butterfly. And that side read as follows (I regret that the splendours of the original cannot be here reproduced):

LANGHAM HOTEL,
MAY 20, 1875.

Dinner in Honour of Literature, Science, and Art,

GIVEN BY

GILEAD P. BECK,

AN OBSCURE AMERICAN CITIZEN RAISED AT LEXINGTON,
WHO STRUCK ILE IN A MOST SURPRISING MANNER
BY THE HELP OF

THE GOLDEN BUTTERFLY,

BUT WHO DESPISES SHODDY AND RESPECTS GENIUS.

Representatives of Literature, Art, and Science.

THOMAS CARLYLE,
ALFRED TENNYSON,
JOHN RUSKIN,
ALGERNON SWINBURNE,

GEORGE AUGUSTUS SALA,
CHARLES DARWIN,
PROFESSOR HUXLEY,
FREDERICK LEIGHTON, R.A.,
CORNELIUS JAGENAL, AND
HUMPHREY JAGENAL,

WITH CAPTAIN LADDS, THE HON. RONALD DUNQUERQUE,
AND GILEAD P. BECK.

After this preamble, which occupied a whole side of the double card,
followed the *menu* itself.

I unwillingly suppress this. There are weaker brethren who might
on reading it feel dissatisfied with the plain lamb and rhubarb-tart of
the sweet spring season. As a present dignitary of the Church, now
a colonial bishop, once a curate, observed to me many years ago, *à
propos* of thirst, university reminiscences, a neighbouring public-house,
a craving for tobacco, and the fear of being observed, "These weaker
brethren are a great nuisance."

Let it suffice that at the Langham they still speak of Gilead Beck's
great dinner with tears in their eyes. I believe a copy of the green and
gold card is framed, and hung in the office so as to catch the eye of
poorer men when they are ordering dinners. It makes those of lower
nature feel envious, and even takes the conceit out of the nobler kind.

Gilead Beck, dressed for the banquet, was nervous and restless.
It seemed as if, for the first time, his wealth was about to bring him
something worth having. His face, always grave, was as solemn as if he
were fixing it for his own funeral. From time to time he drew a paper
from his pocket and read it over. Then he replaced it, and with lips and
arms went through the action of speaking. It was his speech of the
evening, which he had carefully written and imperfectly committed to
memory. Like a famous American lawyer, the attitude he assumed was
to stand bent a little forward, the feet together, the left hand hanging
loosely at his side, while he brandished the right above his head.

In this attitude he was surprised by the Twins, who came a quarter of
an hour before the time. They were dressed with great care, having each
the sweetest little eighteenpenny bouquet, bought from the little shop at
the right hand of the Market as you go in, where the young lady makes it

up before your eyes, sticks the wire into it, and pins it at your buttonhole with her own fair hands. Each brother in turn winked at her during the operation. A harmless wink, but it suggested no end of possible devilries should these two young gentlemen of fifty find themselves loose upon the town. Those who saw it thought of Mohocks, and praised the Lord for the new police.

They both looked very nice; they entered with a jaunty step, a careless backward toss of the head, parted lips, and bright eyes which faced fearlessly a critical but reverent world. Nothing but the crow's-feet showed that the first glow of youth was over; nothing but a few streaks of grey in Humphrey's beard and in Cornelius's hair showed that they were nearing the Indian summer of life. Mr. Beck, seeing them enter so fresh, so bright, and so beaming, was more than ever puzzled at their age. He was waiting for them in a nervous and rather excitable state of mind, as becomes one who is about to find himself face to face with the greatest men of his time.

"You, gentlemen," he said, "will sit near me, one each side, if you will be so kind, just to lend a helping-hand to the talk when it flags. Phew! it will be a rasper, the talk of today. I've read all their works, if I can only remember them, and I bought the *History of English Literature* yesterday to get a grip of the hull subject. No use. I haven't got farther than Chaucer. Do you think they can talk about Chaucer? He wrote the *Canterbury Tales*."

"Cornelius," said Humphrey, "you will be able to lead the conversation to the Anglo-Saxon period."

"That period is too early, brother Humphrey," said Cornelius. "We shall trust to you to turn the steam in the direction of the Renaissance."

Humphrey shifted in his seat uneasily. Why this unwillingness in either Twin to assume the lead on a topic which had engaged his attention for twenty years?

Mr. Beck shook his head.

"I most wish now," he said, "that I hadn't asked them. But it's a thundering great honour. Mr. Dunquerque did it all for me. That young gentleman met these great writers, I suppose, in the baronial halls of his brother, the Earl of Isleworth."

"Do we know Lord Isleworth?" asked Cornelius of Humphrey.

"Lord Isleworth, Cornelius? No; I rather think we have never met him," said Humphrey to Cornelius.

"None of your small names tonight," said Gilead Beck, with serious and even pious joy. "The Lord Mayor may have them at Guildhall.

Mine are the big guns. I did want to get a special report for my own *Gazette*, but Mr. Dunquerque thought it better not to have it. P'r'aps 'twould have seemed kind o' shoddy. I ought to be satisfied with the private honour, and not want the public glory of it. What would they say in Boston if they knew, or even in New York?"

"You should have a dinner for poets alone," said Humphrey, anxious for his brother.

"Or for Artists only," said Cornelius.

"Wal, gentlemen, we shall get on. As there's five minutes to spare, would you like to give an opinion on the wine-list, and oblige me by your advice?"

The Twins perused the latter document with sparkling eyes. It was a noble list. Gilead Beck's plan was simple. He just ordered the best of everything. For Sauterne, he read Château Iquem: for Burgundy, he took Chambertin; for Claret, Château Lafite; for Champagne, Heidsieck; for Sherry, Montilla; a Box Boutel wine for Hock; and for Port the '34. Never before, in all its experiences of Americans, Russians, and returned colonials, had the management of the Langham so "thorough" a wine-bill to make out as for this dinner.

"Is that satisfactory, gentlemen?"

"Cornelius, what do you think?"

"Humphrey, I think as you do; and that is, that this princely selection shows Mr. Beck's true appreciation of Literature and Art."

"It is kind of you, gentlemen, to say so. I talked over the dinner with the *chef*, and I have had the menou printed, as you see it, in gilt and colours, which I am given to understand is the correct thing at the Guildhall. Would you like to look at that?"

They showed the greatest desire to look at it. Humphrey read it aloud with emphasis. While he read and while his brother listened, Mr. Beck thought they seemed a good deal older than before. Perhaps that was before their faces were turned to the light, and the reflection through an open window of the sinking sun showed up the crow's-feet round their eyes.

"Humph! Plovers' eggs. Clear mulligatawny; clear, Cornelius. Turtle-fins. Salmon—I translate the French. Turbot. Lochleven trout—"

"Very good indeed, so far," said Cornelius, with a palpable smack of his lips.

"Lamb-cutlets with peas—a simple but excellent dish; aspic of *foie gras*—ah, two or three things which I cannot translate; a preparation of pigeon; haunch of venison; yes—"

"An excellent dinner, indeed," said Cornelius. "Pray go on, Humphrey."

He began to feel like Sancho in Barataria. So good a dinner seemed really impossible.

"Duckling; cabob curry of chicken-liver with Bombay ducks—really, Mr. Beck, this dinner is worth a dukedom."

"It is indeed," said Cornelius feelingly.

"Canvas-back—ah!—from Baltimore—Cornelius, this is almost too much; apricots in jelly, ice-pudding, grated Parmesan, strawberries, melons, peaches, nectarines, (and only May, Cornelius!), pines, West India bananas, custard apples from Jamaica, and dried litchis from China, Cornelius."

Humphrey handed the document to his brother with a look of appeal which said volumes. One sentence in the volumes was clearly, "Say something appropriate."

Quoth Cornelius deeply moved—

"This new Mæcenas ransacks the corners of the earth to find a fitting entertainment for men of genius. Humphrey, you shall paint him."

"Cornelius, you shall sing his praises."

By a simultaneous impulse the Twins turned to their patron, and presented each a right hand. Gilead Beck had only one right hand to give. He gave that to Cornelius, and the left to Humphrey.

While this sacrament of friendship was proceeding was heard a sound as of many men simultaneously stifling much laughter. The door opened, and the other guests arrived in a body. They were preceded by Jack Dunquerque, and on entering the room dropped, as if by word of command, into line, like soldiers on parade. Eight of them were strangers, but Captain Ladds brought up the rear.

They were, as might be expected of such great men, a remarkable assemblage. At the extreme right stood a tall well-set-up old man, with tangled grey locks, long grey eye-brows, and an immense grey beard. His vigorous bearing belied the look of age, and what part of his face could be seen had a remarkably youthful appearance.

Next to him were other two aged men, one of whom was bent and bowed by the weight of years. They also had large eyebrows and long grey beards; and Mr. Beck remarked at once that so far as could be judged from the brightness of their eyes they had wonderfully preserved their mental strength. The others were younger men, one of them being apparently a boy of eighteen or so.

Then followed a ceremony like a *levée*. Gilead Beck stood in the centre of the room, the table having been pushed back into the corner.

He was supported, right and left, by the Twins, who formed a kind of Court, and above whom he towered grandly with his height of six-feet-two. He held himself as erect, and looked as solemn as if he were the President of the United States. The Twins, for their part, looked a little as if they were his sons.

Jack Dunquerque acted as Lord Chamberlain or Master of the Ceremonies. He wore an anxious face, and looked round among the great men whom he preceded, as soon as they had all filed in, with a glance which might have meant admonition, had that been possible. And, indeed, a broad smile, which was hovering like the sunlight upon their venerable faces, disappeared at the frown of this young gentleman. It was very curious.

It was in the Grand Manner—that peculiar to Courts—in which Jack Dunquerque presented the first of the distinguished guests to Mr. Beck.

"Sir," he said, with low and awe-struck voice, "before you stands Thomas Carlyle."

A thrill ran through the American's veins as he grasped the hand which had written so many splendid things, and looked into the eyes which harboured such splendid thought. Then he said, in softened tones, because his soul was moved; "This is a proud moment, sir, for Gilead P. Beck. I never thought to have shaken by the hand the author of the *French Revolution* and the *Stones of Venice*."

(It really was unfortunate that his reading had been so miscellaneous during the four days preceding the dinner.)

The venerable Philosopher opened his mouth and spake. His tones were deep and his utterance slow.

"You are proud, Mr. Beck? The only Pride should be the pride of work. Beautiful the meanest thing that works; even the rusty and unmusical Meatjack. All else belongs to the outlook of him whom men call Beelzebub. The brief Day passes with its poor paper crowns in tinsel gilt; Night is at hand with her silences and her veracities. What hast thou done? All the rest is phantasmal. Work only remains. Say, brother, what is thy work?"

"I have struck Ile," replied Gilead proudly, feeling that his Work (with a capital W) had been well and thoroughly done.

The Philosopher stepped aside.

Jack Dunquerque brought up the next.

"Mr. Beck, Alfred Tennyson, the Poet Laureate."

This time it was a man with robust frame and strongly-marked features. He wore a long black beard, streaked with grey and rather ragged, with a ragged mass of black hair, looking as he did at Oxford when they made him an honorary D.C.L., and an undergraduate from the gallery asked him politely, "*Did* they wake and call you early?"

"Mr. Tennyson," said Mr. Beck, "I do assure you, sir, that this is the kindest thing that has been done to me since I came to England. I hope I see you well, sir. I read your *Fifine at the Fair*, sir—no, that was the other man's—I mean, sir, your *Songs before Sunrise*; and I congratulate you. We've got some poets on our side of the water, sir. I've written poetry myself for the papers. We've got Longfellow and Lowell, and take out you and Mr. Swinburne, with them we'll meet your lot."

Mr. Tennyson opened his mouth to speak, but shut it again in silence, and looking at Jack mournfully as if he had forgotten something, he stepped aside.

Jack presented another.

"Mr. John Ruskin."

A sharp-featured, clever-looking man, with grey locks and shaven face. He seized Mr. Beck by the hand and spoke first, not giving his host time to utter his little set speech.

"I welcome," he said, "one of our fellow-workers from the other side of the Atlantic. I cannot utter to you what I would. We all see too dimly as yet what are our great world-duties, for we try and outline their enlarging shadows. You in America do not seek peace as Menahem sought it, when he gave the King of Assyria a thousand pieces of silver. You fight for your peace and have it. You do not buy what you want; you take it. That is strength; that is harmony. You do not sit at home lisping comfortable prayers; you go out and work. For many a year to come, sir, the sword of your nation shall be whetted to save and to subdue."

He stopped suddenly, and closed his lips with a snap.

Mr. Beck turned rather helplessly to the Twins. He wanted a diversion to this utterly unintelligible harangue. They stared straight before them, and pretended to be absorbed in meditation.

"Mr. Beck, Mr. Swinburne. Deaf people think Mr. Browning is musical, sir; but all people allow Mr. Swinburne to be the most musical of poets."

It was the very young man. He stood before his host and laughed aloud.

"Sir," said Mr. Beck, "I have read some of your verses. I can't say what they were about, but I took to singin' them softly as I read them, and I seemed to be in a green field, lyin' out among the flowers, while the bees were bummin' around, and the larks were liftin' their hymns in the sky."

Mr. Swinburne laughed again and made way for the next comer.

"Mr. Beck, let me introduce Mr. George Augustus Sala."

"This," said the Man of Oil, "is indeed a pleasure. Mr. Sala, when I say that I am an old and personal friend of Colonel Quagg, you will be glad to meet me."

Contrary to reasonable expectation, the face of Mr. Sala showed no sign of joy at the reminiscence. He only looked rather helplessly at Jack Dunquerque, who turned red, and brought up the rest of his men together, as if to get the introductions over quickly.

"Mr. Beck, these gentlemen are Mr. Darwin, Professor Huxley, and Mr. Frederick Leighton. Ladds you know well enough already. Step up, Tommy."

Gilead Beck shook hands with each, and then, drawing himself up to his full height, laid his left hand within his waistcoat, brandished his right above his head with a preliminary flourish, and began his speech.

"Gentlemen all," he said, "I am more than proud to make your acquaintance. Across the foaming waves of the mighty Atlantic there is a land whose institootions—known to Mr. Sala—air not unlike your own, whose literature is your own up to a hundred years ago ["Hear, hear!" from Cornelius], whose language is the same as yours. We say hard things of each other, gentlemen; but the hard things are said on the low levels, not on the heights where you and your kindred spirits dwell. No, gentlemen,"—here he raised both arms and prepared for a rhetorical burst,—"when the American eagle, proudly bearing the stars and stripes—"

"Dinner on the table, sir!" bawled the head waiter, throwing open the doors with the grandest flourish and standing in the open doorway.

"Hear, hear!" cried Humphrey a little late, because he meant the cheer for the speech, and it sounded like a joy bell ringing for the announcement of dinner. Mr. Beck thought it rather rude, but he did not say so, and vented his wrath upon the waiter.

"Great Jehoshaphat!" he cried, "can't you see when a gentleman is on the stump? Who the devil asked you to shove in?"

"Never mind," said Jack irreverently. "Spout the rest after dinner."

A sigh of relief escaped the lips of all, and the party, headed, after some demur, by the host, who was escorted, one on each side, like a great man with his private secretary, by the Twins, passed into the dining-room.

Oddly enough, when their host passed on before them, the guests turned to each other, and the same extraordinary smile which Jack Dunquerque checked on their first appearance passed from one to the other. Why should Alfred Tennyson look in the face of Thomas Carlyle and laugh? What secret relationship is there between John Ruskin, Swinburne, and George Augustus Sala, that they should snigger and grin on catching each other's eyes? And, if one is to go on asking questions, why did Jack Dunquerque whisper in an agitated tone, "For Heaven's sake, Tom, and you fellows, keep it up?"

There was some little difficulty in seating the guests, because they all showed a bashful reluctance to sitting near their host, and crowded together to the lower end. At last, however, they were settled down. Mr. Carlyle, who, with a modesty worthy of his great name, seized the lowest chair of all—on the left of Jack Dunquerque, who was to occupy the end of the table—was promptly dragged out and forcibly led to the right of the host. Facing him was Alfred Tennyson. The Twins, one on each side, came next. Mr. Sala faced John Ruskin. The others disposed themselves as they pleased.

A little awkwardness was caused at the outset by the host, who, firm in the belief that Professor Huxley was in the Moody and Sankey line, called upon him to say Grace. The invitation was warmly seconded by all the rest, but the Professor, greatly confused, blushed, and after a few moments of reflection was fain to own that he knew no Grace. It was a strange confession, Gilead Beck thought, for a clergyman. The singers, however—Miss Claribelle, Signors Altotenoro, Bassoprofondo, and Mr. Plantagenet Simpkins—performed *Non nobis* with great feeling and power, and dinner began.

It was then that Gilead Beck first conceived, against his will, suspicion of the Twins. So far from being the backbone and stay of the whole party, so far from giving a lead to the conversation, and leading up to the topics loved by the guests, they gave themselves unreservedly and from the very first to "tucking in." They went at the dinner with the go of a Rugby boy—a young gentleman of Eton very soon teaches himself that the stomach is not to be trifled with. So did the rest. Considering the overwhelming amount of genius at the table, and the number of years represented by the guests collectively, it was really wonderful to contemplate the vigour with which all, including the octogenarian, attacked the courses, sparing none. Could it have been believed by an outsider that the author of *Maud* was so passionately critical over the wine? It is sad to be disillusioned, but pleasant, on the other hand, to think that you are no longer an outsider. Individually the party would have disappointed their host, but he did not allow himself to be disappointed. Mr. Beck expected a battery of wit. He heard nothing but laudation of the wine and remarks upon the cookery. No anecdotes, no criticism, no literary talk, no poetical enthusiasm.

"In my country, sir," he began, glancing reproachfully at the Twins, whose noses were over their plates, and feeling his way feebly to a conversation with Carlyle,—"in my country, sir, I hope we know how to appreciate what we cannot do ourselves."

Mr. Carlyle stared for a moment. Then he replied—

"Hope you do, Mr. Beck, I'm sure. Didn't know you'd got so good a *chef* at the Langham."

This was disheartening, and for a space no one spoke.

Presently Mr. Carlyle looked round the table as if he was about to make an utterance.

Humphrey Jagenal, who happened at the moment to have nothing before him, raised his hand and said solemnly, "Hush!" Cornelius bent forward in an attitude of respectful attention.

Said the Teacher—

"Clear mulligatawny's about the best thing I know to begin a dinner upon. Some fellows like Palestine soup. That's a mistake."

"The greatest minds," said Cornelius to the Poet Laureate, "condescend to the meanest things—"

"'Gad!" said Tennyson, "if you call such a dinner as this mean, I wonder what you'd call respectable."

Cornelius felt snubbed. But he presently rallied and went on again. It was between the courses.

"Pray, Mr. Carlyle," he asked, with the sweetest smile, "what was the favourite soup of Herr Teufelsdröckh?"

"Who?" asked the Philosopher. "Beg your pardon, Herr how much?"

"From your own work, Mr. Carlyle," Jack sang out from his end. It was remarkable to notice how anxiously he followed the conversation.

"Oh, ah! quite so," said Mr. Carlyle. "Well, you see, the fact is that— Jack Dunquerque knows."

This was disconcerting too, and the more because everybody began to laugh. What did they laugh at?

The dinner went on. Gilead Beck, silent and grave, sat at the head of the table, watching his guests. He ought, he said to himself, to be a proud man that day. But there were one or two crumpled rose-leaves in his bed. One thing was that he could not for the life of him remember each man's works, so as to address him in honeyed tones of adulation. And he also rightly judged that the higher a man's position in the world of letters, the more you must pile up the praise. No doubt the lamented George the Fourth, the Fourteenth Louis, and John Stuart Mill, grew at last to believe in the worth of the praise-painting which surrounded their names.

And then the Twins were provoking. Only one attempt on the part of Cornelius, at which everybody laughed. And nothing at all from Humphrey.

Carlyle and Tennyson, for their part, sat perfectly silent. Lower down—below the Twins, that is—Sala, Huxley, and the others were conversing freely, but in a low tone. And when Gilead Beck caught a few words it seemed to him as if they talked of horse-racing.

Presently, to his relief, John Ruskin leaned forward and spoke to him.

"I have been studying lately, Mr. Beck, the Art growth of America."

"Is that so, sir? And perhaps you have got something to tell my countrymen?"

"Perhaps, Mr. Beck. You doubtless know my principle, that Art should interpret, not create. You also know that I have preached all my life the doctrine that where Art is followed for Art's own sake, there infallibly ensues a distinction of intellectual and moral principles, while, devoted honestly and self-forgetfully to the clear statement and record of the facts of the universe, Art is always helpful and beneficial to mankind. So much you know, Mr. Beck, I'm sure."

"Well, sir, if you would not mind saying that over again—slow—I might be able to say I know it."

"I have sometimes gone on to say," pursued Mr. Ruskin, "that a time has always hitherto come when, having reached a singular perfection, Art begins to contemplate that perfection and to deduce rules from it. Now all this has nothing to do with the relations between Art and mental development in the United States of America."

"I am glad to hear that, sir," said Gilead Beck, a little relieved.

He looked for help to the Twins, but he leaned upon a slender reed, for they were both engaged upon the duckling, and proffered no help at all. They did not even seem to listen. The dinner was far advanced, their cheeks were red, and their eyes were sparkling.

"What is it all about?" Mr. Carlyle murmured across the table to Tennyson.

"Don't know," replied the Maker. "Didn't think he had it in him."

Could these two great men be jealous of Mr. Ruskin's fame?

"Your remarks, Mr. Ruskin," said the host, "sound very pretty. But I should like to have them before me in black and white, so I could tackle them quietly for an hour. Then I'd tell you what I think. I was reading, last week, all your works."

"All my works in a week!" cried Ruskin. "Sir, my works require loving thought and lingering tender care. You must get up early in the morning with them, you must watch the drapery of the clouds at sunrise when you read them, you must take them into the fields at spring-time and mark, as you meditate on the words of the printed page, the young leaflets breathing low in the sunshine. Then, as the thoughts grow and glow in the pure ether of your mind—hock, if you please—you will rise above the things of the earth, your wings will expand, you will care for nothing of the mean and practical—I will take a little more duckling—your faculties will be woven into a cunning subordination with the wondrous works of Nature, and all will be beautiful alike, from a blade of grass to a South American forest."

"There are very good forests in the Sierra Nevada," said Mr. Beck, who had just understood the last words; "we needn't go to South America for forests, I guess."

"That, Mr. Beck, is what you will get from a study of my works. But a week—a week, Mr. Beck!"

He shook his head with a whole library of reproach.

"My time was limited, Mr. Ruskin, and I hope to go through your books with more study, now I have had the pleasure of meeting you. What I was going to say was, that I am sorry not to be able to talk with you gentlemen on the subjects you like best, because things have got mixed, and I find I can't rightly remember who wrote what."

"Thank goodness!" murmured Mr. Tennyson, under his breath.

Presently the diners began to thaw, and something like general conversation set in.

About the grated Parmesan period, Mr. Beck observed with satisfaction that they were all talking together. The Twins were the loudest. With flushed faces and bright eyes they were laying down the law to their neighbours in Poetry and Art. Cornelius gave Mr. Tennyson some home truths on his later style, which the Poet Laureate received without so much as an attempt to defend himself. Humphrey, from the depth of his Roman experiences, treated Mr. Ruskin to a brief treatise on his imperfections as a critic, and Mr. Leighton to some remarks on his paintings, which those great men heard with a polite stare. Gilead Beck observed also that Jack Dunquerque was trying hard to keep the talk in literary grooves, though with small measure of success. For as the dinner went on the conversation resolved itself into a general discussion on horses, events, Aldershot, Prince's, polo, the drama from its lightest point of view, and such topics as might perhaps be looked for at a regimental mess, but hardly at a dinner of Literature. It was strange that the two greatest men among them all, Carlyle and Tennyson, appeared as interested as any in this light talk.

The Twins were out of it altogether. If there was one thing about which they were absolutely ignorant, it was the Turf. Probably they had never seen a race in their lives. They talked fast and a little at random, but chiefly to each other, because no one, Mr. Beck observed, took any notice of what they said. Also, they drank continuously, and their host remarked that to the flushed cheeks and the bright eyes was rapidly being added thickness of speech.

Mr. Beck rose solemnly, at the right moment, and asked his guests to allow him two or three toasts only. The first, he said, was England and America. Ile, he said briefly, had not yet been found in the old country, and so far she was behind America. But she did her best; she bought what she could not dig.

By special request of the host Mademoiselle Claribelle sang "Old John Brown lies a-mouldering in his grave."

The next toast, Mr. Beck said, was one due to the peculiar position of himself. He would not waste their time in telling his own story, but he would only say that until the Golden Butterfly brought him to Limerick City and showed him Ile, he was but a poor galoot. Therefore, he asked them to join him in a sentiment. He would give them, "More Ile."

Signor Altotenoro, an Englishman who had adopted an Italian name, sang "The Light of other Days."

Then Mr. Beck rose for the third time and begged the indulgence of his friends. He spoke slowly and with a certain sadness.

"I am not," he said, "going to orate. You did not come here, I guess, to hear me pay out chin music. Not at all. You came to do honour to an American. Gentlemen, I am an obscure American; I am half educated; I am a man lifted out of the ranks. In our country—and I think in yours as well, though some of you have got handles to your names—that is not a thing to apologise for. No, gentlemen. I only mention it because it does me the greater honour to have received you. But I can read and I can think. I see here tonight some of the most honoured names in England and I can tell you all what I was goin' to say before dinner, only the misbegotten cuss of a waiter took the words out of my mouth: that I feel this kindness greatly, and I shall never forget it. I did think, gentlemen, that you would have been too many for me in the matter of tall talk, but exceptin' Mr. Ruskin, to whom I am grateful for his beautiful language, though it didn't all get in, not one of you has made me feel my own uneducated ignorance. That is kind of you, and I thank you for it. It was true feeling, Mr. Carlyle, which prompted you, sir, to give the conversation such a turn that I might join in without bein' ashamed or makin' myself feel or'nary. Gentlemen, what a man like me has to guard against is shoddy. If I talk Literature, it's shoddy. If I talk Art, it's shoddy. Because I know neither Literature nor Art. If I pretend to be what I am not, it's shoddy. Therefore, gentlemen, I thank you for leavin' the tall talk at home, and tellin' me about your races and your amusements. And I'll not ask you, either, to make any speeches; but if you'll allow me, I will drink your healths. Mr. Carlyle, sir, the English-speaking race is proud of you. Mr. Tennyson, our gells, I'm told, love your poems more than any others in this wide world. What an American gell loves is generally worth lovin', because she's no fool. Mr. Ruskin, if you'd come across the water you might learn a wrinkle yet in the matter of plain speech. Mr. Sala, we know you already over thar, and I shall be glad to tell the Reverend Colonel Quagg of your welfare when I see him. Mr. Swinburne, you air young, but you air getting on. Professor Huxley and Mr. Darwin, I shall read your sermons and your novels, and I shall be proud to have seen you at my table. Mr. Cornelius and Mr. Humphrey Jagenal, I would drink your healths, too, if you were not sound asleep." This was unfortunately the case; the Twins, having succumbed to the mixture and quantity of the drinks almost before the wine went round once, were now leaning back in their chairs, slumbering with the sweetest of smiles. "Captain Ladds, you know, sir, that you are always welcome. Mr. Dunquerque, you have done me another favour. Gentlemen all, I drink your health."

"Jack," whispered Mr. Swinburne, "I call this a burning shame. He's a rattling good fellow, this, and you must tell him."

"I will, sometime; not now," said Jack, looking remorseful. "I haven't the heart. I thought he would have found us out long ago. I wonder how he'll take it."

They had coffee and cigars, and presently Gilead Beck began telling about American trotting matches, which was interesting to everybody.

It was nearly twelve when Mr. Beck's guests departed.

Mr. Carlyle, in right of his seniority, solemnly "up and spake."

"Mr. Beck," he said, "you are a trump. Come down to the Derby with me, and we will show you a race worth twenty of your trotting. Goodnight, sir, you've treated us like a prince."

He grasped his hand with a grip which had all its youthful vigour, and strode out of the room with the step of early manhood.

"A wonderful man!" said Mr. Beck. "Who would have thought it?"

The rest shook hands in silence, except Mr. Ruskin.

"I am sorry, Mr. Beck," he said meekly, "that the nonsense I talked at dinner annoyed you. It's always the way if a fellow tries to be clever; he overdoes it, and makes himself an ass. Goodnight, sir, and I hope we shall meet on the racecourse next Wednesday."

Mr. Beck was left alone with Jack Dunquerque, the waiter, and the Twins still sleeping.

"What am I to do with these gentlemen, sir?" asked the waiter.

Mr. Beck looked at them with a little disdain.

"Get John, and yank them both to bed, and leave a brandy-and-soda at their elbows in case they're thirsty in the night. Mr. Dunquerque and Captain Ladds, don't go yet. Let us have a cigar together in the little room."

They sat in silence for a while. Then Jack said, with a good deal of hesitation:

"I've got something to tell you, Beck."

"Then don't tell it tonight," replied the American. "I'm thinking over the evening, and I can't get out of my mind that I might have made a better speech. Seems as if I wasn't nigh grateful enough. Wal, it's done. Mr. Dunquerque, there is one thing which pleases me. Great authors are like the rest of us. They are powerful fond of racing; they shoot, they ride, and they hunt; they know how to tackle a dinner; and all of 'em, from Carlyle to young Mr. Swinburne, seem to love the gells alike. That's a healthy sign, sir. It shows that their hearts air in the right place. The world's bound to go on well, somehow, so long as its leaders like to talk of a pretty woman's eyes; because it's human. And then for me to hear these great men actually doing it! Why, Captain Ladds, it adds six inches to my stature to feel sure that they like what I like, and that, after all said and done, Alfred Tennyson and Gilead P. Beck are men and brothers."

XXVII

"Greater humanity."

The world, largely as it had unfolded itself to Phillis, consisted as yet to her wholly of the easy classes. That there were poor people in the country was a matter of hearsay. That is, she had caught a glimpse during a certain walk with Cæsar of a class whose ways were clearly not her ways, nor their manner of thought hers. She had now to learn—as a step to that wider sympathy first awakened by the butter-woman's baby—that there is a kind of folk who are more dangerous than picturesque, to be pitied rather than to be painted, to be schooled and disciplined rather than to be looked at.

She learned this lesson through Mrs. L'Estrange, whose laudable custom it was to pay periodical visits to a certain row of cottages. They were not nice cottages, but nasty. They faced an unrelenting ditch, noisome, green, and putrid. They were slatternly and out at elbows. The people who lived in them were unpleasant to look at or to think of; the men belonged to the riverside—they were boat-cads and touts; and if there is anyone pursuit more demoralising than another, it is that of launching boats into the river, handing the oars, and helping out the crew.

In the daytime the cottages were in the hands of the wives. Towards nightfall the men returned: those who had money enough were drunk; those who were sober envied those who were drunk. Both drunk and sober found scolding wives, squalid homes, and crying children. Both drunk and sober lay down with curses, and slept till the morning, when they awoke, and went forth again with the jocund curse of dawn.

Nothing so beautiful as the civilisation of the period. Half a mile from Agatha L'Estrange and Phillis Fleming were these cottages. Almost within earshot of a house where vice was unknown, or only dimly seen like a ghost at twilight, stood the hovels where virtue was impossible, and goodness a dream of an unknown land. What notion do they have of the gentle life, these dwellers in misery and squalor? What fond ideas of wealth's power to procure unlimited gratification for the throat do they conceive, these men and women whose only pleasure is to drink beer till they drop?

One day Phillis went there with Agatha.

It was such a bright warm morning, the river was so sparkling, the skies were so blue, the gardens were so sunny, the song of the birds so loud, the laburnums so golden, and the lilacs so glorious to behold, that the girl's heart was full of all the sweet thoughts which she had learned of others or framed for herself—thoughts of poets, which echoed in her brain and flowed down the current of her thoughts like the swans upon the river; happy thoughts of youth and innocence.

She walked beside her companion with light and elastic tread; she looked about her with the fresh unconscious grace that belongs to childhood; it was her greatest charm. But the contentment of her soul was rudely shaken—the beauty went out of the day—when Mrs. L'Estrange only led her away from the leafy road and took her into her "Row." There the long arms of the green trees were changed into protruding sticks, on which linen was hanging out to dry; the songs of the birds became the cry of children and the scolding of women, for flowers there was the iridescence on the puddles of soap-suds; for greenhouse were dirty windows and open doors which looked into squalid interiors.

"I am going to see old Mr. Medlicott," said Mrs. L'Estrange cheerfully, picking her accustomed way among the cabbage-stalks, wash-tubs, and other evidences of human habitation.

The women looked out of their houses and retired hastily. Presently they came out again, and stood everyone at her door with a clean apron on, each prepared to lie like an ambassador for the good of the family.

In a great chair by a fire there sat an old woman—a malignant old woman. She looked up and scowled at the ladies; then she looked at the fire and scowled; then she pointed to the corner and scowled again.

"Look at him," she growled in a hoarse crescendo. "Look at him, lying like a pig—like a pig. Do you hear?"

"I hear."

The voice came from what Phillis took at first to be a heap of rags. She was right, because she could not see beneath the rags the supine form of a man.

Mrs. L'Estrange took no notice of the old woman's introduction to the human pig. That phenomenon repeated his answer:

"I hear. I'm her beloved grandson, ladies. I'm Jack-in-the-Water."

"Get up and work. Go down to your river. Comes home and lies down, he does—yah! ye lazy pig; says he's goin' to have the horrors, he does—yah! ye drunken pig; prigs my money for drink—yah! ye thievin' pig. Get up and go out of the place. Leave me and the ladies to talk. Go, I say!"

Jack-in-the-Water arose slowly. He was a long-legged creature with shaky limbs, and when he stood upright his head nearly touched the rafters of the low unceiled room. And he had a face at sight of which Phillis shuddered—an animal face with no forehead; a cruel, bad, selfish face, all jowl and no front. His eyes were bloodshot and his lips were thick. He twitched and trembled all over—his legs trembled; his hands trembled; his cheeks twitched.

"'Orrors!" he said in a husky voice. "And should ha' had the 'orrors if I hadn't a took the money. Two-and-tuppence."

He pushed past Phillis, who shrank in alarm, and disappeared.

"Well, Mrs. Medlicott, and how are we?" asked Mrs. L'Estrange in a cheerful voice—she took no manner of notice of the man.

"Worse. What have you got for me? Money? I want money. Flannel? I want flannel. Physic? I want physic. Brandy? I want brandy very bad; I never wanted it so bad. What have you got? Gimme brandy and you shall read me a tract."

"You forget," said Agatha, "that I never read to you."

"Let the young lady read, then. Come here, missy. Lord, Lord! Don'tee be afraid of an old woman as has got no teeth. Come now. Gimme your hand. Ay, ay, ay! Eh, eh, eh! Here's a pretty little hand."

"Now, Mrs. Medlicott, you said you would not do that anymore. You know it is all foolish wickedness.

"Foolish wickedness," echoed the Witch of Endor. "Never after today, my lady. Come, my pretty lass, take off the glove and gimme the hand."

Without knowing what she did, Phillis drew off the glove from her left hand. The old woman leaned forward in her chair and looked at the lines. She was a fierce and eager old woman. Life was strong in her yet, despite her fourscore years; her eyes were bright and fiery; her toothless gums chattered without speaking; her long lean fingers shook as they seized on the girl's dainty palm.

"Ay, ah! Eh, eh! The line of life is long. A silent childhood! a love-knot hindered; go, on, girl—go on, wife and mother; happy life and happy age, but far away—not here—far away; a lucky lot with him you love; to sleep by his side for fifty years and more; to see your children and your grandchildren; to watch the sun rise and set from your door—a happy life, but far away."

WALTER BESANT AND JAMES RICE

She dropped the girl's hand as quickly as she had seized it, and fell back in her chair mumbling and moaning.

"Gimme brandy, Mrs. L'Estrange—you are a charitable woman—gimme brandy. And port-wine!—ah! lemme have some port-wine. Tea? Don't forget the tea. And Jack-in-the-Water drinks awful, he does. Worse than his father; worse than his grandfather—and they all went off at five-and-thirty."

"I will send you up a basket, Mrs. Medlicott. Come, Phillis, I have got to go to the next cottage."

But Phillis stayed behind a moment.

She touched the old woman on the forehead with her fingers and said softly—

"Tell me, are you happy? Do you suffer?"

"Happy? only the rich are happy. Suffer? of course I suffer. All the pore suffers."

"Poor thing! May I come and see you and bring you things?"

"Of course you may."

"And you will tell me about yourself?"

"Child, child!" cried the old woman impatiently. "Tell you about myself? There, there, you're one of them the Lord loves—wife and mother; happy life and happy death; childer and grandchilder; but far away, far away."

Mrs. Medlicott gave Phillis her first insight into that life so near and yet so distant from us. She should have been introduced to the ideal cottage, where the stalwart husband supports the smiling wife, and both do honour to the intellectual curate with the long coat and the lofty brow. Where are they—lofty brow of priest and stalwart form of virtuous peasant? Remark that Phillis was a child; the first effect of the years upon a child is to sadden it. Philemon and Baucis in their cot would have rejoiced her; that of old Mrs. Medlicott set her thinking.

And while she drew from memory the old fortune-teller in her cottage, certain words of Abraham Dyson's came back to her:

"Life is a joy to one and a burden to ninety-nine. Remember in your joy as many as you can of the ninety-nine.

"Learn that you cannot be entirely happy, because of the ninety-nine who are entirely wretched.

"When you reach this knowledge, Phillis, be sure that the Coping-stone is not far-off."

XXVIII

"Non possidentem multa vocaveris
Recte beatum."

The manner in which Mr. Cassilis conveyed his advice, or rather instructions, to Gilead Beck inspired the American with a blind confidence. He spoke slowly, grimly, and with deliberation. He spoke as one who knew. Most men speak as those who only half know, like the Frenchman who said, "Ce que je sais, je le sais mal; ce que j'ignore, je l'ignore parfaitement."

Mr. Cassilis weighed each word. While he spoke his eyes sought those of his friend, and looked straight in them, not defiantly, but meditatively. He brought Mr. Beck bills, which he made him accept; and he brought prospectuses, in which the American, finding they were English schemes, invested money at his adviser's suggestion.

"You have now," said Mr. Cassilis, "a very large sum invested in different companies; you must consider now how long to hold the shares—when to sell out in fact."

"Can't I sell my shares at once, if I please?"

"You certainly can, and so ruin the companies. Consider my undertaking to my friends on the allotment committees."

"Yes, sir."

"You forget, Mr. Beck, that you are a wealthy man. We do not manage matters in a hole and corner. The bears have sold on expectation of an allotment. Now as they have not got an allotment, and we have, they must buy. When such men as you buy largely, the effect is to run shares up; when you sell largely, you run them down."

Mr. Cassilis did not explain that he had himself greatly profited by this tidal influence, and proposed to profit still more.

"Many companies, perfectly sound in principle, may be ruined by a sudden decrease in the price of shares; a panic sets in, and in a few hours the shareholders may lose all. And if you bring this about by selling without concert with the other favoured allottees, you'll be called a black sheep."

Mr. Beck hesitated. "It's a hard thing—" he began.

His adviser went on:

"You have thus two things to think of—not to lose your own profit, and not to spread disaster over a number of other people by the very magnitude of your transactions."

This was a new light to Gilead.

"Then why sell at all? Why not keep the shares and secure the dividend? It's a hard hank, all this money."

And this was a new light for the financier.

Hold the shares? When they were, scores of them, at 16 premium? "You can certainly do that, if you please," he said slowly. "That, however, puts you in the simple position of investor."

"I thought I was that, Mr. Cassilis?"

"Not at all, Mr. Beck. The wise man distrusts all companies, but puts his hope in a rise or fall. You are not conversant with the way business is done. A company is formed—the A B C let us say. Before any allotment of shares is made, influential brokers, acting in the interest of the promoters, go on to the Stock Exchange, and make a market."

"How is that, sir?"

"They purchase as many shares as they can get. Persons technically called 'bears' in London or in New York sell these shares on the chance of allotment."

"Well?"

"To their astonishment they don't get any shares allotted. Millions of money in a year are allotted to clerks, Mr. Beck—to anybody, in fact—a market is established, and our shares figure at a pretty premium. Then begins the game of backing and filling—to and fro, backward and forward—and all this time we are gradually unloading the shares on the public, the real holders of everything."

"I begin to see," said Mr. Beck slowly.

"By this time you will perceive," Mr. Cassilis continued, "the bears are at the mercy of the favoured allottees. Then up go the shares; the public have come in. I recollect an old friend of mine who made a fortune on 'Change—small compared with yours, Mr. Beck, but a great fortune—used to say, talking of shares in his rather homely style, 'When they rise, the people buys; when they fa's, they lets 'em goes.' Ha, ha! it's so true. I have but a very poor opinion of the Isle of Holyhead Inland Navigation Company; but I thought their shares would go up, and I bought for you. You hold twenty out of fifty thousand. Wait till 'the people buys,' and then unload cautiously."

"And leave the rest in the lurch? No, sir, I can't do that."

"Then, Mr. Beck, I can advise you no more."

"I hold twenty thousand shares; and if I sell out, that company will bust up."

"I do not say so much. I say that if you sell out gradually you take advantage of the premium, and the company is left exactly where it was before you joined, to stand or fall upon its merits. But if you will sell your shares without concert with our colleagues in these companies you are in, we shall be very properly called black sheep."

"Then, Mr. Cassilis," said Gilead, "in God's name, let us have done with companies."

"Very well; as you please. You have only to give me a power of attorney, and I will dispose of all your shares in the best way possible for your interests. Will you give me that power of attorney?"

"Sir, I am deeply obliged to you for all the trouble you are taking."

"A power of attorney conveys large powers. It will put into my hands the management of your great revenues. This is not a thing to be done in a moment. Think well, Mr. Beck, before you sign such a document."

"I have thought, sir," said Gilead, "and I will sign it with gratitude."

"In that case, I will have the document—it is only a printed form, filled up and sent on to you for signature immediately."

"Thank you, Mr. Cassilis."

"And as for the shares in the various companies which you have acquired by my advice, I will, if you please, take them all over one with another at the price you gave for them, without considering which have gone up and which down."

They had all gone up, a fact which Mr. Cassilis might have remembered had he given the thing a moment's thought. The companies on paper were doing extremely well.

"Sir," said Mr. Beck, starting to his feet "you heap coals of fire on my head. When a gentleman like you advises me, I ought to be thankful, and not go worrying around like a hen in a farmyard. The English nation are the only people who can raise a man like you, sir. Honour is your birthright. Duty is your instinct. Truth is your nature. We, Americans, sir, come next to you English in that respect. The rest of the world are nowhere." He was walking backwards and forwards, with his hands in his pockets, while Mr. Cassilis looked at him through his gold eyeglasses as if he was a little amused at the outburst. "Nowhere, sir. Truth lives only among us. The French lie to please you. The Germans lie to get something for themselves. The Russians lie because they imitate the French and have caught the bad tricks of the Germans. Sir, no one but an Englishman would have made me the generous offer you have just made, and I respect you for it, Mr. Cassilis, I respect you, sir."

Gabriel Cassilis looked a little, a very little, confused at all these compliments. Then he held out his hand.

"My dear friend, the respect is mutual," he said, with a forced smile. "Do not, however, act always upon your belief in the honesty of Englishmen. It may lead you into mischief."

"As for the shares," said Beck, "they will stay as they are, if you please, or they will be sold, as you will. And no more companies, Mr. Cassilis, for me."

"You shall have no more," said his adviser.

In his pocket was a beautiful prospectus, brand new, of a company about to be formed for the purpose of lighting the town of La Concepcion Immaculata on the Amazon River in Brazil with gas. A concession of land had been obtained, engineers had been out to survey the place, and their prospects were most bright.

Now, he felt, that project must be released. He turned the paper in his fingers nervously round and round, and the muscles of his cheek twitched. Then he looked up and smiled, but in a joyless way. Mr. Beck did not smile. He was growing more serious.

"You shall have no more shares," said the adviser. "Those that you have already shall be disposed of as soon as possible. Remains the question, what am I to do with the money?"

"You have placed yourself," he went on, "in my hands by means of that promised power of attorney. I advised, first of all, certain shares my influence enabled me to get allotted to you. You have scruples about selling shares at a profit. Let us respect your scruples, Mr. Beck. Instead of shares, you will invest your money in Government stocks."

"That, sir," said Mr. Beck, "would meet my wishes."

"I am glad of it. There are two or three ways of investing money in stocks. The first, your way, is to buy in and take the interest. The next, my way, is to buy in when they are low and sell out when they go up."

"You may buy in low and sell out lower," said the astute Beck.

"Not if you can afford to wait. This game, Mr. Beck, as played by the few who understand it, is one which calls into play all the really valuable qualities of the human intellect."

Mr. Cassilis rose as he spoke and drew himself up to his full height. Then he began to walk backwards and forwards, turning occasionally to jerk a word straight in the face of his client, who was now leaning against the window with an unlighted cigar between his lips, listening gravely.

"Foolish people think it a game of gambling. So it is—for them. What is it to us? It is the forecasting of events. It is the pitting of our experience, our sagacity, against what some outsiders call chance and some Providence. We anticipate events; we read the future by the light of the present."

"Then it isn't true about Malachi," said Mr. Beck. "And he wasn't the last prophet."

Mr. Cassilis went on without regarding this observation:

"There is no game in the world so well worth playing. Politics? You stake your reputation on the breath of the mob. War? You throw away your life at the stockade of savages before you can learn it. Trade? It is the lower branch of the game of speculation. In this game those who have cool heads and iron nerve win. To lose your head for a moment is to lose the results of a lifetime—unless," he murmured, as if to himself—"unless you can wait."

"Well, sir," said Gilead, "I am a scholar, and I learn something new everyday. Do you wish me to learn this game? It seems to me—"

"You?" Contempt that could not be repressed flashed for a moment across the thin features of the speculator. "You? No. Perhaps, Mr. Beck, I do not interest you." He resumed his habitually cold manner, and went on: "I propose, however, to give you my assistance in investing your money, to such advantage as I can, in English and foreign stocks, including railway companies, but not in the shares of newly-formed trading companies."

"Sir, that is very kind."

"You trust me, then, Mr. Beck?"

Again the joyless smile, which gleamed for a moment on his lips and disappeared.

"That is satisfactory to both of us," he said. "And I will send up the power of attorney today."

Mr. Cassilis departed. By the morning's work he had acquired absolute control over a quarter of a million of money. Before this he had influence, but he required persuasion for each separate transaction. Now he had this great fortune entirely in his own control. It was to be the same as his own. And by its means he had the power which every financier wants—that of waiting. He could wait. And Gilead Beck, this man of unparalleled sharpness and unequalled experience, was a Fool.

We have been Christians for nearly two thousand years, and yet he who trusts another man is a Fool. It seems odd.

Mr. Cassilis felt young again. He held his head erect as he walked down the steps of the Langham Hotel. He lost his likeness to old Father Time, or at least resembled that potentate in his younger days, when he used to accommodate himself to people, moving slowly for the happy, sometimes sitting down for a few weeks in the case of young lovers, and galloping for the miserable. He strode across the hall with the gait of a Field-Marshal Commanding-in-Chief, and drove off to the City with the courage of five-and-twenty and the wisdom of sixty.

Before him stretched an endless row of successes, bigger than anything he had ever yet tried. For him the glory of the *coup* and the profit; for Gilead Beck the interest on his money.

In his inner room, after glancing at the pile of letters and telegrams, noting instructions, and reserving a few for private reply, he rang his bell.

The private secretary of Mr. Gabriel Cassilis did not disdain personally to answer that bell. He was a middle-aged man, with a sleek appearance, and a face which, being fat, shiny, and graced only with a slight fringe of whisker lying well behind, somehow conveyed the impression of a Particular Baptist who was also in the oil-trade. That was not the case, because Mr. Mowll was a member of the Church of England and a sidesman. He lived at Tulse Hill, and was a highly-respectable man. Mr. Cassilis gave him a fair salary, and a small amount—a very small amount—of his confidence. He also, when anything good in a humble way offered, tossed the information to his secretary, who was thus enabled to add materially to his salary.

In the outer world Mr. Mowll was the right-hand man of Gabriel Cassilis, his factotum, and the man, according to some, by whose advice he walked. Gabriel Cassilis walked by no man's advice save his own.

"For you, Mowll," said his employer briefly. "These I will attend to. Telegraph to—wherever his address is—to the man Wylie—the writing man"—newspaper people and writers of articles were "writing men" to Gabriel Cassilis—"I want him at once."

Then he absorbed himself again in his papers.

When he was left alone he pulled some printed documents out of a drawer, and compared them with letters which had the New York post-mark upon them. He read carefully, and made notes at various points with a stump of a blue crayon pencil. And he was still engaged on them when, half an hour later, his secretary asked him through a tube whether he would see Mr. Wylie.

Mr. Wylie was an elderly man—a man of sixty—and he was a man on whose face many years of rum-and-water were beginning to tell. He was a man of letters, as he said himself; he had some kind of name, in virtue of certain good things he had written, in his early manhood, before the rum-and-water period set in. Now he went up and down, doing odd jobs of literary work, such as are always wanting someone to do them in this great city. He was a kind of literary cab.

"You are free today, Mr. Wylie?"

"I am, Mr. Cassilis."

"Good. Do you remember last year writing a short political pamphlet—I think at my suggestion—on the prospects of Patagonian bond-holders?"

"You gave me all the information, you know."

"That is, you found the papers in my outer office, to which all the world has access, and on them you based your opinion."

"Quite so," said the pamphleteer. "I also found five-and-twenty pounds in gold on your secretary's table the day after the pamphlet appeared."

"Ah! Possibly—perhaps my secretary had private reasons of his own for—"

"Let us talk business, Mr. Cassilis," said the author a little roughly. "You want me to do something. What is it?"

"Do you know the affairs of Eldorado?"

"I have heard of Eldorado bonds. Of course, I have no bonds either of Eldorado or any other stock."

"I have here certain papers—published papers—on the resources of the country," said Mr. Cassilis. "I think it might pay a clever man to read them. He would probably arrive at the conclusion that the Republic, with its present income, cannot hope to pay its dividends—"

"Must smash up, in short."

"Do not interrupt. But with any assurance of activity and honesty in the application of its borrowed money, there seems, if this paper is correct—it is published in New York—no doubt that the internal resources would be more than sufficient to carry the State triumphantly through any difficulty."

"Is it a quick job, or a job that may wait?"

"I dislike calling things jobs, Mr. Wylie. I give you a suggestion which may or may not be useful. If it is useful—it is now half-past twelve o'clock—the pamphlet should be advertised in tomorrow's papers, in the printer's hand by four, and ready on every counter by ten o'clock in the morning. Make your own arrangements with printers, and call on me tomorrow with the pamphlet. On me, mind, not Mr. Mowll."

"Yes—and—and—"

"And, perhaps, if the pamphlet is clever, and expresses a just view of Eldorado and its obligations, there may be double the sum that you once found on my secretary's table."

Mr. Wylie grasped the papers and departed.

The country of Eldorado is one of the many free, happy, virtuous, and enlightened republics of Central America. It was constituted in the year 1839, after the Confederation broke up. During the thirty years which form its history, it has enjoyed the rule of fifteen Presidents. Don Rufiano Grechyto, its present able administrator, a half-blood Indian by birth, has sat upon the chair of state for nearly a year and a half, and approaches the period of two years, beyond which no previous President has reigned. He is accordingly ill at ease. Those who survive of his fourteen predecessors await his deposition, and expect him shortly in their own happy circle, where they sit like Richard II, and talk of royal misfortunes. Eldorado is a richly-endowed country to look at. It has mountains where a few inches of soil separate the feet of the rare wayfarer from rich lodes of silver; forests of mahogany cover its plains; indigo and tobacco flourish in its valleys; everywhere roam cattle waiting to be caught and sent to the London market. Palms and giant tree-ferns rise in its woods; creepers of surpassing beauty hang from tree to tree; in its silent recesses stand, covered with inscriptions which no man can read, the ruins of a perished civilization. Among these ruins roam the half-savage Indians who form nine-tenths of the population. And in the hot seaboard towns loll and lie the languid whites and half-castes who form the governing class. They never do govern at all; they never improve; they never work; they are a worthless hopeless race; they hoard their energies for the excitement of a pronunciamiento; their favourite occupation is a game of monte; they consider thought a wicked waste of energy, save for purposes of cheating. They ought all, and without exception, to be rubbed out. And it is most unfortunate, in the interests of humanity, that their only strong feeling is an objection to be rubbed out. Otherwise we could plant in Eldorado a colony of Germans; kill the pythons, alligators, jaguars, and other impediments to free civilisation; open up the mines, and make it a country green with sugar-canes and as sweet as Rimmel's shop by reason of its spicy breezes. There are about five thousand of the dominant class; they possess altogether a revenue of about £60,000 a year, a good deal less than a first-class fortune in England. As every man of the five thousand likes to have his share of the £60,000 there is not much saved in the year. Consequently, when one reads that the Republic of Eldorado owes the people of Great Britain and France, the only two European States which have money to lend, the sum of six millions, one feels sorry for the people of Eldorado. It must be a dreadful thing for a high-minded republican to have so little and to owe so much. Fancy a man with £600 a year in debt to the tune of £60,000.

It all grew by degrees. Formerly the Eldoradians owed nothing. In those days champagne was unknown, claret never seen, and the native drink was rum. Nothing can be better for the natives than their rum, because it kills them quickly, and so rids the earth of a pestilent race. In an evil moment it came into the head of an enterprising Eldoradian President to get up a loan. He asked for a million, which is, of course, a trifle to a nation which has nothing, does nothing, and saves nothing. They got so much of their million as enabled them to raise everybody's salary and the pay of the standing army, also to make the dividend certain for a few years. After this satisfactory transaction, somebody boldly ordered the importation of a few cases of brandy. The descent of Avernus is easy and pleasant. Next year they asked for two millions and a half. They got this small trifle conceded to them on advantageous terms—10 percent, which is nothing to a Republic with £60,000 a year, and the stock at 60. The pay of every official was doubled, the army had new shirts issued, and there were fireworks at San Mercurio, the principal town. They promised to build railways leading from nowhere into continental space, to carry passengers who did not exist, and goods not yet invented. The same innovator who had introduced the brandy now went farther, and sent for claret and champagne. Then they asked for more loans, and went ahead quite like a First-class Power.

When there was no more money to pay the dividends with, and no more loans to be raised, Eldorado busted up.

The gallant officers who commanded the standing army are now shirtless and bootless; the men of the standing army have disappeared; grass grows around the house of the importer of European luxuries; but content has not returned to San Mercurio. The empty bottles remain to remind the populace of lost luxuries; the national taste in drink is hopelessly perverted; San Mercurio is ill at ease; and Don Rufiano trembles in his marble palace.

But a year ago the country was not quite played out. There seemed a chance yet to those who had not the materials at hand for a simple sum in Arithmetic.

The next morning saw the appearance of the pamphlet—a short but telling pamphlet of thirty-two pages—called "Eldorado and her Resources. Addressed to the Holders of Eldorado Stock, by Oliver St. George Wylie."

The author took a gloomy but not a despairing view. He mentioned that where there was no revenue there could be no dividends. Therefore, he said, it behooved Eldorado stock-holders to be sure that something was being done with their money. Then he gave pages of facts and figures which proved the utter insolvency of the State unless something could be done. And he then proceeded to point out the amazing resources of the country, could only a little energy be introduced into the Council. He drew a lively picture of millions of acres, the finest ground in the world, planted with sugar-cane; forests of mahogany; silver mines worked by contented and laborious Indians; ports crowded with merchant fleets, each returning home with rich argosies; and a luxurious capital of marble made beautiful by countless palaces.

At eleven Mr. Wylie called on Gabriel Cassilis again. He brought with him his pamphlet.

"I have read it already," said Mr. Cassilis. "It is on the whole well done, and expresses my own view, in part. But I think you have piled it up too much towards the end."

"Why did you not give me clearer instructions, then?"

"I dare say it will have a success. Meantime," said the financier, pushing over a little bag, "you can count that. There ought to be fifty sovereigns. Good-morning, Mr. Wylie."

"Good-morning, Mr. Cassilis. I don't know"—he turned the bag of gold over in his hands—"I don't know; thirty years ago I should have looked with suspicion on such a job as this; thirty years ago—"

"Good-morning, Mr. Wylie."

"Thirty years ago I should have thought that a man who could afford fifty pounds for a pamphlet—"

"Well?"

"Well—that he had his little game. And I should have left that man to play it by himself. Good-morning again, Mr. Cassilis. You know my address, I believe, in case of any other little job turning up."

That afternoon Eldorado stock went down. It was lucky for Mr. Gabriel Cassilis, because he wished to buy—and did—largely.

XXIX

"It is my lady! Oh, it is my love—
Would that she knew she were!"

J ack is late," said Phillis.

She was making the prettiest picture that painter ever drew, standing in the sunlight, with the laburnums and lilacs behind her in their fresh spring glory. Her slender and shapely figure, clad in its black riding habit, stood out in relief against the light and shade of the newly-born foliage; she wore one of the pretty hats of last year's fashion, and in her hand she carried the flowers she had just been gathering. Her face was in repose, and in its clear straight lines might have served for a model Diana, chaste and fair. It was habitually rather a grave face, that came of much solitude and long companionship with an old man. And the contrast was all the greater when she lit up with a smile that was like a touch of tender sunshine upon her face and gave the statue a soul. But now she stood waiting, and her eyes were grave.

Agatha L'Estrange watched her from her shady garden seat. The girl's mind was full of the hidden possibilities of things—for herself; the elder lady—to whom life had given, as she thought, all it had to give—was thinking of these possibilities too—for her charge. Only they approached the subject from different points of view. To the girl, an eager looking forward to new joys which were yet not the ordinary joys of London maidenhood. Each successive day was to reveal to her more secrets of life; she was born for happiness and sunshine; the future was brighter in some dim and misty fashion, far brighter than the present; it was like a picture by Claude, where the untrained eye sees nothing but mist and vapour, rich with gorgeous colour, blurring the outlines which lie behind. But the elder lady saw the present and feared the future. Every man thinks he will succeed till he finds out his own weakness; every woman thinks she is born for the best of this world's gifts—to happiness, to be lapped in warmth and comfort, to be clothed with the love of husband and children as with a garment. Some women get it. Agatha had not received this great happiness. A short two years of colourless wedded life with a man old enough to be her father, and twenty years of widowhood. It was not the lot she might have chosen; not the lot she wished for Phillis. And then she thought of Jack Dunquerque. Oddly enough, the future, in whatever shape it was present to the brain of Phillis, was never without the figure of Jack Dunquerque.

"Jack is late," said Phillis.

"Come here, dear, out of the sun; we must take a little care of our complexion. Sit down and let us talk."

Agatha took Phillis's hand in hers, as the girl sat upon the grass at her feet.

"Let us talk. Tell me, dear Phillis, don't you think a little too much about Mr. Dunquerque?"

"About Jack? How can I, Agatha? Is he not my first friend?"

She did not blush; she did not hesitate; she looked frankly in Agatha's face. The light of love which the elder lady expected was not there yet.

"Changed as you are, my dear, in somethings, you are only a child still," said Agatha.

"Am I only a child?" asked Phillis. "Tell me why you say so now, dear Agatha. Is it because I am fond of Jack?"

"No, dear," Mrs. L'Estrange laughed. What was to be said to this *jeune ingénue*? "Not quite that."

"I have learned a great deal—oh, a great deal—since I came here. How ignorant I was! How foolish!"

"What have you learned, Phillis?"

"Well, about people. They are not all so interesting as they seemed at first. Agatha, it seems like a loss not to think so much of people as I did. Some are foolish, like the poor curate—are all curates foolish, I wonder?— some seem to say one thing and mean another, like Mr. Cassilis; some do not seem to care for anything in the world except dancing; some talk as if china was the only thing worth living for; but some are altogether lovely and charming, like yourself, my dear."

"Go on, Phillis, and tell me more."

"Shall I? I am foolish, perhaps, but most of our visitors have disappointed me. How *can* people talk about china as if the thing could be *felt*, like a picture? What is it they like so much in dancing and skating-rinks, and they prefer them to music and painting, and—and— the beautiful river?"

"Wait till you come out, dear Phillis," said Agatha.

For all the things in which young ladies do most delight were to her a vanity and foolishness. She heard them talk and she could not understand. She was to wait till she came out. And was her coming out to be the putting on of the Coping-stone?

"Jack is late," said Phillis.

It was a little expedition. Mrs. L'Estrange and Gilead Beck were to drive to Hampton Court, while Jack and Phillis rode. It was the first of such expeditions. In late May and early June the Greater London, as the Registrar calls it, is a marvel and a miracle of loveliness; in all the world there are no such meadows of buttercups, with fragrant hedges of thorn; there are no such generous and luxuriant growths of wisteria, with purple clusters; there are no such woods of horse-chestnuts, with massive pyramids of white blossom; there are no such apple-orchards and snow-clad forests of white blossomed plum-trees as are to be seen around this great city of ours. Colonials returned from exile shed tears when they see them, and think of arid Aden and thirsty Indian plains; the American owns that though Lake George with its hundred islets is lovely, and the Hudson River a thing to dream of, there is nothing in the States to place beside the incomparable result of wealth and loving care which the outlying suburbs of south and western London show.

If it was new to Phillis—if every new journey made her pulses bound, and every new place seen was another revelation—it was also new to the American, who looked so grave and smiled so kindly, and sometimes made such funny observations.

Gilead Beck was more silent with the ladies than with Jack, which was natural, because his only experience of the sex was that uncomfortable episode in his life when he taught school and fought poor Pete Conkling. And to this adventurer, this man who had been at all trades—who had roamed about the world for thirty years; who had habitually consorted with miners and adventurers, whom the comic American books have taught us to regard as a compound of drunkard, gambler, buccaneer, blasphemer, and weeping sentimentalist—his manner of life had not been able to destroy the chivalrous respect for women with which an American begins life. Only he had never known a lady at all until now; never any lady in America.

In spite of his life, this man was neither coarse nor vulgar. He was modest, knowing his defects, and he was humble. Nevertheless, he had the self-respect which none of his countrymen are without. He was an undeniable "ranker," a fact of which he was proud, because, if he had a weakness, it was to regard himself as another Cromwell, singled out and chosen. He had two languages, of one of which he made sparing use, save when he narrated his American experiences. This, as we have seen, was a highly ornamental tongue, a gallery of imagery, a painted chamber of decorated metaphor—the language of wild California, an *argot* which, on occasions, he handled with astounding vigour. The other was the tongue of the cultivated American. In England we bark; in the States they speak. We fling out our conversation in jerks; the man of the States shapes his carefully in his brain before he speaks. Gilead Beck spoke like a gentleman of Boston, save that his defective education did not allow him to speak so well.

His great terror was the word Shoddy. He looked at Shoddy full in the face; he made up his mind what Shoddy was—the thing which pretends to be what it is not, a branch of the great family which has the Prig at one end and the Snob at the other—and he was resolute in avoiding the slightest suspicion of Shoddy.

If he was of obscure birth, with antecedents which left him nothing to boast of but honesty, he was also soft-hearted as a girl, quick in sympathy, which Adam Smith teaches us is the groundwork of all morals, and refined in thought. After many years, a man's habitual thoughts are stamped upon his face. The face of Gilead Beck was a record of purity and integrity. Such a man in England would, by the power of circumstances, have been forced into taprooms, and slowly dragged downwards into that beery morass in which, as in another Malebolge, the British workman lies stupefied and helpless. Some wicked cynic—was it Thackeray?—said that below a certain class no English woman knows the meaning of virtue. He might have said, with greater truth, that below a certain class no Englishman knows the meaning of self-respect.

To go into that orderly house at Twickenham, where the higher uses of wealth were practically illustrated by a refinement new to the good ex-miner, was to this American in itself an education, and none the less useful because it came late in life. To be with the ladies, to see the tender graces of the elder and the sweetness of the younger, filled his heart with emotion.

"The Luck of the Golden Butterfly, Mrs. L'Estrange," he said, "is more than what the old squaw thought. It began in dollars, but it has brought me—this."

They were sitting in the garden, Agatha and Gilead Beck, while Jack Dunquerque and Phillis were watering flowers, or gathering them, or always doing something which would keep Jack close to the girl.

"If by 'this' you mean friendship, Mr. Beck," said Agatha, "I am very glad of it. Dollars, as you call money, may take to themselves wings and fly away, but friends do not."

It will be observed that Agatha L'Estrange had never seen reason to abandon the old-fashioned rules invented by those philosophers who lived before Rochefoucauld.

"I sometimes think I should like to try," said Gilead Beck. "Poor men have no friends; they have mates on our side of the water, and pals on yours."

"Mates and pals?" cried Phillis, laughing. "Jack, do you know mates and pals?"

"I ought to," said Jack, "because I'm poor enough."

"Friends come to rich folk naturally, like the fruit to the tree, or—or—the flower to the rose," Gilead added poetically.

"Or the mud to the wheel," said Jack.

"Suppose all my dollars were suddenly to vamose—I mean, to vanish away," Gilead Beck went on solemnly; "would the friends vanish away too?"

"Jack would not," said Phillis promptly, "and Agatha would not. Nor should I."

She held out her hand in the free frank manner which was her greatest charm. Gilead Beck took the little fingers in his big rough hand the bones of which seemed to stick out all over it, so rugged and hard it was, and looked in her face with the solemn smile which made Phillis trust in him, and raised her fingers to his lips.

Then she blushed with a pretty confusion which drove poor Jack to the verge of madness. Indeed, the ardour of his passion and the necessity for keeping silence were together making the young man thin and pale.

They were gradually exploring, this party of four, the outside gardens, parks, castles, and views of London. Of course, they were as new to Jack and Mrs. L'Estrange as they were to Phillis and the American. Jack knew Greenwich, where he had dined; and Richmond, where he had dined; and the Crystal Palace, where he had also dined, revealed to him one summer evening an unknown stretch of fair country; more than that he knew not.

Perhaps more exciting pleasures might have been found, but this simple party found their own unsophisticated delight in driving and riding through green lanes.

"Phillis will have to come out next year," said Agatha, half apologising to herself for enjoying such things. "We must amuse her while we can."

They went to Virginia Water, where Mr. Beck made some excellent observations on the ruins and on the flight of time, insomuch that it was really sad to discover that they were only, so to speak, new ruins.

They went to Hampton Court, where they strolled through the picture galleries and looked at the Lely beauties; walked up the long avenues, and saw that quaint old mediæval garden which lies hidden away at the side of the Palace, marked by few. Gilead Beck said that if he was the Queen and had such a place he should sometimes live in it, if only for the sake of giving a dinner in the great Hall. But Phillis liked best the gardens, with their old-fashioned flowers, and the peace which reigns perpetually in the quaint old courts. And Gilead Beck asked Jack privately if he thought the Palace might be bought, and if so, for how much.

They visited Windsor. Mr. Beck said that if he had such a location he should always live there; he speculated on the probable cost of erecting such a fortress on the banks of the Hudson River; and then he cast his imagination backwards up the stream of time and plunged into history.

Phillis allowed him to go on, while he jumbled kings, mixed up cardinals, and tried, by the recovery of old associations, to connect the venerable pile with the past.

"From one of those windows, I guess," he said, pointing his long arm vaguely round the narrow lattices, "Charles came out to be beheaded, while Oliver Cromwell spurted ink in his face. It was rough on the poor king. Seems to me, kings very often do have a rough time. And perhaps, too, that Cardinal Thomas à Beckett, when he told Henry IV that he wished he'd served his country as well as he'd loved his God, it was on this very terrace. Perhaps—"

"O Mr. Beck! when *did* you learn English history," cried Phillis.

Then, like a little pedant as she was, she began to unfold all that she knew about the old fortress and its history. Its history is not so grim as that of the Tower of London, which she had once narrated to Jack Dunquerque; but it has a picturesque story of its own, which the girl somehow made out from the bare facts of English history—all she knew. But these her imagination converted into living and indisputable truths, pictures whose only fault was that the lights were too bright and the shadows too intense.

Alas, this is the way with posterity! The dead are to be judged as they seem from such acts as have remained on record. The force of circumstances, the mixture of motives, the general muddle of good and bad together, are lost in the summing-up; and history, which after all only does what Phillis did, but takes longer to do it, paints Nero black and Titus white, with the clear and hard outline of an etching.

Gilead Beck, after the lecture, looked round the place with renewed interest.

"I am more ignorant than I thought," he said humbly. "But I am trying to read, Miss Fleming."

"Are you!" she cried, with a real delight in finding, as she thought, one other person in the world as ignorant of that art as herself. "And how far have you got?"

"I've got so far," he said, "that I've lost my way, and shall have to go back again. It was all through Robert Browning. My dear young lady,—" he said this in his most impressive tones,—"if you should chance upon one of his books with a pretty title, such as *Red Cotton Nightcap Country*, or *Fifine at the Fair*, don't read it, don't try it. It isn't a fairy story, nor a love story. It's a story without an end, it's a story told upsy-down; it's like wandering in a forest without a path. It gets into your brain and makes it go round; it gets into your eyes and makes you see ghosts. Don't you look at that book.

"Reading in a general way, and if you don't take too much of it, is a fine thing," he continued. "The difficulty is to keep the volumes separate in your head. Anybody can write a book. I've written columns enough in the *Clearville Roarer* for a dozen books; but it takes a man to read one."

"Ah, but it is different with you," said Phillis. "I am only in words of two syllables. I've just got through the first reading-book. 'The cat has drunk up all the milk.' I suppose I must go on with it, but I think it is better to have someone to read for you. I am sure Jack would read for me whenever I asked him."

"I never thought of that," said Gilead Beck. "Why not keep a clerk to read for you, and pay out the information in small chunks? I should like to tackle Mr. Carlyle that way."

"Agatha is reading a novel to me now," Phillis went on. "There is a girl in it; but somehow I think my own life is more interesting than hers. She belongs to a part of the country where the common people say clever things!—Oh, very clever things!—and she herself says all sorts of clever things."

"Mr. Dunquerque," interrupted Gilead Beck, who was not listening, "would read to you all the days of his life, I think, if you would let him."

Phillis made no reply. As she neither blushed, nor smiled, nor gave any of the ordinary signs of apprehension with which most young ladies would have received this speech, it is to be presumed that she did not take in the full meaning of it.

"There is one thing about Mr. Dunquerque," Gilead Beck went on, "that belongs, I reckon, to you English people only. He is not a young man—"

"Jack not a young man? Why, Mr. Beck—"

"Not what we call a young man. Our young men are sixteen and seventeen. Mr. Dunquerque is five-and-twenty. Our men of five-and-twenty are grave and full of care. Mr. Dunquerque is light-hearted and laughs. That is what I like him for."

"Yes; Jack laughs. I should not like to see Jack grave."

She spoke of him as if he were her own property. To be sure, he was her first and principal friend. She could talk to him as she could talk to no one else. And she loved him with the deep and passionless love, as yet, of a sister.

"Yes," said Gilead Beck, looking round him, "England is a great country. Its young men are not all mad for dollars; they can laugh and be happy; and the land is one great garden. Miss Fleming, that is the happiest country, I guess, whose people the longest keep their youth."

She only half understood him, but she looked in his face with her sweet smile.

"It is like a dream. That I should be walking here with you, such as you, in this grand place—I, Gilead P. Beck. To be with you and Mr. Dunquerque is like getting back the youth I never had: youth that isn't always thinkin' about the next day; youth that isn't always plannin' for the future; youth that has time to enjoy the sunshine, to look into a sweet gell's eyes and fall in love—like you, my pretty, and Mr. Dunquerque—who saved my life."

He added these last words as an after-thought, and as if he was reminded of some duty forgotten.

Phillis was silent, because his words fell upon her heart and made her think. It was not her youth that was prolonged; it was her childhood. And that was dropping from her now like the shell of the chrysalis. She thought how, somewhere in the world, there were people born to be unhappy, and she felt humiliated when she was selfishly enjoying what they could not. Somewhere in the world—and where? Close to her, in the cottages where Mrs. L'Estrange had taken her.

For until then the poor, who are always with us, were not unhappy, to Phillis, nor hungry, nor deserving of pity and sympathy; they were only picturesque.

They went to St. George's Chapel, after over-ruling Gilead Beck's objections to attending divine service—for he said he hadn't been to meetin' for more than thirty years; also, that he had not yet "got religion"—and when he stood in the stall under the banner of its rightful owner he looked on from an outsider's point of view.

The ceremonial of the ancient Church of England was to him a pageant and a scenic display. The picture, however, was very fine; the grand chapel with its splendor of ornamentation; the banners and heraldry; the surpliced sweet-voiced boys; the dignified white-robed clergy-men; the roll of the organ; the sunlight through the painted glass; even the young subaltern who came clanking into the chapel as the service began,—there was nothing, he said, in America which could be reckoned a patch upon it. Church in avenue 39, New York, was painted and gilded in imitation of the Alhambra; that was considered fine, but could not be compared with St. George's, Windsor. And the performance of the service, he said, was so good as to have merited a larger audience.

Jack Dunquerque, I grieve to say, did not attend to the service. He was standing beside Phillis, and he watched her with hungry eyes. For she was looking before her in a sort of trance. The beauty of the place intoxicated her. She listened with soft eyes and parted lips. All was artistic and beautiful. The chapel was peopled again with mailed knights; the voices of the anthem sang the greatness and the glory of England; the sunshine through the painted glass gave colour to the picture in her brain; and when the service was over she came out with dazed look, as one who is snatched too suddenly from a dream of heaven.

This too, like everything else, was part of her education. She had learned the beauty of the world and its splendours. She was to see the things she had only dreamed of, but by dreaming had wrapped in a cloud of coloured mist.

When was it to be completed, her education? Phillis waited for that Coping-stone for which Joseph Jagenal was vainly searching. She laughed when she thought of it, the mysterious completion of Abraham Dyson's great fabric. What was it?

She had not long to wait.

"I love her, Mrs. L'Estrange," said Jack Dunquerque passionately, on the evening of the last of their expeditions: "I love her!"

"I have seen it for sometime," Agatha replied. "And I wanted to speak to you before, but I did not like to. I am afraid I have been very wrong in encouraging you to come here so often."

"Who could help loving her?" he cried "Tell me, Mrs. L'Estrange, you who have known so many, was there ever a girl like Phillis—so sweet, so fresh, so pretty, and so good?"

"Indeed, she is all that you say," Agatha acknowledged.

"And will you be my friend with Colquhoun? I am going to see him tomorrow about it, because I cannot stand it any longer."

"He knows that you visit me; he will be prepared in a way. And—Oh, Mr. Dunquerque, why are you in such a hurry? Phillis is so nice and you are so young."

"I am five-and-twenty, and Phillis is nineteen."

"Then Phillis is so inexperienced."

"Yes; she is inexperienced," Jack repeated. "And if experience comes, she may learn to love another man."

"That is what all the men say. Why, you silly boy, if Phillis were to love you first, do you think a thousand men could make her give you up?"

"You are right: but she does not love me; she only likes me; she does not know what love means. That is bad enough to think of. But even that isn't the worst."

"What more is there?"

"I am so horribly, so abominably poor. My brother Isleworth is the poorest peer in the kingdom, and I am about the poorest younger son. And Colquhoun will think I am coming after Phillis's money."

"As you are poor, it will be a great comfort for everybody concerned," said Agatha, with good sense, "to think that, should you marry Phillis, she has some money to help you with. Go and see Lawrence Colquhoun, Mr. Dunquerque, and—and if I can help your cause, I will. There! Now let us have no more."

"They will make a pretty pair," said Mr. Gilead Beck presently to Mrs. L'Estrange.

"O Mr. Beck, you are all in a plot! And perhaps after all—and Mr. Dunquerque is so poor."

"Is that so?" Mr. Beck asked eagerly. "Will the young lady's guardian refuse the best man in the world because he is poor? No, Mrs. L'Estrange, there's only one way out of this muss, and perhaps you will take that way for me."

"What is it, Mr. Beck?"

"I can't say myself to Mr. Dunquerque, 'What is mine is yours.' And I can't say to Mr. Colquhoun—not with the delicacy that you would put into it—that Mr. Dunquerque shall have all I've got to make him happy. I want you to say that for me. Tell him there is no two ways about it—that Jack Dunquerque *must* marry Miss Fleming. Lord, Lord! why, they are made for each other! Look at him now, Mrs. L'Estrange, leanin' towards her, with a look half respectful and half hungry. And look at her, with her sweet innocent eyes; she doesn't understand it, she doesn't know what he's beatin' down with all his might: the strong honest love of a man—the best thing he's got to give. Wait till you give the word, and she feels his arms about her waist, and his lips close to hers. It's a beautiful thing, love. I've never been in love myself, but I've watched those that were; and I venture to tell you, Mrs. L'Estrange, that from the Queen down to the kitchen-maid, there isn't a woman among them all that isn't the better for being loved. And they know it, too, all of them, except that pretty creature."

XXX

"Pictoribus atque Poetis
Quidlibet audendi semper fuit æqua potestas."

With commissions"—Cornelius Jagenal spoke as if Gilead Beck was a man of multitude, signifying many, and as if one commission was a thousand—"with commissions pouring in as they should, Brother Humphrey—"

"And the great Epic, the masterpiece of the century about to be published in the Grand Style, brother Cornelius, the only style which is worthy of its merits—"

"Something definite should be attempted, Humphrey—"

"You mean, brother—"

"With regard to—"

"With regard to Phillis Fleming."

They looked at each other meaningly and firmly. The little table was between them; it was past twelve o'clock; already two or three soda-water bottles were lying on it empty; and the world looked rosy to the poetic pair.

Humphrey was the first to speak after the young lady's name was mentioned. He removed the pipe from his mouth, threw back his head, stroked his long brown beard, and addressed the ceiling.

"She is," he said, "she is indeed a charming girl. Her outlines finely but firmly drawn; her colouring delicate, but strongly accentuated; the grouping to which she lends herself always differentiated artistically; her single attitudes designed naturally and with freedom; her flesh-tints remarkably pure and sweet; her draperies falling in artistic folds; her atmosphere softened as by the perfumed mists of morning; her hair tied in the simple knot which is the admiration and despair of many painters;—you agree with my rendering, brother Cornelius"—he turned his reflective gaze from the ceiling, and fixed his lustrous eyes, perhaps with the least little look of triumph, upon his brother—"my rendering of this incomparable Work?"

He spoke of the young lady as if she were a picture. This was because, immediately after receiving his commission, he bethought him of reading a little modern criticism, and so bought the *Academy* for a few weeks. In that clear bubbling fount of modern English undefiled,

WALTER BESANT AND JAMES RICE

the Art criticisms are done with such entire freedom from cant and affectation that they are a pleasure to read; and from its pages every Prig is so jealously kept out, that the paper is as widely circulated and as popular as *Punch*; thus Humphrey Jagenal acquired a new jargon of Art criticism, which he developed and made his own.

Cornelius had been profiting by the same delightful and genial enemy to Mutual Admiration Societies. He was a little taken aback for a moment by the eloquence and fidelity of his brother's word-picture, but stimulated to rivalry. He made answer, gazing into the black and hollow depths of the empty fireplace, and speaking slowly as if he enjoyed his words too much to let them slip out too fast—

"She is all that you say, Humphrey. From your standpoint nothing could be better. I judge her, however, from my own platform. I look on her as one of Nature's sweetest poems; such a poem as defies the highest effort of the greatest creative genius; where the cadenced lines are sunlit, and as they ripple on make music in your soul. You are rapt with their beauty; you are saddened with the unapproachable magic of their charm; you feel the deepest emotions of the heart awakened and beating in responsive harmony. And when, after long and patient watching, the Searcher after the Truth of Beauty feels each verse sink deeper and deeper within him, till it becomes a part of his own nature, there arises before him, clad in mystic and transparent Coan robe, the spirit of subtle wisdom, long lying perdu in those magic utterances. She is a lyric; she is a sonnet; she is an epigram—"

"At least," interrupted Humphrey unkindly, cutting short his brother's freest flow, "at least she doesn't carry a sting."

"Then let us say an Idyl—"

"Cornelius, make an Idyl yourself for her," Humphrey interrupted again, because really his brother was taking an unfair advantage of a paltry verbal superiority. "Now that we have both described her—and I am sure, brother," he added out of the kindness of his heart, "no description could be more poetically true than your own—it would make even a stranger see Phillis standing in a vision before his eyes. But let us see what had better be done."

"We must act at once, Humphrey. We must call upon her at her guardian's, Mrs. L'Estrange, at Twickenham. Perhaps that lady does not know so many men of genius as to render the accession of two more to her circle anything but a pleasure and an honour. And as for our next steps, they must be guided by our finesse, by our knowledge of the world, our insight into a woman's heart, our—shall I say our power of intrigue, Humphrey?"

Then the Artist positively winked. It is not a gesture to be commended from an artistic point of view, but he did it. Then he chuckled and wagged his head.

Then the Poet in his turn also winked, chuckled, and wagged his head too.

"We understand each other, Humphrey. We always do."

"We must make our own opportunity," said the Artist thoughtfully. "Not together, but separately."

"Surely separately. Together would never do."

"We will go to bed early tonight, in order to be fresh tomorrow. Have you—did you—can you give me any of your own experiences in this way, Cornelius?"

The Poet shook his head.

"I may have been wooed," he said. "Men of genius are always run after. But as I am a bachelor, you see it is clear that I never proposed."

Humphrey had much the same idea in his own mind, and felt as if the wind was a little taken out of his sails. This often happens when two sister craft cruise so very close alongside of each other.

"Do not let us be nervous, Humphrey," the elder brother went on kindly. "It is the simplest thing in the world, I dare say, when you come to do it. Love finds out a way."

"When I was in Rome—" Humphrey said, casting his thoughts backwards thirty years.

"When I was in Heidelberg—" said Cornelius, in the same mood of retrospective meditation.

"There was a model—a young artist's model—"

"There was a little country girl—"

"With the darkest eyes, and hair of a deep blue-black, the kind of colour one seems only to read of or to see in a picture."

"With blue eyes as limpid as the waters of the Neckar, and light-brown hair which caught the sunshine in a way that one seldom seems to see, but which we poets sometimes sing of."

Then they both started and looked at each other guiltily.

"Cornelius," said Humphrey, "I think that Phillis would not like these reminiscences. We must offer virgin hearts."

"True, brother," said Cornelius with a sigh, "We must. Yet the recollection is not unpleasant."

They went to bed early, only concentrating into two hours the brandy-and-soda of four. It was a wonderful thing that neither gave the other the least hint of a separate and individual preference for Phillis. They were running together, as usual, in double harness, and so far as might be gathered from their conversation they were proposing to themselves that both should marry Phillis.

They dressed with more than usual care in the morning, and, without taking their customary walk, sat each in his own room till two o'clock, when Humphrey sought Cornelius in the Workshop.

They surveyed each other with admiration. They were certainly a remarkable pair, and, save for that little redness of the nose already alluded to, they were more youthful than one could conceive possible at the age of fifty. Their step was elastic; their eyes were bright; Humphrey's beard was as brown and silky, Cornelius's cheek as smooth, as twenty years before. This it is to lead a life unclouded and devoted to contemplation of Art. This it is to have a younger brother, successful, and never tired of working for his seniors.

"We are not nervous, brother?" asked Cornelius with a little hesitation.

"Not at all," said Humphrey sturdily, "not at all. Still, to steady the system, perhaps—"

"Yes," said Cornelius; "you are quite right, brother. We will."

There was no need of words. The reader knows already what was implied.

Humphrey led the way to the dining-room, where he speedily found a pint of champagne. With this modest pick-me-up, which no one surely will grudge the brethren, they started on their way.

"What we need, Cornelius," said Humphrey, putting himself outside the last drop—"What we need. Not what we wish for."

Then he straightened his back, smote his chest, stamped lustily with his right foot, and looked like a war-horse before the battle.

Unconscious of the approaching attack of these two conquering heroes, Phillis and Agatha L'Estrange were sitting in the shade and on the grass: the elder lady with some work, the younger doing nothing. It was a special characteristic with her that she could sit for hours doing nothing. So the modern Arabs, the gipsies, niggerdom in general, and all that large section of humanity which has never learned to read and write, are contented to fold their hands, lie down, and think away the golden hours. What they think about, these untutored tribes, the Lord only knows. Whether by degrees, and as they grow old, some faint intelligence of the divine order sinks into their souls, or whether they become slowly enwrapped in the beauty of the world, or whether their thoughts, always turned in the bacon-and-cabbage direction, are wholly gross and earthly, I cannot tell. Phillis's thoughts were still as the thoughts of a child, but as those of a child passing into womanhood: partly selfish, inasmuch as she consciously placed her own individuality, as every child does, in the centre of the universe, and made the sun, the moon, the planets, and all the minor stars revolve around her; partly unselfish, because they hovered about the forms of two or three people she loved, and took the shape of devising means of pleasing these people; partly artistic, because the beauty of the June afternoon cried aloud for admiration, while the sunshine lay on the lawns and the flower-beds, threw up the light leaves and blossoms of the passion-flower on the house-side, and made darker shadows in the gables, while the glorious river ran swiftly at her feet. The river of which she never tired. Other things lost their novelty, but the river never.

"I wish Jack Dunquerque were here," she said at last.

"I wish so, too," said Agatha. "Why did we not invite him, Phillis?"

Then they were silent again.

"I wish Mr. Beck would call," remarked Phillis.

"My dear, we do nothing but wish. But here is somebody—two young gentlemen. Who are they, I wonder?"

"O Agatha, they are the Twins!"

Phillis sprang from her seat, and ran to meet them with a most unaffected pleasure.

"This is Mr. Cornelius Jagenal," she said, introducing them to Agatha. "The Poet, you know." And here she laughed, because Agatha did not know, and Cornelius perked up his head and tried to look unconscious of his fame. "And this is Mr. Humphrey, the Artist." And then she laughed again, because Humphrey did exactly the same as Cornelius, only with an air of deprecation, as one who would say, "Never mind my fame for the present."

It was embarrassing for Mrs. L'Estrange, because she could not for her life recollect any Poet or Artist named Jagenal. The men and their work were alike unknown to her. And why did Phillis laugh? And what did the pair before her look so solemn about?

They were solemn partly from vanity, which is the cause of most of the grave solemnity we so much admire in the world, and partly because, finding themselves face to face with Phillis, they became suddenly and painfully aware that they had come on a delicate errand. Cornelius looked furtively at Humphrey, and the Artist glanced at the Poet, but neither found any help from his brother. Their courage, as evanescent as that of Mr. Robert Acres, was rapidly oozing out at their boots.

Phillis noted their embarrassment, and tried to put them at their ease. This was difficult; they were so inordinately vain, so self-conscious, so unused to anything beyond their daily experience, that they were as awkward as a pair of fantoccini. People who live alone get into the habit of thinking and talking about themselves; the Twins were literally unable to think or speak on any other subject.

Phillis, they saw, to begin with, was altered. Somehow she looked older. Certainly more formidable. And it was awkward to feel that she was taking them in a manner under her own protection before a stranger. And why did she laugh? The task which they discussed with such an airy confidence over the brandy-and-soda assumed, in the presence of the young lady herself, dimensions quite out of proportion to their midnight estimate. All these considerations made them feel and look ill at ease.

Also it was vexatious that neither of the ladies turned the conversation upon the subject nearest to each man's heart—his own Work. On the contrary, Phillis asked after Joseph, and sent him an invitation to come and see her; Mrs. L'Estrange talked timidly about the weather, and tried them on the Opera, on the Academy, and on the last volume of Browning. It was odd in so great an Artist as Humphrey that he had not yet seen the Academy, and in so great a Poet as Cornelius that he had not read any recent poetry. Then they tried to talk about flowers. The two city-bred artists knew a wall-flower from a cabbage and a rose from a sprig of asparagus, and that was all.

Phillis would not help either the Twins or Agatha, so that the former grew more helpless every moment. In fact, the girl was staring at them, and wondering to feel how differently she regarded men and manners since that first evening in Carnarvon Square, when they produced champagne in her honour, and drank it all up themselves.

She remembered how she had looked at them with awe; how, after a day or two, this reverence vanished; how she found them to be mere shallow wind-bags and humbugs, and regarded them with contempt; how she made fun of them with Jack Dunquerque; and how she drew their portraits.

And now—it was a mark of her advanced education—she looked at them with pity. They were so dependent on each other for admiration; they were so childishly vain; they were so full of themselves; and their daily life of sleep, drink, and boastful pretension showed itself to her experienced head as so mean and sordid a thing.

She came to the help of the whole party, and took the Twins for a walk among the flowers, flattering them, asking how Work got on, congratulating them on their good looks, and generally making things comfortable for them.

Presently she found herself on the sloping bank of the river, where she was wont to sit with Jack. Cornelius Jagenal alone was by her side. She looked round, and saw Humphrey standing before Mrs. L'Estrange, and occasionally glancing over his shoulder. And she noticed, then, a curiously nervous motion of her companion's hand; also that his cheek was twitching with some secret emotion. He looked older, too, she thought; perhaps that was the bright sunlight, which brought out the dells and valleys and the crow's-feet round his eyes.

He cleared his voice with an effort, and opened his mouth to speak, but shut it again, silent.

"You were going to say, Mr. Cornelius?"

"Yes. Will you sit down, Miss Fleming?"

"He is going to tell me about the *Upheaving of Ælfred*" thought Phillis. "And how does the Workshop get on?" she asked.

"Fairly well," he replied modestly. "We publish in the autumn. The work is to be brought out, you will be glad to learn, with all the luxury of the best illustrations, paper, print, and binding that money can procure."

"So that all you want is the poem itself," said Phillis, with a mischievous light in her eyes.

"Ye-es—" he winced a little. "As you say, the Epic itself alone is wanting, and that advances with mighty strides. My brother Humphrey—a noble creature is Humphrey, Miss Fleming—"

She bowed and smiled.

"Is he still hard at work? Always hard at work?" She laughed as she asked the question.

"His work is crushing him, Miss Fleming—may I call you Phillis?" He spoke very solemnly—"His work is crushing him."

"Of course you may, Mr. Cornelius. We are quite old friends. But I am sorry to hear that your brother is being crushed."

"Yesterday, Phillis—I feel to you already like a brother," pursued the Poet—"yesterday I discovered the secret of Humphrey's life. May I tell it to you?"

"If you please." She began to be a little bored. Also she noticed that Agatha wore a look of mute suffering, as if the Artist was getting altogether too much for her. "If you please; but be quick, because I think Mrs. L'Estrange wants me."

"I will tell you the secret in a few words. My brother Humphrey adores you with all the simplicity and strength of a noble artistic nature."

"Does he? You mean he likes me very much. How good he his! I am glad to hear it, Mr. Cornelius, though why it need be a secret I do not know."

"Then my poor brother—he is all loyalty, and brings you a virgin heart," (O Cornelius! and the model with the blue black hair!) "an unsullied name, and the bright prospects of requited genius—my brother may hope?"

Phillis did not understand one word.

"Certainly," she said; "I am sure I would like to see him hoping."

"I will tell him, sister Phillis," said Cornelius, nodding with a sunny smile. "You have made two men happy, and one at least grateful."

His mission was accomplished, his task done. It will hardly be believed that this treacherous bard, growing more and more nervous as he reflected on the uncertainty of the wedded life, actually came to a sudden resolution to plead his brother's cause. Humphrey was the younger. Let him bear off the winsome bride.

"It will be a change in our lives," he said. "You will allow me to have my share in his happiness?"

Phillis made no reply. Decidedly the Poet was gone distraught with overmuch reading and thought.

Cornelius, smiling, crowing, and laughing almost like a child, pressed her hand and left her, stepping with a youthful elasticity across the lawn. Humphrey, sitting beside Mrs. L'Estrange, was bewildering that good lady with a dissertation on colour à propos of a flower which he held in his hand. Agatha could not understand this strange pair, who looked so youthful until you came to see them closely, and then they seemed to be of any age you pleased to name. Nor could she understand their talk, which was pedantic, affected, and continually involved the theory that the speaker was, next to his brother, the greatest of living men.

If it was awkward and stupid sitting with Humphrey on a bench while he discoursed on Colour, it was still more awkward when the other one appeared with a countenance wreathed with smiles, and sat on the other side. Nor did there appear any reason why the one with the beard should suddenly break off his oration, turn very red in the face, get up, and walk slowly across the lawn to take his brother's place. But that is what he did, and Cornelius took up the running.

Humphrey sat down beside Phillis without speaking. She noticed in him the same characteristics of nervousness as in his brother. Twice he attempted to speak, and twice his tongue clave to the roof of his mouth.

"He is going to tell me that Cornelius adores me," she thought.

It was instinct. That was exactly what Humphrey—the treacherous Humphrey—had determined on doing. Matrimony, contemplated at close quarters and in the presence of the enemy, so to speak, lost all its charms. Humphrey thought of the pleasant life in Carnarvon Square, and determined, at the very last moment, that if either of them was to marry it should not be himself. Cornelius was the elder. Let him be married first.

"You are peaceful and happy here, Miss Fleming—may I call you Phillis?"

"Certainly, Mr. Humphrey. We are old friends, you know. And I am very happy here."

"I am glad"—he sighed heavily—"I am very glad indeed to hear that."

"Are you not happy, Mr. Humphrey? Why do you look so gloomy? And how is the Great Picture getting on?"

"The 'Birth of the Renaissance' is advancing rapidly—rapidly," he said. "It will occupy a canvas fourteen feet long by six high."

"If you have got the canvas, and the frame, and the purchaser, all you want now is the Picture."

"True, as you say, the Picture. It is all that I want. And that is striding—literally striding, *I* am happy, dear Miss Fleming, dear Phillis, since I may call you by your pretty Christian name. It is of my brother that I think. It is on his account that I feel unhappy."

"What is the matter with him?"

She tried very hard not to laugh, but would not trust herself to look in his face. So that he thought she was modestly guessing his secret.

"He is a great, a noble fellow, His life is made up of sacrifices and devoted to hard work. No one works so conscientiously as Cornelius. Now, at length the prospect opens up, and he will take immediately his true position among English poets."

"Indeed, I am glad of it."

"Thank you. Yet he is not happy. There is a secret sorrow in his life."

"Oh, dear!" Phillis cried impatiently, "do let me know it, and at once. Was there ever such a pair of devoted brothers?"

Humphrey was disconcerted for the moment, but went on again:

"A secret which no one has guessed but myself."

"I know what it is." She laughed and clapped her hands.

"Has he told you, Phillis? The secret of his life is that my brother Cornelius is attached to you with all the devotion of his grand poetic soul."

"Why, that was what I thought you were going to say!"

"You knew it?" Humphrey was as solemn as an eight-day clock, while Phillis's eyes danced with mirth. "And you feel the response of a passionate nature? He shall be your Petrarch. You shall read his very soul. But Cornelius brings you a virgin heart, a virgin heart, Phillis" (O Humphrey! and after what you know about Gretchen!). "May he hope that—"

"Certainly he may hope, and so may you. And now we have had quite enough of devotion and secrets and great poetic souls. Come, Mr. Humphrey."

She rose from the grass and looked him in the face, laughing. For a moment the thought crossed the Artist's brain that he had made a mess of it somehow.

"Now," she said, joining the other two, "let us have some tea, and be real."

Neither of them understood her desire to be real, and the Twins declined tea. That beverage they considered worthy only of late breakfast, and to be taken as a morning pick-me-up. So they departed, taking leave with a multitudinous smile and many tender hand-pressures. As they left the garden together arm-in-arm they straightened their backs, held up their heads, and stuck out their legs like the Knave of Spades. And they looked so exactly like a pair of triumphant cocks that Phillis almost expected them to crow.

"*Au revoir*," said Cornelius, taking off his hat, with a whole wreath of smiles, for a final parting at the gate.

"*Sans dire adieu*," said Humphrey, doing the same, with a light in his eyes which played upon his beard like sunshine.

"Phillis, my dear," said Agatha, "they really are the most wonderful pair I ever saw."

"They *are* so funny," said Phillis, laughing. "They sleep all day, and when they wake up they pretend to have been working. And they sit up all night. And, O Agatha! each one came to me just now, and told me he had a secret to impart to me."

"What was that, my dear?"

"That the other one adored me, and might he hope?"

"But, Phillis, this is beyond a joke. And actually here, before my very eyes!"

"I said they might both hope. Though I don't know what they are to hope. It seems to me that if those two lazy men, who never do anything but pretend to be exhausted with work, were only to hope for anything at all it might wake them up a little. And they each said that the other would bring me a virgin heart, Agatha. What did they mean?"

Agatha laughed.

"Well, my dear, it is a most uncommon thing to find in a man of fifty, and I should say, if it were true, which I don't believe, that it argued extreme insensibility. Such an offering is desirable at five-and-twenty, but very, very rare, my dear at any age. And at their time of life I should think that it was like an apple in May—kept too long, Phillis, and tasting of the straw. But then you don't understand."

Phillis thought that a virgin heart might be one of the things to be understood when the Coping-stone was achieved, and asked no more.

At the Richmond railway-station the brothers, who had not spoken a word to each other since leaving the house, turned into the refreshment-room by common consent and without consultation. They had, as usual, a brandy-and-soda, and on taking the glasses in their hands they looked at each other and smiled.

"Cornelius."

"Humphrey."

"Shall we"—the Artist dropped his voice, so that the attendant damsel might not hear—"shall we drink the health and happiness of Phillis?"

"We will, Humphrey," replied the Poet, with enthusiasm.

When they got into the train and found themselves alone in the carriage they dug each other in the ribs once, with great meaning.

"She knows," said the Poet, with a grin worthy of Mephistopheles, "that she has found a virgin heart."

"She does," said Humphrey. "O Cornelius, and the little Gretchen and the milkpails? Byronic Rover!"

"Ah, Humphrey, shall I tell her of the contadina, the black-eyed model, and the old wild days in Rome, eh? Don Giovanni!"

Then they both laughed, and then they fell asleep in the carriage, because it was long past their regular hour for the afternoon nap, and slept till the guard took their tickets at Vauxhall.

XXXI

"This fellow's of exceeding honesty,
And knows all qualities."

It was the night of the Derby of 1875. The great race had been run, and the partisans of Galopin were triumphant. Those who had set their affections on other names had finished their weeping, because by this time lamentation, especially among those of the baser sort was changed for a cheerful resignation begotten of much beer. The busy road was deserted, save for the tramps who plodded their weary way homeward; the moon, now in its third quarter, looked with sympathetic eye upon the sleeping forms which dotted the silent downs. These lay strewn like unto the bodies on a battle-field—they lay in rows, they lay singly; they were protected from the night-dews by canvas tents, or they were exposed to the moon-light and the wind. All day long these people had plied the weary trade of amusing a mob; the Derby, when most hearts are open, is the harvest-day of those who play instruments, those who dance, those who tumble, those who tell fortunes. Among these honest artists sleeps the 'prentice who is going to rob the till to pay his debt of honour; the seedy betting-man in a drunken stupor; the boy who has tramped all the way from town to pick up a sixpence somehow; the rustic who loves a race; and the sharp-fingered lad with the restless eye and a pocketful of handkerchiefs. The holiday is over, and few are the heads which will awake in the morning clear and untroubled with regrets, remorse, or hot coppers. It is two in the morning, and most of the revellers are asleep. A few, still awake, are at the Burleigh Club; and among these are Gilead Beck, Ladds, and Jack Dunquerque.

They have been to Epsom. On the course the two Englishmen seemed, not unnaturally, to know a good many men. Some, whose voices were, oddly enough, familiar to Gilead Beck, shook hands with him and laughed. One voice—it belonged to a man in a light coat and a white hat—reminded him of Thomas Carlyle. The owner of the voice laughed cheerfully when Beck told him so. Another made him mindful of John Ruskin. And the owner of that voice, too, laughed and changed the subject. They were all cheerful, these friends of Jack Dunquerque; they partook with affability of the luncheon and drank freely of the champagne. Also there was a good deal of quiet betting.

Jack Dunquerque, Gilead Beck observed, was the least adventurous. Betting and gambling were luxuries which Jack's income would not allow him. Most other things he could share in, but betting was beyond him. Gilead Beck plunged and won. It was a part of his Luck that he should win; but, nevertheless, when Galopin carried his owner's colours past the winning-post, Gilead gave a great shout of triumph, and felt for once the pleasures of the Turf.

Now it was all over. Jack and he were together in the smoking-room, where half a dozen lingered. Ladds was somewhere in the club, but not with them.

"It was a fine sight," said Gilead Beck, on the subject of the race generally; "a fine sight. In the matter of crowds you beat us: that I allow. And the horses were good: that I allow too. But let me show you a trotting-race, where the sweet little winner goes his measured mile in two minutes and a half. That seems to me better sport. But the Derby is a fine race, and I admit it. When I go back to America," he went on, "I shall institute races of my own—with a great National Dunquerque Cup—and we will have an American Derby, with trotting thrown in. There's room for both sports. What do you think, Mr. Dunquerque, of having sports from all countries?"

"Seems a bright idea. Take your bull-fights from Spain; your fencing from France; your racing from England—what will you have from Germany?"

"Playing at soldiers, I guess. They don't seem to care for any other game."

"And Russia?"

"A great green table with a pack of cards and a roulette. We can get a few Egyptian bonds for the Greeks to exhibit their favourite game with. We may import a band of brigands for the Italian sports. Imitation murder will represent Turkish Delights, and the performers shall camp in Central Park. It wouldn't be bad fun to go out at night and hunt them. Say, Mr. Dunquerque, we'll do it. A permanent Exhibition of the Amusements of all Nations. You shall come over if you like, and show them English fox-hunting. Where is Captain Ladds?"

"I left him hovering round the card-tables. I will bring him up."

Presently Jack returned.

"Ladds is hard at work at *écarté* with a villainous-looking stranger. And I should think, from the way Tommy is sticking at it, that Tommy is dropping pretty heavily."

WALTER BESANT AND JAMES RICE

"It's an American he's playing with," said one of the other men in the room. "Don't know who brought him; not a member; a Major Hamilton Ruggles—don't know what service."

Mr. Beck looked up quietly, and reflected a moment. Then he said softly to Jack—

"Mr. Dunquerque, I think we can have a little amusement out of this. If you were to go now to Captain Ladds, and if you were to bring him up to this same identical room with Major Hamilton Ruggles, I think, sir,—I do think you would see something pleasant."

There was a sweet and winning smile on the face of Mr. Beck when he spoke these words. Jack immediately understood that there was going to be a row, and went at once on his errand, in order to promote it to the best of his power.

"You know Major Ruggles?" asked the first speaker.

"No, sir, no—I can hardly say that I know Major Ruggles. But I think he knows me."

In ten minutes Ladds and his adversary at *écarté* came upstairs. Ladds wore the heavy impenetrable look in which, as in a mask, he always played; the other, who had a limp in one leg and a heavy scar across his face, came with him. He was laughing in a high-pitched voice. After them came Jack.

At sight of Mr. Beck, Major Ruggles stopped suddenly.

"I beg your pardon, Captain Ladds," he said. "I find I have forgotten my handkerchief."

He turned to go. But, Jack, the awkward, was in his way.

"Handkerchief sticking out of your pocket," said Ladds.

"So it is, so it is!"

By a sort of instinct the half-dozen men in the smoking-room seemed to draw their chairs and to close in together. There was evidently something going to happen.

Mr. Beck rose solemnly—surely nobody ever had so grave a face as Gilead P. Beck—and advanced to Major Ruggles.

"Major Ruggles," he said, "I gave you to understand, two days ago, that I didn't remember you. I found out afterwards that I was wrong. I remember you perfectly well."

"You used words, Mr. Beck, which—"

"Ay, ay—I know. You want satisfaction, Major. You shall have it. Sit down now, sit down, sir. We are all among gentlemen here, and this is a happy meeting for both of us. What will you drink?—I beg your pardon,

Mr. Dunquerque, but I thought we were at the Langham. Perhaps you would yourself ask Major Ruggles what he will put himself outside of?"

The Major, who did not seem quite at his ease, took a seltzer-and-brandy and a cigarette. Then he looked furtively at Gilead Beck. He understood what the man was going to say and why he was going to say it.

"Satisfaction, Major? Wal, these gentlemen shall be witnesses. Yesterday mornin', as I was walkin' down the steps of the Langham Hotel, this gentleman, this high-toned, whole-souled pride of the American army, met me and offered his hand. 'Hope you are well, Mr. Beck,' were his affable words. 'Hope you are quite well. Met you last at Delmonico's, in with Boss Calderon.' Now, gentlemen, you'll hardly believe me when I tell you I answered this politeness by askin' the Major if he had ever heard of a Banco Steerer, and if he knew the meanin' of a Roper. He did not reply, doubtless because he was wounded in his feelin's—being above all things a man of honour *and* the boast of his native country. I then left him with a Scriptural reference, which p'r'aps he's overhauled since, and now understands what I meant when I said that, if I was to meet him goin' around arm-in-arm with Ananias and Sapphira, I'd say he was in good company."

Here the Major jumped in his chair, and put his right hand to his shirt-front.

"No, sir," said Beck, unmoved. "I can tackle more'n one wild cat at once, if you mean fightin',' which you do not. And it's no use, no manner o' use, feelin' in that breast-pocket of yours, because the shootin' irons in this country are always left at home. You sit still, Major, and take it quiet. I'm goin' to be more improvin' presently."

"Perhaps, Beck," said Jack, "you would explain what a Banco Steerer and a Roper are."

"I was comin' to that, sir. They air one and the same animal. The Roper or the Banco Steerer, gentlemen, will find you out the morning after you land in Chicago or Saint Louis. He will accost you—very friendly, wonderful friendly—when you come out of your hotel, by your name, and he will remind you—which is most surprising, considerin' you never set eyes on his face before—how you have dined together in Cincinnati, or it may be Orleans, or perhaps Francisco, because he finds out where you came from last. And he will shake hands with you: and he will propose a drink; and he will pay for that drink. And presently he will take you somewhere else, among his pals, and he will strip you so clean that there won't be left the price of a four cent paper to throw around your face and hide your blushes. In London, gentlemen, they do, I believe, the confidence trick. Perhaps Major Ruggles will explain his own method presently."

But Major Ruggles preserved silence.

"So, gentlemen, after I'd shown my familiarity with the Ax of the Apostles, I went down town, thinkin' how mighty clever I was—that's a way of mine, gentlemen, which generally takes me after I've made a durned fool of myself. All of a sudden I recollected the face of Major Ruggles, and where I'd seen him last. Yes, Major, you *did* know me— you were quite right, and I ought to have kept Ananias out of the muss—you *did* know me, and I'd forgotten it. Those words of mine, Major, required explanation, as you said just now."

"Satisfaction, I said," objected the Major, trying to recover himself a little.

"Sir, you air a whole-souled gentleman; and your sense of honour is as keen as a quarter-dollar razor. Satisfaction you shall have; and if you are not satisfied when I have done with you, ask these gentlemen around what an American nobleman—one of the noblemen like yourself that we do sometimes show the world—wants more, and the more you shall git.

"You did know me, Major; but you made a little mistake. It was not with Boss Calderon that you met me, because I do not know Boss Calderon; nor was it at Delmonico's. And where it was I am about to tell this company."

He hesitated a moment.

"Gentlemen, I believe it is a rule that strangers in your clubs must be introduced by members. I was introduced by my friend Mr. Dunquerque, and I hope I shall not disgrace that introduction. May I ask who introduced Major Ruggles?"

Nobody knew. In fact, he had passed in with an acquaintance picked up somehow, and stayed there.

The Major tried again to get away. "This is fooling," he said. "Captain Ladds, do you wish me to be insulted? If you do, sir, say so. You will find that an American officer—"

"Silence, sir!" said Mr. Beck. "An American officer! Say that again, and I will teach you to respect the name of an American officer. I've been a private soldier myself in that army," he added, by way of explanation. "Now, Major Ruggles, I am going to invite you to remain while I tell these gentlemen a little story—a very little story—but it concerns you.

And if Captain Ladds likes when that story is finished, I will apologise to you, and to him, and to all this honourable company."

"Let us hear the story," said Jack. "Nothing could be fairer."

"Nothing!" echoed the little circle of listeners.

Beck addressed the room in general, occasionally pointing the finger of emphasis at the unfortunate Major. His victim showed every sign of bodily discomfort and mental agitation. First he fidgeted in the chair; then he threw away his cigarette; then he folded his arms and stared defiantly at the speaker. Then he got up again.

"What have I to do with you and your story? Let me go. Captain Ladds, you have my address. And as for you, sir, you shall hear from me tomorrow."

"Sit down, Major." Gilead Beck invited him to resume his chair with a sweet smile. "Sit down. The night's young. May be Captain Ladds wants his revenge."

"Not I," said Ladds. "Had enough. Go to bed. Not a revengeful man."

"Then," said Gilead Beck, his face darkening and his manner suddenly changing, "I will take your revenge for you. Sit down, sir!"

It was an order he gave this time, not an invitation, and the stranger obeyed with an uneasy smile.

"It is not gambling, Major Ruggles," Beck went on. "Captain Ladds' revenge is going to be of another sort, I reckon."

He drew close to Major Ruggles, and sitting on the table, placed one foot on a chair which was between the stranger and the door.

"Delmonico's, was it, where we met last? And with Joe Calderon— Boss Calderon? Really, Major Ruggles, I was a great fool not to remember that at once. But I always am weak over faces, even such a striking face as yours. So we met last when you were dining with Boss Calderon, eh?"

Then Mr. Beck began his little story.

"Six years ago, gentlemen,—long before I found my Butterfly, of which you may have heard,—I ran up and down the Great Pacific Railway between Chicago and Francisco for close upon six months. I did not choose that way of spendin' the golden hours, because, if one had a choice at all, a Pullman's sleeping-car on the Pacific Railway would be just one of the last places you would choose to pass your life in. I should class it, as a permanent home, with a first-class saloon in a Cunard steamer. No, gentlemen, I was on board those cars in an official capacity. I was conductor. It is not a proud position, not an office which you care to magnify; it doesn't lift your chin in the air and stick out your toes like the proud title of Major does for our friend squirmin' in the chair before us. Squirm on, Major; but listen, because this is interestin'. On those cars and on that railway there is a deal of time to be got through. I am bound to say that time kind of hangs heavy on the hands. You can't be always outside smokin'; you can't sleep more'n a certain time, because the nigger turns you out and folds up the beds; and you oughtn't to drink more'n your proper whack. Also, you get tired watchin' the scenery. You may make notes if you like, but you get tired o' that. And you get mortal tired of settin' on end. Mostly, therefore, you stand around the conductor, and you listen to his talk.

"But six years ago the dullness of that long journey was enlivened by the presence of a few sportsmen like our friend the Major here. They were so fond of the beauties of Nature, they were so wrapped up in the pride of bein' American citizens and ownin' the biggest railway in the world, that they would travel all the way from New York to San Francisco, stay there a day, and then travel all the way back again. And the most remarkable thing was, that when they got to New York again they would take a through ticket all the way back to San Fran. This attachment to the line pleased the company at first. It did seem as if good deeds was going to meet their recompense at last, even in this world, and the spirited conduct of the gentlemen, when it first became known, filled everybody with admiration.—You remember, Major, the very handsome remarks made by you yourself on the New York platform.

"Lord, is it six years ago? Why, it seems to me but yesterday, Major Ruggles, that I saw you standin' erect and bold—lookin' like a senator in a stove pipe hat, store boots, and go-to-meetin' coat—shakin' hands with the chairman. 'Sir,' you said, with tears in your eyes, 'you represent the advance of civilisation. We air now, indeed, ahead of the hull creation. You have united the Pacific and the Atlantic. And, sir, by the iron road the West and the East may jine hands and defy the tyranny of Europe.' Those, gentlemen, were the noble sentiments of Major Hamilton Ruggles.—Did I say, Major, that I would give you satisfaction? Wait till I have done, and you shall bust with satisfaction."

The Major did not look, at all events, like being satisfied so far.

"One day an ugly rumor got about—you know how rumours spread— that the Great Pacific Railroad was a big gamblin' shop. The enthusiastic travellers up and down that line were one mighty confederated gang. They were up to every dodge: they travelled together, and they travelled separate; they had dice, and those dice were loaded; they had cards, and those cards were marked; they played on the square, but behind every man's hand was a confederate, and he gave signs, so that the honest sportsman knew how to play. And by these simple contrivances, gentlemen, they always won. So much did they win, that I have conducted a through train in which, when we got to Chicago, there wasn't a five-dollar piece left among the lot. And all the time strangers to each other. The gang never, by so much as a wink, let out that they had met before. And no one could tell them from ordinary passengers. But I knew; and I had a long conversation with the Directors one day, the result of which—Major Ruggles, perhaps you can tell these gentlemen what was the result of that conversation."

The man was sallow. His sharp eyes gleamed with an angry light as he looked from one to the other, as if in the hope of finding an associate. There was none. Only Ladds, his adversary, moved quietly around the room and sat near to Gilead Beck, on the table, but *nearer the door*. The Major saw this manoeuvre with a sinking heart, because his pockets were heavy with the proceeds of the evening game.

"Well, gentlemen, a general order came for all the conductors. It was 'No play.' We were to stop that. And another general order was—an imperative order, Major, so that I am sure you will not bear malice—'If they won't leave off, chuck 'em out.' That was the order, Major, 'Chuck 'em out.'

"It was on the journey back from San Francisco that the first trouble began. You were an upright man to look at then, Major; you hadn't got the limp you've got now, and you hadn't received that unfort'nate scar across your handsome face. You were a most charmin' companion for a long railway journey, but you had that little weakness—that you *would* play. I warned you at the time. I said, 'Cap'en, this must stop.' You were only a Cap'en then. But you would go on. 'Cap'en,' I said, 'if you will not stop, you will be chucked out.' You will acknowledge, Major, that I gave you fair warnin'. You laughed. That was all you did. You laughed and you shuffled the cards. But the man who was playing with you got up. He saw reason. Then you drew out a revolver and used bad language. So I made for you.

"Gentlemen, it was not a fair fight. But orders had to be observed. In half a minute I had his pistol from him, and in two minutes more he was flyin' from the end of the train. We were goin' twenty miles an hour, and we hadn't time to stop to see if he was likely to get along somehow.

And the last I saw of Captain Ruggles—I beg your pardon, Major—was his two heels in the air as he left the end of the train. I s'pose, Major, it was stoppin' so sudden gave you that limp and ornamented your face with that beautiful scar. The ground was gritty, I believe?"

Everybody's eyes were turned on the Major, whose face was livid.

"Gentlemen," Mr. Beck continued, "that ærial flight of Captain Ruggles improved the moral tone of the Pacific Railroad to a degree that you would hardly believe. I don't think there has been a single sportsman chucked out since. Major Ruggles, sir, you were the blessed means, under Providence and Gilead P. Beck conjointly, of commencing a new and moral era for the Great Pacific Railroad.

"And now, Major, that my little story is told, may I ask if you are satisfied? Because if there is any other satisfaction in my power you shall have that too. Have I done enough for honour, gentlemen all?"

The men laughed.

"Now for a word with me," Ladds began.

"Cap'en," said Gilead Beck, "let me work through this contract, if you have no objection—Major Ruggles, you will clear out all your pockets."

The miserable man made no reply.

"Clear out everyone, and turn them inside out, right away."

He neither moved nor spoke.

"Gentlemen," Mr. Beck said calmly, "you will be kind enough not to interfere."

He pulled a penknife out of his pocket and laid it on a chair open. He then seized Major Ruggles by the collar and arm. The man fought like a wild cat, but Beck's grasp was like a vice. It seemed incredible to the bystanders that a man should be so strong, so active, and so skilled. He tossed, rather than laid, his victim on the table, and then, holding both his hands in one grip of his own enormous fist, he deliberately ripped open the Major's trousers, waistcoat, and coat pockets, and took out the contents. When he was satisfied that nothing more was left in them he dragged him to the ground.

On the table lay the things which he had taken possession of.

"Take up those dice," he said to Ladds; "Try them; if they are not loaded, I will ask the Major's pardon."

They were loaded.

"Look at these cards," he went on. "They are the cards you have been playing with, when you thought you had a new pack of club-cards. If they are not marked, I will ask the Major to change places with me."

They were marked.

"And now, gentlemen, I think I may ask Captain Ladds what he has lost, and invite him to take it out of that heap."

There was a murmur of assent.

"I lost twenty pounds in notes and gold," said Ladds. "And I gave an I O U for sixty more."

There were other I O U's in the heap, and more gold when Ladds had recovered his own. The paper was solemnly torn up, but the coin restored to the Major, who now stood, abject, white, and trembling, but with the look of a devil in his eyes.

"Such men as you, Major," said Gilead the Moralist, "are the curse of our country. You see, gentlemen, we travel about, we make money fast; we are sometimes a reckless lot; the miners have got pockets full; there's everything to encourage such a crew as Major Ruggles belonged to. And when we find them out, we lynch them.—Lynch is the word, isn't it, Major?—do you want to know the end of this man, gentlemen? I am not much in the prophetic line, but I think I see a crowd of men in a minin' city, and I see a thick branch with a rope over it. And at the end of that rope is Major Ruggles's neck, tightened in a most unpleasant and ungentlemanly manner.—It's inhospitable, but what can you expect, Major? We like play, but we like playin' on the square. Now, Major, you may go. And you may thank the Lord on your knees before you go to sleep that this providential interference has taken place in London instead of the States. For had I told my interestin' anecdote at a bar in any city of the Western States, run up you would have been. You may go, Major Ruggles; and I daresay Cap'en Ladds, in consideration of the damage done to those bright and shinin' store clothes of yours, will forego the British kicking which I see tremblin' at the point of his toes."

Ladds did forego that revenge, and the Major slunk away.

XXXII

*"Nulla fere causa est in qua non femina
litem Moverit."*

When Mr. Wylie, the pamphleteer, left Gabriel Cassilis, the latter resumed with undisturbed countenance his previous occupation of reading the letters and telegrams he had laid aside. Among them was one which he took up gingerly, as if it were a torpedo.

"Pshaw!" he cried impatiently, tossing it from him. "Another of those anonymous letters. The third." He looked at it with disgust, and then half involuntarily his hand reached out and took it up again. "The third, and all in the same handwriting. 'I have written you two letters, and you have taken no notice. This is the third. Beware! Your wife was with Mr. Colquhoun yesterday; she will be with him again today and tomorrow. Ask her, if you dare, what is her secret with him. Ask him what hold he has over her. Watch her, and caution her lest something evil befall you.—Your well-wisher.'

"I am a fool," he said, "to be disquieted about an anonymous slander. What does it matter to me? As if Victoria—she did know Colquhoun before her marriage—their names were mentioned—I remember hearing that there had been flirtation—flirtation! As if Victoria could ever flirt! She was no frivolous silly girl. No one who knows Victoria could for a moment suspect—suspect! The word is intolerable. One would say I was jealous."

He pushed forward his papers and leaned back in his chair, casting his thoughts behind him to the days of his stiff and formal wooing. He remembered how he said, sitting opposite to her in her cousin's drawing-room—there was no wandering by the river-bank or in pleasant gardens on summer evenings for those two lovers—

"You bring me fewer springs than I can offer you, Victoria"; which was his pretty poetical way of telling her that he was nearly forty years older than herself: "but we shall begin life with no trammels of previous attachments on either hand."

He called it—and thought it—at sixty-five, beginning life; and it was quite true that he had never before conceived an attachment for any woman.

"No, Mr. Cassilis," she replied; "we are both free, quite free; and the disparity of age is only a disadvantage on my side, which a few years will remedy."

This cold stately woman conducting a flirtation before her marriage? This Juno among young matrons causing a scandal after her marriage? It was ridiculous.

He said to himself that it was ridiculous so often, that he succeeded at last in persuading himself that it really was. And when he had quite done that, he folded up the anonymous document, docketed it, and placed it in one of the numerous pigeon-holes of his desk, which was one of those which shut up completely, covering over papers, pigeon-holes, and everything.

Then he addressed himself again to business, and, but for an occasional twinge of uneasiness, like the first throb which presages the coming gout, he got through an important day's work with his accustomed ease and power.

The situation, as Lawrence Colquhoun told Victoria, was strained. There they were, as he put it, all three—himself, for some reason of his own, put first; the lady; and Gabriel Cassilis. The last was the one who did not know. There was no reason, none in the world, why things should not remain as they were, only that the lady would not let sleeping dangers sleep, and Lawrence was too indolent to resist. In other words, Victoria Cassilis, having once succeeded in making him visit her, spared no pains to bring him constantly to her house, and to make it seem as if he was that innocent sort of *cicisbeo* whom English society allows.

Why?

The investigation of motives is a delicate thing at the best, and apt to lead the analyst into strange paths. It may be discovered that the philanthropist acts for love of notoriety; that the preacher does not believe in the truths he proclaims; that the woman of self-sacrifice and good works is consciously posing before an admiring world. This is disheartening, because it makes the cynic and the worldly-minded man to chuckle and chortle with an open joy. St. Paul, who was versed in the ways of the world, knew this perfectly when he proclaimed the insufficiency of good works. It is at all times best to accept the deed, and never ask the motive. And, after all, good deeds are something practical. And as for a foolish or a bad deed, the difficulty of ascertaining an adequate motive only becomes more complicated with its folly or its villainy. Mrs. Cassilis had everything to gain by keeping her old friend on the respectful level of a former acquaintance; she had everything to lose by treating him as a friend. And yet she forced her friendship upon him.

Kindly people who find in the affairs of other people sufficient occupation for themselves, and whose activity of intellect obtains a useful vent in observation and comment, watched them. The man was always the same; indolent, careless, unmoved by any kind of passion for any other man's wife or for any maid. That was a just conclusion. Lawrence Colquhoun was not in love with this lady. And yet he suffered himself to obey orders; dropped easily in the position; allowed himself to be led by her invitations; went where she told him to go; and all the time half laughed at himself and was half angry to think that he was thus enthralled by a siren who charmed him not. To have once loved a woman; to love her no longer; to go about the town behaving as if you did: this, it was evident to him, was not a position to be envied or desired. Few false positions are. Perhaps he did not know that Mrs. Grundy talked; perhaps he was only amused when he heard of remarks that had been made by Sir Benjamin Backbite; and although the brief sunshine of passion which he only felt for this woman was long since past and gone, nipped in its very bud by the lady herself perhaps, he still liked her cold and cynical talk. Colquhoun habitually chose the most pleasant paths for his lounge through life. From eighteen to forty there had been but one disagreeable episode, which he would fain have forgotten. Mrs. Cassilis revived it; but, in her presence, the memory was robbed somehow of half its sting.

Sir Benjamin Backbite remarked that though the gentleman was languid, the lady was shaken out of her habitual coldness. She was changed. What could change her, asked the Baronet, but passion for this old friend of her youth? Why, it was only four years since he had followed her, after a London season, down to Scotland, and everybody said it would be a match. She received his attentions coldly then, as she received the attentions of every man. Now the tables were turned; it was the man who was cold.

These social observers are always right. But they never rise out of themselves; therefore their conclusions are generally wrong. Victoria Cassilis was not, as they charitably thought, running after Colquhoun through the fancy of a wayward heart. Not at all. She was simply wondering where it had gone—that old power of hers, by which she once twisted him round her finger—and why it was gone. A woman cannot believe that she has lost her power over a man. It is an intolerable thought. Her power is born of her beauty and her grace; these may vanish, but the old attractiveness remains, she thinks, if only as a tradition. When she is no longer beautiful she loves to believe that her lovers are faithful still. Now Victoria Cassilis remembered this man as a lover and a slave; his was the only pleading she had ever heard which could make her understand the meaning of man's passion; he was the only suitor whom a word could make wretched or a look happy. For he had once loved her with all his power and all his might. Between them there was the knowledge of a thing which, if any knowledge could, should have crushed out and beaten down the memory of this love. She had made it, by her own act and deed, a crime to remember it. And yet, in spite of all, she could not bring herself to remember that the old power was dead. She tried to bring him again under influence. She failed, but she succeeded in making him come back to her as if nothing had ever happened. And then she said to herself that there must be another woman, and she set herself to find out who that woman was.

Formerly many men had hovered—marriageable men, excellent *partis*—round the cold and statuesque beauty of Victoria Pengelley. She was an acknowledged beauty; she brought an atmosphere of perfect taste and grace into a room with her; men looked at her and wondered; foolish girls, who knew no better, envied her. Presently the foolish girls, who had soft faces and eyes, which could melt in love or sorrow, envied her no longer, because they got engaged and married. And of all the men who came and went, there was but one who loved her so that his pulse beat quicker when she came; who trembled when he took her hand; whose nerves tingled and whose blood ran swifter through his veins when he asked her, down in that quiet Scotch village, with no one to know it but her maid, to be his wife.

The man was Lawrence Colquhoun. The passion had been his. Now love and passion were buried in the ashes of the past. The man was impassable, and the woman, madly kicking against the fetters which she had bound around herself, was angry and jealous.

It is by some mistake of Nature that women who cannot love can yet be jealous. Victoria Pengelley's pulse never once moved the faster for all the impetuosity of her lover. She liked to watch it, this curious yearning after her beauty, this eminently masculine weakness, because it was a tribute to her power; it is always pleasant for a woman to feel that she is loved as women are loved in novels—men's novels, not the pseudo-passionate school-girls' novels, or the calmly respectable feminine tales where the young gentlemen and the young ladies are superior to the instincts of common humanity. Victoria played with this giant as an engineer will play with the wheels of a mighty engine. She could do what she liked with it. Samson was not more pliable to Delilah; and Delilah was not more unresponsive to that guileless strong man. She soon got tired of her toy, however. Scarcely were the morning and the evening of the fifth day, when by pressing some unknown spring she smashed it altogether.

Now, when it was quite too late, when the thing was utterly smashed, when she had a husband and child, she was actually trying to reconstruct it. Some philosopher, probing more deeply than usual the mysteries of mankind, once discovered that it was at all times impossible to know what a woman wants. He laid that down as a general axiom, and presented it as an irrefragable truth for the universal use of humanity. One may sometimes, however, guess what a woman does not want. Victoria Cassilis, one may be sure, did not want to sacrifice her honour, her social standing, or her future. She was not intending to go off, for instance, with her old lover, even if he should propose the step, which seemed unlikely. And yet she would have liked him to propose it, because then she would have felt the recovery of her power. Now her sex, as Chaucer and others before him pointed out, love power beyond all other earthly things. And the history of queens, from Semiramis to Isabella, shows what a mess they always make of it when they do get power.

A curious problem. Given a woman, no longer in the first bloom of youth, married well, and clinging with the instincts of her class to her reputation and social position. She has everything to lose and nothing to gain. She cannot hope even for the love of the man for whom she is incurring the suspicions of the world, and exciting the jealousy of her husband. Yet it is true, in her case, what the race of evil-speakers, liars, and slanderers say of her. She is running after Lawrence Colquhoun. He is too much with her. She has given the enemy occasion to blaspheme.

As for Colquhoun, when he thought seriously over the situation, he laughed when it was a fine day, and swore if it was raining. The English generally take a sombre view of things because it is so constantly raining. We proclaim our impotence, the lack of national spirit, and our poverty, until other nations actually begin to believe us. But Colquhoun, though he might swear, made no effort to release himself, when a word would have done it.

"You may use harsh language to me, Lawrence," said Mrs. Cassilis— he never had used harsh language to any woman—"you may sneer at me, and laugh in your cold and cruelly impassive manner. But one thing I can say for you, that you understand me."

"I have seen all your moods, Mrs. Cassilis, and I have a good memory. If you will show your husband that the surface of the ocean may be stormy sometimes, he will understand you a good deal better. Get up a little breeze for him."

"I am certainly not going to have a vulgar quarrel with Mr. Cassilis."

"A vulgar quarrel? Vulgar? Ah, vulgarity changes every five years or so. What a pity that vulgar quarrels were in fashion six years ago, Mrs. Cassilis!"

"Some men are not worth losing your temper about."

"Thank you. I was, I suppose. It was very kind of you, indeed, to remind me of it, as you then did, in a manner at once forcible and not to be forgotten. Mr. Cassilis gets nothing, I suppose, but east wind, with a cloudless sky which has the sun in it, but only the semblance of warmth. I got a good sou'-wester. But take care, take care, Mrs. Cassilis! You have wantonly thrown away once what most women would have kept—kept, Mrs. Cassilis! I remember when I was kneeling at your feet years ago, talking the usual nonsense about being unworthy of you. Rubbish! I was more than worthy of you, because I could give myself to you loyally, and you—you could only pretend!"

"Go on, Lawrence. It is something that you regret the past, and something to see that you *can* feel, after all."

She stopped and laughed carelessly.

"Prick me and I sing out. That is natural. But we will have no heroics. What I mean is, that I am well out of it; and that you, Victoria Cassilis, are—forgive the plain speaking—a foolish woman."

"Lawrence Colquhoun has the right to insult me as he pleases, and I must bear it."

It was in her own room. Colquhoun was leaning on the window; she was sitting on a chair before him. She was agitated and excited. He, save for the brief moments when he spoke as if with emotion, was languid and calm.

"I have no right," he replied, "and you know it. Let us finish. Mrs. Cassilis, keep what you have, and be thankful."

"What I have! What have I?"

"One of the best houses in London. An excellent social position. A husband said to be the ablest man in the City. An income which gives you all that a woman can ask for. The confidence and esteem of your husband—and a child. Do these things mean nothing?"

"My husband—Oh, my husband! He is insufferable sometimes, when I remember, Lawrence."

WALTER BESANT AND JAMES RICE

"He is a man who gives his trust after a great deal of doubt and hesitation. Then he gives it wholly. To take it back would be a greater blow, a far greater blow, than it would ever be to a younger man—to such a man as myself."

"Gabriel Cassilis only suffers when he loses money."

"That is not the case. You cannot afford to make another great mistake. Success isn't on the cards after two such blunders, Mrs. Cassilis."

"What do I want with success? Let me have happiness."

"Take it; it is at your feet," said Lawrence. "It is in this house. It is the commonest secret. Every simple country woman knows it."

"No one will ever understand me," she sighed. "No one."

"It is simply to give up forever thinking about yourself. Go and look after your baby, and find happiness there."

Why superior women are always so angry if they are asked to look after their babies, I cannot understand. There is no blinking the fact that they have them. The maternal instinct makes women who cannot write or talk fine language about the domestic affections, take to the tiny creatures with a passion of devotion which is the loveliest thing to look upon in all this earth. The *femme incomprise* alone feels no anguish if her baby cries, no joy if he laughs, and flies into a divine rage if you remind her that she is a mother.

"My baby!" cried Victoria, springing to her feet. "You see me yearning for sympathy, looking to you as my oldest—once my dearest—friend, for a little—only a little—interest and pity, and you send me to my baby! The world is all selfish and cold-hearted, but the most selfish man in it is Lawrence Colquhoun!"

He laughed again. After all, he had said his say.

"I am glad you think so, because it simplifies matters. Now, Mrs. Cassilis, we have had our little confidential talk, and I think, under the circumstances, that it had better be the last. So, for a time, we will not meet, if you please. I do take a certain amount of interest in you— that is, I am always curious to see what line you will take next. And if you are at all concerned to have my opinion and counsel, it is this: that you've got your chance; and if you give that man who loves you and trusts you any unhappiness through your folly, you will be a much more heartless and wicked woman than even I have ever thought you. And, by Gad! I ought to know."

He left her. Mrs. Cassilis heard his step in the hall and the door close behind him. Then she ran to the window, and watched him strolling in his leisurely, careless way down the road. It made her mad to think that she could not make him unhappy, and made her jealous to think that she could no longer touch his heart. Not in love with him at all—she never had been; but jealous because her old power was gone.

Jealous! There must be another girl. Doubtless Phillis Fleming. She ordered her carriage and drove straight to Twickenham. Agatha was having one of her little garden-parties. Jack Dunquerque was there with Gilead Beck. Also Captain Ladds. But Lawrence Colquhoun was not. She stayed an hour; she ascertained from Phillis that her guardian seldom came to see her, and went home again in a worse temper than before, because she felt herself on the wrong track.

Tomlinson, her maid, had a very bad time of it while she was dressing her mistress for dinner. Nothing went right, somehow. Tomlinson, the hard-featured, was long suffering and patient. She made no reply to the torrent which flowed from her superior's angry lips. But when respite came with the dinner-bell, and her mistress was safely downstairs, the maid sat down to the table and wrote a letter very carefully. This she read and re-read, and, being finally satisfied with it, she took it out to the post herself. After that, as she would not be wanted till midnight at least, she took a cab and went to the Marylebone Theatre, where she wept over the distresses of a lady, ruined by the secret voice of calumny.

It was at the end of May, and the season was at its height. Mrs. Cassilis had two or three engagements, but she came home early, and was even sharper with the unfortunate Tomlinson than before dinner. But Tomlinson was very good, and bore all in patience. It is Christian to endure.

Next morning Gabriel Cassilis found among his letters another in the same handwriting as that of the three anonymous communications he had already received.

He tore it open with a groan.

"This is the fourth letter. You will have to take notice of my communications, and to act upon them, sooner or later. All this morning Mr. Colquhoun was locked up with your wife in her boudoir. He came at eleven and went away at half-past one. No one was admitted. They talked of many things—of their Scotch secret especially, and how to hide it from you. I shall keep you informed of what they do. At half past two Mrs. Cassilis ordered the carriage and drove to Twickenham. Mr. Colquhoun has got his ward there, Miss Fleming. So that doubtless she went to meet him again. In the evening she came home in a very bad temper, because she had failed to meet him. She had hoped to see him three times at least this very day. Surely, surely even your blind confidence cannot stand a continuation of this kind of thing. All the world knows it except yourself. You may be rich and generous to her, but she doesn't love you. And she doesn't care for her child. She hasn't asked to see it for three days—think of that! There is a pretty mother for you! She ill-treats her maid, who is *a most faithful person, and devoted to your interests*. She is hated by every servant in the house. She is a cold-hearted, cruel woman. And even if she loves Mr. Colquhoun, it can only be through jealousy, and because she won't let him marry anybody else, even if he wanted to. But things are coming to a crisis. Wait!"

Mr. Mowll came in with a packet of papers, and found his master staring straight before him into space. He spoke to him but received no answer. Then he touched him gently on the arm. Mr. Cassilis started, and looked round hastily. His first movement was to lay his hand upon a letter on the desk.

"What is it, Mowll—what is it? I was thinking—I was thinking. I am not very well today, Mowll."

"You have been working too hard, sir," said his secretary.

"Yes—yes. It is nothing. Now, then, let us look at what you have brought."

For two hours Mr. Cassilis worked with his secretary. He had the faculty of rapid and decisive work. And he had the eye of a hawk. They were two hours of good work, and the secretary's notes were voluminous. Suddenly the financier stopped—the work half done. It was as if the machinery of a clock were to go wrong without warning.

"So," he said, with an effort, "I think we will stop for today. Put all these matters at work, Mowll. I shall go home and rest."

A thing he had never done before in all his life.

He went back to his house. His wife was at home and alone. They had luncheon together, and drove out in the afternoon. Her calm and stately pride drove the jealous doubts from his troubled mind as the sun chases away the mists of morning.

XXXIII

"An excellent play."

Such things as dinners to Literature were the relaxations of Gilead Beck's serious life. His real business was to find an object worthy of that enormous income of which he found himself the trustee. The most sympathetic man of his acquaintance, although it was difficult to make him regard any subject seriously, was Jack Dunquerque, and to him he confided his anxieties and difficulties.

"I can't fix it," he groaned. "I can't fix it anyhow."

Jack knew what he meant, but waited for further light, like him who readeth an acrostic.

"The more I look at that growin' pile—there's enough now to build the White House over again—the more I misdoubt myself."

"Where have you got it all?"

"In Government Stocks—by the help of Mr. Cassilis. No more of the unholy traffic in shares which you buy to sell again. No, sir. That means makin' the widow weep and the minister swear; an' I don't know which spectacle of those two is the more melancholy for a Christian man. All in stocks—Government Stocks, safe and easy to draw out, with the interest comin' in regular as the chant of the cuckoo-clock."

"Well, can't you let it stay there?"

"No, Mr. Dunquerque, I can't. There's the voice of that blessed Inseck in the box there, night and day in my ears. And it says, plain as speech can make it, 'Do something with the money.'"

"You have bought a few pictures."

"Yes, sir: I have begun the great Gilead P. Beck collection. And when that is finished, I guess there'll be no collection on this airth to show a candle to it. But that's personal vanity. That's not what the Golden Butterfly wants."

"Would he like you to have a yacht? A good deal may be chucked over a yacht. That is, a good deal for what we Englishmen call a rich man."

"When I go home again I mean to build a yacht, and sail her over here and race you people at Cowes—all the same as the America, twenty years ago. But not yet."

"There are a few trifles going about which run away with money. Polo, now. If you play polo hard enough, you may knock up a pony

WALTER BESANT AND JAMES RICE

every game. But I suppose that would not be expensive enough for you. You couldn't ride two ponies at once, I suppose, like a circus fellow."

"Selfish luxury, Mr. Dunquerque," said Gilead, with an almost prayerful twang, "is not the platform of the Golden Butterfly. I should like to ride two ponies at once, but it's not to be thought of. And my legs are too long for any but a Kentucky pony."

"Is the Turf selfish luxury, I wonder?" asked Jack. "A good deal of money can be got through on the Turf. Nothing, of course, compared with your pile; but still, you might make a sensible hole in it by judicious backing."

Gilead Beck was as free from ostentation, vanity, and the desire to have his ears tickled as any man. But still he did like to feel that by the act of Providence, he was separated from other men. An income of fifteen hundred pounds a day, which does not depend upon harvests, or on coal, or on iron, or anything to eat and drink, but only on the demand for rock-oil, which increases, as he often said, with the march of civilisation, does certainly separate a man from his fellows. This feeling of division saddened him; it imparted something of the greatness of soul which belongs even to the most unworthy emperors; he felt himself bound to do something for the good of mankind while life and strength were in him. And it was not unpleasant to know that others recognised the vastness of his Luck. Therefore, when Jack Dunquerque spoke as if the Turf were a gulf which might be filled up with his fortune, while it swallowed, without growing sensibly more shallow, all the smaller fortunes yearly shot into it like the rubbish on the future site of a suburban villa, Gilead Beck smiled. Such recognition from this young man was doubly pleasant to him on account of his unbounded affection for him. Jack Dunquerque had saved his life. Jack Dunquerque treated him as an equal and a friend. Jack Dunquerque wanted nothing of him, and, poor as he was, would accept nothing of him. Jack Dunquerque was the first, as he was also the most favourable, specimen he had met of the class which may be poor, but does not seem to care for more money; the class which no longer works for increase of fortune.

"No, sir," said Gilead. "I do not understand the Turf. When I go home I shall rear horses and improve the breed. Maybe I may run a horse in a trotting-match at Saratoga."

In the mornings this American, in search of a Worthy Object, devoted his time to making the round of hospitals, London societies, and charities of all kinds. He asked what they did, and why they did it. He made remarks which were generally unpleasant to the employés of the societies; he went away without offering the smallest donation; and he returned moodily to the Langham Hotel.

"The English," he said, after a fortnight of these investigations, "air the most kind-hearted people in the hull world. We are charitable, and I believe the Germans, when they are not officers in their own army, are a well-disposed folk. But in America, when a man tumbles down the ladder, he falls hard. Here there's every contrivance for makin' him fall soft. A man don't feel handsome when he's on the broad of his back, but it must be a comfort for him to feel that his backbone isn't broke. Lord, Mr. Dunquerque! to look at the hospitals and refuges, one would think the hull Bible had got nothin' but the story of the Prodigal Son, and that every other Englishman was that misbehaved boy. I reckon if the young man had lived in London, he'd have gone home very slow—most as slow as ever he could travel. There'd be the hospitals, comfortable and warm, when his constitootion had broke down with too many drinks: there'd have been the convalescent home for him to enjoy six months of happy meditation by the seaside when he was pickin' up again; and when he got well, would he take to the swine-herdin', or would he tramp it home to the old man? Not he, sir; he would go back to the old courses and become a Roper. Then more hospitals. P'r'aps when he'd got quite tired, and seen the inside of a State prison, and been without his little comforts for a spell, he'd have gone home at last—just as I did, for I was the prodigal son without the riotous livin'—and found the old man gone, leavin' him his blessin'. The elder one would hand him the blessin' cheerfully, and stick to the old man's farm. Then the poor broken down sportsman—he'd tramp it back to London, get into an almshouse, with an allowance from a City charity, and die happy.

"There's another kind o' prodigal," Mr. Beck went on, being in a mood for moralising. "She's of the other sex. Formerly she used to repent when she thought of what was before her. There's a refuge before her now, and kind women to take her by the hand and cry over her. She isn't in any hurry for the cryin' to begin, but it's comfortable to look forward to; and so she goes on until she's ready. Twenty years fling, maybe, with nothing to do for her daily bread; and then to start fair on the same level as the woman who has kept her self-respect and worked.

"I can't see my way clear, Mr. Dunquerque; I can't. It wouldn't do any kind of honour to the Golden Butterfly to lay out all of these dollars in helpin' up them who are bound to fall—bound to fall. There's only two classes of people in this world—those who are goin' up, and those who are goin' down. It's no use tryin' to stop those who are on their way down. Let them go; let them slide; give them a shove down, if you like, and all the better, because they will the sooner get to the bottom, and then go up again till they find their own level."

It was in the evening, at nine o'clock, when Gilead Beck made the oration. He was in his smaller room, which was lit only by the twilight of the May evening and by the gas-lamp in the street below. He walked up and down, talking with his hands in his pockets, and silencing Jack Dunquerque, who had never thought seriously about these or any other things, by his earnestness. Every now and then he went to the window and looked into the street below. The cabs rattled up and down, and on the pavement the customary sight of a West-end street after dark perhaps gave him inspiration.

"Their own level," he repeated it. "Yes, sir, there's a proper level for everyone of us somewhere, if only we can find it. At the lowest depth of all, there's the airth to be ploughed, the hogs to be drove, and the corn to be reaped. I read the other day, when I was studying for the great dinner, that formerly, if a man took refuge in a town, he might stay there for a year and a day. If then he could not keep himself, they opened the gates and they ran him out on a plank; same way as I left Clearville City. Back to the soil he went—back to the plough. Let those who are going down hill get down as fast as they can, and go back to the soil.

"I've sometimes thought," he went on, "that there's a kind of work lower than agriculture. It is to wear a black coat and do copying. You take a boy and you make him a machine; tell him to copy, that is all. Why, sir, the rustic who feeds the pigs is a Solomon beside that poor critter. Make your poor helpless paupers into clerks, and make the men who've got arms and legs and no brains into farm labourers. Perhaps I shall build a city and conduct it on those principles."

Then he stopped because he had run himself down, and they began to talk of Phillis.

But it seemed to Jack a new and singular idea. The weak must go to the wall; but they might be helped to find their level. He was glad for once that he had that small four hundred a year of his own, because, as he reflected, his own level might be somewhere on the stage where the manufacture by hand, say, of upper leathers, represents the proper occupation of the class. A good many other fellows, he thought, among his own acquaintance, might find themselves accommodated with boards for the cobbling business near himself. And he looked at Gilead Beck with increased admiration as a man who had struck all this, as well as Ile, out of his own head.

Jack Dunquerque suggested educational endowments. Mr. Beck made deliberate inquiries into the endowments of Oxford and Cambridge, with a view of founding a grand National American University on the old lines, to be endowed in perpetuity with the proceeds of his perennial oil-fountains. But there were things about these ancient seats of learning which did not commend themselves to him. In his unscholastic ignorance he asked what was the good of pitting young men against each other, like the gladiators in the arena, to fight, like them, with weapons of no earthly modern use. And when he was told of fellowships given to men for life as a prize for a single battle, he laughed aloud.

He went down to Eton. He was mean enough to say of the masters that they made their incomes by over-charging the butchers' and the grocers' bills, and he said that ministers, as he called them, ought not to be grocers; and of the boys he said that he thought it unwholesome for them that some should have unlimited pocket-money, and all should have unlimited tick. Also someone told him that Eton boys no longer fight, because they funk one another. So that he came home sorrowful and scornful.

"In my country," he said, "we have got no scholarships, and if the young men can't pay their professors they do without them and educate themselves. And in my country the boys fight. Yes, Mr. Dunquerque, you bet they do fight."

It was after an evening at the Lyceum that Gilead Beck hit upon the grand idea of his life.

The idea struck him as they walked home. It fell upon him like an inspiration, and for the moment stunned him. He was silent until he reached the hotel. Then he called a waiter.

"Get Mr. Dunquerque a key," he said. "He will sleep here. That means, Mr. Dunquerque, that we can talk all night if you please. I want advice."

Jack laughed. He always did laugh.

"It is a great privilege," he said, "advising Fortunatus."

"It is a great privilege, Mr. Dunquerque," returned Fortunatus, "having an adviser who wants nothing for himself. See that pile of letters. Everyone a begging-letter, except that blue one on the top, which is from a clergyman. He's a powerful generous man, sir. He offers to conduct my charities at a salary of three hundred pounds a year."

Mr. Beck then proceeded to unfold the great idea which had sprung up, full grown, in his brain.

"That man, sir," he said, meaning Henry Irving, "is a grand actor. And they are using him up. He wants rest."

"I was an actor myself once, and I've loved the boards ever since. I was not a great actor. I am bound to say that I did not act like Mr. Henry Irving. Quite the contrary. Once I was the hind legs of an elephant. Perhaps Mr. Irving himself, when he was a 'prentice, was the fore legs. I was on the boards for a month, when the company busted up. Most things did bust up that I had to do with in those days. I was the lawyer in *Flowers of the Forest*. I was the demon with the keg to Mr. Jefferson's Rip Van Winkle. Once I played Horatio. That was when the Mayor of Constantinople City inaugurated his year of office by playin' Hamlet. He'd always been fond of the stage, that Mayor, but through bein' in the soft-goods line never could find time to go on. So when he got the chance, bein' then a matter of four-and-fifty, of course he took it. And he elected to play Hamlet, just to show the citizens what a whole-souled Mayor they'd got, and the people in general what good play-actin' meant. The corporation attended in a body, and sat in the front row of what you would call the dress circle. All in store clothes and go-to-meetin' gloves. It was a majestic and an imposing spectacle. Behind them was the fire brigade in uniform. The citizens of Constantinople and their wives and daughters crowded out the house.

"Wal, sir, we began. Whether it was they felt jealous or whether they felt envious, that corporation laughed. They laughed at the sentinels, and they laughed at the moon. They laughed at the Ghost, and they laughed at me—Horatio. And then they laughed at Hamlet.

"I watched the Mayor gettin' gradually riz. Any man's dander would. Presently he rose to that height that he went to the footlights, and stood there facin' his own town council like a bull behind a gate.

"They left off laughing for a minute, and then they began again. We are a grave people, Mr. Dunquerque, I am told, and the sight of those town councillors all laughin' together like so many free niggers before the war was most too much for anyone.

"The Mayor made a speech that wasn't in the play.

"'Hyar,' he said, lookin' solemn. 'You jest gether up your traps and skin out of this. I've got the say about this house, and I arn't a goin' to have the folks incited to make game of their Mayor. So—you—kin—jist—light.'

"They hesitated.

"The Mayor pointed to the back of the theatre.

"'Git,' he said again.

"One of the town councillors rose and spoke.

"'Mr. Mayor,' he began, 'or Hamlet, Prince of Denmark'—

"'Wal, sir,' said the Mayor, 'didn't Nero play in his own theaytre?'

"'Mr. Mayor, or Hamlet, or Nero,' e went on, 'we came here on the presumption that we were paying for our places, and bound to laugh if we were amused at the performance. Now, sir, this performance does amuse us considerable.'

"'You may presump,' said the Mayor, 'what you dam please. But git. Git at once, or I'll turn on the pumps.'

"It was the Ghost who came to the front with the hose in his hands ready to begin.

"The town council disappeared before he had time to play on them and we went on with the tragedy.

"But it was spoiled, sir, completely spoiled. And I have never acted since then.

"So you see Mr. Dunquerque, I know somethin' about actin. 'Tisn't as if I was a raw youngster starting a theatrical idea all at once. I thought of it tonight, while I saw a man actin who has the real stuff in him, and only wants rest. I mean to try an experiment in London, and if it succeeds I shall take it to New York, and make the American Drama the greatest in all the world."

"What will you do?"

"I said to myself in that theatre: 'We want a place where we can have a different piece acted every week; we want to give time for rehearsals and for alteration; we want to bring up the level of the second-rate actors; we want more intelligence; and we want more care.' Now, Mr. Dunquerque, how would you tackle that problem?"

"I cannot say."

"Then I will tell you, sir. You must have three full companies. You must give up expecting that Theatre to pay its expenses; you must find a rich man to pay for that Theatre; and he must pay up pretty handsome."

"Lord de Molleteste took the Royal Hemisphere last year."

"Had he three companies, sir?"

"No; he only had one; and that was a bad one. Wanted to bring out a new actress, and no one went to see her. Cost him a hundred pounds a week till he shut it up."

"Well, we will bring along new actresses too, but in a different fashion. They will have to work their way up from the bottom of the ladder. My Theatre will cost me a good deal more than a hundred pounds a week, I expect. But I am bound to run it. The idea's in my head strong. It's the thing to do. A year or two in London, and then for the States. We shall have a Grand National Drama, and the Ile shall pay for it."

He took paper and pen, and began to write.

"Three companies, all complete, for tragedy and comedy. I've been to every theatre in London, and I'm ready with my list. Now, Mr. Dunquerque, you listen while I write them down.

"I say first company; not that there's any better or worse, but because one must begin with something.

"In the first I will have Mr. Irving, Mr. Henry Neville, Mr. William Farren, Mr Toole, Mr. Emery, Miss Bateman, and Miss Nelly Farren.

"In the second, Mr. George Rignold—I saw him in *Henry V* last winter in the States—Mr. Hare, Mr. Kendal, Mr. Lionel Brough, Mrs. Kendal, and that clever little lady, Miss Angelina Claude.

"In the third I will have Mr. Phelps, Mr. Charles Matthews, Mr. W. J. Hill, Mr. Arthur Cecil, Mr. Kelly, Mr. and Mrs. Bancroft, and Mrs. Scott-Siddons, if you could only get her.

"I should ask Mr. Alfred Wigan to be a stage-manager and general director, and I would give him absolute power.

"Every company will play for a week and rehearse for a fortnight. The principal parts shall not always be played by the best actors. And I will not have any piece run for more than a week at a time."

"And how do you think your teams would run together?"

"Sir, it would be a distinction to belong to that Theatre. And they would be well paid. They will run together just for the very same reason as everybody runs together—for their own interest."

"I believe," said Jack, "that you have at last hit upon a plan for getting rid even of your superfluous cash."

"It will cost a powerful lot, I believe. But Lord, Mr. Dunquerque! what better object can there be than to improve the Stage? Think what it would mean. The House properly managed; no loafin' around behind the scenes; every actor doing his darn best, and taking time for study and rehearsal; people comin' down to a quiet evening, with the best artists to entertain them, and the best pieces to play. The Stage would revive, sir. We should hear no more about the decay of the Drama. The Drama decay! That's bunkum, sir. That's the invention of the priests and the ministers, who go about down-cryin' what they can't have their own fingers in."

"But I don't see how your scheme will encourage authors."

"I shall pay them too, sir. I should say to Mr. Byron: 'Sir, you air a clever and a witty man. Go right away, sir. Sit down for a twelvemonth, and do nothin' at all. Then write me a play; put your own situations in it, not old jokes; put your own situations in it, not old ones. Give me somethin' better.' Then I should say to Mr. Gilbert: 'Your pieces have got the real grit, young gentleman; but you write too fast. Go away too for six months and do nothin'. Then sit down for six months more, and write a piece that will be pretty and sweet, and won't be thin.' And there's more dramatists behind—only give them a chance. They shall have it at my house."

"And what will the other houses do?"

"The other houses, sir, may go on playing pieces for four hundred nights if they like. I leave them plenty of men to stump their boards, and my Theatre won't hold more than a certain number. I shall only take a small house to begin with, such a house as the Lyceum, and we shall gradually get along. But no profit can be made by such a Stage, and I am ready to give half my Ile to keep it goin'. Of course," he added, "when it is a success in London I shall carry it away, company and all, to New York."

He rose in a burst of enthusiasm.

"Gilead P. Beck shall be known for his collection of pictures. He shall be known for his Golden Butterfly, and the Luck it brought him. But he shall be best known, Mr. Dunquerque, because he will be the first man to take the Stage out of the mud of commercial enterprise, and raise it to be the great educator of the people. He shall be known as the founder of the Grand National American Drama. And his bust shall be planted on the top of every American stage."

XXXIV

"In such a cause who would not give? What heart
But leaps at such a name?"

People of rank and position are apt to complain of begging-letters. Surely England must be a happy country since its rich people complain mostly of begging-letters; for they are so easily dropped into the waste-paper basket. A country squire—any man with a handle to his name and place for a permanent address—is the natural prey and victim of the beggars. The lithographed letter comes with every post, trying in vain to look like a written letter. And though in fervid sentences it shows the danger to your immortal soul if you refuse the pleading, most men have the courage to resist. The fact is that the letter is not a nuisance at all, because it is never read. On the other hand, a new and very tangible nuisance is springing up. It is that of the people who go round and call. Sir Roger de Coverly in his secluded village is free from the women who give you the alternative of a day with Moody and Sankey or an eternity of repentance; he never sees the pair of Sisters got up like Roman Catholic nuns, who stand meekly before you, arms crossed, mutely refusing to go without five shillings at least for their Ritualist hot-house. But he who lives in chambers, he who puts up at a great hotel and becomes known, he who has a house in any address from Chester Square to Notting Hill, understands this trouble.

In some mysterious way Gilead Beck had become known. Perhaps this was partly in consequence of his habit of going to institutions, charities, and the like, and wanting to find out everything. In some vague and misty way it became known that there was at the Langham Hotel an American named Gilead P. Beck, who was asking questions philanthropically. Then all the people who live on philanthropists, with all those who work for their pleasure among philanthropists, began to tackle Gilead P. Beck. Letters came in the morning, which he read but did not answer. Circulars were sent to him, of which he perhaps made a note. Telegrams were even delivered to him—people somehow *must* read telegrams—asking him for money. Those wonderful people who address the Affluent in the *Times* and ask for £300 on the security of an honest man's word; those unhappy ladies whose father was a gentleman and an officer, on the strength of which fact they ask the Benevolent to help them in their undeserved distress, poor things; those disinterested advertisers who want a few hundreds, and who will give fifteen percent. on the security of a splendid piano, a small gallery of undoubted pictures, and some unique china; those tradesmen who try to stave off bankruptcy by asking the world generally for a loan on the strength of a simple reference to the clergyman of St. Tinpot, Hammersmith; those artful dodgers, Mr. Ally Sloper and his friends, when they have devised a new and ingenious method of screwing money out of the rich,—all these people got hold of our Gilead, and pelted him with letters. Did they know, the ingenious and the needy, how the business is overdone, they would change their tactics and go round calling.

It requires a front of brass, entire absence of self-respect, and an epidermis like that of the rhinoceros for toughness, to undertake this work. Yet ladies do it. You want a temperament off which insults, gibes, sneers, and blank refusals fall like water off a nasturtium-leaf to go the begging-round. Yet women do it. They do it not only for themselves, but also for their cause. From Ritualism down to Atheism, from the fashionable enthusiasm to the nihilism which the British workman is being taught to regard as the hidden knowledge, there are women who will brave anything, dare anything, say anything, and endure anything. They love to be martyred, so long especially as it does not hurt; they are angry with the lukewarm zeal of their male supporters, forgetting that a man sees the two sides of a question, while a woman never sees more than one; they mistake notoriety for fame, and contempt for jealous admiration.

And here, in the very heart of London, was a man who seemed simply born for the Polite Beggar. A man restless because he could not part with his money. Not seeking profitable investments, not asking for ten and twenty percent.; but anxious to use his money for the best purposes; a man who was a philanthropist in the abstract, who considered himself the trustee of a gigantic gift to the human race, and was desirous of exercising that trust to the best advantage.

In London; and at the same time, in the same city, thousands of people not only representing their individual distresses or their society's wants, but also plans, schemes, and ideas for the promotion of civilisation in the abstract. Do we not all know the projectors? I myself know at this moment six men who want each to establish a daily paper; at least a dozen who would like a weekly; fifty who see a way, by the formation of a new society, to check immorality, kill infidelity once for all, make men sober and women clean, prevent strikes and destroy Republicanism. There is one man who would "save" the Church of England by establishing the preaching order; one who knows how to restore England to her place among the nations without a single additional soldier; one who burns to abolish bishops' aprons, and would make it penal to preach in a black gown. The land teems with idea'd men. They yearn, pray, and sigh daily for the capitalist who will reduce their idea to practice.

And besides the projectors, there are the inventors. I once knew a man who claimed to have invented a means for embarking and setting down passengers and goods on a railway without stopping the trains. Think of the convenience. Why no railways have taken up the invention, I cannot explain. Then there are men who have inventions which will reform the whole system of domestic appliances; there are others who are prepared on encouragement to reform the whole conduct of life by new inventions. There are men by thousands brooding over experiments which they have no money to carry out; there are men longing to carry on experiments whose previous failure they can now account for. All these men are looking for a capitalist as for a Messiah. Had they known—had they but dimly suspected—that such a capitalist was in June of last year staying at the Langham Hotel, they would have sought that hotel with one consent, and besieged its portals. The world in general did not know Mr. Beck's resources. But they were beginning to find him out. The voice of rumour was spreading abroad his reputation. And the people wrote letters, sent circulars, and called.

"Twenty-three of them came yesterday morning," Gilead Beck complained to Jack Dunquerque. "Three-and-twenty, and all with a tale to tell. No, sir,"—his voice rose in indignation—"I did not give one of them so much as a quarter-dollar. The Luck of the Golden Butterfly is not to be squandered among the well-dressed beggars of Great Britain. Three-and-twenty, counting one little boy, who came by himself. His mother was a widow, he said, and he sat on the chair and sniffed. And they all wanted money. There was one man in a white choker who had found out a new channel for doing good—and one man who wished to recommend a list of orphans. The rest were women. And talk? There's no name for it. With little books, and pencils, and bundles of tracts."

While he spoke there was a gentle tap at the door.

"There's another of them," he groaned. "Stand by me, Mr. Dunquerque. See me through with it. Come in, come in! Good Lord!" he whispered, "a brace this time. Will you tackle the young one, Mr. Dunquerque?"

A pair of ladies. One of them a lady tall and thin, stern of aspect, sharp of feature, eager of expression. She wore spectacles: she was apparently careless of her dress, which was of black silk a little rusty. With her was a girl of about eighteen, perhaps her daughter, perhaps her niece; a girl of rather sharp but pretty features, marked by a look of determination, as if she meant to see the bottom of this business, or know the reason why.

"You are Mr. Beck, sir?" the elder lady began.

"I am Gilead P. Beck, madam," he replied.

He was standing before the fireplace, with his long hands thrust into his pocket, one foot on an adjacent chair, and his head thrown a little back—defiantly.

"You have received two letters from me, Mr. Beck, written by my own hand, and—how many circulars, child?'

"Twenty," said the girl.

"And I have had no answer. I am come for your answer, Mr. Beck. We will sit down, if you please, while you consider your answer."

Mr. Beck took up a waste paper basket which stood at his feet, and tossed out the whole contents upon the table.

"Those are the letters of yesterday and today," he said. "What was yours, madam? Was it a letter asking for money?"

"It was."

"Yesterday there were seventy-four letters asking for money. Today there are only fifty-two. May I ask, madam, if you air the widow who wants money to run a mangle?"

"Sir, I am unmarried. A mangle!"

He dug his hand into the pile, and took out one at random.

"You air, perhaps, the young lady who writes to know if I want a housekeeper, and encloses her carte-de-visite? No; that won't do. Is it possible you are the daughter of the Confederate general who lost his life in the cause?"

"Really, sir!"

"Then, madam, we come to the lady who"—here he read from another letter—"who was once a governess, and now is reduced to sell her last remaining garments."

"Sir!"

There was a withering scorn on the lady's lips.

"I represent a Cause, Mr. Beck. I am not a beggar for myself. My cause is the sacred one of Womanhood. You, sir, in your free and happy Republic—"

Mr. Beck bowed.

"Have seen woman partially restored to her proper place—on a level with man."

"A higher level," murmured the girl, who had far-off eyes and a sweet voice. "The higher level reached by the purer heart."

"Only partially restored at present. But the good work goes on. Here we are only beginning. Mr. Beck, the Cause wants help—your help."

He said nothing and she went on.

"We want our rights; we want suffrage; we want to be elected for the Houses of Parliament; we insist on equality in following the professions and in enjoying the endowments of Education. We shall prove that we are no whit inferior to men. We want no privileges. Let us stand by ourselves."

"Wal, madam, their air helpers who shove up, and I guess there air helpers who shove down."

She did not understand him, and went on with increasing volubility.

" The subjection of the Sex is the most monstrous injustice of all those which blot the fair fame of manhood. What is there in man's physical strength that he should use it to lord over the weaker half of humanity? Why has not our sex produced a Shakespeare?"

"It has, madam," said Mr. Beck gravely. "It has produced all our greatest men."

She was staggered.

"Your answer, if you please, Mr. Beck."

"I have no answer, madam."

"I have written you two letters, and sent you twenty circulars, urging upon you the claims of the Woman's Rights Association. I have the right to ask for a reply. I expect one. You will be kind enough sir, to give categorically your answer to the several heads. This you will do of your courtesy to a lady. We can wait here while you write it. I shall probably, I ought to tell you, publish it."

"We can wait," said the young lady.

They sat with folded hands in silence.

Mr. Beck shifted his foot from the chair to the carpet. Then he took his hands out of his pockets and stroked his chin. Then he gazed at the ladies steadily.

Jack Dunquerque sat in the background, and rendered no help whatever.

"Did you ever, ladies," asked Mr. Beck, after a few moments of reflection, "hear of Paul Deroon of Memphis? He was the wickedest man in that city. Which was allowed. He kept a bar where the whisky was straight and the language was free, and where Paul would tell stories, once you set him on, calculated to raise on end the hair of your best sofa. When the Crusade began—I mean the Whisky Crusade—the ladies naturally began with Paul Deroon's saloon."

"This is very tedious, my dear," said the elder lady in a loud whisper.

"How did Paul Deroon behave? Some barkeepers came out and cursed while the Whisky War went on; some gave in and poured away the Bourbon: some shut up shop and took to preachin'. Paul just did nothing. You couldn't tell from Paul's face that he even knew of the forty women around him prayin' all together. If he stepped outside he walked through as if they weren't there, and they made a lane for him. If he'd been blind and deaf and dumb, Paul Deroon couldn't have taken less notice."

"We shall not keep our appointment, I fear," the younger lady remarked.

"They prayed, preached, and sang hymns for a whole week. On Sunday they sang eighty strong. And on the seventh day Paul took no more notice than on the first. Once they asked him if he heard the singin'. He said he did: and it was very soothin' and pleasant. Said, too, that he liked music to his drink. Then they asked him if he heard the prayers. He said he did; said, too, that it was cool work sittin' in the shade and listenin'; also that it kinder seemed as if it was bound to do somebody or other good some day. Then they told him that the ladies were waitin' to see him converted. He said it was very kind of them, and, for his own part, he didn't mind meetin' their wishes half way, and would wait as long as they did."

The ladies rose. Said the elder lady viciously: "You are unworthy, sir, to represent your great country. You are a common scoffer."

"General Schenck represents my country, madam."

"You are unworthy of being associated with a great Cause. We have wasted our time upon you."

Their departure was less dignified than their entry.

As they left the room another visitor arrived. It was a tall and handsome man, with a full flowing beard and a genial presence.

He had a loud voice and a commanding manner.

"Mr. Beck? I thought so. I wrote to you yesterday, Mr. Beck. And I am come in person—in person, sir—for your reply."

"You air the gentleman, sir, interested in the orphan children of a colonial bishop?"

"No, sir, I am not. Nothing of the kind."

"Then you air perhaps the gentleman who wrote to say that unless I sent him a ten-pound note by return of post he would blow out his brains?"

"I am Major Borington. I wrote to you, sir, on behalf of the Grand National Movement for erecting International Statues."

"What is that movement, sir?"

"A series of monuments to all our great men, Mr. Beck. America and England, have ancestors in common. We have our Shakespeare, sir, our Milton."

"Yes, sir, so I have heard. I did not know those ancestors myself, having been born too late, and therefore I do not take that interest in their stone figures you do."

"Positively, Mr. Beck, you must join us."

"It is your idea, Colonel, is it?"

"Mine, Mr. Beck. I am proud to say it is my own."

"I knew a man once, Colonel, in my country, who wanted to be a great man. He had that ambition, sir. He wasn't particular how he got his greatness. But he scorned to die and be forgotten, and he yearned to go down to posterity. His name, sir, was Hiram Turtle. First of all, he ambitioned military greatness. We went into Bull's Run together. And we came out of it together. We came away from that field side by side. We left our guns there, too. If we had had shields, we should have left them as well. Hiram concluded, sir, after that experience, to leave military greatness to others."

Major Borington interposed a gesture.

"One moment, Brigadier. The connection is coming. Hiram Turtle thought the ministry opened up a field. So he became a preacher. Yes; he preached once. But he forgot that a preacher must have something to say, and so the elders concluded not to ask Hiram Turtle anymore. Then he became clerk in a store while he looked about him. For a year or two he wrote poetry. But the papers in America, he found, were in a league against genius. So he gave up that lay. Politics was his next move; and he went for stump-orating with the Presidency in his eye. Stumpin' offers amusement as well as gentle exercise, but it doesn't pay unless you get more than one brace of niggers and a bubbly-jock to listen. Wal, sir, how do you think Hiram Turtle made his greatness? He figured around, sir, with a List, and his own name a-top, for a Grand National Monument to the memory of the great men who fell in the Civil War. They air still subscribing, and Hiram Turtle is the great Patriot. Now, General, you see the connection."

"If you mean, sir," cried Major Borington, "to imply that my motives are interested—"

"Not at all, sir," said Mr. Beck; "I have told you a little story. Hiram Turtle's was a remarkable case. Perhaps you might ponder on it."

"Your language is insulting, sir!"

"Colonel, this is not a country where men have to take care what they say. But if you should ever pay a visit out West, and if you should happen to be about where tar and feathers are cheap, you would really be astonished at the consideration you would receive. No, sir, I shall not subscribe to your Grand National Association. But go on, Captain, go on. This is a charitable country, and the people haven't all heard the story of Hiram Turtle. And what'll you take, Major?"

But Major Borington, clapping on his hat, stalked out of the room.

The visits of the strong-minded female and Major Borington which were typical, took place on the day which was the first and only occasion on which Phillis went to the theatre. Gilead Beck took the box, and they went—Jack Dunquerque being himself the fourth, as they say in Greek exercise-books—to the Lyceum, and saw Henry Irving play Hamlet.

Phillis brought to the play none of the reverence with which English people habitually approach Shakespeare, insomuch that while we make superhuman efforts to understand him we have lost the power of criticism. To her, George III's remark that there was a great deal of rubbish in Shakspeare would have seemed a perfectly legitimate conclusion. But she knew nothing about the great dramatist.

The house, with its decorations, lights, and crowd, pleased her. She liked the overture, and she waited with patience for the first scene. She was going to see a representation of life done in show. So much she understood. Instead of telling a story the players would act the story.

The Ghost—perhaps because the Lyceum Ghost was so palpably flesh and blood—inspired her with no terror at all. But gradually the story grew into her, and she watched the unfortunate Prince of Denmark torn by his conflicting emotions, distraught with the horror of the deed that had been done and the deed that was to do, with a beating heart and trembling lip. When Hamlet with that wild cry threw himself upon his uncle's throne, she gasped and caught Agatha by the hand. When the play upon the stage showed the King how much of the truth was known, she trembled, and looked to see him immediately confess his crime and go out to be hanged. She was indignant with Hamlet for the

WALTER BESANT AND JAMES RICE

slaughter of Polonius; she was contemptuous of Ophelia, whom she did not understand; and she was impatient when the two Gravediggers came to the front, resolute to spare the audience none of their somewhat musty old jokes and to abate nothing of the stage-business.

When they left the theatre Phillis moved and spoke as in a dream. War, battle, conspiracy, murder, crime—all these things, of which her guardian had told her, she saw presented before her on the stage. She had too much to think of; she had to fit all these new surroundings in her mind with the stories of the past. As for the actors, she had no power whatever of distinguishing between them and the parts they played. Irving was Hamlet; Miss Bateman was Ophelia; and they were all like the figures of a dream, because she did not understand how they could be anything but Hamlet, Ophelia, and the Court of Denmark.

And this, too, was part of her education.

XXXV

"Love in her eyes lay hiding,
His time in patience biding."

S quare it with Colquhoun before you go any farther," said Ladds.
Square it with the guardian—speak to the young lady's father—
make it all right with the authorities; what excellent advice to give, and
how easy to follow it up! Who does not look forward with pleasure, or
backward as to an agreeable reminiscence, to that half hour spent in a
confidential talk with dear papa? How calmly critical, how severely judicial,
was his summing up! With what a determined air did he follow up the
trail, elicited in cross-examination, of former sins! With how keen a scent
did he disinter forgotten follies, call attention to bygone extravagances, or
place the finger of censure upon debts which never ought to have been
incurred, and economies which ought to have been made!

Remember his "finally"—a word which from childhood has been
associated with sweet memories, because it brings the sermon to an
end, but which henceforth will awake in your brain the ghost of that
mauvais quart d'heure. In that brief peroration he tore the veil from the
last cherished morsel of self-illusion; he showed you that the furnishing
of a house was a costly business, that he was not going to do it for you,
that servants require an annual income of considerable extent, that his
daughter had been brought up a lady, that lady's dress is a serious affair,
that wedlock in due season brings babies, and that he was not so rich
as he seemed.

Well, perhaps he said "Yes" reluctantly, in spite of drawbacks. Then
you felt that you were regarded by the rest of the family as the means of
preventing dear Annabella from making a brilliant match. That humbled
you for life. Or perhaps he said "No." In that case you went away sadly
and meditated suicide. And whether you got over the fit, or whether
you didn't—though of course you did—the chances were that Annabella
never married at all, and you are still regarded by the family as the cause
of that sweet creature not making the exceptionally splendid alliance
which, but for you, the disturbing influence, would have been her lot.

However, the thing is necessary, unless people run away, a good old
fashion by which such interviews, together with wedding-breakfasts,
wedding-garments, and wedding-presents were avoided.

Running away is out of fashion. It would have been the worst form possible in Jack Dunquerque even to propose such a thing to Phillis, and I am not at all certain that he would ever have made her understand either the necessity or the romance of the thing. And I am quite sure that she would never understand that Jack Dunquerque was asking her to do a wrong thing.

Certainly it was not likely that this young man would proceed further in the path of irregularity—which leads to repentance—than he had hitherto done. He had now to confess before the young lady's guardian something of the part he played.

Looked at dispassionately, and unsoftened by the haze of illusion, this part had, as he acknowledged with groans, an appearance far from pleasing to the Christian moralist.

He had taken advantage of the girl's total ignorance to introduce himself at the house where she was practically alone for the whole day; he found her like a child in the absence of the reserve which girls are trained to; he stepped at once into the position of a confidential friend; he took her about for walks and drives, a thing which might have compromised her seriously; he allowed Joseph Jagenal, without, it is true, stating it in so many words, to believe him an old friend of Phillis's; he followed her to Twickenham and installed himself at Mrs. L'Estrange's as an *ami de famille*; he had done so much to make the girl's life bright and happy, he was so dear to her, that he felt there was but one step to be taken to pass from a brother to a lover.

It was a black record to look at, and it was poor consolation to think that any other man would have done the same.

Jack Dunquerque, like Phillis herself, was changed within a month. Somehow the fun and carelessness which struck Gilead Beck as so remarkable in a man of five-and-twenty were a good deal damped. For the first time in his life he was serious; for the first time he had a serious and definite object before him. He was perfectly serious in an unbounded love for Phillis. Day by day the sweet beauty of the girl, her grace, her simple faith, her child-like affection, sank into his heart and softened him. Day after day, as he rowed along the meadows of the Thames, or lazied under the hanging willows by the shore, or sat with her in the garden, or rode along the leafy roads by her side, the sincerity of her nature, as clear and cloudless as the blue depths of heaven; its purity, like the bright water that leaps and bubbles and flows beneath the shade of Lebanon; its perfect truthfulness, like the midday sunshine in June; the innocence with which, even as another Eve, she bared her very soul for him to read—these things, when he thought of them, brought the unaccustomed tears to his eyes, and made his spirit rise and bound within him as to unheard of heights. For love, to an honest man, is like Nature to a poet or colour to an artist—it makes him see great depths, and gives him, if only for once in his life, a Pisgah view of a Land far, far holier, a life far, far higher, a condition far, far sweeter and nobler than anything in this world can give us—except the love of a good woman. In such a vision the ordinary course of our life is suspended; we move on air; we see men as trees walking, and regard them not. Happy the man who once in his life has been so lifted out of the present, and knows not afterwards whether he was in the flesh or out of the flesh.

Jack, with the influence of this great passion upon him, was transformed. Fortunately for us this emotion had its ebb and flow. Else that great dinner to Literature had never come off. But at all times he was under its sobering influence. And it was in a penitent and humble mood that he sought Lawrence Colquhoun, in the hope of "squaring it" with him as Ladds advised. Good fellow, Tommy; none better; but wanting in the higher delicacy. Somehow the common words and phrases of everyday use applied to Phillis jarred upon him. After all, one feels a difficulty in offering a princess the change for a shilling in coppers. If I had to do it, I should fall back on a draught upon the Cheque Bank.

Lawrence was full of his own annoyances—most of us always are, and it is one of the less understood ills of life that one can never get, even for five minutes, a Monopoly of Complaint. But he listened patiently while Jack—Jack of the Rueful Countenance—poured out his tale of repentance, woe, and prayer.

"You see," he said, winding up, "I never thought what it would come to. I dropped into it by accident and then—then—"

"When people come to flirt they stay to spoon," said Lawrence. "In other words, my dear fellow, you are in love. Ah!"

Jack wondered what was meant by the interjection. In all the list of interjections given by Lindley Murray, or the new light Dr. Morris, such as Pish! Phaw! Alas! Humph! and the rest which are in everybody's mouth, there is none which blows with such an uncertain sound as this. Impossible to tell whether it means encouragement, sympathy, or cold distrust.

"Ah!" said Lawrence. "Sit down and be comfortable, Jack. When one is really worried, nothing like a perfect chair. Take my own. Now, then, let us talk it over."

"It doesn't look well," thought Jack.

"Always face the situation," said Lawrence (he had got an uncommonly awkward situation of his own to face, and it was a little relief to turn to someone else's). "Nothing done by blinking facts. Here we are. Young lady of eighteen or so—just released from a convent; ignorant of the world; pretty; attractive ways; rich, as girls go—on the one hand. On the other, you: good-looking, as my cousin Agatha L'Estrange says, though I can't see it; of a cheerful disposition—*aptus ludere*, fit to play, *cum puellâ*, all the day—"

"Don't chaff, Colquhoun; it's too serious."

But Colquhoun went on:

"An inflammable young man. Well, with any other girl the danger would have been seen at once; poor Phillis is so innocent that she is supposed to be quite safe. So you go on calling. My cousin Agatha writes me word that she has been looking for the light of love, as she calls it, in Phillis's eyes; and it isn't there. She is a sentimentalist, and therefore silly. Why didn't she look in your eyes, Jack? That would have been very much more to the purpose."

"She has, now. I told her yesterday that I—I—loved Phillis."

"Did she ask you to take the young lady's hand and a blessing at once? Come, Jack, look at the thing sensibly. There are two or three very strong reasons why it can't be."

"Why it can't be!" echoed Jack dolefully.

"First, the girl hasn't come out. Now, I ask you, would it not be simply sinful not to give her a fair run? In any case you could not be engaged till after she has had one season. Then her father, who did not forget that he was grandson of a Peer, wanted his daughter to make a good match, and always spoke of the fortune he was to leave her as a guarantee that she would marry well. He never thought he was going to die, of course; but all events I know so much of his wishes. Lastly, my dear Jack Dunquerque, you are the best fellow in the world, but, you know—but—"

"But I am not Lord Isleworth."

"That is just it. You are his lordship's younger brother, with one or two between you and the title. Now don't you see? Need we talk about it anymore?"

"I suppose Phil—I mean Miss Fleming—will be allowed to choose for herself. You are not going to make her marry a man because he happens to have a title and an estate, and offers himself?"

"I suppose," said Lawrence, laughing, "that I am going to lock Phillis up in a tower until the right man comes. No, no, Jack; there shall be no compulsion. If she sets her heart upon marrying you—she is a downright young lady—why, she must do it; but after she has had her run among the ball-rooms, not before. Let her take a look round first; there will be other Jack Dunquerques ready to look at, be sure of that. Perhaps she will think them fairer to outward view than you. If she does, you will have to give her up in the end, you know."

"I have said no word of love to her, Colquhoun, I give you my honour," said Jack hotly, "I don't think she would understand it if I did."

"I am glad of that at least."

"If I am to give her up and go away, I dare say," the poor youth went on, with a little choking in his throat, "that she will regret me at first and for a day or two. But she will get over that; and—as you say, there are plenty of fellows in the world better than myself—and—"

"My dear Jack, there will be no going away. You tell me you have not told her all the effect that her *beaux yeux* have produced upon you. Well, then—and there has been nothing to compromise her at all?"

"Nothing; that is, once we went to the Tower in a hansom cab."

"Oh, that is all, is it? Jack Dunquerque—Jack Dunquerque!"

"And we have been up the river a good many times in a boat."

"I see. The river is pleasant at this time of the year."

"And we have been riding together a good deal. Phil rides very well, you know."

"Does she? It seems to me, Jack, that my cousin Agatha is a fool, and that you have been having rather a high time in consequence. Surely you can't complain if I ask you to consider the innings over for the present?"

"No; I can't complain, if one may hope—"

"Let us hope nothing. Sufficient for the day. He who hopes nothing gets everything. Come out of it at once, Jack, before you get hit too hard."

"I think no one was ever hit so hard before," said Jack. "Colquhoun, you don't know your ward. It is impossible for anyone to be with her without falling in love with her. She is—" Here he stopped, because he could not go any farther. Anybody who did not know the manly nature of Jack Dunquerque might have thought he was stopped by emotion.

"We all get the fever sometime or other. But we worry through. Look at me, Jack. I am forty, and, as you see, a comparatively hale and hearty man, despite my years. It doesn't shorten life, that kind of fever; it doesn't take away appetite; it doesn't interfere with your powers of enjoyment. There is even a luxury about it. You can't remember Geraldine Arundale, now Lady Newladegge, when she came out, of course. You were getting ready for Eton about that time. Well, she and I carried on for a whole season. People talked. Then she got engaged to her present husband, after seeing him twice. She wanted a Title, you see. I was very bad, that journey; and I remember that Agatha, who was in my confidence, had a hot time of it over the faithlessness of shallow hearts. But I got over the attack, and I have not been dangerously ill, so to speak since. That is, I have made a contemptible ass of myself on several occasions, and I dare say I shall go on making an ass of myself as long as I live. Because the older you grow, somehow, the sweeter do the flowers smell."

Jack only groaned. It really is no kind of consolation to tell a suffering man that you have gone through it yourself. Gilead Beck told me once of a man who lived in one of the Southern States of America: he was a mild, and placid creature, inoffensive as a canary bird, quiet as a mongoose, and much esteemed for his unusual meekness. This harmless being once got ear-ache—very bad ear-ache. Boyhood's ear-aches are awful things to remember; but those of manhood, when they do come, which is seldom, are the Devil. To him in agony came a friend, who sat down beside him, like Eliphaz the Temanite, and sighed. This the harmless being who had the ear-ache put up with, though it was irritating. Presently the friend began to relate how he once had the ear-ache himself. Then the harmless creature rose up suddenly, and, seizing an adjacent chunk of wood, gave that friend a token of friendship on the head with such effect that he ceased the telling of that and all other stories, and has remained quite dumb ever since. The jury acquitted that inoffensive and meek creature, who wept when the ear-ache was gone, and often laid flowers on the grave of his departed friend.

Jack did not heave chunks of wood at Colquhoun. He only looked at him with ineffable contempt.

"Lady Newladegge! why, she's five-and-thirty! and she's fat!"

"She wasn't always five-and-thirty, nor was she always fat. On the contrary, when she was twenty, and I was in love with her, she was slender, and, if one may so speak of a Peeress, she was cuddlesome!"

"Cuddlesome!" Jack cried, his deepest feelings outraged. "Good Heavens! to think of comparing Phil with a woman who was once cuddlesome!"

Lawrence Colquhoun laughed.

"In fifteen years, or thereabouts, perhaps you will take much the same view of things as I do. Meantime Jack, let things remain as they are. You shall have a fair chance with the rest; and you must remember that you have had a much better chance than anybody else, because you have had the first running. Leave off going to Twickenham quite so much; but don't stop going altogether, or Phillis may be led to suspect. Can't you contrive to slack off by degrees?"

Jack breathed a little more freely. The house, then, was not shut to him.

"The young lady will have her first season next year. I don't say I hope she will marry anybody else, Jack, but I am bound to give her the chance. As soon as she really understands a little more of life she will find out for herself what is best for her, perhaps. Now we've talked enough about it."

Jack Dunquerque went away sorrowful. He expected some such result of this endeavour to "square" it with Colquhoun, but yet he was disappointed.

"Hang it all, Jack," said Ladds, "what can you want more? You are told to wait a year. No one will step in between you and the young lady till she comes out. You are not told to discontinue your visits—only not to go too often, and not to compromise her. What more does the man want?"

"You are a very good fellow, Tommy," sighed the lover; "a very good fellow in the main. But you see, you don't know Phil. Let me call her Phil to you, old man. There's not another man in the world that I *could* talk about her to—not one, by Jove; it would seem a desecration."

"Go on, Jack—talk away; and I'll give you good advice."

He did talk away! What says Solomon? "Ointment and perfume rejoice the soul; so doth the sweetness of a man's friend by hearty counsel." The Wise Man might have expressed himself more clearly, but his meaning can be made out.

Meantime Lawrence Colquhoun, pulling himself together after Jack went away, remembered that he had not once gone near his ward since he drove her to Twickenham.

"It is too bad," said Conscience; "a whole month."

"It is all that woman's fault," he pleaded. "I have been dangling about, in obedience to her, like a fool."

"Like a fool!" echoed Conscience.

He went that very day, and was easily persuaded to stay and dine with the two ladies.

He said very little, but Agatha observed him watching his ward closely. After dinner she got a chance.

It was a pleasant evening, early in June. They had strawberries on a garden table. Phillis presently grew tired of sitting under the shade, and strolled down to the river-side, where she sat on the grass and threw biscuits to the swans.

"What do you think, Lawrence?"

He was watching her in silence.

"I don't understand it, Agatha. What have you done to her?"

"Nothing. Are you pleased?"

"You are a witch; I believe you must have a familiar somewhere. She is wonderful—wonderful!"

"Is she a ward to be proud of and to love, Lawrence? Is she the sweetest and prettiest girl you ever saw? My dear cousin, I declare to you that I think her faultless. At least, her very faults are attractive. She is impetuous and self-willed, but she is full of sympathy. And that seems to have grown up in her altogether in the last few months."

"Her manner appears to be more perfect than anything I have ever seen."

"It is because she has no self-consciousness. She is like a child still, my dear Phillis, so far."

"I wonder if it is because she cannot read? Why should we not prohibit the whole sex from learning to read?"

"Nonsense, Lawrence. What would the novelists do? Besides, she is learning to read fast. I put her this morning into the Third Lesson Book—two syllables. And it is not as if she were ignorant, because she knows a great deal."

"Then why is it?"

"I think her sweet nature has something to do with it; and, besides, she has been shielded from many bad influences. We send girls to school, and—and—well, Lawrence, we cannot all be angels, anymore than men. If girls learn about love, and establishments, and flirtations, and the rest of it, why, they naturally want their share of these good things. Then they get self-conscious."

"What about Jack Dunquerque?" asked Lawrence abruptly. "He has been to me about her."

Agatha blushed as prettily as any self-conscious young girl.

"He loves Phillis," she said; "but Phillis only regards him as a brother."

"Agatha, you are no wiser than little Red Riding Hood. Jack Dunquerque is a wolf."

"I am sure he is a most honourable, good young man."

"As for good, goodness knows. Honourable no doubt, and a wolf. You are a matchmaker, you bad, bad woman. I believe you want him to marry that young Princess over there."

"And what did you tell poor Jack?"

"Told him to wait. Acted the stern guardian. Won't have an engagement. Must let Phillis have her run. Mustn't come here perpetually trying to gobble up my dainty heiress. Think upon that now, Cousin Agatha."

"She could not marry into a better family."

"Very true. The Dunquerques had an Ark of their own, I believe, at the Deluge. But then Jack is not Lord Isleworth; and he isn't ambitious, and he isn't clever, and he isn't rich."

"Go on, Lawrence; it is charming to see you in a new character— Lawrence the Prudent!"

"Charmed to charm *la belle cousine*. He is in love, and he is hit as hard as any man I ever saw. But Phillis shall not be snapped up in this hasty and inconsiderate manner. There are lots of better *partis* in the field."

Then Phillis came back, dangling her hat by its ribbons. The setting sun made a glory of her hair, lit up the splendour of her eyes, and made a clear outline of her delicate features and tall shapely figure.

"Come and sit by me, Phillis," said her guardian. "I have neglected you. Agatha will tell you that I am a worthless youth of forty, who neglects all his duties. You are so much improved, my child, that I hardly knew you. Prettier and—and—everything. How goes on the education?"

"Reading and writing," said Phillis, "do not make education. Really, Lawrence, you ought to know better. A year or two with Mr. Dyson would have done you much good. I am in words of two syllables; and Agatha thinks I am getting on very nicely. I am in despair about my painting since we have been to picture-galleries. And to think how conceited I was once over it! But I *can* draw, Lawrence; I shall not give up my drawing."

"And you liked your galleries?"

"Some of them. The Academy was tiring. Why don't they put all the portraits in one room together, so that we need not waste time over them?"

"What did you look at?"

"I looked at what all the other people pressed to see, first of all. There was a picture of Waterloo, with the French and English crowded together so that they could shake hands. It was drawn beautifully; but somehow it made me feel as if War was a little thing. Mr. Dyson used to say that women take the grandeur and strength out of Art. Then there was a brown man with a sling on a platform. The platform rested on stalks of corn; and if the man were to throw the stone he would topple over, and tumble off his platform. And there was another one, of a row of women going to be sold for slaves; a curious picture, and beautifully painted, but I did not like it."

"What did you like?"

"I liked some that told their own story, and made me think. There was a picture of a moor—take me to see a moor, Lawrence—with a windy sky, and a wooden fence, and a light upon. Oh, I liked all the landscapes. I think our artists feel trees and sunshine. But what is my opinion worth?"

"Come with me tomorrow, Phillis; we will go through the pictures together, and you shall teach me what to like. Your opinion worth? Why, child, all the opinions of all the critics together are not worth yours."

XXXVI

"What is it that has been done?"

These anonymous letters and this fit of jealousy, the more dangerous because it was a new thing, came at an awkward time for Gabriel Cassilis. He had got "big" things in hand, and the eyes of the City, he felt, were on him. It was all-important that he should keep his clearness of vision and unclouded activity of brain. For the first time in his life his operations equalled, or nearly approached, his ambition. For the first time he had what he called a considerable sum in his hands. That is to say, there was his own money—he was reported to be worth three hundred thousand pounds—Gilead Beck's little pile, with his unlimited credit, and smaller sums placed in his hands for investment by private friends, such as Colquhoun, Ladds, and others. A total which enabled him to wait. And the share-market oscillating. And telegrams in cipher reaching him from all quarters. And Gabriel Cassilis unable to work, tormented by the one thought, like Io by her gad-fly, attacked by fits of giddiness which made him cling to the arms of his chair, and relying on a brain which was active, indeed, because it was filled with a never-ending succession of pictures, in which his wife and Colquhoun always formed the principal figures, but which refused steady work.

Gabriel Cassilis was a gamester who played to win. His game was not the roulette-table, where the bank holds one chance out of thirty, and must win in the long run; it was a game in which he staked his foresight, knowledge of events, financial connections, and calm judgment against greed, panic, enthusiasm, and ignorance. It was his business to be prepared against any turn of the tide. He would have stood calmly in the Rue Quincampoix, buying in and selling out up to an hour before the smash. And that would have found him without a single share in Law's great scheme. A great game, but a difficult one. It requires many qualities, and when you have got these, it requires a steady watchfulness and attention to the smallest cloud appearing on the horizon.

There were many clouds on the horizon. His grand *coup* was to be in Eldorado Stock. Thanks to Mr. Wylie's pamphlet they went down, and Gabriel Cassilis bought in—bought all he could; and the Stock went up. There was a fortnight before settling day.

They went up higher, and yet higher. El Señor Don Bellaco de la Carambola, Minister of the Eldorado Republic at St. James's, wrote a strong letter to the daily papers in reply to Mr. Wylie's pamphlet. He called attention to the rapid—the enormous—advance made in the State. As no one had seen the place, it was quite safe to speak of buildings, banks, commercial prosperity, and "openings up." It appeared, indeed from his letter that the time of universal wealth, long looked for by mankind, was actually arrived for Eldorado.

The Stock went higher. Half the country clergy who had a few hundreds in the bank wanted to put them in Eldorado Stock. Still Gabriel Cassilis made no move, but held on.

And everyday to get another of those accursed letters, with some new fact; everyday to groan under fresh torture of suspicion; everyday to go home and dine with the calm cold creature whose beauty had been his pride, and try to think that this impassive woman could be faithless.

This torture lasted for weeks; it began when Colquhoun first went to his house, and continued through May into June. His mental sufferings were so great that his speech became affected. He found himself saying wrong words, or not being able to hit upon the right word at all. So he grew silent. When he returned home, which was now early, he hovered about the house. Or he crept up to his nursery, and played with his year-old child. And the nurses noticed how, while he laughed and crowed to please the baby, the tears came into his eyes.

The letters grew more savage.

He would take them out and look at them. Some of the sentences burned into his brain like fire.

"As Mr. Lawrence Colquhoun is the only man she ever loved. Ask her for the secret. They think no one knows it.

"Does she care for the child—your child? Ask Tomlinson how often she sees it.

"When you go to your office, Mr. Colquhoun comes to your house. When you come home, he goes out of it. Then they meet somewhere else.

"Ask him for the secret. Then ask her, and compare what they say.

"Five years ago Mr. Lawrence Colquhoun and Miss Pengelley were going to be married. Everybody said so. She went to Scotland. He went after her. Ask him why.

"You are an old fool with a young wife. She loves your money, not you; she despises you because you are a City man; and she loves Mr. Colquhoun."

He sat alone in his study after dinner, reading these wretched things, in misery of soul. And a thought came across him.

"I will go and see Colquhoun," he said. "I will talk to him, and ask him what is this secret."

It was about ten o'clock. He put on his hat and took a cab to Colquhoun's chambers.

On that day Lawrence Colquhoun was ill at ease. It was borne in upon him with especial force—probably because it was one of the sultry and thunderous days when Conscience has it all her own disagreeable way—that he was and had been an enormous Ass. By some accident he was acquainted with the fact that he had given rise to talk by his frequent visits to Victoria Cassilis.

"And to think," he said to himself, "that I only went there at her own special request, and because she likes quarrelling!"

He began to think of possible dangers, not to himself, but to her and to her husband, even old stories revived and things forgotten and brought to light. And the thing which she had done came before him in its real shape and ghastliness—a bad and ugly thing; a thing for whose sake he should have fled from her presence and avoided her; a thing which he was guilty in hiding. No possible danger to himself? Well, in some sense none; in every other sense all dangers. He had known of this thing, and yet he sat at her table; he was conscious of the crime, and yet he was seen with her in public places; he was almost *particeps criminis*, because he did not tell what he knew; and yet he went day after day to her house—for the pleasure of quarrelling with her.

He sat down and wrote to her. He told her that perhaps she did not wholly understand him when he told her that the renewed acquaintance between them must cease; that, considering the past and with an eye to the future, he was going to put it out of her power to compromise herself by seeing her no more. He reminded her that she had a great secret to keep unknown, and a great position to lose; and then he begged her to give up her wild attempts at renewing the old ties of friendship.

The letter, considering what the secret really was, seemed a wretched mockery to the writer, but he signed it and sent it by his servant.

Then he strolled to his club, and read the papers before dinner. But he was not easy. There was upon him the weight of impending misfortune. He dined, and tried to drown care in claret, but with poor success, Then he issued forth—it was nine o'clock and still light—and walked gently homewards.

He walked so slowly that it was half-past nine when he let himself into his chambers in the Albany. His servant was out, and the rooms looked dismal and lonely. They were not dismal, being on the second floor, where it is light and airy, and being furnished as mediæval bachelorhood with plenty of money alone understands furniture. But he was nervous tonight, and grim stories came into his mind of spectres and strange visitors to lonely men in chambers. Such things happen mostly, he remembered, on twilight evenings in midsummer. He was quite right. The only ghost I ever saw myself was in one of the Inns of Court, in chambers, at nine o'clock on a June evening.

He made haste to light a lamp—no such abomination as gas was permitted in Lawrence Colquhoun's chambers: it was one of the silver reading-lamps, good for small tables, and provided with a green shade, so that the light might fall in a bright circle, which was Cimmertian blackness shading off into the sepia of twilight. It was his habit, too, to have lighted candles on the mantelshelf and on a table; but tonight he forgot them, so that, except for the light cast upwards by the gas in the court and an opposite window illuminated, and for the half-darkness of the June evening, the room was dark. It was very quiet, too. There was no footsteps in the court below, and no voices or steps in the room near him. His nearest neighbour, young Lord Orlebar, would certainly not be home, much before one or two, when he might return with a few friends connected with the twin services of the army and the ballet for a little cheerful supper. Below him was old Sir Richard de Counterpane, who was by this time certainly in bed, and perhaps sound asleep. Very quiet—he had never known it more quiet; and he began to feel as if it would be a relief to his nerves were something or somebody to make a little noise.

He took a novel, one that he had begun a week ago. Whether the novel of the day is inferior to the novel of Colquhoun's youth, or whether he was a bad reader of fiction, certainly he had been more than a week over the first volume alone.

Now it interested him less than ever.

He threw it away and lit a cigar. And then his thoughts went back to Victoria. What was the devil which possessed the woman that she could not rest quiet? What was the meaning of this madness upon her?

"A cold—an Arctic woman," Lawrence murmured. "Cold when I told her how much I loved her; cold when she engaged herself to me; cold in her crime; and yet she follows me about as if she was devoured by the ardour of love, like another Sappho."

It was not that, Lawrence Colquhoun; it was the *spretæ injuria formæ*, the jealousy and hatred caused by the lost power.

"I wish," he said, starting to his feet, and walking like the Polar bear across his den and back again, "I wish to heaven I had gone on living in the Empire City with my pair of villainous Chinamen. At least I was free from her over there. And when I saw her marriage, by Gad! I thought it was a finisher. Then I came home again."

He stopped in his retrospection, because he heard a foot upon the stairs.

A woman's foot; a light step and a quick step.

"May be De Counterpane's nurse. Too early for one of young Orlebar's friends. Can't be anybody for me."

But it was; and a woman stopped at his doorway, and seeing him alone, stepped in.

She had a hooded cloak thrown about an evening-dress; the hood was drawn completely over her face, so that you could see nothing of it in the dim light. And she came in without a word.

Then Colquhoun, who was no coward, felt his blood run cold, because he knew by her figure and by her step that it was Victoria Cassilis.

She threw back the hood with a gesture almost theatrical, and stood before him with parted lips and flashing eyes.

His spirits rallied a little then, because he saw that her face was white, and that she was in a royal rage. Lawrence Colquhoun could tackle a woman in a rage. That is indeed elementary, and nothing at all to be proud of. The really difficult thing is to tackle a woman in tears and distress. The stoutest heart quails before such an enterprise.

"What is this?" she began, with a rush as of the liberated whirlwind. "What does this letter mean, Lawrence?"

"Exactly what it says, Mrs. Cassilis. May I ask, is it customary for married ladies to visit single gentlemen in their chambers, and at night?"

"It is not usual for—married—ladies—to visit—single—gentlemen, Lawrence. Do not ask foolish questions. Tell me what this means, I say."

"It means that my visits to your house have been too frequent, and that they will be discontinued. In other words, Mrs. Cassilis, the thing has gone too far, and I shall cease to be seen with you. I suppose you know that people will talk."

"Let them talk. What do I care how people talk? Lawrence, if you think that I am going to let you go like this, you are mistaken."

"I believe this poor lady has gone mad," said Lawrence quietly. It was not the best way to quiet and soothe her, but he could not help himself.

"You think you are going to play fast and loose with me twice in my life, and you are mistaken. You shall not. Years ago you showed me what you are—cold, treacherous, and crafty—"

"Go on, Victoria; I like that kind of thing, because now I know that you are not mad. Quite in your best style."

"And I forgave you when you returned, and allowed you once more to visit me. What other woman would have acted so to such a man?"

"Yet she must be mad," said Lawrence. "How else could she talk such frightful rubbish?"

"Once more we have been friends. Again you have drawn me on, until I have learned to look to you, for the second time, for the appreciation denied to me by my—Mr. Cassilis. No, sir; this second desertion must not and shall not be."

"One would think," said Lawrence helplessly, "that we had not quarrelled everytime we met. Now, Mrs. Cassilis, you have my resolution. What you please, in your sweet romantic way, to call second desertion must be and shall be."

"Then I will know the reason why?"

"I have told you the reason why. Don't be a fool, Mrs. Cassilis. Ask yourself what you want. Do you want me to run away with you? I am a lazy man, I know, and I generally do what people ask me to do; but as for that thing, I am damned if I do it!"

"Insult me, Lawrence!" she cried, sinking into a chair. "Swear at me, as you will."

"Do you wish me to philander about your house like a ridiculous tame cat, till all the world cries out?"

She started to her feet.

"No!" she cried. "I care nothing about your coming and going. But I know why—Oh, I know why!—you make up this lame excuse about my good name—*my* good name! As if you cared about that!"

"More than you cared about it yourself," he retorted, "But pray go on."

"It is Phillis Fleming; I saw it from the very first. You began by taking her away from me and placing her with your cousin, where you could have her completely under your own influence. You let Jack Dunquerque hang about her at first, just to show the ignorant creature what was meant by flirtation, and then you send him about his business. Lawrence, you are more wicked than I thought you."

"Jealousy, by Gad!" he cried. "Did ever mortal man hear of such a thing? Jealousy! And after all that she has done—"

"I warn you. You may do a good many things. You may deceive and insult me in anyway except one. But you shall never, never marry Phillis Fleming!"

Colquhoun was about to reply that he never thought of marrying Phillis Fleming, but it occurred to him that there was no reason for making that assertion. So he replied nothing.

"I escaped," she said, "under pretence of being ill. And I made them fetch me a cab to come away in. My cab is at the Burlington Gardens end of the court now. Before I go you shall make me a promise, Lawrence—you used to keep your promises—to act as if this miserable letter had not been written."

"I shall promise nothing of the kind."

"Then remember, Lawrence—you *shall never marry Phillis Fleming*! Not if I have to stop it by proclaiming my own disgrace—you shall not marry that girl, or any other girl. I have that power over you, at any rate. Now I shall go."

"There is someone on the stairs," said Lawrence quietly.

"Perhaps he is coming here. You had better not be seen. Best go into the other room and wait."

There was only one objection to her waiting in the other room, and that was that the door was on the opposite side; that the outer oak was wide open; that the step upon the stairs was already the step upon the landing; and that the owner of the step was already entering the room.

Mrs. Cassilis instinctively shrank back into the darkest corner—that near the window. The curtains were of some light-coloured stuff. She drew them closely round her and cowered down, covering her head with the hood, like Guinevere before her injured lord. For the late caller was no other than her own husband, Gabriel Cassilis.

As he stood in the doorway the light of the reading-lamp—Mrs. Cassilis in one of her gestures had tilted up the shade—fell upon his pale face and stooping form. Colquhoun noticed that he stooped more than usual, and that his grave face bore an anxious look—such a look as one sees sometimes in the faces of men who have long suffered grievous bodily pain. He hesitated for a moment, tapping his knuckles with his double eyeglasses, his habitual gesture.

"I came up this evening, Colquhoun. Are you quite alone?"

"As you see, Mr. Cassilis," said Colquhoun. He looked hastily round the room. In the corner he saw the dim outline of the crouching form. He adjusted the shade, and turned the lamp a little lower. The gas in the chambers on the other side of the narrow court was put out, and the room was almost dark. "As you see, Mr. Cassilis. And what gives me the pleasure of this late call from you?"

"I thought I would come—I came to say—" he stopped helplessly, and threw himself into a chair. It was a chair standing near the corner in which his wife was crouching; and he pushed it back until he might have heard her breathing close to his ear, and, if he had put forth his hand, might have touched her.

"Glad to see you always, Mr. Cassilis. You came to speak about some money matters? I have an engagement in five minutes; but we shall have time, I dare say."

"An engagement? Ah! a lady, perhaps." This with a forced laugh, because he was thinking of his wife.

"A lady? Yes—yes, a lady."

"Young men—young men—" said Gabriel Cassilis. "Well, I will not keep you. I came here to speak to you about—about my wife."

"O Lord!" cried Lawrence. "I beg your pardon—about Mrs. Cassilis?"

"Yes; it is a very stupid business. You have known her for a long time."

"I have, Mr. Cassilis; for nearly eight years."

"Ah, old friends; and once, I believe, people thought—"

"Once, Mr. Cassilis, I myself thought—I cannot tell you what I thought Victoria Pengelley might be to me. But that is over long since."

"One for her," thought Lawrence, whose nerves were steady in danger. His two listeners trembled and shook, but from different causes.

"Over long since," repeated Gabriel Cassilis. "There was nothing in it, then?"

"We were two persons entirely dissimilar in disposition, Mr. Cassilis," Lawrence replied evasively. "Perhaps I was not worthy of her—her calm, clear judgment."

"Another for her," he thought, with a chuckle. The situation would have pleased him but that he felt sorry for the poor man.

"Victoria is outwardly cold, yet capable of the deepest emotions. It is on her account, Colquhoun, that I come here. Foolish gossip has been at work, connecting your names. I think it the best thing, without saying anything to Victoria, who must never suspect—"

"Never suspect," echoed Colquhoun.

"That I ever heard this absurdity. But we must guard her from calumny, Colquhoun. Cæsar's wife, you know; and—and—I think that, perhaps, if you were to be a little less frequent in your calls—and—"

"I quite understand, Mr. Cassilis; and I am not in the least offended. I assure you most sincerely—I wish Mrs. Cassilis were here to listen— that I am deeply sorry for having innocently put you to the pain of saying this. However, the world shall have no further cause of gossip."

No motion or sign from the dark corner where the hiding woman crouched.

Mr. Cassilis rose and tapped his knuckles with his glasses. "Thank you, Colquhoun. It is good of you to take this most unusual request so kindly. With such a wife as mine jealousy would be absurd. But I have to keep her name from even a breath—even a breath."

"Quite right, Mr. Cassilis."

He looked round the room.

"Snug quarters for a bachelor—ah! I lived in lodgings always myself. I thought I heard a woman's voice as I came upstairs."

"From Sir Richard de Counterpane's rooms down stairs, perhaps. His nurses, I suppose. The poor old man is getting infirm."

"Ay—ay; and your bedroom is there, I suppose?"

Lawrence took the lamp and opened the door. It was a bare, badly furnished room, with a little camp-bedstead, and nothing else hardly. For Lawrence kept his luxurious habits for the day.

Was it pure curiosity that made Gabriel Cassilis look all round the room?

"Ah, hermit-like. Now, I like a large bed. However, I am very glad I came. One word, Colquhoun, is better than a thousand letters; and you are sure you do not misunderstand me?"

"Quite," said Lawrence, taking his hat. "I am going out, too."

"No jealousy at all," said Gabriel Cassilis, going down the stairs.

"Certainly not."

"Nothing but a desire to—to—"

"I understand perfectly," said Lawrence.

As they descended, Lawrence heard steps on the stairs behind them. They were not yet, then, out of danger.

"Very odd," said Mr. Cassilis. "Coming up I heard a woman's voice. Now it seems as if there were a woman's feet."

"Nerves, perhaps," said Colquhoun. The steps above them stopped. "I hear nothing."

WALTER BESANT AND JAMES RICE

"Nor do I. Nerves—ah, yes—nerves."

Mr. Cassilis turned to the left, Colquhoun with him. Behind them he saw the cloaked and hooded figure of Victoria Cassilis. At the Burlington Gardens end a cab was waiting. Near the horse's head stood a woman's figure which Lawrence thought he knew. As they passed her this woman, whoever she was, covered her face with a handkerchief. And at the same moment the cab drove by rapidly. Gabriel Cassilis saw neither woman nor cab. He was too happy to notice anything. There was nothing in it; nothing at all except mischievous gossip. And he had laid the Ghost.

"Dear me!" he said to himself presently, "I forgot to ask about the Secret. But of course there is none. How should there be?"

Next morning there came another letter.

"You have been fooled worse than ever," it said. "Your wife was in Mr. Colquhoun's chambers the whole time that you were there. She came down the stairs after you; she passed through the gate, almost touching you, and she drove past you in a hansom cab. *I know the number*, and will give it to you when the time comes. Mr. Colquhoun lied to you. How long? How long?"

It should have been a busy day in the City. To begin with, it only wanted four days to settling-day. Telegrams and letters poured in, and they lay unopened on the desk at which Gabriel Cassilis sat, with this letter before him, mad with jealousy and rage.

XXXVII

"'Come now,' the Master Builder cried,
'The twenty years of work are done;
Flaunt forth the Flag, and crown with pride
The Glory of the Coping-Stone.'"

J ack Dunquerque was to "slack off" his visits to Twickenham. That is to say, as he interpreted the injunction, he was not wholly to discontinue them, in order not to excite suspicion. But he was not to haunt the house; he was to make less frequent voyages up the silver Thames; he was not to ride in leafy lanes side by side with Phillis—without having Phillis by his side he cared little about leafy lanes, and would rather be at the club; further, by these absences he was to leave off being necessary to the brightness of her life.

It was a hard saying. Nevertheless, the young man felt that he had little reason for complaint. Other fellows he knew, going after other heiresses, had been quite peremptorily sent about their business for good, particularly needy young men like himself. All that Colquhoun extorted of him was that he should "slack off." He felt, in a manner, grateful, although had he been a youth of quicker perception, he would have remembered that the lover who "slacks off" can be no other than the lover who wishes he had not begun. But nobody ever called Jack a clever young man.

He was not to give her up altogether. He was not even to give up hoping. He was to have his chance with the rest. But he was warned that no chance was to be open to him until the young lady should enter upon her first season.

Not to give up seeing her. That was everything. Jack Dunquerque had hitherto lived the life of all young men, careless and *insouciant*, with its little round of daily pleasures. He was only different from other young men that he had learned, partly from a sympathetic nature and partly by travel, not to put all his pleasure in that life about town and in country houses which seems to so many the one thing which the world has to offer. He who has lived out on the Prairies for weeks has found that there are other pleasures besides the gas-light joys of Town. But his life had been without thought and purposeless—a very chaos of a life. And now he felt vaguely that his whole being was changed. To be with

WALTER BESANT AND JAMES RICE

Phillis day after day, to listen to the outpourings of her freshness and innocence, brought to him the same sort of refreshment as sitting under the little cataract of a mountain stream brings to one who rambles in a hot West Indian island. Things for which he once cared greatly he now cared for no more; the club-life, the cards, and the billiards ceased to interest him; he took no delight in them. Perhaps it was a proof of a certain weakness of nature in Jack Dunquerque that he could not at the same time love things in which Phillis took no part and the things which made the simple pleasures of her every-day life.

He might have been weak, and yet, whether he was weak or strong, he knew that she leaned upon him. He was so sympathetic; he seemed to know so much; he decided so quickly; he was in his way so masterful, that the girl looked up to him as a paragon of wisdom and strength.

I think she will always so regard him, because the knowledge of her respect raises Jack daily in moral and spiritual strength, and so her hero approaches daily to her ideal. What is the highest love worth if it have not the power of lifting man and woman together up to the higher levels, where the air is purer, the sunshine brighter, the vision clearer?

But Colquhoun's commands had wrought a further change in him; that ugly good-looking face of his, which Agatha L'Estrange admired so much, and which was wont to be wreathed with a multitudinous smile, was now doleful. To the world of mankind—male mankind— the chief charm of Jack Dunquerque, the main cause of his popularity— his unvarying cheerfulness—was vanished.

"You ought to be called Doleful Jack," said Ladds. "Jack of Rueful Countenance."

"You don't know, Tommy," replied the lover, sorrowfully wagging his head. "I've seen Colquhoun; and he won't have it. Says I must wait."

"He's waited till forty. I've waited to five and thirty, and we're both pretty jolly. Come, young un, you may take courage by our examples."

"You never met Phil when you were five and twenty," said Jack. "Nobody ever saw a girl like Phillis."

Five and thirty seems so great an age to five and twenty. And at five and thirty one feels so young, that it comes upon the possessor of so many years like a shock of cold water to be reminded that he is really no longer young.

One good thing—Lawrence Colquhoun did not reproach him. Partly perhaps because, as a guardian, he did not thoroughly realize Jack's flagitious conduct; partly because he was an easy-going man, with a notion in his head that he had nothing to do with the work of Duennas and Keepers of the Gynæceum. He treated the confessions of the remorseful lover with a cheery contempt—passed them by; no great harm had been done; and the girl was but a child.

His own conscience it was which bullied Jack so tremendously. One day he rounded on his accuser like the poor worm in the proverb, who might perhaps have got safe back to its hole but for that ill-advised turning. He met the charges like a man. He pleaded that, criminal as he had been, nefarious and inexcusable as his action was, this action had given him a very high time; and that, if it was all to do over again, he should probably alter his conduct only in degree, but not in kind; that is to say, he would see Phillis oftener and stay with her longer. Conscience knocked him out of time in a couple of rounds; but still he did have the satisfaction of showing fight.

Of course he would do the same thing again. There has never been found by duenna, by guardian, by despotic parent, or by interested relation, any law of restraint strong enough to keep apart two young people of the opposite sex and like age, after they have once become attracted towards each other. Prudence and prudery, jealousy and interest, never have much chance. The ancient dames of duennadom may purse their withered lips and wrinkle their crow's-footed eyes; Love, the unconquered, laughs and conquers again.

It is of no use to repeat long explanations about Phillis. Such as she was, we know her—a law unto herself; careless of prohibitions and unsuspicious of danger. Like Una, she wandered unprotected and fearless among whatever two-legged wolves, bears, eagles, lions, vultures and other beasts and birds of prey might be anxiously waiting to snap her up. Jack was the great-hearted lion who was to bear her safely through the wistful growls of the meaner beasts. The lion is not clever like the fox or the beaver, but one always conceives of him as a gentleman, and therefore fit to be entrusted with such a beautiful maiden as Una or Phillis. And if Jack was quietly allowed to carry off his treasure it was Agatha L'Estrange who was chiefly to blame; and she, falling in love with Jack herself, quite in a motherly way, allowed the wooing to go on under her very nose. "A bad, bad woman," as Lawrence Colquhoun called her.

But such a wooing! Miss Ethel Citybredde, when she sees Amandus making a steady but not an eagerly impetuous advance in her direction at a ball, feels her languid pulses beat a little faster. "He is coming after

Me," she says to herself, with pride. They snatch a few moments to sit together in a conservatory. He offers no remark worthy of repetition, nor does she; yet she thinks to herself, "He is going to ask me to marry him; he will kiss me; there will be a grand wedding; everybody will be pleased; other girls will be envious; and I shall be delighted. Papa knows that he is well off and well connected. How charming!"

Now Phillis allowed her lover to woo her without one thought of love or marriage, of which, indeed, she knew nothing. But if the passion was all on one side, the affection was equally divided. And when Jack truly said that Phillis did not love him, he forgot that she had given him already all that she knew of love; in that her thoughts, which on her first emancipation leaped forth, bounding and running in all directions with a wild yearning to behold the Great Unknown, were now returning to herself, and mostly flowed steadily, like streams of electric influence, in the direction of Jack; inasmuch as she referred unconsciously everything to Jack, as she dressed for him, drew for him, pored diligently over hated reading books for him, and told him all her thoughts.

I have not told, nor can I tell, of the many walks and talks these two young people had together. Day after day Jack's boat—that comfortable old tub, in which he could, and often did, cut a crab without spilling the contents into the river—lay moored off Agatha's lawn, or rolled slowly up and down the river, Jack rowing, while Phillis steered, sang, talked, and laughed. This was pleasant in the morning; but it was far more pleasant in the evening, when the river was so quiet, so still and so black, and when thoughts crowded into the girl's brain, which fled like spirits when she tried to put them into words.

Or they rode together along the leafy roads through Richmond Park, and down by that unknown region, far away from the world, where heron rise up from the water's edge, where the wild fowl fly above the lake in figures which remind one of Euclid's definitions, and the deer collect in herds among great ferns half as high as themselves. There they would let the horses walk, while Phillis, with the slender curving lines of her figure, her dainty dress which fitted it so well, and her sweet face, made the heart of her lover hungry; and when she turned to speak to him, and he saw in the clear depths of her eyes his own face reflected, his passion grew almost too much for him to bear.

A delicate dainty maiden, who was yet of strong and healthy *physique*; one who did not disdain to own a love for cake and strawberries, cream and ices, and other pleasant things; who had no young-ladyish affectations; who took life eagerly, not languidly. And not a coward, as many maidens boast to be; she ruled her horse with a rein as firm as Jack Dunquerque, and sat him as steadily; she clinched her little fingers and set her lips hard when she heard a tale of wrong; her eyes lit up and her bosom heaved when she heard of heroic gest; she was strong to endure and to do. Not every girl would, as Phillis did, rise in the morning at five to train her untaught eyes and hand over those little symbols by which we read and write; not every girl would patiently begin at nineteen the mechanical drudgery of the music-lesson. And she did this in confidence, because Jack asked her everyday about her lessons, and Agatha L'Estrange was pleased.

The emotion which is the next after, and worse than that of love, is sympathy. Phillis passed through the stages of curiosity and knowledge before she arrived at the stage of sympathy. Perhaps she was not far from the highest stage of all.

She learned something everyday, and told Jack what it was. Sometimes it was an increase in her knowledge of evil. Jack, who was by no means so clever as his biographer, thought that a pity. His idea was the common one—that a maiden should be kept innocent of the knowledge of evil. I think Jack took a prejudiced, even a Philistine, view of the case. He put himself on the same level as the Frenchman who keeps his daughter out of mischief by locking her up in a convent. It is not the knowledge of evil that hurts, anymore than the knowledge of black-beetles, earwigs, slugs, and other crawling things; the pure in spirit cast it off, just as the gardener who digs and delves among his plants washes his hands and is clean. The thing that hurts is the suspicion and constant thought of evil; the loveliest and most divine creature in the world is she who neither commits any ill, nor thinks any, nor suspects others of ill—who has a perfect pity for backsliders, and a perfect trust in the people around her. Unfortunate it is that experience of life turns pity to anger, and trust into hesitation.

Or they would be out upon Agatha's lawn, playing croquet, to which that good lady still adhered, or lawn-tennis, which she tolerated. There would be the curate—he had abandoned that design of getting up *all* about Laud, but was madly, ecclesiastically madly, in love with Phillis; there would be occasionally Ladds, who, in his heavy, kindly way, pleased this young May Queen. Besides, Ladds was fond of Jack. There would be Gilead Beck in the straightest of frock coats, and on the most careful behaviour; there would be also two or three young ladies, compared with whom Phillis was as Rosalind at the court of her uncle, or as Esther among the damsels of the Persian king's seraglio, so fresh and so incomparably fair.

"Mrs. L'Estrange," Jack whispered one day, "I am going to say a rude thing. Did you pick out the other girls on purpose to set off Phillis?"

"What a shame, Jack!" said Agatha, who like the rest of the world called him by what was not his Christian name. "The girls are very nice—not so pretty as Phillis, but good-looking, all of them. I call them as pretty a set of girls as you would be likely to see on any lawn this season."

"Yes," said Jack; "only you see they are all alike, and Phillis is different."

That was it—Phillis was different. The girls were graceful, pleasant, and well bred. But Phillis was all this, and more. The others followed the beaten track, in which the strength of life is subdued and its intensity forbidden. Phillis was in earnest about everything, quietly in earnest; not openly bent on enjoyment, like the young ladies who run down Greenwich Hill, for instance, but in her way making others feel something of what she felt herself. Her intensity was visible in the eager face, the mobile flashes of her sensitive lips, and her brightening eyes. And, most unlike her neighbours, she even forgot her own dress, much as she loved the theory and practice of dress, when once she was interested, and was careless about theirs.

It was not pleasant for the minor stars. They felt in a vague uncomfortable way that Phillis was far more attractive; they said to each other that she was strange; one who pretended to know more French than the others said that she was *farouche*.

She was not in the least *farouche*, and the young lady her calumniator did not understand the adjective; but *farouche* she continued to be among the maidens of Twickenham and Richmond.

Jack Dunquerque heard the epithet applied on one occasion, and burst out laughing.

Phillis *farouche*! Phillis, without fear and without suspicion!

But then they do teach French so badly at girls' schools. And so poor Phillis remained ticketed with the adjective which least of any belonged to her.

A pleasant six weeks from April to June, while the late spring blossomed and flowered into summer; a time to remember all his life afterwards with the saddened joy which, despite Dante's observation, does still belong to the memory of past pleasures.

But every pleasant time passes, and the six weeks were over.

Jack was to "slack off." The phrase struck him, applied to himself and Phillis, as simply in bad taste; but the meaning was plain. He was to present himself at Twickenham with less frequency.

Accordingly he began well by going there the very next day. The new *régime* has to be commenced somehow, and Jack began his at once. He pulled up in his tub. It was a cloudy and windy day; drops of rain fell from time to time; the river was swept by sudden gusts which came driving down the stream, marked by broad black patches; there were no other boats out, and Jack struggled upwards against the current; the exercise at least was a relief to the oppression of his thoughts.

What was he to do with himself after the "slacking off" had begun—after that day, in fact? The visits might drop to twice a week, then once a week, and then? But surely Colquhoun would be satisfied with such a measure of self-denial. In the intervals—say from Saturday to Saturday—he could occupy himself in thinking about her. He might write to her—would that be against the letter of the law? It was clearly against the spirit. And—another consideration—it was no use writing unless he wrote in printed characters, and in words of not more than two syllables. He thought of such a love-letter, and of Phillis gravely spelling it out word by word to Mrs. L'Estrange. For poor Phillis had not as yet accustomed herself to look on the printed page as a vehicle for thought, although Agatha read to her everyday. She regarded it as the means of conveying to the reader facts such as the elementary reading-book delights to set forth; so dry that the adult reader, if a woman, presently feels the dust in her eyes, and if a man, is fain to get up and call wildly for quarts of bitter beer. No; Phillis was not educated up to the reception of a letter.

He would, he thought, sit in the least-frequented room of his club—the drawing-room—and with a book of some kind before him, just for a pretence, would pass the leaden hours in thinking of Phillis's perfections. Heavens! when was there a moment, by day or by night, that he did not think of them?

Bump! It was the bow of the ship, which knew by experience very well when to stop, and grounded herself without any conscious volition on his part at the accustomed spot.

Jack jumped out, and fastened the painter to the tree to which Phillis had once tied him. Then he strode across the lawns and flower-beds, and made for the little morning-room, where he hoped to find the ladies.

He found one of them. Fortune sometimes favors lovers. It was the younger one—Phillis herself.

She was bending over her work with brush and colour-box, looking as serious as if all her future depended on the success of that particular picture; beside her, tossed contemptuously aside, lay the much-despised Lesson-Book in Reading; for she had done her daily task. She did not hear Jack step in at the open window, and went on with her painting.

She wore a dress made of that stuff which looks like brown holland till you come close to it, and then you think it is silk, but are not quite certain, and I believe they call it Indian tussore. Round her dainty waist was a leathern belt set in silver with a châtelaine, like a small armoury of deadly weapons; and for colour she had a crimson ribbon about her neck. To show that the ribbon was not entirely meant for vanity, but had its uses, Phillis had slung upon it a cross of Maltese silver-work, which I fear Jack had given her himself. And below the cross, where her rounded figure showed it off, she had placed a little bunch of sweet peas. Such a dainty damsel! Not content with the flower in her dress, she had stuck a white jasmine-blossom in her hair. All these things Jack noted with speechless admiration.

Then she began to sing in a low voice, all to herself, a little French ballad which Mrs. L'Estrange had taught her—one of the sweet old French songs.

She was painting in the other window, at a table drawn up to face it. The curtains were partly pulled together, and the blind was half drawn down, so that she sat in a subdued light, in which only her face was lit up, like the faces in a certain kind of photograph, while her hair and figure lay in shadow. The hangings were of some light-rose hue, which tinted the whole room, and threw a warm colouring over the old-fashioned furniture, the pictures, the books, the flowers on the tables, and the ferns in their glasses. Mrs. L'Estrange was no follower after the new school. Neutral tints had small charms for her; she liked the warmth and glow of the older fashion in which she had been brought up.

It looked to Jack Dunquerque like some shrine dedicated to peace and love, with Phillis for its priestess—or even its goddess. Outside the skies were grey; the wind swept down the river with driving rain; here was warmth, colour, and brightness. So he stood still and watched.

And as he waited an overwhelming passion of love seized him. If the world was well lost for Antony when he threw it all away for a queen no longer young, and the mother of one son at least almost grown up, what would it have been had his Cleopatra welcomed him in all the splendour of her white Greek beauty at sweet seventeen? There was no world to be lost for this obscure cadet of a noble house, but all the world to be won. His world was before his eyes; it was an unconscious maid, ignorant of her own surpassing worth, and of the power of her beauty. To win her was to be the lord of all the world he cared for.

Presently she laid down her brush, and raised her head. Then she pushed aside the curtains, and looked out upon the gardens. The rain drove against the windows, and the wind beat about the branches of the lilacs on the lawn. She shivered, and pulled the curtains together again.

"I wish Jack were here," she said to herself.

"He is here, Phil," Jack replied.

She looked round, and darted across the room, catching him by both hands.

"Jack! Oh, I am glad! There is nobody at home. Agatha has gone up to town, and I am quite alone. What shall we do this afternoon?"

Clearly the right thing for him to propose was that he should instantly leave the young lady, and row himself back to Richmond. This, however, was not what he did propose. On the contrary, he kept Phillis's hands in his, and held them tight, looking in her upturned face, where he saw nothing but undisguised joy at his appearance.

"Shall we talk? Shall I play to you? Shall I draw you a picture? What shall we do, Jack?"

"Well, Phil, I think—perhaps—we had better talk."

Something in his voice struck her; she looked at him sharply.

"What has happened, Jack? You do not look happy."

"Nothing, Phil—nothing but what I might have expected." But he looked so dismal that it was quite certain he had not expected it.

"Tell me, Jack."

He shook his head.

"Jack, what *is* the good of being friends if you won't tell me what makes you unhappy?"

"I don't know how to tell you, Phil. I don't see a way to begin."

"Sit down, and begin somehow." She placed him comfortably in the largest chair in the room, and then she stood in front of him, and looked in his face with compassionate eyes. The sight of those deep-brown orbs, so full of light and pity, smote her lover with a kind of madness. "What is it makes people unhappy? Are you ill?"

He shook his head, and laughed.

WALTER BESANT AND JAMES RICE

"No, Phil; I am never ill. You see, I am not exactly unhappy—"

"But Jack, you look so dismal."

"Yes, that is it; I am a little dismal. No. Phil—no. I am really unhappy, and you are the cause."

"I the cause? But, Jack, why?"

"I had a talk with your guardian, Lawrence Colquhoun, yesterday. It was all about you. And he wants me—not to come here so often, in fact. And I musn't come."

"But why not? What does Lawrence mean?"

"That is just what I cannot explain to you. You must try to forgive me."

"Forgive you, Jack?"

"You see, Phil, I have behaved badly from the beginning. I ought not to have called upon you as I did in Carnarvon Square; I ought not to have let you call me Jack, nor should I have called you Phil. It is altogether improper in the eyes of the world."

She was silent for a while.

"Perhaps I have known, Jack, that it was a little unusual. Other girls haven't got a Jack Dunquerque, have they? Poor things! That is all you mean, isn't it, Jack?"

"Phil, don't look at me like that! You don't know—you can't understand—No; it is more than unusual; it is quite wrong."

"I have done nothing wrong," the girl said proudly. "If I had, my conscience would make me unhappy. But I do begin to understand what you mean. Last week Agatha asked me if I was not thinking too much about you. And the curate made me laugh because he said, quite by himself in a corner, you know, that Mr. Dunquerque was a happy man; and when I asked him, why he turned very red, and said it was because I had given to him what all the world would long to have. He meant, Jack—"

"I wish he was here," Jack cried hotly, "for me to wring his neck!"

"And one day Laura Herries—"

"That's the girl who said you were *farouche*, Phil. Go on."

"Was talking to Agatha about some young lady who had got compromised by a gentleman's attentions. I asked why, and she replied quite sharply that if I did not know, no one could know. Then she got up and went away. Agatha was angry about it, I could see; but she only said something about understanding when I come out."

"Miss Herries ought to have her neck wrung, too, as well as the curate," said Jack.

"Compromise—improper." Phil beat her little foot on the floor. "What does it all mean? Jack, tell me—what is this wrong thing that you and I have done?"

"Not you, Phil; a thousand times not you."

"Then I do not care much what other people say," she replied simply. "Do you know, Jack, it seems to me as if we never ought to care for what people, besides people we love, say about us."

"But it is I who have done wrong," said Jack.

"Have you, Jack? Oh, then I forgive you. I think I know you. You should have come to me with an unreal smile on your face, and pretended the greatest deference to my opinion, even when you knew it wasn't worth having. That is what the curate does to young ladies. I saw him yesterday taking Miss Herries's opinion on Holman Hunt's picture. She said it was 'sweetly pretty.' He said, 'Do you really think so?' in such a solemn voice, as if he wasn't quite sure that the phrase summed up the whole picture, but was going to think it over quietly. Don't laugh, Jack, because I cannot read like other people, and all I have to go by is what Mr. Dyson told me, and Agatha tells me, and what I see—and—and what you tell me, Jack, which is worth all the rest to me."

The tears came into her eyes, but only for a moment, and she brushed them aside.

"And I forgive you, Jack, all the more because you did not treat me as you would have treated the girls who seem to me so lifeless and languid, and—Jack, it may be wrong to say it, but Oh, so small! What compliment could you have paid me better than to single me out for your friend—you who have seen so much and done so much—my friend—mine? We were friends from the first, were we not? And I have never since hidden anything from you, Jack, and never will."

He kept it down still, this mighty yearning that filled his heart, but he could not bear to look her in the face. Every word that she said stabbed him like a knife, because it showed her childish innocence and her utter unconsciousness of what her words might mean.

And then she laid her little hand in his.

"And now you have compromised me, as they would say? What does it matter Jack? We can go on always just the same as we have been doing, can we not?"

He shook his head and answered huskily, "No, Phil. Your guardian will not allow it. You must obey him. He says that I am to come here less frequently; that I must not do you—he is quite right, Phil—anymore mischief; and that you are to have your first season in London without any ties or entanglements."

"My guardian leaves me alone here with Agatha. It is you who have been my real guardian, Jack. I shall do what you tell me to do."

"I want to do what is best for you, Phil—but—Child"—he caught her by the hands, and she half fell, half knelt at his feet, and looked up in his eyes with her face full of trouble and emotion—"child, must I tell you? Could not Agatha L'Estrange tell you that there is something in the world very different from friendship? Is it left for me to teach you? They call it Love, Phil."

He whispered the last words.

"Love? But I know all about it, Jack."

"No, Phil, you know nothing. It isn't the love that you bear to Agatha that I mean."

"Is it the love I have for you, Jack?" she asked in all innocence.

"It may be, Phil. Tell me only"—he was reckless now, and spoke fast and fiercely—"tell me if you love me as I love you. Try to tell me. I love you so much that I cannot sleep for thinking of you; and I think of you all day long. It seems as if my life must have been a long blank before I saw you; all my happiness is to be with you; to think of going on without you maddens me."

"Poor Jack!" she said softly. She did not offer to withdraw her hands, but let them lie in his warm and tender grasp.

"My dear, my darling—my queen and pearl of girls—who can help loving you? And even to be with you, to have you close to me, to hold your hands in mine, that isn't enough."

"What more—O Jack, Jack! what more?"

She began to tremble, and she tried to take back her hands. He let them go, but before she could change her position he bent down, threw his arms about her, and held her face close to his while he kissed it a thousand times.

"What more? My darling, my angel, this—and this! Phil, Phil! wake at last from your long childhood; leave the Garden of Eden where you have wandered so many years, and come out into the other world—the world of love. My dear, my dear! can you love me a little, only a little, in return? We are all so different from what you thought us; you will find out some day that I am not clever and good at all; that I have only one thing to give you—my love. Phil, Phil, answer me—speak to me—forgive me!"

He let her go, for she tore herself from him and sprang to her feet, burying her face in her hands and sobbing aloud.

"Forgive me—forgive me!" It was all that he could say.

"Jack, what is it? what does it mean? O Jack!"—she lifted her face and looked about her, with hands outstretched as one who feels in the darkness; her cheeks were white and her eyes wild—"what does it mean? what is it you have said? what is it you have done?"

"Phil!"

"Yes! Hush! don't speak to me—not yet, Jack. Wait a moment. My brain is full of strange thoughts"—she put out trembling hands before her, like one who wakes suddenly in a dream, and spoke with short, quick breath. "Something seems to have come upon me. Help me, Jack! Oh, help me! I am frightened."

He took her in his arms and soothed and caressed her like a child, while she sobbed and cried.

"Look at me, Jack," she said presently. "Tell me, am I the same? Is there any change in me?"

"Yes, Phil; yes, my darling. You are changed. Your sweet eyes are full of tears, like the skies in April; and your cheeks are pale and white. Let me kiss them till they get their own colour again."

He did kiss them, and she stood unresisting. But she trembled.

"I know, Jack, now," she said softly. "It all came upon me in a moment, when your lips touched mine. O Jack, Jack! it was as if something snapped; as if a veil fell from my eyes. I know now what you meant when you said just now that you loved me."

"Do you, Phil? And can you love me, too?"

"Yes, Jack. I will tell you when I am able to talk again. Let me sit down. Sit with me, Jack."

She drew him beside her on the sofa and murmured low, while he held her hands.

"Do you like to sit just so, holding my hands? Are you better now, Jack?

"Do you think, Jack, that I can have always loved you—without knowing it all—just as you love me? O my poor Jack!

"My heart beats so fast. And I am so happy. What have you said to me, Jack, that I should be so happy?

"See, the sun has come out—and the showers are over and gone—and the birds are singing—all the sweet birds—they are singing for me, Jack, for you and me—Oh, for you and me!"

Her voice broke down again, and she hid her face upon her lover's shoulder, crying happy tears.

He called her a thousand endearing names; he told her that they would be always together; that she had made him the happiest man in all the world; that he loved her more than any girl ever had been loved in the history of mankind; that she was the crown and pearl and queen of all the women who ever lived; and then she looked up, smiling through her tears.

Ah, happy, happy day! Ah, day forever to be remembered even when, if ever, the years shall bring its fiftieth anniversary to an aged pair, whose children and grandchildren stand around their trembling feet? Ah, moments that live forever in the memory of a life! They die, but are immortal. They perish all too quickly, but they bring forth the precious fruits of love and constancy, of trust, affection, good works, peace, and joy, which never perish.

"Take me on the river, Jack," she said presently. "I want to think it all over again, and try to understand it better."

He fetched cushion and wrapper, for the boat was wet, and placed her tenderly in the boat. And then he began to pull gently up the stream.

The day had suddenly changed. The morning had been gloomy and dull, but the afternoon was bright; the strong wind was dropped for a light cool breeze; the swans were cruising about with their lordly pretence of not caring for things external; and the river ran clear and bright.

They were very silent now; the girl sat in her place, looking with full soft eyes on the wet and dripping branches or in the cool depths of the stream.

Presently they passed an old gentleman fishing in a punt; he was the same old gentleman whom Phillis saw one morning—now so long ago—when he had that little misfortune we have narrated, and tumbled backwards in his ark. He saw them coming, and adjusted his spectacles.

"Youth and Beauty again," he murmured. "And she's been crying. That young fellow has said something cruel to her. Wish I could break his head for him. The pretty creature! He'll come to a bad end, that young man." Then he impaled an immense worm savagely and went on fishing.

A very foolish old gentleman this.

"I am trying to make it all out quite clearly, Jack," Phillis presently began. "And it is so difficult." Her eyes were still bright with tears, but she did not tremble now, and the smile was back upon her lips.

"My darling, let it remain difficult. Only tell me now, if you can, that you love me."

"Yes, Jack," she said, not in the frank and childish unconsciousness of yesterday, but with the soft blush of a woman who is wooed. "Yes, Jack, I know now that I do love you, as you love me, because my heart beat when you kissed me, and I felt all of a sudden that you were all the world to me."

"Phil, I don't deserve it. I don't deserve you."

"Not deserve me? O Jack, you make me feel humble when you say that! And I am so proud.

"So proud and so happy," she went on, after a pause. "And the girls who know all along—how do they find it out?—want everyone for herself this great happiness, too. I have heard them talk and never understood till now. Poor girls! I wish they had their—their own Jack, not my Jack."

Her lover had no words to reply.

"Poor boy! And you went about with your secret so long. Tell me how long, Jack?"

"Since the very first day I saw you in Carnarvon Square, Phil."

"All that time? Did you love me on that day—not the first day of all, Jack? Oh, surely not the very first day?"

"Yes; not as I love you now—now that I know you so well, my Phillis—mine—but only then because you were so pretty."

"Do men always fall in love with a girl because she is pretty?"

"Yes, Phil. They begin because she is pretty, and they love her more everyday when she is so sweet and so good as my darling Phil."

All this time Jack had been leaning on his oars, and the boat was drifting slowly down the current. It was now close to the punt where the old gentleman sat watching them.

"They have made it up," he said. "That's right." And he chuckled.

She looked dreamy and contented; the tears were gone out of her eyes, and a sweet softness lay there, like the sunshine on a field of grass.

"She is a rose of Sharon and a lily of the valley," said this old gentleman. "That young fellow ought to be banished from the State for making other people envious of his luck. Looks a good-tempered rogue, too."

He observed with delight that they were thinking of each other while the boat drifted nearer to his punt. Presently—bump—bump!

Jack seized his sculls and looked up guiltily. The old gentleman was nodding and smiling to Phillis.

"Made it up?" he asked most impertinently. "That is right, that is right. Give you joy, sir, give you joy. Wish you both happiness. Wish I had it to do all over again. God bless you, my dear!"

His jolly red face beamed like the setting sun under his big straw hat, and he wagged his head and laughed.

Jack laughed too; at other times he would have thought the old angler an extremely impertinent person. Now he only laughed.

Then he turned the boat's head, and rowed his bride swiftly homewards.

"Phil, I am like Jason bringing home Medea," he said, with a faint reminiscence of classical tradition. I have explained that Jack was not clever.

"I hope not," said Phil; "Medea was a dreadful person."

"Then Paris bringing home Helen—No, Phil; only your lover bringing home the sweetest girl that ever was. And worth five and thirty Helens."

When they landed, Agatha L'Estrange was on the lawn waiting for them. To her surprise, Phillis, on disembarking, took Jack by the arm, and his hand closed over hers. Mrs. L'Estrange gasped. And in Phillis's tear-bright eyes, she saw at last the light and glow of love; and in Phillis's blushing face she saw the happy pride of the celestial Venus who has met her only love.

"Children—children!" she said, "what is this?"

Phillis made answer, in words which Abraham Dyson used to read to her from a certain Book, but which she never understood till now—made answer with her face upturned to her lover—

"I am my beloved's, and his desire is toward me."

THEY WERE A QUIET PARTY that evening. Jack did not want to talk. He asked Phillis to sing; he sat by in a sort of rapture while her voice, in the songs she most affected, whispered and sang to his soul not words, but suggestions of every innocent delight. She recovered something of her gaiety, but their usual laughter was hushed as if by some unexpressed thought. It will never come back to her again, that old mirth and light heart of childhood. She felt while she played as if she was in some great cathedral; the fancies of her brain built over her head a pile more mystic and wonderful than any she had seen. Its arches towered to the sky; its aisles led far away into dim space. She was walking slowly up the church hand-in-hand with Jack, towards a great rose light in the east. An anthem of praise and thanksgiving echoed along the corridors, and pealed like thunder among the million rafters of the roof. Round them floated faces which looked and smiled. And she heard the voice of Abraham Dyson in her ear—

"Life should be two-fold, not single. That, Phillis, is the great secret of the world. Every man is a priest; every woman is a priestess; it is a sacrament which you have learned of Jack this day. Go on with him in faith and hope. Love is the Universal Church and Heaven is everywhere. Live in it; die in it; and dying begin your life of love again."

"Phil," cried Jack, "what is it? You look as if you had seen a vision."

"I have heard the voice of Abraham Dyson," she said solemnly. "He is satisfied and pleased with us, Jack."

That was nothing to what followed, for presently there occurred a really wonderful thing.

On Phillis's table—they were all three sitting in the pleasant morning-room—lay among her lesson-books and drawing materials a portfolio. Jack turned it over carelessly. There was nothing at all in it except a single sheet of white paper, partly written over. But there had been other sheets, and these were torn off.

"It is an old book full of writing," said Phillis carelessly. "I have torn out all the leaves to make rough sketches at the back. There is only one left now."

Jack took it up and read the scanty remnant.

"Good heavens!" he cried. "Have you really destroyed all these pages, Phil?"

Then he laughed.

"What is it, Jack? Yes I have torn them all out, drawn rough things on them, and then burnt them, everyone."

"Is it anything important?" asked Mrs. L'Estrange.

"I should think it was important!" said Jack. "Ho, ho! Phillis has destroyed the whole of Mr. Dyson's lost chapter on the Coping-stone. And now his will is not worth the paper it is written on."

It was actually so. Bit by bit, while Joseph Jagenal was leaving no corner unturned in the old house at Highgate in search of the precious document, without which Mr. Dyson's will was so much waste paper, this young lady was contentedly cutting out the sheets one by one and using them up for her first unfinished groups. Of course she could not read one word of what was written. It was a fitting Nemesis to the old man's plans that they were frustrated through the very means by which he wished to regenerate the world.

And now nothing at all left but a tag end, a bit of the peroration, the last words of the final summing-up. And this was what Jack read aloud—

". . . these provisions and no other. Thus will I have my College for the better Education of Women founded and maintained. Thus shall it grow and develop till the land is full of the gracious influence of womankind at her best and noblest. The Coping-stone of a girl's Education should be, and must be, Love. When Phillis Fleming, my ward, whose example shall be taken as the model for my college, feels the passion of Love, her education is finally completed. She will have much afterwards to learn. But self-denial, sympathy, and faith come best through Love. Woman is born to be loved; that woman only approaches the higher state who has been wooed and who has loved. When Phillis loves, she will give herself without distrust and wholly to the man who wins her. It is my prayer, my last prayer for her, that he may be worthy of her." Here Jack's voice faltered for a moment. "Her education has occupied my whole thoughts for thirteen years. It has been the business of my later years. Now I send her out into the world prepared for all, except treachery, neglect, and ill treatment. Perhaps her character would pass through these and come out the brighter. But we do not know; we cannot tell beforehand. Lord, lead her not into temptation; and so deal with her lover as he shall deal with her."

"Amen," said Agatha L'Estrange.

But Phillis sprang to her feet and threw up her arms.

"I have found it!" she cried. "Oh, how often did he talk to me about the Coping-stone. Now I have nothing more to learn. O Jack, Jack!" she fell into his arms, and lay there as if it was her proper place. "We have found the Coping-stone—you and I between us—and it is here, it is here!"

XXXVIII

"'Tis well to be off with the old love,
Though you never get on with a new."

During the two of three weeks following their success with Gilead
Beck the Twins were conspicuous, had anyone noticed them, for
a recklessness of expenditure quite without parallel in their previous
history. They plunged as regarded hansoms, paying whatever was asked
with an airy prodigality; they dined at the club everyday, and drank
champagne at all hours; they took half-guinea stalls at theatres: they
went down to Greenwich and had fish-dinners; they appeared with new
chains and rings; they even changed their regular hours of sleep, and
sometimes passed the whole day broad awake, in the pursuit of youthful
pleasures. They winked and nodded at each other in a way which
suggested all kinds of delirious delights; and Cornelius even talked
of adding an episode to the Epic, based on his own later experiences,
which he would call, he said, the Jubilee of Joy.

The funds for this fling, all too short, were provided by their
American patron. Gilead Beck had no objection to advance them
something on account; the young gentlemen found it so pleasant
to spend money, that they quickly overcame scruples about asking
for more; perhaps they would have gone on getting more, but for
a word of caution spoken by Jack Dunquerque. In consequence of
this unkindness they met each other one evening in the Studio with
melancholy faces.

"I had a letter today from Mr. Gilead Beck," said Cornelius to
Humphrey.

"So had I," said Humphrey to Cornelius.

"In answer to a note from me," said Cornelius.

"In reply to a letter of mine," said Humphrey.

"It is sometimes a little awkward, brother Humphrey," Cornelius
remarked with a little temper, "that our inclinations so often prompt us
to do the same thing at the same time."

Said Humphrey, "I suppose then, Cornelius, that you asked him for
money?"

"I did, Humphrey. How much has the Patron advanced you already
on the great Picture?"

"Two hundred only. A mere trifle. And now he refuses to advance anymore until the Picture is completed. Some enemy, some jealous brother artist, must have corrupted his mind."

"My case, too. I asked for a simple fifty pounds. It is the end of May, and the country would be delightful if one could go there. I have already drawn four or five cheques of fifty each, on account of the Epic. He says, this mercenary and mechanical patron, that he will not lend me anymore until the Poem is brought to him finished. Some carping critic has been talking to him."

"How much of the Poem is finished?"

"How much of the Picture is done?"

The questions were asked simultaneously, but no answer was returned by either.

Then each sat for a few moments in gloomy silence.

"The end of May," murmured Humphrey. "We have to be ready by the beginning of October. June—July—only four months. My painting is designed for many hundreds of figures. Your poem for—how many lines, brother?"

"Twenty cantos of about five hundred lines each."

"Twenty times five hundred is ten thousand."

Then they relapsed into silence again.

"Brother Cornelius," the Artist went on, "this has been a most eventful year for us. We have been rudely disturbed from the artistic life of contemplation and patient work into which we had gradually dropped. We have been hurried—hurried, I say, brother—into Action, perhaps prematurely—"

Cornelius grasped his brother's hand, but said nothing.

"You, Cornelius, have engaged yourself to be married."

Cornelius dropped his brother's hand. "Pardon me, Humphrey; it is you that is engaged to Phillis Fleming."

"I am nothing of the sort, Cornelius," the other returned sharply. "I am astonished that you should make such a statement."

"One of us certainly is engaged to the young lady. And as certainly it is not I. 'Let your brother Humphrey hope,' she said. Those were her very words. I do think, brother, that it is a little ungenerous, a little ungenerous of you, after all the trouble I took on your behalf, to try to force this young lady on me."

Humphrey's cheek turned pallid. He plunged his hands into his silky beard, and walked up and down the room gesticulating.

"I went down on purpose to tell Phillis about him. I spoke to her of his ardour. She said she appreciated—said she appreciated it, Cornelius. I even went so far as to say that you offered her a virgin heart—perilling my own soul by those very words—a virgin heart"—he laughed melodramatically. "And after that German milkmaid! Ha, ha! The Poet and the milkmaid!"

Cornelius by this time was red with anger. The brothers, alike in so many things, differed in this, that, when roused to passion, while Humphrey grew white Cornelius grew crimson.

"And what did I do for you?" he cried out. The brothers were now on opposite sides of the table, walking backwards and forwards with agitated strides. "I told her that you brought her a heart which had never beat for another—that, after your miserable little Roman model! An artist not able to resist the charms of his own model!"

"Cornelius!" cried Humphrey, suddenly stopping and bringing his fist with a bang upon the table.

"Humphrey!" cried his brother, exactly imitating his gesture.

Their faces glared into each other's; Cornelius, as usual, wrapped in his long dressing-gown, his shaven cheeks purple with passion; Humphrey in his loose velvet jacket, his white lips and cheeks, and his long silken beard trembling to every hair.

It was the first time the brothers had ever quarrelled in all their lives. And like a tempest on Lake Windermere, it sprang up without the slightest warning.

They glared in a steady way for a few minutes, and then drew back and renewed their quick and angry walk side by side, with the table between them.

"To bring up the old German business!" said Cornelius.

"To taunt me with the Roman girl!" said Humphrey.

"Will you keep your engagement like a gentleman, and marry the girl?" cried the Poet.

"Will you behave as a man of honour, and go to the Altar with Phillis Fleming?" asked the Artist.

"I will not," said Cornelius. "Nothing shall induce me to get married."

"Nor will I," said Humphrey. "I will see myself drawn and quartered first."

"Then," said Cornelius, "go and break it to her yourself, for I will not."

"Break what?" asked Humphrey passionately. "Break her heart, when I tell her, if I must, that my brother repudiates his most sacred promises?"

Cornelius was touched. He relented. He softened.

"Can it be that she loves us both?"

They were at the end of the table, near the chairs, which as usual were side by side.

"Can that be so, Cornelius?"

They drew nearer the chairs; they sat down; they turned, by force of habit, lovingly towards each other; and their faces cleared.

"Brother Humphrey," said Cornelius, "I see that we have mismanaged this affair. It will be a wrench to the poor girl, but it will have to be done. I thought you *wanted* to marry her."

"I thought *you* did."

"And so we each pleaded the other's cause. And the poor girl loves us both. Good heavens! What a dreadful thing for her."

"I remember nothing in fiction so startling. To be sure, there is some excuse for her."

"But she can't marry us both?"

"N—n—no. I suppose not. No—certainly not. Heaven forbid! And as you will not marry her—"

Humphrey shook his head in a decided manner.

"And I will not—"

"Marry?" interrupted Humphrey. "What! And give up this? Have to get up early; to take breakfast at nine; to be chained to work; to be inspected and interfered with while at work—Phillis drew me once, and pinned the portrait on my easel; to be restricted in the matter of port; to have to go to bed at eleven; perhaps, Cornelius, to have babies; and beside, if they should be Twins! Fancy being shaken out of your poetic dream by the cries of Twins!"

"No sitting up at night with pipes and brandy-and-water," echoed the Poet. "And, Humphrey"—here he chuckled, and his face quite returned to its brotherly form—"should we go abroad, no flirting with Roman models—eh, eh, eh?"

"Ho, ho, ho!" laughed the Artist melodiously. "And no carrying milk-pails up the Heidelberg hills—eh, eh, eh?"

"Marriage be hanged!" cried the Poet, starting up again. "We will preserve our independence, Humphrey. We will be free to woo, but not to wed."

Was there ever a more unprincipled Bard? It is sad to relate that the Artist echoed his brother.

"We will, Cornelius—we will. *Vive la liberté!*" He snapped his fingers, and began to sing:

> *"Quand on est a Paris*
> *On ecrit a son pere,*
> *Qui fait reponse, 'Brigand,*
> *Tu n'en as—'"*

He broke short off, and clapped his hands like a school-boy. "We will go to Paris next week, brother."

"We will, Humphrey, if we can get anymore money. And now—how to get out of the mess?"

"Do you think Mrs. L'Estrange will interfere?"

"Or Colquhoun?"

"Or Joseph?"

"The best way would be to pretend it was all a mistake. Let us go tomorrow, and cry off as well as we can."

"We will, Cornelius."

The quarrel and its settlement made them thirsty, and they drank a whole potash-and-brandy each before proceeding with the interrupted conversation.

"Poor little Phillis!" said the Artist, filling his pipe. "I hope she won't pine much."

"Ariadne, you know," said the Poet; and then he forgot what Ariadne did, and broke off short.

"It isn't our fault, after all. Men of genius are always run after. Women are made to love men, and men are made to break their hearts. Law of nature, dear Cornelius—law of Nature. Perhaps the man is a fool who binds himself to one. Art alone should be our mistress—glorious Art!"

"Yes," said Cornelius; "you are quite right. And what about Mr. Gilead Beck?"

This was a delicate question, and the Artist's face grew grave.

"What are we to do, Cornelius?"

"I don't know, Humphrey."

"Will the Poem be finished?"

"No. Will the Picture?"

"Not a chance."

"Had we not better, Humphrey, considering all the circumstances, make up our minds to throw over the engagement?"

"Tell me, Cornelius—how much of your Poem remains to be done?"

"Well, you see, there is not much actually written."

"Will you show it to me—what there is of it?"

"It is all in my head, Humphrey. Nothing is written."

He blushed prettily as he made the confession. But the Artist met him half-way with a frank smile.

"It is curious, Cornelius, that up to the present I have not actually drawn any of the groups. My figures are still in my head."

Both were surprised. Each, spending his own afternoons in sleep, had given the other credit for working during that part of the day. But they were too much accustomed to keep up appearances to make any remark upon this curious coincidence.

"Then, brother," said the Poet, with a sigh of relief, "there really is not the slightest use in leading Mr. Beck to believe that the works will be finished by October, and we had better ask for a longer term. A year longer would do for me."

"A year longer would, I think, do for me," said Humphrey, stroking his beard, as if he was calculating how long each figure would take to put in. "We will go and see Mr. Beck tomorrow."

"Better not," said the sagacious Poet.

"Why not?"

"He might ask for the money back."

"True, brother. He must be capable of that meanness, or he would have given us that cheque we asked for. Very true. We will write."

"What excuse shall we make?"

"We will state the exact truth, Brother. No excuse need be invented. We will tell our Patron that Art cannot—must not—be forced."

This settled, Cornelius declared that a weight was off his mind, which had oppressed him since the engagement with Mr. Beck was first entered into. Nothing, he said, so much obstructed the avenues of fancy, checked the flow of ideas, and destroyed grasp of language, as a slavish time-engagement. Now, he went on to explain, he felt free; already his mind, like a garden in May, was blossoming in a thousand sweet flowers. Now he was at peace with mankind. Before this relief he had been—Humphrey would bear him out—inclined to lose his temper over trifles; and the feeling of thraldom caused him only that very evening to use harsh words even to his twin brother. Here he held out his hand, which Humphrey grasped with effusion.

They wrote their letters next day—not early in the day, because they prolonged their evening parliament till late, and it was one o'clock when they took breakfast But they wrote the letters after breakfast, and at two they took the train to Twickenham.

Phillis received them in her morning-room. They appeared almost as nervous and agitated as when they called a week before. So shaky were their hands that Phillis began by prescribing for them a glass of wine each, which they took, and said they felt better.

"We come for a few words of serious explanation," said the Poet.

"Yes," said Phillis. "Will Mrs. L'Estrange do?"

"On the contrary, it is with you that we would speak."

"Very well," she replied. "Pray go on."

They were sitting side by side on the sofa, looking as grave as a pair of owls. There was something Gog and Magogish, too, in their proximity.

Phillis found herself smiling when she looked at them. So, to prevent laughing in their very faces, she changed her place, and went to the open window.

"Now," she said.

Cornelius, with the gravest face in the world, began again.

"It is a delicate and, I fear, a painful business," he said. "Miss Fleming, you doubtless remember a conversation I had with you last week on your lawn?"

"Certainly. You told me that your brother, Mr. Humphrey, adored me. You also said that he brought me a virgin heart. I remember perfectly. I did not understand your meaning then. But I do now. I understand it now." She spoke the last words with softened voice, because she was thinking of the Coping-stone and Jack Dunquerque.

Humphrey looked indignantly at his brother. Here was a position to be placed in! But Cornelius lifted his hand, with a gesture which meant, "Patience; I will see you through this affair," and went on—

"You see, Miss Fleming, I was under a mistake. My brother, who has the highest respect, in the abstract, for womanhood, which is the incarnation and embodiment of all that is graceful and beautiful in this fair world of ours, does not—does not—after all—"

Phillis looked at Humphrey. He sat by his brother, trembling with a mixture of shame and terror. They were not brave men, these Twins, and they certainly drank habitually more than is good for the nervous system.

She began to laugh, not loudly, but with a little ripple of mirth which terrified them both, because in their vanity they thought it the first symptoms of hysterical grief. Then she stepped to the sofa, and placed both her hands on the unfortunate Artist's shoulder.

He thought that she was going to shake him, and his soul sank into his boots.

"You mean that he does not, after all, adore me. O Mr. Humphrey, Mr. Humphrey! was it for this that you offered me a virgin heart? Is this your gratitude to me for drawing your likeness when you were hard at work in the Studio? What shall I say to your brother Joseph, and what will he say to you?"

"My dear young lady," Cornelius interposed hastily, "there is not the slightest reason to bring Joseph into the business at all. He must not be told of this unfortunate mistake. Humphrey does adore you—speak, brother—do you not adore Miss Fleming?"

Humphrey was gasping and panting.

"I do," he exclaimed, "I do Oh, most certainly."

Then Phillis left him and turned to his brother.

"But there is yourself, Mr. Cornelius. You are not an artist; you are a poet; you spend your days in the Workshop, where Jack Dunquerque and I found you rapt in so poetic a dream that your eyes were closed and your mouth open. If you made a mistake about Humphrey, it is impossible that he could have made a mistake about you."

"This is terrible," said Cornelius. "Explain, brother Humphrey. Miss Fleming, we—no, you as well—are victims of a dreadful error."

He wiped his brow and appealed to his brother.

Released from the terror of Phillis's hands upon his shoulder, the Artist recovered some of his courage and spoke. But his voice was faltering. "I, too," he said, "mistook the respectful admiration of my brother for something dearer. Miss Fleming, he is already wedded."

"Wedded? Are you a married man, Mr. Cornelius? Oh, and where is the virgin heart?"

"Wedded to his art," Humphrey explained. Then he went a little off his head, I suppose, in the excitement of this crisis, because he continued in broken words, "Wedded—long ago—object of his life's love—with milk-pails on the hills of Heidelberg, and light blue eyes—the Muse of Song. But he regards you with respectful admiration."

"Most respectful," said Cornelius. "As Petrarch regarded the wife of the Count de Sade. Will you forgive us, Miss Fleming, and—and—try to forget us?"

"So, gentlemen," the young lady said, with sparkling eyes, "you come to say that you would rather not marry me. I wonder if that is usual with men?"

"No, no!" they both cried together. "Happy is the man—"

"You may be the happy man, Humphrey," said Cornelius.

"No; you, brother—you."

Never had wedlock seemed so dreadful a thing as it did now, with a possible bride standing before them, apparently only waiting for the groom to make up his mind.

"I will forgive you both," she said; "so go away happy. But I am afraid I shall never, never be able to forget you. And if I send you a sketch of yourselves just as you look now, so ashamed and so foolish, perhaps you will hang it up in the Workshop or the Studio, to be looked at when you are awake; that is, when you are not at work."

They looked guiltily at each other and drew a little apart. It was the most cruel speech that Phillis had ever made; but she was a little angry with this vain and conceited pair of windbags.

"I shall not tell Mr. Joseph Jagenal, because he is a sensible man and would take it ill, I am sure. And I shall not tell my guardian, Lawrence Colquhoun, because I do not know what he might say or do. And I shall not tell Mrs. L'Estrange; that is, I shall not tell her the whole of it, for your sakes. But I must tell Jack Dunquerque, because I am engaged to be married to Jack, and because I love him and must tell him everything."

They cowered before her as they thought of the possible consequences of this information.

"You need not be frightened," she went on; "Jack will not call to see you and disturb you at your work."

Her eyes, that began by dancing with fun, now flashed indignation. It was not that she felt angry at what most girls would have regarded as a deliberate insult, but the unmanliness of the two filled her with contempt. They looked so small and so mean.

"Go," she said, pointing to the door. "I forgive you. But never again dare to offer a girl each other's virgin heart."

They literally slunk away like a pair of beaten hounds. Then Phillis suddenly felt sorry for them as they crept out of the door, one after the other. She ran after them and called them back.

"Stop," she cried; "we must not part like that. Shake hands, Cornelius. Shake hands, Humphrey. Come back and take another glass of wine. Indeed you want it; you are shaking all over; come."

WALTER BESANT AND JAMES RICE

She led them back, one in each hand, and poured out a glass of sherry for each.

"You could not have married me, you know," she said, laughing, "because I am going to marry Jack. There—forgive me for speaking unkindly, and we will remain friends."

They took her hand, but they did not speak, and something like a tear stood in their eyes. When they left her Phillis observed that they did not take each other's arm as usual, but walked separate. And they looked older.

XXXIX

"What is it you see?
A nameless thing—a creeping snake in the grass."

Who was the writer of the letters? They were all in one hand, and that a feigned hand. Gabriel Cassilis sat with these anonymous accusations against his wife spread out upon the table before him. He compared one with another; he held them up to the light; he looked for chance indications which a careless moment might leave behind; there were none—not a stroke of the pen; not even the name of the shop where the paper was sold. They were all posted at the same place; but that was nothing.

The handwriting was large, upright, and perhaps designedly ill-formed; it appeared to be the writing of a woman, but of this Mr. Cassilis was not sure.

Always the same tale; always reference to a secret between Colquhoun and his wife. What was that secret?

In Colquhoun's room—alone with him—almost under his hand. But where? He went into the bedroom, which was lighted by the gas of the court; an open room, furnished without curtains; there was certainly no one concealed, because concealment was impossible. And in the sitting-room—then he remembered that the room was dimly lighted; curtains kept out the gas-light of the court; Colquhoun had on his entrance lowered the silver lamp; there was a heavy green shade on this; it was possible that she might have been in the room while he was there, and listening to every word.

The thought was maddening. He tried to put it all before himself in logical sequence, but could not; he tried to fence with the question, but it would not be evaded; he tried to persuade himself that suspicions resting on an anonymous slander were baseless, but everytime his mind fell back upon the voice which proclaimed his wife's dishonour.

A man on the rack might as well try to dream of soft beds and luxurious dreamless sleep; a man being flogged at the cart-tail might as well try to transport his thoughts to boyhood's games upon a village green; a man at the stake might as well try to think of deep delicious draughts of ice-cold water from a shady brook. The agony and shame of the present are too much for any imagination.

WALTER BESANT AND JAMES RICE

It was so to Gabriel Cassilis. The one thing which he trusted in, after all the villainies and rogueries he had learned during sixty-five years mostly spent among men trying to make money, was his wife's fidelity. It was like the Gospel—a thing to be accepted and acted upon with unquestioning belief. Good heavens! if a man cannot believe in his wife's honesty, in what is he to believe?

Gabriel Cassilis was not a violent man; he could not find relief in angry words and desperate deeds like a Moor of Venice; his jealousy was a smouldering fire; a flame which burned with a dull fierce heat; a disease which crept over body and mind alike, crushing energy, vitality, and life out of both.

Everything might go to ruin round him; he was no longer capable of thought and action. Telegrams and letters lay piled before him on the table, and he left them unopened.

Outside, his secretary was in dismay. His employer would receive no one, and would attend to nothing. He signed mechanically such papers as were brought him to sign, and then he motioned the secretary to the door.

This apathy lasted for four days—the four days most important of any in the lives of himself, of Gilead Beck, and of Lawrence Colquhoun. For the fortunes of all hung upon his shaking it off, and he did not shake it off.

On the second day, the day when he got the letter telling him that his wife had been in Colquhoun's chambers while he was there, he sent for a private detective.

He put into his hands all the letters.

"Written by a woman," said the officer. "Have you any clue, sir?"

"None—none whatever. I want you to watch. You will watch my wife and you will watch Mr. Colquhoun. Get every movement watched, and report to me every morning. Can you do this? Good. Then go, and spare neither pains nor money."

The next morning's report was unsatisfactory. Colquhoun had gone to the Park in the afternoon, dined at his club, and gone home to his chambers at eleven. Mrs. Cassilis, after dining at home, went out at ten, and returned early—at half-past eleven.

But there came a letter from the anonymous correspondent.

"You are having a watch set on them. Good. But that won't find out the Scotch secret. She *was* in his room while you were there—hidden somewhere, but I do not know where."

He went home to watch his wife with his own eyes. He might as well have watched a marble statue. She met his eyes with the calm cold look to which he was accustomed. There was nothing in her manner to show that she was other than she had always been. He tried in her presence to realise the fact, if it was a fact. "This woman," he said to himself, "has been lying hidden in Colquhoun's chambers listening while I talked to him. She was there before I went; she was there when I came away. What is her secret?"

What, indeed! She seemed a woman who could have no secrets, a woman whose life from her cradle might have been exposed to the whole world, who would have found nothing but cause of admiration and respect.

In her presence, under her influence, his jealousy lost something of its fierceness. He feared her too much to suspect her while in his sight. It was at night, in his office, away from her, that he gave full swing to the bitterness of his thoughts. In the hours when he should have been sleeping he paced his room, wrapped in his dressing-gown—a long lean figure, with eyes aflame, and thoughts that tore him asunder; and in the hours when he should have been waking he sat with bent shoulders, glowering at the letters of her accuser, gazing into a future which seemed as black as ink.

His life, he knew, was drawing to its close. Yet a few more brief years, and the summons would come for him to cross the River. Of that he had no fear; but it was dreadful to think that his age was to be dishonoured. Success was his; the respect which men give to success was his; no one inquired very curiously into the means by which success was commanded; he was a name and a power. Now that name was to be tarnished; by no act of his own, by no fault of his; by the treachery of the only creature in the world, except his infant child, in whom he trusted.

He would have, perhaps, to face the publicity of an open court; to hear his wrongs set forth to a jury; to read his "case" in the daily papers.

And he would have to alter his will.

Oddly enough, of all the evil things which seemed about to fall on him, not one troubled him more than the last.

His detective brought him no news on the next day. But his unknown correspondent did.

"She is tired," the letter said, "of not seeing Mr. Colquhoun for three whole days. She will see him tomorrow. There is to be a garden-party at Mrs. L'Estrange's Twickenham villa. Mr. Colquhoun will be there, and she is going, too, to meet him. If you dared, if you had the heart of a mouse, you would be there too. You would arrive late; you would watch and see for yourself, unseen, if possible, how they meet, and what they say to each other. An invitation lies for you, as well as your wife upon the table. Go!"

While he was reading this document his secretary came in, uncalled.

"The Eldorado Stock," he said, in his usual whisper. "Have you decided what to do? Settling day on Friday. Have you forgotten what you hold, sir?"

"I have forgotten nothing," Gabriel Cassilis replied. "Eldorado stock? I never forget anything. Leave me. I shall see no one today; no one is to be admitted. I am very busy."

"I don't understand it," the secretary said to himself. "Has he got information that he keeps to himself? Has he got a deeper game on than I ever gave him credit for? What does it mean? Is he going off his head?"

More letters and more telegrams came. They were sent in to the inner office; but nothing came out of it.

That night Gabriel Cassilis left his chair at ten o'clock. He had eaten nothing all day. He was faint and weak; he took something at a City railway station, and drove home in a cab. His wife was out.

In the hall he saw her woman, the tall woman with the unprepossessing face.

"You are Mrs. Cassilis's maid?" he asked.

"I am, sir."

"Come with me."

He took her to his own study, and sat down. Now he had the woman with him he did not know what to ask her.

"You called me, sir," she said. "Do you want to know anything?"

"How long have you been with your mistress?"

"I came to her when her former maid, Janet, died, sir. Janet was with her for many years before she married."

"Janet—Janet—a Scotch name."

"Janet was with my mistress in Scotland."

"Yes—Mrs. Cassilis was in Scotland—yes. And—and—Janet was in your confidence?"

"We had no secrets from each other, sir. Janet told me everything.

"What was there to tell?"

"Nothing, sir. What should there be?"

This was idle fencing.

"You may go," he said. "Stay. Let them send me up something—a cup of tea, a slice of meat—anything."

Then he recommenced his dreary walk up and down the room.

Later on a curious feeling came over him—quite a strange and novel feeling. It was as if, while he thought, or rather while his fancies like so many devils played riot in his brain, he could not find the right words in which to clothe his thoughts. He struggled against the feeling. He tried to talk. But the wrong words came from his lips. Then he took a book; yes—he could read. It was nonsense; he shook off the feeling. But he shrank from speaking to any servant, and went to bed.

That night he slept better, and in the morning was less agitated. He breakfasted in his study, and then he went down to his office.

It was the fourth day since he had opened no letters and attended to no business. He remembered this, and tried to shake off the gloomy fit. And then he thought of the coming *coup*, and tried to bring his thoughts back to their usual channel. How much did he hold of Eldorado Stock? Rising higher day by day. But three days, three short days, before settling-day.

The largest stake he had ever ventured; a stake so large that when he thought of it his spirit and nerve came back to him.

For once—for the last time—he entered his office, holding himself erect, and looking brighter than he had done for days; and he sat down to his letters with an air of resolution.

Unfortunately, the first letter was from the anonymous correspondent.

"She wrote to him today; she told him that she could bear her life no longer; she threatened to tell the secret right out; she will have an explanation with him tomorrow at Mrs. L'Estrange's. Do you go down and you will hear the explanation. Be quiet, and the secret."

He started from his chair, the letter in his hand, and looked straight before him. Was it, then, all true? Would that very day give him a chance of finding out the secret between Lawrence Colquhoun and his wife?

He put up his glasses and read the letter—the last of a long series, everyone of which had been a fresh arrow in his heart—again and again.

Then he sat down and burst into tears.

A young man's tears may be forced from him by many a passing sorrow, but an old man's only by the reality of a sorrow which cannot be put aside. The deaths of those who are dear to the old man fall on him as so many reminders that his own time will soon arrive; but it is not for such things as death that he laments.

"I loved her," moaned Gabriel Cassilis. "I loved her, and I trusted her; and this the end!"

He did not curse her, nor Colquhoun, nor himself. It was all the hand of Fate. It was hard upon him, harder than he expected or knew, but he bore it in silence.

He sat so, still and quiet, a long while.

Then he put together all the letters, which the detective had brought back, and placed them in his pocket. Then he dallied and played with the paper and pencils before him, just as one who is restless and uncertain in his mind. Then he looked at his watch—it was past three; the garden party was for four; and then he rose suddenly, put on his hat, and passed out. His secretary asked him as he went through his office, if he would return, and at what time.

Mr. Cassilis made a motion with his hand, as if to put the matter off for a few moments, and replied nothing. When he got into the street it occurred to him that he could not answer the secretary because that same curious feeling was upon him again, and he had lost the power of speech. It was strange, and he laughed. Then the power of speech as suddenly returned to him. He called a cab and told the driver where to go. It is a long drive to Twickenham. He was absorbed in his thoughts, and as he sat back, gazing straight before him, the sensation of not being able to speak kept coming and going in his brain. This made him uneasy, but not much, because he had graver things to think about.

At half-past four he arrived within a few yards of Mrs. L'Estrange's house, where he alighted and dismissed his cab. The cabman touched his hat and said it was a fine day, and seasonable weather for the time of the year.

"Ay," replied Gabriel Cassilis mechanically. "A fine day, and seasonable weather for the time of the year."

And as he walked along under the lime-trees he found himself saying over again, as if it was the burden of a song:

"A fine day, and seasonable weather for the time of the year."

XL

"How green are you and fresh in this old world!"

On the morning of the garden party Joseph Jagenal called on Lawrence Colquhoun.

"I have two or three things to say," he began, "if you can give me five minutes."

"Twenty," said Lawrence. "Now then."

He threw himself back in his easiest chair and prepared to listen.

"I am in the way of hearing things sometimes," Joseph said. "And I heard a good deal yesterday about Mr. Gabriel Cassilis."

"What?" said Lawrence, aghast, "he surely has not been telling all the world about it!"

"I think we are talking of different things," Joseph answered after a pause. "Don't tell me what you mean, but what I mean is that there is an uneasy feeling about Gabriel Cassilis."

"Ay? In what way?"

"Well, they say he is strange; does not see people; does not open letters; and is evidently suffering from some mental distress."

"Yes."

"And when such a man as Gabriel Cassilis is in mental distress, money is at the bottom of it."

"Generally. Not always."

"It was against my advice that you invested any of your money by his direction."

"I invested the whole of it; and all Phillis's too. Mr. Cassilis has the investment of our little all," Lawrence added, laughing.

But the lawyer looked grave.

"Don't do it," he said; "get it in your own hands again; let it lie safely in the three percents. What has a pigeon like you to do among the City hawks? And Miss Fleming's money, too. Let it be put away safely, and give her what she wants, a modest and sufficient income without risk."

"I believe you are right, Jagenal. In fact, I am sure you are right. But Cassilis would have it. He talked me into an ambition for good investments which I never felt before. I will ask him to sell out for me, and go back to the old three percents. and railway shares—which is what I have been brought up to. On the other hand, you are quite

WALTER BESANT AND JAMES RICE

wrong about his mental distress. That is—I happen to know—you are a lawyer and will not talk—it is not due to money matters; and Gabriel Cassilis is, for what I know, as keen a hand as ever at piling up the dollars. The money is all safe; of that I am quite certain."

"Well, if you think so—But don't let him keep it," said Joseph the Doubter.

"After all, why not get eight and nine percent. if you can?"

"Because it isn't safe, and because you ought not to expect it. What do you want with more money than you have got? However, I have told you what men say. There is another thing. I am sorry to say that my brothers have made fools of themselves, and I am come to apologise for them."

"Don't if it is disagreeable, my dear fellow."

"It is not very disagreeable, and I would rather. They are fifty, but they are not wise. In fact, they have lived so much out of the world that they do not understand things. And so they went down and proposed for the hand of your ward, Phillis Fleming."

"Oh! Both of them? And did she accept?"

"The absurd thing is that I cannot discover which of them wished to be the bridegroom, nor which Phillis thought it was. She is quite confused about the whole matter. However, they went away and thought one of them was accepted, which explains a great deal of innuendo and reference to some unknown subject of mirth which I have observed lately. I say one of them, because I find it impossible to ascertain which of them was the man. Well, whether they were conscience-stricken or whether they repented, I do not know, but they went back to Twickenham and solemnly repudiated the engagement."

"And Phillis?"

"She laughed at them, of course. Do not fear; she wasn't in the least annoyed. I shall speak to my brothers this evening."

Colquhoun thought of the small, fragile-looking pair, and inwardly hoped that their brother would be gentle with them.

"And there is another thing, Colquhoun. Do you want to see your ward married?"

"To Jack Dunquerque?"

"Yes."

"Not yet. I want her to have her little fling first. Why the poor child is only just out of the nursery, and he wants to marry her off-hand—it's cruel. Let her see the world for a year, and then we will consider it. Jagenal, I wish I could marry the girl myself."

"So do I," said Joseph, with a sigh.

"I fell in love with her," said Lawrence, "at first sight. That is why," he added, in his laziest tones, "I suppose that is why I told Jack Dunquerque not to go there anymore. But he has gone there again, and he has proposed to her, I hear, and she has accepted him. So that I can't marry her, and you can't, and we are a brace of fogies."

"And what have you said to Mr. Dunquerque?"

"I acted the jealous guardian, and I ordered him not to call on my ward anymore for the present. I shall see how Phillis takes it, and give in, of course, if she makes a fuss. Then Beck has been here offering to hand over all his money to Jack, because he loves the young man."

"Quixotic," said the lawyer.

"Yes. The end of it will be a wedding, of course. You and I may shake a leg at it if we like. As for me, I never can marry anyone; and as for you—"

"As for me, I never thought of marrying her. I only remarked that I had fallen in love, as you say, with her. That's no matter to anybody."

"Well, things go on as they like, not as we like. What nonsense it is to say that man is master of his fate! Now, what I should like would be to get rid of the reason that prevents my marrying; to put Jack Dunquerque into the water-butt and sit on the lid; and then for Phillis to fall in love with me. After that, strawberries and cream with a little champagne for the rest of my Methuselah-like career. And I can't get any of these things. Master of his fate?"

"Have you heard of the Coping-stone chapter? It is found."

"Agatha told me something, in a disjointed way. What is the effect of it?"

Joseph laughed.

"It is all torn up but the last page. A righteous retribution, because if Phillis had been taught to read this would not have happened. Now, I suspect the will must be set aside, and the money will mostly go to Gabriel Cassilis, the nearest of kin, who doesn't want it."

XLI

"La langue des femmes est leur epee,
et elles ne la laissent pas rouiller."

The grounds of the house formed a parallelogram, of which the longer sides were parallel with the river. In the north-east corner stood the house itself, its front facing west. It was not a large house, as has been explained. A conservatory was built against nearly the whole length of the front. The lawns and flower-beds spread to west and south, sloping down to the river's edge. The opposite angle was occupied by stables, kitchen-garden, and boat-house. Gabriel Cassilis approached it from the east. An iron railing and a low hedge, along which were planted limes, laburnums, and lilacs, separated the place from the road. But before reaching the gate—in fact, at the corner of the kitchen garden—he could, himself, unseen, look through the trees and observe the party. They were all there. He saw Mrs. L'Estrange, Phillis, his own wife—Heavens! how calm and cold she looked, and how beautiful he thought her!—with half a dozen other ladies. The men were few. There was the curate. He was dangling round Phillis, and wore an expression of holiness-out-for-a-holiday, which is always so charming in these young men. Gabriel Cassilis also noticed that he was casting eyes of longing at the young lady. There was Lawrence Colquhoun. Gabriel Cassilis looked everywhere for him, till he saw him, lying beneath a tree, his head on his hand. He was not talking to Victoria, nor was he looking at her. On the contrary, he was watching Phillis. There was Captain Ladds. He was talking to one of the young ladies, and he was looking at Phillis. The young lady evidently did not like this. And there was Gilead Beck. He was standing apart, talking to Mrs. L'Estrange, with his hands in his pockets, leaning against a tree. But he, too, was casting furtive glances at Phillis.

They all seemed, somehow, looking at the girl. There was no special reason why they should look at her, except that she was so bright, so fresh, and so charming for the eye to rest upon. The other girls were as well dressed, but they were nowhere compared with Phillis. The lines of their figures, perhaps, were not so fine; the shape of their heads more commonplace; their features not so delicate; their pose less graceful. There are some girls who go well together. Helena and Hermia are a foil to each other; but when Desdemona shows all other beauties pale like lesser lights. And the other beauties do not like it.

Said one of the fair guests to another—

"What do they see in her?"

"I cannot tell," replied her friend. "She seems to me more *farouche* than ever."

For, having decided that *farouche* was the word to express poor Phillis's distinguishing quality, there was no longer any room for question, and *farouche* she continued to be. If there is anything that Phillis never was, it is that quality of fierce shy wildness which requires the adjective *farouche*. But the word stuck, because it sounded well. To this day—to be sure, it is only a twelvemonth since—the girls say still, "Oh, yes! Phillis Fleming. She was pretty, but extremely *farouche*."

Gabriel Cassilis stood by the hedge and looked through the trees. He has come all the way from town to attend this party, and now he hesitated at the very gates. For he became conscious of two things: first, that the old feeling of not finding his words was upon him again; and secondly, that he was not exactly dressed for a festive occasion. Like most City men who have long remained bachelors, Gabriel Cassilis was careful of his personal appearance. He considered a garden-party as an occasion demanding something special. Now he not only wore his habitual pepper-and-salt suit, but the coat in which he wrote at his office—a comfortable easy old frock, a little baggy at the elbows. His mind was strung to such an intense pitch, that such a trifling objection as his dress—because Gabriel Cassilis never looked other than a gentleman—appeared to him insuperable. He withdrew from the hedge, and retraced his steps. Presently he came to a lane. He left the road, and turned down the path. He found himself by the river. He sat down under a tree, and began to think.

He thought of the time when his lonely life was wearisome to him, when he longed for a wife and a house of his own. He remembered how he pictured a girl who would be his darling, who would return his caresses and love him for his own sake. And how, when he met Victoria Pengelley, his thoughts changed, and he pictured that girl, stately and statuesque, at the head of the table. There would be no pettings and caressings from her, that was quite certain. On the other hand, there would be a woman of whom he would be proud—one who would wear his wealth properly. And a woman of good family, well connected all round. There were no caresses, he remembered now; there was the coldest acceptance of him; and there had been no caresses since. But he had been proud of her; and as for her honour—how was it possible that the doubt should arise? That man must be himself distinctly of the lower order of men who would begin by doubting or suspecting his wife.

To end in this: doubt so strong as to be almost certainty: suspicion like a knife cutting at his heart; his brain clouded; and he himself driven to creep down clandestinely to watch his wife.

He sat there till the June sun began to sink in the west. The river was covered with the evening craft. They were manned by the young City men but just beginning the worship of Mammon, who would have looked with envy upon the figure sitting motionless in the shade by the river's edge had they known who he was. Presently he roused himself, and looked at his watch. It was past seven. Perhaps the party would be over by this time; he could go home with his wife; it would be something, at least, to be with her, to keep her from that other man. He rose,—his brain in a tumult—and repaired once more to his point of vantage at the hedge. The lawn was empty; there was no one there. But he saw his own carriage in the yard, and therefore his wife was not yet gone.

In the garden, no one. He crept in softly, and looked round him. No one saw him enter the place; and he felt something like a burglar as he walked, with a stealthy step which he vainly tried to make confident, across the lawn.

Two ways of entrance stood open before him. One was the porch of the house, covered with creepers and hung with flowers. The door stood open, and beyond it was the hall, looking dark from the bright light outside. He heard voices within. Another way was by the conservatory, the door of which was also open. He looked in. Among the flowers and vines there stood a figure he knew—his wife's. But she was alone. And she was listening. On her face was an expression which he had never seen there, and never dreamed of. Her features were distorted; her hands were closed in a tight clutch; her arms were stiffened—but she was trembling. What was she doing. To whom was she listening?

He hesitated a moment, and then he stepped through the porch into the hall. The voices came from the right, in fact, from the morning room,—Phillis's room,—which opened by its single window upon the lawn, and by its two doors into the hall on one side and the conservatory on the other.

And Gabriel Cassilis, like his wife, listened. He put off his hat, placed his umbrella in the stand, and stood in attitude, in case he should be observed, to push open the door and step in. He was so abject in his jealousy that he actually did not feel the disgrace and degradation of the act. He was so keen and eager to lose no word, that he leaned his head to the half-open door, and stood, his long thin figure trembling with excitement, like some listener in a melodrama of the transpontine stage.

There were two persons in the room, and one was a woman; and they were talking together. One was Lawrence Colquhoun and the other was Phillis Fleming.

Colquhoun was not, according to his wont, lying on a sofa, nor sitting in the easiest of the chairs. He was standing, and he was speaking in an earnest voice.

"When I saw you first," he said, "you were little Phillis—a wee toddler of six or seven. I went away and forgot all about you—almost forgot your very existence, Phillis,—till the news of Mr. Dyson's death met me on my way home again. I fear that I have neglected you since I came home; but I have been worried."

"What has worried you, Lawrence?" asked the girl.

She was sitting on the music-stool before the piano; and as she spoke she turned from the piano, her fingers resting silently on the notes. She was dressed for the party,—which was over now, and the guests departed,—in a simple muslin costume, light and airy, which became her well. And in her hair she had placed a flower. There were flowers all about the room, flowers at the open window, flowers in the conservatory beyond, flowers on the bright green lawns beyond.

"How pretty you are, Phillis!" answered her guardian.

He touched her cheek with his finger as she sat.

"I am your guardian," he said, as if in apology.

"And you have been worried about things?" she persisted. "Agatha says you never care what happens."

"Agatha is right, as a rule. In one case, of which she knows nothing, she is wrong. Tell me, Phillis, is there anything you want in the world that I can get for you?"

"I think I have everything," she said, laughing. "And what you will not give me I shall wait for till I am twenty-one."

"You mean—"

"I mean—Jack Dunquerque, Lawrence."

Only a short month ago, and Jack Dunquerque was her friend. She could speak of him openly and friendly, without change of voice or face.

Now she blushed, and her voice trembled as she uttered his name. That is one of the outward and visible signs of an inward and spiritual state known to the most elementary observers.

"I wanted to speak about him. Phillis, you are very young, you have seen nothing of the world; you know no other men. All I ask you is to wait. Do not give your promise to this man till you have at least had an opportunity of—of comparing—of learning your own mind."

She shook her head.

"I have already given my promise," she said.

"But it is a promise that may be recalled," he urged. "Dunquerque is a gentleman; he will not hold you to your word when he feels that he ought not to have taken it from you. Phillis, you do not know yourself. You have no idea of what it is that you have given, or its value. How can I tell you the truth?"

"I think you mean the best for me, Lawrence," she said. "But the best is—Jack."

Then she began to speak quite low, so that the listeners heard nothing.

"See, Lawrence, you are kind, and I can tell you all without being ashamed. I think of Jack all day long and all night. I pray for him in the morning and in the evening. When he comes near me I tremble; I feel that I must obey him if he were to order me in anything. I have no more command of myself when he is with me—"

"Stop, Phillis," Lawrence interposed; "you must not tell me anymore. I was trying to act for the best; but I will make no further opposition. See, my dear"—he took her hand in his in a tender and kindly way—"if I write to Jack Dunquerque today, and tell the villain he may come and see you whenever he likes, and that he shall marry you whenever you like, will that do for you?"

She started to her feet, and threw her left hand—Lawrence still holding the right—upon his shoulder, looking him full in the face.

"Will it do? O Lawrence! Agatha always said you were the kindest man in the world; and I—forgive me!—I did not believe it, I could not understand it. O Jack, Jack, we shall be so happy, so happy! He loves me, Lawrence, as much as I love him."

The listeners in the greenhouse and the hall craned their necks, but they could hear little, because the girl spoke low.

"Does he love you as much as you love him, Phillis? Does he love you a thousand times better than you can understand? Why, child, you do not know what love means. Perhaps women never do quite realise what it means. Only go on believing that he loves you, and love him in return, and all will be well with you."

"I do believe it, Lawrence! and I love him, too."

Looking through the flowers and the leaves of the conservatory glared a face upon the pair strangely out of harmony with the peace which breathed in the atmosphere of the place—a face violently distorted by passion, a face in which every evil feeling was at work, a face dark with rage. Phillis might have seen the face had she looked in that direction, but she did not; she held Lawrence's hand, and she was shyly pressing it in gratitude.

"Phillis," said Lawrence hoarsely, "Jack Dunquerque is a lucky man. We all love you, my dear; and I almost as much as Jack. But I am too old for you; and besides, besides—" He cleared his throat, and spoke more distinctly. "I do love you, however, Phillis; a man could not be long beside you without loving you."

There was a movement and a rustle in the leaves.

The man at the door stood bewildered. What was it all about? Colquhoun and a woman—not his wife—talking of love. What love? what woman? And his wife in the conservatory, looking as he never saw her look before, and listening. What did it all mean? what thing was coming over him? He pressed his hand to his forehead, trying to make out what it all meant, for he seemed to be in a dream; and, as before, while he tried to shape the words in his mind for some sort of an excuse, or a reassurance to himself, he found that no words came, or, if any, then the wrong words.

The house was very quiet; no sounds came from any part of it,—the servants were resting in the kitchen, the mistress of the house was resting in her room, after the party,—no voices but the gentle talk of the girl and her guardian.

"Kiss me, Phillis," said Lawrence. "Then let me hold you in my arms for once, because you are so sweet, and—and I am your guardian, you know, and we all love you."

He drew her gently by the hands. She made no resistance; it seemed to her right that her guardian should kiss her if he wished. She did not know how the touch of her hand, the light in her eyes, the sound of her voice, were stirring in the man before her depths that he thought long ago buried and put away, awakening once more the possibilities, at forty, of a youthful love.

His lips were touching her forehead, her face was close to his, he held her two hands tight, when the crash of a falling flower-pot startled him, and Victoria Cassilis stood before him.

Panting, gasping for breath, with hands clenched and eyes distended—a living statue of the *femina demens*. For a moment she paused to take breath, and then, with a wave of her hand which was grand because it was natural and worthy of Rachel—because you may see it any day among the untutored beauties of Whitechapel, among the gipsy camps, or in the villages where Hindoo women live and quarrel—Victoria Cassilis for once in her life was herself, and acted superbly, because she did not act at all.

"Victoria!" The word came from Lawrence.

Phillis, with a little cry of terror, clung tightly to her guardian's arm.

"Leave him!" cried the angry woman. "Do you hear?—leave him!"

"Better go, Phillis," said Lawrence.

At the prospect of battle the real nature of the man asserted itself. He drew himself erect, and met her wild eyes with a steady gaze, which had neither terror nor surprise in it—a gaze such as a mad doctor might practise upon his patients, a look which calms the wildest outbreaks, because it sees in them nothing but what it expected to find, and is only sorry.

"No! she shall not go," said Victoria, sweeping her skirts behind her with a splendid movement from her feet; "she shall not go until she has heard me first. You dare to make love to this girl, this schoolgirl, before my very eyes. She shall know, she shall know our secret!"

"Victoria," said Lawrence calmly, "you do not understand what you are saying. *Our* secret? Say your secret, and be careful."

The door moved an inch or two; the man standing behind it was shaking in every limb. "Their secret? her secret?" He was going to learn at last; he was going to find the truth; he was going—And here a sudden thought struck him that he had neglected his affairs of late, and that, this business once got through, he must look into things again; a thought without words, because, somehow, just then he had no words—he had forgotten them all.

The writer of the anonymous letters had done much mischief, as she hoped to do. People who write anonymous letters generally contrive so much. Unhappily, the beginning of mischief is like the boring of a hole in a dam or dyke, because very soon, instead of a trickling rivulet of water, you get a gigantic inundation. Nothing is easier than to have your revenge; only it is so very difficult to calculate the after consequences of revenge. If the writer of the letters had known what was going to happen in consequence, most likely they would never have been written.

"Their secret? her secret?" He listened with all his might. But Victoria, his wife Victoria, spoke out clearly; he could hear without straining his ears.

"Be careful," repeated Lawrence.

"I shall not be careful; the time is past for care. You have sneered and scoffed at me; you have insulted me; you have refused almost to know me,—all that I have borne, but this I will not bear."

"Phillis Fleming." She turned to the girl. Phillis did not shrink or cower before her; on the contrary, she stood like Lawrence, calm and quiet, to face the storm, whatever storm might be brewing. "This man takes you in his arms and kisses you. He says he loves you; he dares to tell you he loves you. No doubt you are flattered. You have had the men round you all day long, and now you have the best of them at your feet, alone, when they are gone. Well, the man you want to catch, the excellent *parti* you and Agatha would like to trap, the man who stands there—"

"Victoria, there is still time to stop," said Lawrence calmly.

"That man is my husband!"

Phillis looked from one to the other, understanding nothing. The man stood quietly stroking his great beard with his fingers, and looking straight at Mrs. Cassilis.

"My husband. We were married six years ago and more. We were married in Scotland, privately; but he is my husband, and five days after our wedding he left me. Is that true?"

"Perfectly. You have forgotten nothing, except the reason of my departure. If you think it worth while troubling Phillis with that, why—"

"We quarrelled; that was the reason. He used cruel and bitter language. He gave me back my liberty."

"We separated, Phillis, after a row, the like of which you may conceive by remembering that Mrs. Cassilis was then six years younger, and even more ready for such encounters than at present. We separated; we agreed that things should go on as if the marriage, which was no marriage, had never taken place. Janet, the maid, was to be trusted. She stayed with her mistress; I went abroad. And then I heard by accident that my wife had taken the liberty I gave her, in its fullest sense, by marrying again. Then I came home, because I thought that chapter was closed; but it was not, you see; and for her sake I wish I had stayed in America."

Mrs. Cassilis listened as if she did not hear a word; then she went on—

"He is my husband still. I can claim him when I want him; and I claim him now. I say, Lawrence, so long as I live you shall marry no other woman. You are mine; whatever happens, you are mine."

The sight of the man, callous, immovable, suddenly seemed to terrify her. She sank weeping at his knees.

"Lawrence, forgive me, forgive me! Take me away. I never loved anyone but you. Forgive me!"

He made no answer or any sign.

"Let me go with you, somewhere, out of this place; let us go away together, we two. I have never loved anyone but you—never anyone but you, but you!"

She broke into a passion of sobs. When she looked up, it was to meet the white face of Gabriel Cassilis. He was stooping over her, his hands spread out helplessly, his form quivering, his lips trying to utter something; but no sound came through them. Beyond stood Lawrence, still with the look of watchful determination which had broken down her rage. Then she sprang to her feet.

"You here? Then you know all. It is true; that is my legal husband. For two years and more my life has been a lie. Stand back, and let me go to my husband!"

But he stood between Colquhoun and herself. Lawrence saw with a sudden terror that something had happened to the man. He expected an outburst of wrath, but no wrath came. Gabriel Cassilis turned his head from one to the other, and presently said, in a trembling voice—

"A fine day, and seasonable weather for the time of year."

"Good God!" cried Lawrence, "you have destroyed his reason!"

Gabriel Cassilis shook his head, and began again—

"A fine day, and seasonable—"

Here he threw himself upon the nearest chair, and buried his face in his hands.

XLII

"Then a babbled of green fields."

A nd then there was silence. Which of them was to speak! Not the woman who had wrought this mischief; not the man who knew of the wickedness but had not spoken; not the innocent girl who only perceived that something dreadful—something beyond the ordinary run of dreadful events—had happened, and that Victoria Cassilis looked out of her senses. Lawrence Colquhoun stood unmoved by her tears; his face was hardened; it bore a look beneath which the guilty woman cowered. Yet she looked at him and not at her husband.

Presently Colquhoun spoke. His voice was harsh, and his words were a command.

"Go home!" he said to Victoria. "There is no more mischief for you to do—go!"

She obeyed without a word. She threw the light wrapper which she carried on her arm round her slender neck, and walked away, restored, to outward seeming, to all her calm and stately coldness. The coachman and the footman noticed nothing. If any of her acquaintances passed her on the road, they saw no change in her. The woman was impassive and impenetrable.

Did she love Colquhoun? No one knows. She loved to feel that she had him in her power; she was driven to a mad jealousy when that power slipped quite away; and although she had broken the vows which both once swore to keep, she could not bear even to think that he should do the same. And she did despise her husband, the man of shares, companies, and stocks. But could she love Colquhoun? Such a woman may feel the passion of jealousy; she may rejoice in the admiration which gratifies her vanity; but she is far too cold and selfish for love. It is an artful fable of the ancients which makes Narcissus pine away and die for the loss of his own image, for thereby they teach the great lesson that he who loves himself destroys himself.

The carriage wheels crunched over the gravel, and Gabriel Cassilis raised a pale and trembling face—a face with so much desolation and horror, such a piteous gaze of questioning reproach at Colquhoun, that the man's heart melted within him. He seemed to have grown old suddenly; his hair looked whiter; he trembled as one who has the palsy; and his eyes mutely asked the question, "Is this thing true?"

Lawrence Colquhoun made answer. His voice was low and gentle; his eyes were filled with tears.

"It is true, Mr. Cassilis. God knows I would have spared you the knowledge. But it is true."

Gabriel Cassilis opened his lips as if to speak. But he refrained, stopping suddenly, because he recollected that he could no longer utter what he wished to say. Then he touched his mouth with his fingers like a dumb man. He was worse than a dumb man, who cannot speak at all, because his tongue, if he allowed it, uttered words which had no connection with his thoughts. Men that have been called possessed of the devil have knelt at altars, uttering blasphemous impieties when their souls were full of prayer.

"Do you understand me, Mr. Cassilis? Do you comprehend what I am saying?"

He nodded his head.

Colquhoun took a piece of notepaper from the writing-table, and laid it before him with a pencil. Mr. Cassilis grasped the pencil eagerly, and began to write. From his fingers, as from his tongue, came the sentence which he did *not* wish to write—

"A fine day, and seasonable weather for the time of year."

He looked at this result with sorrowful heart, and showed it to Colquhoun, shaking his head.

"Good heavens?" cried Colquhoun, "his mind is gone."

Gabriel Cassilis touched him on the arm and shook his head.

"He understands you, Lawrence," said Phillis; "but he cannot explain himself. Something has gone wrong with him which we do not know."

Gabriel Cassilis nodded gratefully to Phillis.

"Then Mr. Cassilis," Colquhoun began, "it is right that you should know all. Six years ago I followed Victoria Pengelley into Scotland. We were married privately at a registrar's office under assumed names. If you ever want to know where and by what names, you have only to ask me, and I will tell you. There were reasons, she said,—I never quite understood what they were, but she chose to be a *fille romanesque* at the time,—why the marriage should be kept secret. After the wedding ceremony—such as it was—she left the office with her maid, who was the only witness, and returned to the friends with whom she was staying. I met her everyday; but always in that house and among other people.

A few days passed. She would not, for some whim of her own, allow the marriage to be disclosed. We quarrelled for that, and other reasons—my fault, possibly. Good God! what a honeymoon! To meet the woman you love—your bride—in society; if for half an hour alone, then in the solitude of open observation; to quarrel like people who have been married for forty years— Well, perhaps it was my fault. On the fifth day we agreed to let things be as if they had never been. I left my bride, who was not my wife, in anger. We used bitter words—perhaps I the bitterest. And when we parted, I bade her go back to her old life as if nothing had been promised on either side. I said she should be free; that I would never claim the power and the rights given me by a form of words; that she might marry again; that, to leave her the more free, I would go away and never return till she was married, or till she gave me leave. I was away for four years; and then I saw the announcement of her marriage in the paper, and I returned. That is the bare history, Mr. Cassilis. Since my return, on my honour as a gentleman, you have had no cause for jealousy in my own behaviour towards—your wife, not mine. Remember, Mr. Cassilis, whatever else may be said, she never was my wife. And yet, in the eye of the law, I suppose she is my wife still. And with all my heart I pity you."

He stopped, and looked at the victim of the crime. Gabriel Cassilis was staring helplessly from him to Phillis. Did he understand? Not entirely, I think. Yet the words which he had heard fell upon his heart softly, and soothed him in his trouble. At last his eyes rested on Phillis, as if asking, as men do in times of trouble, for the quick comprehension of a woman.

"What can I do, Mr. Cassilis?" asked the girl. "If you cannot speak, will you make some sign? Any little sign that I can understand?"

She remembered that among her lesson-books was a dictionary. She put that into his hand, and asked him to show her in the dictionary what he wished to say.

He took the book in his trembling hands, turned over the leaves, and presently, finding the page he wanted, ran his fingers down the lines till they rested on a word.

Phillis read it, spelling it out in her pretty little school-girl fashion.

"S, I, si; L, E, N, C, LAME DUCK, lence—silence. Is that what you wish to say, Mr. Cassilis?"

He nodded.

"Silence," repeated Lawrence. "For all our sakes it is the best—the only thing. Phillis, tell no one what you have heard; not even Agatha;

not even Jack Dunquerque. Or, if you tell Jack Dunquerque, send him to me directly afterwards. Do you promise, child?"

"I promise, Lawrence. I will tell no one but Jack; and I shall ask him first if he thinks I ought to tell him another person's secret."

"Thank you, Phillis. Mr. Cassilis, there are only we three and—and one more. You may trust Phillis when she promises a thing; you may trust me, for my own sake; you may, I hope, trust that other person. And as for me, it is my intention to leave England in a week. I deeply regret that I ever came back to this country."

A week was too far ahead for Mr. Cassilis to look forward to in his agitation. Clearly the one thing in his mind at the moment—the one possible thing—was concealment. He took the dictionary again, and found the word "Home."

"Will you let me take you home, sir?" Lawrence asked.

He nodded again. There was no resentment in his face, and none in his feeble confiding manner when he took Lawrence's arm and leaned upon it as he crawled out to the carriage.

Only one sign of feeling. He took Phillis by the hand and kissed her. When he had kissed her, he laid his finger on her lips. And she understood his wish that no one should learn this thing.

"Not even Agatha, Phillis," said Lawrence. "Forget, if you can. And if you cannot, keep silence."

They drove into town together, these men with a secret between them. Lawrence made no further explanations. What was there to explain? The one who suffered the most sat upright, looking straight before him in mute suffering.

It is a long drive from Twickenham to Kensington Palace Gardens. When they arrived, Mr. Cassilis was too weak to step out of the carriage. They helped him—Lawrence Colquhoun and a footman—into the hall. He was feeble with long fasting as much as from the effects of this dreadful shock.

They carried him to his study. Among the servants who looked on was Tomlinson, the middle-aged maid with the harsh face. She knew that her bolt had fallen at last; and she saw, too, that it had fallen upon the wrong person, for upstairs sat her mistress, calm, cold and collected. She came home looking pale and a little worn; fatigued, perhaps, with the constant round of engagements, though the season was little more than half over. She dressed in gentle silence, which Tomlinson could not understand. She went down to dinner alone, and presently went to her drawing-room, where she sat in a window, and thought.

There Colquhoun found her.

"I have told him all," he said. "Your words told him only half, and yet too much. You were never my wife, as you know, and never will be, though the Law may make you take my name. Cruel and heartless woman! to gratify an insensate jealousy you have destroyed your husband."

"Is he—is he—dead?" she cried, almost as if she wished he were.

"No; he is not dead; he is struck with some fit. He cannot speak. Learn, now, that your jealousy was without foundation. Phillis will marry Dunquerque. As for me, I can never marry, as you know."

"He is not dead!" she echoed, taking no notice of the last words. Indeed, Phillis was quite out of her thoughts now. "Does he wish to see me?"

"No; you must not, at present, attempt to see him."

"What will they do to me, Lawrence?" she asked again. "What can they do? I did not mean him to hear. It was all to frighten you."

"To frighten me! What they can do, Mrs. Cassilis, is to put you in the prisoner's box and me in the witness box. What he wants to do, so far as we can yet understand, is to keep silence."

"What is the good of that? He will cry his wrongs all over the town, and Phillis will tell everybody."

"Phillis will tell no one, no one—not even Agatha. It was lucky that Agatha heard nothing; she was upstairs, lying down after her party. Will you keep silence?"

"Of course I shall. What else is there for me to do?"

"For the sake of your husband; for the sake of your boy—"

"It is for my own sake, Lawrence," she interrupted coldly.

"I beg your pardon. I ought to have known by this time that you would have acted for your own sake only. Victoria, it was an evil day for me when I met you; it was a worse day when I consented to a secret marriage, which was no marriage, when there was no reason for any secrecy; it was the worst day of all when I answered your letter, and came here to see you. Everyday we have met has produced more recrimination. That would not have mattered, but for the mischief our meeting has wrought upon your husband. I pray that we may never in this world meet again."

He was gone, and Victoria Cassilis has not met him since, nor do I think now that she ever will meet him again.

The summer night closed in; the moonlight came up and shone upon the Park before her, laying silvery patches of light in ten of thousands upon the young leaves of the trees, and darkening the shadows a deeper black by way of contrast. They brought her tea and lights; then they came for orders. There were none; she would not go out that night. At eleven Tomlinson came.

"I want nothing, Tomlinson. You need not wait up; I shall not want you this evening."

"Yes, madam; no, madam. Mr. Cassilis is asleep, madam."

"Let someone sit up with him. See to that, Tomlinson; and don't let him be disturbed."

"I will sit up with him myself, madam." Tomlinson was anxious to get to the bottom of the thing. What mischief had been done, and how far was it her own doing? To persons who want revenge these are very important questions, when mischief has actually been perpetrated.

Then Victoria was left alone. In that great house, with its troop of servants and nurses, with her husband and child, there was no one who cared to know what she was doing. The master was not popular, because he simply regarded every servant as a machine; but at least he was just, and he paid well, and the house, from the point of view likely to be taken by Mr. Plush and Miss Hairpin, was a comfortable one. The mistress of the house was unpopular. Her temper at times was intolerable, her treatment of servants showed no consideration; and the women-folk regarded the neglect of her own child with the horror of such neglect in which the Englishwoman of all ranks is trained. So she was alone, and remained alone. The hands of the clock went round and round; the moon went down, and over the garden lay the soft sepia twilight of June; the lamp on the little table at her elbow went out; but she sat still, hands crossed in her lap, looking out of window, and thinking.

She saw, but she did not feel the wickedness of it, a cold and selfish girl ripening into a cold and selfish woman—one to whom the outer world was as a panorama of moving objects, meaning nothing, and having no connection with herself. Like one blind, deaf, and dumb, she moved among the mobs who danced and sang, or who grovelled and wept. She had no tears to help the sufferers, and no smiles to encourage the happy; she had never been able to sympathise with the acting of a theatre or the puppets of a novel; she was so cold that she was not even critical. It seems odd, but it is really true, that a critic may be actually too cold. She saw a mind that, like the Indian devotee, was occupied forever in contemplating itself; she saw beauty which would have been irresistible had there been one gleam, just one gleam of womanly tenderness; she saw one man after the other first attracted and then repelled; and then she came to the one man who was not repelled. There was once an unfortunate creature who dared to make love to Diana. His fate is recorded in Lempriére's Dictionary; also in Dr. Smith's later and more expensive work. Lawrence Colquhoun resembled that swain, and his fate was not unlike the classical punishment. She went through the form of marriage with him, and then she drove him from her by the cold wind of her own intense selfishness—a very Mistral. When he was gone she began to regret a slave of such uncomplaining slavishness. Well, no one knew except Janet. Janet did not talk. It was rather a struggle, she remembered, to take Gabriel Cassilis—rather a struggle, because Lawrence Colquhoun might come home and tell the story, not because there was anything morally wrong. She was most anxious to see him when he did come home—out of curiosity, out of jealousy, out of a desire to know whether her old power was gone; out of fear, out of that reason which makes a criminal seek out from time to time the scene and accomplices of his crime, and for the thousand reasons which make up a selfish woman's code of conduct. It was three o'clock and daylight when she discovered that she had really thought the whole thing over from the beginning, and that there was nothing more to think about, except the future—a distasteful subject to all sinners.

"After all," she summed up, as she rose to go to bed, "it is as well. Lawrence and I should never have got along. He is too selfish, much too selfish."

Downstairs they were watching over the stricken man. The doctor came and felt his pulse; he also looked wise, and wrote things in Latin on a paper, which he gave to a servant. Then he went away, and said he would come in the morning again. He was a great doctor, with a title, and quite believed to know everything; but he did not know what had befallen this patient.

When Gabriel Cassilis awoke there was some confusion in his mind, and his brain was wandering—at least it appeared so, because what he said had nothing to do with any possible wish or thought. He rambled at large and at length; and then he grew angry, and then he became suddenly sorrowful, and sighed; then he became perfectly silent. The confused babble of speech ceased as suddenly as it had come; and since that morning Gabriel Cassilis has not spoken.

It was at half-past nine that his secretary called, simultaneously with the doctor.

He heard something from the servants, and pushed into the room where his chief was lying. The eyes of the sick man opened languidly and fell upon his first officer, but they expressed no interest and asked no question.

"Ah!" sighed Mr. Mowll, in the impatience of a sympathy which has but little time to spare. "Will he recover, doctor?"

"No doubt, no doubt. This way, my dear sir." He led the secretary out of the room. "Hush! he understands what is said. This is no ordinary seizure. Has he received any shock?"

"Shock enough to kill thirty men," said the secretary. "Where was he yesterday? Why did he not say something—do something—to avert the disaster?"

"Oh! Then the shock has been of a financial kind? I gathered from Mr. Colquhoun that it was of a family nature—something sudden and distressing."

"Family nature!" echoed the secretary. "Who ever heard of Mr. Cassilis worrying himself about family matters? No, sir; when a man is ruined he has no time to bother about family matters."

"Ruined? The great Mr. Gabriel Cassilis ruined?"

"I should say so, and I ought to know. They say so in the City; they will say so tonight in the papers. If he were well, and able to face things, there might be—no, even then there could be no hope. Settling-day this very morning; and a pretty settling it is."

"Whatever day it is," said the doctor, "I cannot have him disturbed. You may return in three or four hours, if you like, and then perhaps he may be able to speak to you. Just now, leave him in peace."

What had happened was this:

When Mr. Cassilis caused to be circulated a certain pamphlet which we have heard of, impugning the resources of the Republic of Eldorado, he wished the stock to go down. It did go down, and he bought in— bought in so largely that he held two millions of the stock. Men in his position do not buy large quantities of stock without affecting the price—Stock Exchange transactions are not secret—and Eldorado Stock went up. This was what Gabriel Cassilis naturally desired. Also the letter of El Señor Don Bellaco de la Carambola to the *Times*, showing the admirable way in which Eldorado loans were received and administered, helped. The stock went up from 64, at which price

Gabriel Cassilis bought in, to 75, at which he should have sold. Had he done so at the right moment, he would have realised the very handsome sum of two hundred and sixty thousand pounds; but the trouble of the letters came, and prevented him from acting.

While his mind was agitated by these—agitated, as we have seen, to such an extent that he could no longer think or work, or attend to any kind of business—there arrived for him telegram after telegram, in his own cipher, from America. These lay unopened. It was disastrous, because they announced beforehand the fact which only his correspondent knew—the Eldorado bonds were no longer to be paid.

That fact was now public. It was made known by all the papers that Eldorado, having paid the interest out of the money borrowed, had no further resources whatever, and could pay no more. It was stated in leading articles that England should have known all along what a miserable country Eldorado is. The British public were warned too late not to trust in Eldorado promises anymore; and the unfortunates who held Eldorado Stock were actuated by one common impulse to sell, and no one would buy. It was absurd to quote Eldorado bonds at anything; and the great financier had to meet his engagements by finding the difference between stock at 64 and stock at next to nothing for two millions.

Gabriel Cassilis was consequently ruined. When it became known that he had some sort of stroke, people said that it was the shock of the fatal news. He made the one mistake of an otherwise faultless career, they said to each other, in trusting Eldorado, and his brain could not stand the blow. When the secretary, who understood the cipher, came to open the letters and telegrams, he left off talking about the fatal shock of the news. It must have been something else—something he knew nothing of, because he saw the blow might have been averted; and the man's mind, clear enough when he went in for a great coup, had become unhinged during the few days before the smash.

Ruined! Gabriel Cassilis knew nothing about the wreck of his life, as he lay upon his bed afraid to speak because he would only babble incoherently. All was gone from him—money, reputation, wife. He had no longer anything. The anonymous correspondent had taken all away.

XLIII

"This comes of airy visions and the whispers
Of demons like to angels. Brother, weep."

Gilead Beck, returning from the Twickenham party before the explosion, found Jack Dunquerque waiting for him. As we have seen, he was not invited.

"Tell me how she was looking!" he cried. "Did she ask after me?"

"Wal, Mr. Dunquerque, I reckon you the most fortunate individual in the hull world. She looked like an angel, and she talked like a—like a woman, with pretty blushes; and yet she wasn't ashamed neither. Seems as if bein' ashamed isn't her strong point. And what has she got to be ashamed of?"

"Did Colquhoun say anything?"

"We had already got upon the subject, and I had ventured to make him a proposition. You see, Mr. Dunquerque"—he grew confused, and hesitated—"fact is, I want you to look at things just exactly as I do. I'm rich. I have struck Ile; that Ile is the mightiest Special Providence ever given to a single man. But it's given for purposes. And one of those purposes is that some of it's got to go to you."

"To me?"

"To you, Mr. Dunquerque. Who fired that shot? Who delivered me from the Grisly?"

"Why, Ladds did as much as I."

Mr. Beck shook his head.

"Captain Ladds is a fine fellow," he said. "Steady as a rock is Captain Ladds. There's nobody I'd rather march under if we'd the war to do all over again. But the Ile isn't for Captain Ladds. It isn't for him that the Golden Butterfly fills me with yearnin's. No sir. I owe it all to you. You've saved my life; you've sought me out, and gone about this city with me; you've put me up to ropes; you've taken me to that sweet creature's house and made her my friend. And Mrs. L'Estrange my friend, too. If I was to turn away and forget you, I should deserve to lose that precious Inseck."

He paused for a minute.

"I said to Mr. Colquhoun, 'Mr. Dunquerque shall have half of my pile, and more if he wants it. Only you let him come back again to Miss

Fleming.' And he laughed in his easy way; there's no kind of man in the States like that Mr. Colquhoun—seems as if he never wants to get anything. He laughed and lay back on the grass. And then he said, 'My dear fellow, let Jack come back if he likes; there's no fighting against fate; only let him have the decency not to announce his engagement till Phillis has had her first season.' Then he drank some cider-cup, and lay back again. Mrs. Cassilis—she's a very superior woman that, but a trifle cold, I should say—watched him whenever he spoke. She's got a game of her own, unless I am mistaken."

"But, Beck," Jack gasped, "I can't do this thing; I can't take your money."

"I guess, sir, you can, and I guess you will. Come, Mr. Dunquerque, say you won't go against Providence. There's a sweet young lady waiting for you, and a little mountain of dollars."

But Jack shook his head.

"I thank you all the same," he said. "I shall never forget your generosity—never. But that cannot be."

"We will leave it to Miss Fleming," said Gilead. "What Miss Fleming says is to be, shall be—"

He was interrupted by the arrival of two letters.

The first was from Joseph Jagenal. It informed him that he had learned from his brothers that they had received money from him on account of work which he thought would never be done. He enclosed a cheque for the full amount, with many thanks for his kindness, and the earnest hope that he would advance nothing more.

In the letter was his cheque for £400, the amount which the Twins had borrowed during the four weeks of their acquaintance.

Mr. Beck put the cheque in his pocket and opened the other letter. It was from Cornelius, and informed him that the Poem could not possibly be finished in the time; that it was rapidly advancing; but that he could not pledge himself to completing the work by October. Also, that his brother Humphrey found himself in the same position as regarded the Picture. He ended by the original statement that Art cannot be forced.

Mr. Beck laughed.

"Not straight men, Mr. Dunquerque. I suspected it first when they backed out at the dinner, and left me to do the talk. Wal, they may be high-toned, whole-souled, and talented; but give me the man who works. Now Mr. Dunquerque, if you please, we'll go and have some dinner, and you shall talk about Miss Fleming. And the day after tomorrow—you note that down—I've asked Mrs. L'Estrange and Miss Phillis to breakfast. Captain Ladds is coming, and Mr. Colquhoun. And you shall sit next to her. Mrs. Cassilis is coming too. When I asked her she wanted to know if Mr. Colquhoun was to be there. I said yes. Then she wanted to know if Phillis was to be there. I said yes. Then she set her lips hard, and said, 'I will come, Mr. Beck.' She isn't happy, that lady; she's got somethin' on her mind."

That evening Joseph Jagenal had an unpleasant duty to perform. It was at dinner that he spoke. The Twins were just taking their first glass of port. He had been quite silent through dinner, eating little. Now he looked from one to the other without a word.

They changed colour. Instinctively they knew what was coming. He said with a gulp:

"I am sorry to find that my brothers have not been acting honourably."

"What is this, brother Humphrey," asked Cornelius.

"I do not know, brother Cornelius," said the Artist.

"I will tell you," said Joseph, "what they have done. They made a disingenuous attempt to engage the affections of a rich young lady for the sake of her money."

"If Humphrey loved the girl—" began Cornelius.

"If Cornelius was devoted to Phillis Fleming—" began Humphrey.

"I was not, Humphrey," said Cornelius. "No such thing. And I told you so."

"I never did love her," said Humphrey. "I always said it was you."

This was undignified.

"I do not care which it was. It belongs to both. Then you went down to her again, under the belief that she was engaged to—to—the Lord knows which of you—and solemnly broke it off."

Neither spoke this time.

"Another thing. I regret to find that my brothers, having made a contract for certain work with Mr. Gilead Beck, and having been partly paid in advance, are not executing the work."

"There, Joseph," said Humphrey, waving his hand as if this was a matter on quite another footing, "you must excuse us. We know what is right in Art, if we know nothing else. Art, Joseph, cannot be forced."

Cornelius murmured assent.

"We have our dignity to stand upon; we retreat with dignity. We say, 'We will not be forced; we will give the world our best.'"

"Good," said Joseph. "That is very well; but where is the money?"

Neither answered.

"I have returned that money; but it is a large sum, and you must repay me in part. Understand me, brothers. You may stay here as long as I live: I shall never ask more of you than to respect the family name. There was a time when you promised great things, and I believed in you. It is only quite lately that I have learned to my sorrow that all this promise has been for years a pretence. You sleep all day—you call it work. You habitually drink too much at night. You, Cornelius"—the Poet started—"have not put pen to paper for years. You, Humphrey"—the Artist hung his head—"have neither drawn nor painted anything since you came to live with me. I cannot make either of you work. I cannot retrieve the past. I cannot restore lost habits of industry. I cannot even make you feel your fall from the promise of your youth, or remember the hopes of our father. What I can do is to check your intemperate habits by such means as are in my power."

He stopped; they were trembling violently.

"Half of the £400 which you have drawn from Mr. Beck will be paid by household saving. Wine will disappear from my table; brandy-and-soda will have to be bought at your own expense. I shall order the dinners, and I shall keep the key of the wine-cellar."

A year has passed. The Twins have had a sad time; they look forward with undisguised eagerness to the return of the years of fatness; they have exhausted their own little income in purchasing the means for their midnight *séances*; and they have run up a frightful score at the Carnarvon Arms.

But they still keep up bravely the pretence about their work.

WALTER BESANT AND JAMES RICE

XLIV

"So, on the ruins he himself had made.
Sat Marius reft of all his former glory."

"C an you understand me, sir?"

Gabriel Cassilis sat in his own study. It was the day after the garden-party. He slept through the night, and in the morning rose and dressed as usual. Then he took his seat in his customary chair at his table. Before him lay papers, but he did not read them. He sat upright, his frock-coat tightly buttoned across his chest, and rapped his knuckles with his gold eyeglasses as if he was thinking.

They brought him breakfast, and he took a cup of tea. Then he motioned them to take the things away. They gave him the *Times*, and he laid it mechanically at his elbow. But he did not speak, nor did he seem to attend to what was done around him. And his eyes had a far-off look in them.

"Can you understand me, sir?"

The speaker was his secretary. He came in a cab, panting, eager to see if there was still any hope. Somehow or other it was whispered already in the City that Gabriel Cassilis had had some sort of stroke. And there was terrible news besides.

Mr. Mowll asked because there was something in his patron's face which frightened him. His eyes were changed. They had lost the keen sharp look which in a soldier means victory; in a scholar, clearness of purpose; in a priest, knowledge of human nature and ability to use that knowledge in a financier, the power and the intuition of success. That was gone. In its place an expression almost of childish softness. And another thing—the lips, once set firm and close, were parted now and mobile.

The other things were nothing. That a man of sixty-five should in a single night become a man of eighty; that the iron grey hair should become white; that a steady hand should shake, and straight shoulders be bent. It was the look in his face, the far-off look, which made the secretary ask that question before he went on.

Mr. Cassilis nodded his head gently. He could understand.

"You left the telegrams unopened for a week and more!" cried the impatient clerk. "Why—Oh, why!—did you not let me open them?"

There was no reply.

"If I had known, I could have acted. Even the day before yesterday I could have acted. The news came yesterday morning. It was all over the City by three. And Eldorado's down to nothing in a moment."

Mr. Cassilis looked a mild inquiry. No anxiety in that look at all.

"Eldorado won't pay up her interest. It's due next week. Nothing to pay it with. Your agent in New York telegraphed this a week ago. He's been confirming the secret everyday since. O Lord! O Lord! And you the only man who had the knowledge, and all that stake in it! Can you speak, sir?"

For his master's silence was terrible to him.

"Listen, then. Ten days ago Eldorados went down after Wylie's pamphlet. You told him what to write and you paid him, just as you did last year. But you tried to hide it from me. That was wrong, sir. I've served you faithfully for twenty years. But never mind that. You bought in at 64. Then the Eldorado minister wrote to the paper. Stock went up to 75. You stood to win, only the day before yesterday, £260,000; more than a quarter of a million. Yesterday, by three, they were down to 16. This morning they are down to 8. And it's settling-day, and you lose—you lose—your all. Oh, what a day, what a day!"

Still no complaint, not even a sigh from the patient man in the Windsor chair. Only that gentle tapping of the knuckles, and that far-off look.

"The great name of Gabriel Cassilis dragged in the dust! All your reputation gone—the whole work of your life—O sir! can't you feel even that? Can't you feel the dreadful end of it all—Gabriel Cassilis, the great Gabriel Cassilis, a LAME DUCK!"

Not even that. The work of his life was forgotten with all its hopes, and the great financier, listening to his clerk with the polite impatience of one who listens to a wearisome sermon, was trying to understand what was the meaning of that black shadow which lay upon his mind and made him uneasy. For the rest a perfect calm in his brain.

"People will say it was the shock of the Eldorado smash. Well, sir, it wasn't that; I know so much; but it's best to let people think so. If you haven't a penny left in the world you have your character, and that's as high as ever.

"Fortunately," Mr. Mowll went on, "my own little savings were not in Eldorado Stock. But my employment is gone, I suppose. You will recommend me, I hope, sir. And I do think that I've got some little reputation in the City."

It was not for want of asserting himself that this worthy man failed, at any rate, of achieving his reputation. For twenty years he had magnified his office as confidential adviser of a great City light; among his friends and in his usual haunts he successfully posed as one burdened with the weight of affairs, laden with responsibility, and at all times oppressed by the importance of his thoughts. He carried a pocket-book which shut with a clasp; in the midst of a conversation he would stop, become abstracted, rush at the pocket-book, so to speak, confide a jotting to its care, shut it with a snap, and then go on with a smile and an excuse. Some said that he stood in with Gabriel Cassilis; all thought that he shared his secrets, and gave advice when asked for it.

As a matter of fact, he was a clerk, and had always been a clerk; but he was a clerk who knew a few things which might have been awkward if told generally. He had a fair salary, but no confidence, no advice, and not much more real knowledge of what his chief was doing than any outsider. And in this tremendous smash it was a great consolation to him to reflect that the liabilities represented an amount for which it was really a credit to fail.

Mr. Mowll has since got another place where the transactions are not so large, but perhaps his personal emoluments greater. In the evenings he will talk of the great failure.

"We stood to win," he will say, leaning back with a superior smile,—"we stood to win £260,000. We lost a million and a quarter. I told him not to hang on too long. Against my advice he did. I remember—ah, only four days before it happened—he said to me, 'Mowll, my boy,' he said, 'I've never known you wrong yet. But for once I fancy my own opinion. We've worked together for twenty years,' he said, 'and you've the clearest head of any man I ever saw,' he said. 'But here I think you're wrong. And I shall hold on for another day or two,' he said. Ah, little he knew what a day or two would bring forth! And he hasn't spoken since. Plays with his little boy, and goes about in a Bath-chair. What a man he was! and what a pair—if I may say so—we made between us among the bulls and the bears! Dear me, dear me!"

It may be mentioned here that everything was at once given up; the house in Kensington Palace Gardens, with its costly furniture, its carriages, plate, library, and pictures. Mr. Cassilis signed whatever documents were brought for signature without hesitation, provided a copy of his own signature was placed before him. Otherwise he could not write his name.

And never a single word of lamentation, reproach, or sorrow. The past was, and is still, dead to him; all the past except one thing, and that is ever with him.

For sixty years of his life, this man of the City, whose whole desire was to make money, to win in the game which he played with rare success and skill, regarded bankruptcy as the one thing to be dreaded, or at least to be looked upon, because it was absurd to dread it, as a thing bringing with it the whole of dishonour. Not to meet your engagements was to be in some sort a criminal. And now he was proclaimed as one who could not meet his engagements.

If he understood what had befallen him he did not care about it. The trouble was slight indeed in comparison with the other disaster. The honour of his wife and the legitimacy of his child—these were gone; and the man felt what it is that is greater than money gained or money lost.

The blow which fell upon him left his brain clear while it changed the whole course of his thoughts and deprived him partially of memory. But it destroyed his power of speech. That rare and wonderful disease which seems to attack none but the strongest, which separates the brain from the tongue, takes away the knowledge and the sense of language, and kills the power of connecting words with things, while it leaves that of understanding what is said—the disease which doctors call Aphasia—was upon Mr. Gabriel Cassilis.

In old men this is an incurable disease. Gabriel Cassilis will never speak again. He can read, listen, and understand, but he can frame no words with his lips nor write them with his hand. He is a prisoner who has free use of his limbs. He is separated from the world by a greater gulf than that which divides the blind and the deaf from the rest of us, because he cannot make known his thoughts, his wants, or his wishes.

It took sometime to discover what was the matter with him. Patients are not often found suffering from aphasia, and paralysis was the first name given to his disease.

But it was very early found out that Mr. Cassilis understood all that was said to him, and by degrees they learned what he liked and what he disliked.

Victoria Cassilis sat upstairs, waiting for something—she knew not what—to happen. Her maid told her that Mr. Cassilis was ill; she made no reply; she did not ask to see him; she did not ask for any further news of him. She sat in her own room for two days, waiting.

Then Joseph Jagenal asked if he might see her.

WALTER BESANT AND JAMES RICE

She refused at first; but on hearing that he proposed to stay in the house till she could receive him, she gave way.

He came from Lawrence, perhaps. He would bring her a message of some kind; probably a menace.

"You have something to say to me, Mr. Jagenal?" Her face was set hard, but her eyes were wistful. He saw that she was afraid. When a woman is afraid, you may make her do pretty well what you please.

"I have a good deal to tell you, Mrs. Cassilis; and I am sorry to say it is of an unpleasant nature.

"I have heard," he went on, "from Mr. Colquhoun that you made a remarkable statement in the presence of Miss Fleming, and in the hearing of Mr. Cassilis."

"Lawrence informed you correctly, I have no doubt," she replied coldly.

"That statement of course was untrue," said Joseph, knowing that no record ever was more true "And therefore I venture to advise—"

"On the part of Lawrence?"

"In the name of Mr. Colquhoun, partly; partly in your own interest—"

"Go on, if you please, Mr. Jagenal."

"Believing that statement to be untrue," he repeated, "for otherwise I could not give this advice, I recommend to all parties concerned—silence. Your husband's paralysis is attributed to the shock of his bankruptcy—"

"His what?" cried Victoria, who had heard as yet nothing of the City disaster.

"His bankruptcy. Mr. Cassilis is ruined."

"Ruined! Mr. Cassilis!"

She was startled out of herself.

Ruined! The thought of such disaster had never once crossed her brains. Ruined! That Colossus of wealth—the man whom she married for his money, while secretly she despised his power of accumulating money!

"He is ruined, Mrs. Cassilis, and hopelessly. I have read certain papers which he put into my hands this morning. It is clear to me that his mind has been for some weeks agitated by certain anonymous letters which came to him everyday, and accused you—pardon me, Mrs. Cassilis—accused you of—infidelity. The letters state that there is a secret of some kind connected with your former acquaintance with Mr. Colquhoun; that you have been lately in the habit of receiving him or meeting him everyday; that you were in his chambers one evening when Mr. Cassilis called; with other particulars extremely calculated to excite jealousy and suspicion. Lastly, he was sent by the writer to Twickenham. The rest, I believe you know."

She made no reply.

"There can be no doubt, not the least doubt, that had your husband's mind been untroubled, this would never have happened. The disaster is due to his jealousy."

"I could kill her!" said Mrs. Cassilis, clenching her fist. "I could kill her!"

"Kill whom?"

"The woman who wrote those letters. It was a woman. No man could have done such a thing. A woman's trick. Go on."

"There is nothing more to say. How far other people are involved with your husband, I cannot tell. I am going now into the City to find out if I can. Your wild words, Mrs. Cassilis, and your unguarded conduct, have brought about misfortunes on which you little calculated. But I am not here to reproach you."

"You are my husband's man of business, I suppose," she replied coldly—"a paid servant of his. What you say has no importance, nor what you think. What did Lawrence bid you tell me?"

Joseph Jagenal's face clouded for a moment. But what was the good of feeling resentment with such a woman, and in such a miserable business?

"You have two courses open to you," he went on. "You may, by repeating the confession you made in the hearing of Mr. Cassilis, draw upon yourself such punishment as the Law, provided the confession be true, can inflict. That will be a grievous thing to you. It will drive you out of society, and brand you as a criminal; it will lock you up for two years in prison; it will leave a stigma never to be forgotten or obliterated; it means ruin far, far worse than what you have brought on Mr. Cassilis. On the other hand, you may keep silence. This at least will secure the legitimacy of your boy, and will keep for you the amount settled on you at your marriage. But you may choose. If the statement you made is true, of course I can be no party to compounding a felony—"

"And Lawrence?" she interposed. "What does Lawrence say?"

"In any case Mr. Colquhoun will leave England at once."

"He will marry that Phillis girl? You may tell him," she hissed out, "that I will do anything and suffer anything rather than consent to his marrying her, or anyone else."

"Mr. Colquhoun informs me further," pursued the crafty lawyer, "that, for some reason only known to himself, he will never marry during the life of a certain person. Phillis Fleming will probably marry the Honourable Mr. Ronald Dunquerque."

She buried her head in her hands, not to hide any emotion, for there was none to hide, but to think. Presently she rose, and said, "Take me to—my husband, if you please."

Joseph Jagenal, as a lawyer, is tolerably well versed in such wickedness and deceptions as the human heart is capable of. At the same time, he acknowledges to himself that the speech made by Victoria Cassilis to her husband, and the manner in which it was delivered, surpassed anything he had ever experienced or conceived.

Gabriel Cassilis was sitting in an arm-chair near his table. In his arms was his infant son, a child of a year old, for whose amusement he was dangling a bunch of keys. The nurse was standing beside him.

When his wife opened the door he looked up, and there crossed his face a sudden expression of such repulsion, indignation, and horror, that the lawyer fairly expected the lady to give way altogether. But she did not. Then Mrs. Cassilis motioned the nurse to leave them, and Victoria said what she had come to say. She stood at the table, in the attitude of one who commands respect rather than one who entreats pardon. Her accentuation was precise, and her words as carefully chosen as if she had written them down first. But her husband held his eyes down, as if afraid of meeting her gaze. You would have called him a culprit waiting for reproof and punishment.

"I learn today for the first time that you have suffered from certain attacks made upon me by an anonymous writer; I learn also for the first time, and to my great regret, that you have suffered in fortune as well as in health. I have myself been too ill in mind and body to be told anything. I am come to say at once that I am sorry if any rash words of mine have given you pain, or any foolish actions of mine have given you reason for jealousy. The exact truth is that Lawrence Colquhoun and I were once engaged. The breaking off of that engagement caused me at the time the greatest unhappiness. I resolved then that he should never be engaged to any other girl if I could prevent it by any means in my power. My whole action of late, which appeared to you as if I was running after an old lover, was the prevention of his engagement, which I determined to break off, with Phillis Fleming. In the heat of my passion I used words which were not true. They occurred to me at the moment. I said he was my husband. I meant to have said my promised husband. You now know, Mr. Cassilis, the whole secret. I am deeply humiliated in having to confess my revengeful spirit. I am punished in your affliction."

Always herself; always her own punishment.

"We can henceforth, I presume, Mr. Cassilis, resume our old manner of life."

Mr. Cassilis made no answer, but he patted the head of his child, and Joseph Jagenal saw the tears running down his cheeks. For he knew that the woman lied to him.

"For the sake of the boy, Mr. Cassilis," the lawyer pleaded, "let things go on as before."

He made no sign.

"Will you let me say something for you in the interests of the child?"

He nodded.

"Then, Mrs. Cassilis, your husband consents that there shall be no separation and no scandal. But it will be advisable for you both that there shall be as little intercourse as possible. Your husband will breakfast and dine by himself, and occupy his own apartments. You are free, provided you live in the same house, and keep up appearances, to do whatever you please. But you will not obtrude your presence upon your husband."

Mr. Cassilis nodded again. Then he sought his dictionary, and hunted for a word. It was the word he had first found, and was "Silence."

"Yes; you will also observe strict silence on what has passed at Twickenham, here or elsewhere. Should that silence not be observed, the advisers of Mr. Cassilis will recommend such legal measures as may be necessary."

Again Gabriel Cassilis nodded. He had not once looked up at his wife since that first gaze, in which he concentrated the hatred and loathing of his speechless soul.

"Is that all?" asked Victoria Cassilis. "Or have we more arrangements?"

"That is all, madam," said Joseph, opening the door with great ceremony.

She went away as she had come, with cold haughtiness. Nothing seemed to touch her; not her husband's misery; not his ruin; not the sight of her child. One thing only pleased her. Lawrence Colquhoun would not marry during her lifetime. Bah! she would live a hundred years, and he should never marry at all.

In her own room was her maid.

"Tomlinson," said Mrs. Cassilis—in spite of her outward calm, her nerves were strung to the utmost, and she felt that she must speak to someone—"Tomlinson, if a woman wrote anonymous letters about you, if those letters brought misery and misfortune, what would you do to that woman?"

"I do not know, ma'am," said Tomlinson, whose cheeks grew white.

"I will kill her, Tomlinson! I will kill her! I will get those letters and prove the handwriting, and find that woman out. I will devote my life to it, and I will have no mercy on her when I have found her. I will kill her—somehow—by poison—by stabbing—somehow. Don't tremble, woman; I don't mean you. And Tomlinson, forget what I have said."

Tomlinson could not forget. She tottered from the room, trembling in every limb.

The wretched maid had her revenge. In full and overflowing measure. And yet she was not satisfied. The exasperating thing about revenge is that it never does satisfy, but leaves you at the end as angry as at the beginning. Your enemy is crushed; you have seen him tied to a stake, as is the pleasant wont of the Red Indian, and stick arrows, knives, and red-hot things into him. These hurt so much that he is glad to die. But he is dead, and you can do no more to him. And it seems a pity, because if you had kept him alive, you might have thought of other and more dreadful ways of revenge. These doubts will occur to the most revenge-satiated Christian, and they lead to self-reproach. After all, one might just as well forgive a fellow at once.

Mrs. Cassilis was a selfish and heartless woman. All the harm that was done to her was the loss of her great wealth. And what had her husband done to Tomlinson that he should be stricken? And what had others done who were involved with him in the great disaster?

Tomlinson was so terrified, however, by the look which crossed her mistress's face, that she went away that very evening; pretended to have received a telegram from Liverpool; when she got there wrote for boxes and wages, with a letter in somebody else's writing, *for a reason*, to her mistress, and then went to America, where she had relations. She lives now in a city of the Western States, where her brother keeps a store. She is a leader in her religious circle; and I think that if she were to see Victoria Cassilis by any accident in the streets of that city, she would fly again, and to the farthest corners of the earth.

So much for revenge; and I do hope that Tomlinson's example will be laid to heart, and pondered by other ladies'-maids whose mistresses are selfish and sharp-tempered.

XLV

"Farewell to all my greatness."

The last day of Gilead Beck's wealth. He rose as unconscious of his doom as that frolicsome kid whose destiny brought the tear to Delia's eye. Had he looked at the papers he would at least have ascertained that Gabriel Cassilis was ruined. But he had a rooted dislike to newspapers, and never looked at them. He classed the editor of the *Times* with Mr. Huggins of Clearville or Mr. Van Cott of Chicago, but supposed that he had a larger influence. Politics he despised; criticism was beyond him; with social matters he had no concern; and it would wound the national self-respect were he to explain how carelessly he regarded matters which to Londoners seem of world-wide importance.

On this day Gilead rose early because there was a good deal to look after. His breakfast was fixed for eleven—a real breakfast. At six he was dressed, and making, in his mind's eye, the arrangements for seating his guests. Mr. and Mrs. Cassilis, Mrs. L'Estrange and Phillis, Lawrence Colquhoun, Ladds, and Jack Dunquerque—all his most intimate friends were coming. He had also invited the Twins, but a guilty conscience made them send an excuse. They were now sitting at home, sober by compulsion and in great wretchedness, as has been seen.

The breakfast was to be held in the same room in which he once entertained the men of genius, but the appointments were different. Gilead Beck now went in for flowers, to please the ladies: flowers in June do not savour of ostentation. Also for fruit: strawberries, apricots, cherries and grapes in early June are not things quite beyond precedent, and his conscience acquitted him of display which might seem shoddy. And when the table was laid, with its flowers and fruit and dainty cold dishes garnished with all sorts of pretty things, it was, he felt, a work of art which reflected the highest credit on himself and everybody concerned.

Gilead Beck was at great peace with himself that morning. He was resolved on putting into practice at once some of those schemes which the Golden Butterfly demanded as loudly as it could whisper. He would start that daily paper which should be independent of commercial success; have no advertisements; boil down the news; do without long leaders; and always speak the truth, without evasion, equivocation, suppression, or exaggeration. A miracle in journalism. He would run the great National Drama which should revive the ancient glories of the stage. And for the rest he would be guided by circumstances, and when a big thing had to be done he would step in with his Pile, and do that big thing by himself.

There was in all this perhaps a little over-rating the power of the Pile; but Gilead Beck was, after all, only human. Think what an inflation of dignity, brother De Pauper-et-egens, would follow in your own case on the acquisition of fifteen hundred pounds a day.

Another thing pleased our Gilead. He knew that in his own country the difficulty of getting into what he felt to be the best society would be insuperable. The society of shoddy, the companionship with the quickly grown rich, and the friendship of the gilded bladder are in the reach of every wealthy man. But Gilead was a man of finer feelings; he wanted more than this; he wanted the friendship of those who were born in the purple of good breeding. In New York he could not have got this. In London he did get it. His friends were ladies and gentlemen; they not only tolerated him, but they liked him; they were people to whom he could give nothing, but they courted his society, and this pleased him more than any other part of his grand Luck. There was no great merit in their liking the man. Rude as his life had been, he was gifted with the tenderest and kindest heart; lowly born and roughly bred, he was yet a man of boundless sympathies. And because he had kept his self-respect throughout, and was ashamed of nothing, he slipt easily and naturally into the new circle, picking up without difficulty what was lacking of external things. Yet he was just the same as when he landed in England; with the same earnest, almost solemn, way of looking at things; the same gravity; the same twang which marked his nationality. He affected nothing and pretended nothing; he hid nothing and was ashamed of nothing; he paraded nothing and wanted to be thought no other than the man he was—the ex-miner, ex-adventurer, ex-everything, who by a lucky stroke hit upon Ile, and was living on the profits. And perhaps in all the world there was no happier man than Gilead Beck on that bright June morning, which was to be the last day of his grandeur. A purling stream of content murmured and babbled hymns of praise in his heart. He had no fears; his nerves were strong; he expected nothing but a continuous flow of prosperity and happiness.

The first to arrive was Jack Dunquerque. Now, if this youth had read the papers he would have been able to communicate some of the fatal news. But he had not, because he was full of Phillis. And if any rumour of the Eldorado collapse smote his ears, it smote them unnoticed, because he did not connect Eldorado with Gilead Beck. What did it matter to this intolerably selfish young man how many British speculators lost their money by the Eldorado smash when he was going to meet Phillis. After all, the round world and all that is therein do really rotate about a pole—of course invisible—which goes through every man's own centre of gravity, and sticks out in a manner which may be felt by him. And the reason why men have so many different opinions is, I am persuaded, this extraordinary, miraculous, multitudinous, simultaneous revolution of the earth upon her million axes. Enough for Jack that Phillis was coming—Phillis, whom he had not seen since the discovery—more memorable to him than any made by Traveller or Physicist—of the Coping-stone.

Jack came smiling and bounding up the stairs with agile spring—a good-half hour before the time. Perhaps Phillis might be before him. But she was not.

Then came Ladds. Gilead Beck saw that there was some trouble upon him, but forbore to ask him what it was. He bore his heavy inscrutable look, such as that with which he had been wont to meet gambling losses, untoward telegrams from Newmarket, and other buffetings of Fate.

Then came a letter from Mrs. Cassilis. Her husband was ill, and therefore she could not come.

Then came a letter from Lawrence Colquhoun. He had most important business in the City, and therefore he could not come.

"Seems like the Wedding-feast," said Gilead irreverently. He was a little disconcerted by the defection of so many guests; but he had a leaf taken out of the table, and cheerfully waited for the remaining two.

They came at last, and I think the hearts of all three leaped within them at sight of Phillis's happy face. If it was sweet before, when Jack first met her, with the mysterious look of childhood on it, it was far sweeter now with the bloom and blush of conscious womanhood, the modest light of maidenly joy with which she met her lover. Jack rushed, so to speak, at her hand, and held it with a ridiculous shamelessness only excusable on the ground that they were almost in a family circle. Then Phillis shook hands with Gilead Beck, with a smile of gratitude which meant a good deal more than preliminary thanks for the coming breakfast. Then it came to Ladds's turn. He turned very red—I do not know why—and whispered in his deepest bass—

WALTER BESANT AND JAMES RICE

"Know all about it. Lucky beggar, Jack! Wish you happiness!"

"Thank you, Captain Ladds," Phillis replied, in her fearless fashion. "I am very happy already. And so is Jack."

"Wanted yesterday," Ladds went on, in the same deep whisper—"wanted yesterday to offer some slight token of regard—found I couldn't—no more money—Eldorado smash—all gone—locked in boxes—found ring—once my mother's. Will you accept it?"

Phillis understood the ring, but she did not understand the rest of the speech. It was one of those old-fashioned rings set in pearls and brilliants. She was not by any means above admiring rings, and she accepted it with a cheerful alacrity.

"Sell up," Ladds growled,—"go away—do something—earn the daily crust—"

"But I don't understand—" she interrupted.

"Never mind. Tell you after breakfast. Tell you all presently."

And then they went to breakfast.

It was rather a silent party. Ladds was, as might have been expected of a man who had lost his all, disposed to taciturnity. Jack and Phillis were too happy to talk much. Agatha L'Estrange and the host had all the conversation to themselves.

Agatha asked him if the dainty spread before them was the usual method of breakfast in America. Gilead Beck replied that of late years he had been accustomed to call a chunk of cold pork with a piece of bread a substantial breakfast, and that the same luxuries furnished him, as a rule, with dinner.

"The old life," he said, "had its points, I confess. For those who love cold pork it was one long round of delirious joy. And there was always the future to look forward to. Now the future has come I like it better. My experience, Mrs. L'Estrange, is that you may divide men into two classes—those who've got a future, and those who haven't. I belonged to the class who had a future. Sometimes we miss it. And I feel like to cry whenever I think of the boys with a bright future before them, who fell in the War at my side, not in tens, but in hundreds. Sometimes we find it. I found it when I struck Ile. And always, for those men, whether the future come early or whether it come late, it lies bright and shinin' before them, and so they never lose hope."

"And have women no future as well as men, Mr. Beck?" asked Phillis.

"I don't know, Miss Fleming. But I hope you have. Before my Golden Butterfly came to me I was lookin' forward for my future, and I knew it was bound to come in some form or other. I looked forward for thirty years; my youth was gone when it came, and half my manhood. But it is here."

"Perhaps, Mr. Beck," said Mrs. L'Estrange, who was a little *rococo* in her morality, "it is well that this great fortune did not come to you when you were younger."

"You think that, madam? Perhaps it is so. To fool around New York would be a poor return for the Luck of the Butterfly. Yes; better as it is. Providence knows very well what to be about; it don't need promptin' from us. And impatience is no manner of use, not the least use in the world. At the right time the Luck comes; at the right time the Luck will go. Yes,"—he looked solemnly round the table,—"some day the Luck is bound to go. When it goes, I hope I shall be prepared for the change. But if it goes tomorrow, it cannot take away, Mrs. L'Estrange, the memory of these few months, your friendship, and yours, Miss Fleming. There's things which do not depend upon Ile; more things than I thought formerly; things which money cannot do. More than once I thought my pile ought to find it easy to do somethin' useful before the time comes. But the world is a more tangled web than I used to think."

"There are always the poor among us," said the good Agatha.

"Yes, madam, that is true. And there always will be. More you give to the poor, more you make them poor. There's folks goin' up and folks goin' down. You in England help the folks goin' down. You make them fall easy. I want to help the folks goin' up."

At this moment a telegram was brought for him.

It was from his London bankers. They informed him that a cheque for a small sum had been presented, but that his balance was already overdrawn; and that they had received a telegram from New York on which they would be glad to see him.

Gilead Beck read it, and could not understand it. The cheque was for his own weekly account at the hotel.

He laid the letter aside, and went on with his exposition of the duties and responsibilities of wealth. He pointed out to Mrs. L'Estrange, who alone listened to him—Jack was whispering to Phillis, and Ladds was absorbed in thoughts of his own—that when he arrived in London he was possessed with the idea that all he had to do, in order to protect, benefit, and advance humanity, was to found a series of institutions; that, in the pursuit of this idea, he had visited and examined all the British institutions he could hear of; and that his conclusions were that they were all a failure.

"For," he concluded, "what have you done? Your citizens need not save money, because a hospital, a church, an almshouse, a dispensary, and a workhouse stand in every parish; they need not be moral, because there's homes for the repentant in every other street. All around they are protected by charity and the State. Even if they get knocked down in the street, they need not fight, because there's a policeman within easy hail. You breed your poor, Mrs. L'Estrange, and you take almighty care to keep them always with you. In my country he who can work and won't work goes to the wall; he starves, and a good thing too. Here he gets fat."

"Every way," he went on, "you encourage your people to do nothing. Your clever young men get a handsome income for life, I am told, at Oxford and Cambridge, if they pass one good examination. For us the examination is only the beginning. Your clergymen get a handsome income for life, whether they do their work or not. Ours have got to go on preachin' well and livin' well; else we want to know the reason why. You give your subalterns as much as other nations give their colonels; you set them down to a grand mess everyday as if they were all born lords. You keep four times as many naval officers as you want, and ten times as many generals. It's all waste and lavishin' from end to end. And as for your Royal Family, I reckon that I'd find a dozen families in Massachusetts alone who'd run the Royal Mill for a tenth of the money. I own they wouldn't have the same gracious manners," he added. "And your Princess is—wal, if Miss Fleming were Princess, she couldn't do the part better. Perhaps gracious manners are worth paying for."

Here another telegram was brought him.

It was from New York. It informed him in plain and intelligible terms that his wells had all run dry, that his credit was exhausted, and that no more bills would be honoured.

He read this aloud with a firm voice and unfaltering eye. Then he looked round him, and said solemnly—

"The time has come. It's come a little sooner than I expected. But it has come at last."

He was staggered, but he remembered something which consoled him.

"At least," he said, "if the income is gone, the Pile remains. That's close upon half a million of English money. We can do something with that. Mr. Cassilis has got it all for me."

"Who?" cried Ladds eagerly.

"Mr. Gabriel Cassilis, the great English financier."

"He is ruined," said Ladds. "He has failed for two millions sterling. If your money is in his hands—"

"Part of it, I believe, was in Eldorado Stock."

"The Eldoradians cannot pay their interest. And the stock has sunk to nothing. Gabriel Cassilis has lost all my money in it—at least, I have lost it on his recommendation."

"Your money all gone, Tommy?" cried Jack.

"All, Jack—Ladds' Aromatic Cocoa—Fragrant—Nutritious—no use now—business sold twenty years ago. Proceeds sunk in Eldorado Stock. Nothing but the smell left."

And while they were gazing in each other's face with mute bewilderment, a third messenger arrived with a letter.

It was from Mr. Mowll the secretary. It informed poor Gilead that Mr. Gabriel Cassilis had drawn, in accordance with his power of attorney, upon him to the following extent. A bewildering mass of figures followed, at the bottom of which was the total—Gilead Beck's two million dollars. That, further, Gabriel Cassilis, always, it appeared, acting on the wishes of Mr. Beck, had invested the whole sum in Eldorado Stock. That, &c. He threw the letter on the table half unread. Then, after a moment's hesitation, he rose solemnly, and sought the corner of the room in which stood the safe containing the Emblem of his Luck. He opened it, and took out the box of glass and gold which held it. This was covered with a case of green leather. He carried it to the table. They all crowded round while he raised the leathern cover and displayed the Butterfly.

"Has anyone," he lifted his head and looked helplessly round,—"has anyone felt an airthquake?"

For a strange thing had happened The wings of the insect were lying on the floor of the box; the white quartz which formed its body had slipped from the gold wire which held it up, and the Golden Butterfly was in pieces.

He opened the box with a little gold key and took out the fragments of the two wings and the body.

"Gone!" he said. "Broken!"

> *"If this golden Butterfly fall and break,*
> *Farewell the Luck of Gilead P. Beck."'*

"Your own lines, Mr. Dunquerque. Broken into little bits it is. The Ile run dry, the credit exhausted, and the Pile fooled away."

No one spoke.

"I am sorry for you most, Mr. Dunquerque. I am powerful sorry, sir. I had hoped, with the assistance of Miss Fleming, to divide that Pile with you. Now, sir, I've got nothing. Not a red cent left to divide with a beggar.

"Mrs. L'Estrange," he went on, "those last words of mine were prophetic. When I am gone back to America—I suppose the odds and ends here will pay my passage—you'll remember that I said the Luck would some day go."

It was all so sudden, so incomprehensible, that no one present had a word to say, either of sympathy or of sorrow.

Gilead Beck proceeded with his soliloquy:

"I've had a real high time for three months; the best three months of my life. Whatever happens more can't touch the memory of the last three months. I've met English ladies and made friends of English gentlemen. There's Amer'can ladies and Amer'can gentlemen, but I can't speak of them, because I never went into their society You don't find ladies and gentlemen in Empire City. And in all the trades I've turned my attention to, from school-keepin' to editing, there's not been one where Amer'can ladies cared to show their hand. That means that the Stars and Stripes may be as good as the Union Jack—come to know them."

He stopped and pulled himself together with a laugh.

"I can't make it out,—somehow. Seems as if I'm in a dream. Is it real? Is the story of the Golden Butterfly a true story, or is it made up out of some man's brain?"

"It is real, Mr. Beck," said Phillis, softly putting her hand in his. "It is real. No one could have invented such a story. See, dear Mr. Beck, you that we all love so much, there is you in it, and I am in it—and—and the Twins. Why, if people saw us all in a book they would say it was impossible. I am the only girl in all the civilised world who can neither read nor write—and Jack doesn't mind it—and you are the only man who ever found the Golden Butterfly. Indeed it is all real."

"It is all real, Beck," Jack echoed. "You have had the high time, and sorry indeed we are that it is over. But perhaps it is not all over. Surely something out of the two million dollars must have remained."

Mr. Beck pointed sorrowfully to the three pieces which were the fragments of the Butterfly.

"Nothing is left," he said. "Nothing except the solid gold that made his cage. And that will go to pay the hotel-bill."

Mrs. L'Estrange looked on in silence. What was this quiet lady, this woman of even and uneventful life, to say in the presence of such misfortune?

Ladds held out his hand.

"Worth twenty of any of us," he said. "We are in the same boat."

"And you, too, Captain Ladds!" Gilead cried. "It is worse than my own misfortune, because I am a rough man and can go back to the rough life. No, Mrs. L'Estrange—no, my dear young lady—I can't—not with the same light heart as before—you've spoiled me. I must strike out something new—away from Empire City and Ile and gold. I'm spoiled. It's not the cold chunk of pork that I am afraid of; it is the beautiful life and the sweetness that I'm going to lose. I said I hoped I should be prepared to meet the fall of my Luck—when it came. But I never thought it would come like this."

"Stay with us, Mr. Beck," said Phillis. "Don't go back to the old life."

"Stay with us," said Jack. "We will all live together."

"Do not leave us, Mr. Beck," said Mrs. L'Estrange. (Women can blush, although they may be past forty.) "Stay here with your friends."

He looked from one to the other, and something like a tear glittered in his eye. But he shook his head.

Then he took up the wings of the Butterfly, the pretty golden *laminæ* cut in the perfect shape of a wing, marked and veined by Nature as if, for once she was determined to show that she too could be an Artist and imitate her self. They lay in her hands, and he looked fondly at them.

"What shall I do with these?" he said softly. "They have been very good to me. They have given me the pleasantest hours of my life. They have made me dream of power as if I was Autocrat of All the Russians. Say, Mrs. L'Estrange—since my chief pleasure has come through Mr. Dunquerque—may I offer the broken Butterfly to Miss Fleming?"

He laid the wings before her with a sweet sad smile. Jack took them up and looked at them. In the white quartz were the little holes where the wings had fitted. He put them back in their old place—the wings in the quartz. They fitted exactly, and in a moment the butterfly was as it had always been.

Jack deftly bent round it again the golden wire which held it to the golden flower. Singular to relate, the wire fitted like the wings just the same as before, and the Butterfly vibrated on its perch again.

WALTER BESANT AND JAMES RICE

"It's wonderful!" cried Gilead Beck. "It's the Luck I've given away. It's gone to you, Miss Fleming. But it won't take the form of Ile."

"Then take it back, Mr. Beck," cried Phillis.

"No, young lady. The Luck left me of its own accord. That was shown when the Butterfly fell off the wires. It is yours now, yours; and you will make a better use of it.

"I think," he went on, with his hand upon the golden case,—"I think there's a Luck in the world which I never dreamed of, a better Luck than Ile. Mrs. L'Estrange, you know what sort of Luck I mean?"

"Yes, Mr. Beck, I know," she replied.

Phillis laid her hands on Jack's shoulder, while his arm stole round her waist.

"It is Love. Mr. Beck," said the girl. "Yes; that is the best Luck in all the world, and I am sure of it."

Jack stooped and kissed her. The simplicity and innocence of this maiden went to Gilead Beck's heart. They were a religion to him, an education. In the presence of that guileless heart all earthly thoughts dropped from his soul, and he was, like the girl before him, pure in heart and clean in memory. That is indeed the sweet enchantment of innocence; a bewitchment out of which we need never awake unless we like.

"Take the case and all, Miss Fleming," said Gilead Beck.

But she would not have the splendid case with its thick plate glass and solid gold pillars.

Then Gilead Beck brought out the little wooden box, the same in which the Golden Butterfly lay when he ran from the Bear on the slopes of the Sierra Nevada. And Phillis laid her new treasure in the cotton-wool and slung the box by its steel chain round his neck, laughing in a solemn fashion.

While they talked thus sadly, the door opened, and Lawrence Colquhoun stood before them.

Agatha cried out when she saw him, because he was transformed. The lazy insouciant look was gone; a troubled look was in its place. Worse than a troubled look—a look of misery; a look of self-reproach; a look as of a criminal brought to the bar and convicted.

"Lawrence!" cried Mrs. L'Estrange.

He came into the room in a helpless sort of way, his hands shaking before him like those of some half-blind old man.

"Phillis," he said, in hoarse voice, "forgive me!"

"What have I to forgive, Lawrence?"

"Forgive me!" he repeated humbly. "Nay, you do not understand. Dunquerque, it is for you to speak—for all of you—you all love Phillis. Agatha—you love her—you used to love me too. How shall I tell you?"

"I think we guess," said Gilead.

"I did it for the best, Phillis. I thought to double your fortune. Cassilis said I should double it. I thought to double my own. I put all your money, child, every farthing of your money, in Eldorado Stock by his advice, and all my own too. And it is all gone—every penny of it gone."

Jack Dunquerque clasped Phillis tighter by the hand.

She only laughed.

"Why, Lawrence," she said, "what if you have lost all my money? Jack doesn't care. Do you Jack?"

"No, darling, no," said Jack. And at the moment—such was the infatuation of this young man—he really did not care.

"Lawrence," said Agatha, "you acted for the best. Don't dear Lawrence, don't trouble too much. Captain Ladds has lost all his fortune, too—and Mr. Beck has lost all his—and we are all ruined together."

"All ruined together!" echoed Gilead Beck, looking at Mrs. L'Estrange. "Gabriel Cassilis is a wonderful man. I always said he was a wonderful man."

In the evening the three ruined men sat together in Gilead's room.

"Nothing saved, Colquhoun?" asked Ladds, after a long pause.

"Nothing. The stock was 70 when I bought in: 70 at 10 percent. It is now anything you like—4, 6, 8, 16—what you please—because no one will buy it."

"Wal," said Gilead Beck, "it does seem rough on us all, and perhaps it's rougher on you two than it is on me. But to think, only to think, that such an almighty Pile should be fooled away on a darned half-caste State like Eldorado! And for all of us to believe Mr. Gabriel Cassilis a whole-souled, high toned speculator.

"Once I thought," he continued, "that we Amer'cans must be the Ten Tribes; because, I said, nobody but one out of the Ten Tribes would get such a providential lift as the Golden Butterfly. Gentlemen, my opinions are changed since this morning. I believe we're nothing better, not a single cent better, than one of the kicked-out Tribes. I may be an Amalekite, or I may be a Hivite; but I'm darned if I ever call myself again one of the children of Abraham."

Chapter the Last

"Whisper Love, ye breezes; sigh
In Love's content, soft air of morn;
Let eve in brighter sunsets die,
And day with brighter dawn be born."

It is a week since the disastrous day. Gilead Beck has sold the works of art with which he intended to found his Grand National Collection; he has torn up his great schemes for a National Theatre, a Grand National Paper; he has ceased to think, for the delectation of the Golden Butterfly, about improving the human race. His gratitude to that prodigy of Nature has so far cooled that he now considers it more in the light of a capricious sprite, a sort of Robin Good-fellow, than as a benefactor. He has also changed his views as to the construction of the round earth, and all that is therein. Ile, he says, may be found by other lucky adventures; but Ile is not to be depended on for a permanence. He would now recommend those who strike Ile to make their Pile as quickly as may be, and devote all their energies to the safety of that pile. And as to the human race, it may slide.

"What's the good," he says to Jack Dunquerque, "of helpin' up those that are bound to climb? Let them climb. And what's the good of tryin' to save those that are bound to fall? Let them fall. I'm down myself; but I mean to get up again."

It is sad to record that Mr. Burls, the picture-dealer, refused to buy back again the great picture of "Sisera and Jael." No one would purchase the work at all. Mr. Beck offered it to the Langham Hotel as a gift. The directors firmly declined to accept it. When it was evident that this remarkable effort of genius was appreciated by no one, Gilead Beck resolved on leaving it where it was. It is rumoured that the manager of the hotel bribed the owner of a certain Regent Street restaurant to take it away; and I have heard that it now hangs, having been greatly cut down, on the wall of that establishment, getting its tones mellowed day by day with the steam of roast and boiled. As for the other pictures, Mr. Burls expressed his extreme sorrow that temporary embarrassment prevented him purchasing them back at the price given for them. He afterwards told Mr. Beck that the unprincipled picture-dealer who did ultimately buy them, at the price of so much a square foot, and as second-rate copies, was a disgrace to his honourable profession. He, he said, stood high in public estimation for truth, generosity, and fair dealing. None but genuine works came from his own establishment; and what he called a Grooze was a Grooze, and nothing but a Grooze.

As for the Pile, Gilead's power of attorney had effectually destroyed that. There was not a cent left; not one single coin to rub against another. All was gone in that great crash.

He called upon Gabriel Cassilis. The financier smiled upon him with his newly-born air of sweetness and trust; but, as we have seen, he could no longer speak, and there was nothing in his face to express sorrow or repentance.

Gilead found himself, when all was wound up, the possessor of that single cheque which Joseph Jagenal had placed in his hands, and which, most fortunately for himself, he had not paid into the bank.

Four hundred pounds. With that, at forty-five, he was to begin the world again. After all, the majority of mankind at forty five have much less than four hundred pounds.

He heard from Canada that the town he had built, the whole of which belonged to him, was deserted again. There was a quicker rush out of it than into it. It stands there now, more lonely than Empire City—its derricks and machinery rusting and dropping to pieces, the houses empty and neglected, the land relapsing into its old condition of bog and marsh. But Gilead Beck will never see it again.

He kept away from Twickenham during this winding-up and settlement of affairs. It was a week later when, his mind at rest and his conscience clear of bills and doubts, because now there was nothing more to lose, he called at the house where he had spent so many pleasant hours.

Mrs. L'Estrange received him. She was troubled in look, and the traces of tears were on her face.

"It is a most unfortunate time," Gilead said sympathetically; "a most unfortunate time."

"Blow after blow, Mr. Beck," Agatha sobbed. "Stroke upon stroke."

"That is so, madam. They've got the knife well in, this time, and when they give it a twist we're bound to cry out. You've thought me selfish, I know, not to inquire before."

"No, Mr. Beck; no. It is only too kind of you to think of us in your overwhelming disaster. I have never spent so wretched a week. Poor Lawrence has literally not a penny left, except what he gets from the sale of his horses, pictures and things. Captain Ladds is the same; Phillis has no longer a farthing; and now, Oh dear, Oh dear. I am going to lose her altogether!"

"But when she marries Mr. Dunquerque you will see her often."

"No, no. Haven't they told you? Jack has got almost nothing—only ten thousand pounds altogether; and they have made up their minds to emigrate. They are going to Virginia, where Jack will buy a small estate."

"Is that so?" asked Gilead meditatively.

"Lawrence says that he and Captain Ladds will go away together somewhere; perhaps back to Empire City."

"And you will be left alone—you, Mrs. L'Estrange—all alone in this country, and ruined. It mustn't be." He straightened himself up, and looked round the room. "It must not be, Mrs. L'Estrange. You know me partly—that is you know the manner of man I wish to seem and try to be; you know what I have been. You do not know, because you cannot guess, the things which you have put into my head."

Mrs. L'Estrange blushed and began to tremble. Could it be possible that he was actually going to—

He was.

"You and I together, Mrs. L'Estrange, are gone to wreck in this almighty hurricane. I've got one or two thousand dollars left; perhaps you will have as much, perhaps *not*. Mrs. L'Estrange, you will think it presumptuous in a rough American—not an American gentleman by birth and raising—to offer you such protection and care as he can give to the best of women? We, too, will go to Virginia with Mr. Dunquerque and his wife; we will settle near them, and watch their happiness. The Virginians are a kindly folk, and love the English people, especially if they are of gentle birth. Say, Mrs. L'Estrange."

"O Mr. Beck! I am forty years of age!"

"And I am five and forty."

Just then Phillis and Jack burst into the room. They did not look at all like being ruined; they were wild with joy and good spirits.

"And you are going to Virginia, Mr. Dunquerque?" said Gilead. "I am thinking of going, too, if I can persuade this lady to go with me."

"O Agatha! come with us!"

"Come with me," corrected Gilead.

Then Phillis saw how things lay—what a change in Phillis, to see so much?—and half laughing, but more in seriousness than in mirth, threw her arms round Agatha's neck.

"Will you come, dear Agatha? He is a good man, and he loves you; and we will all live near together and be happy."

THREE SHORT SCENES TO CONCLUDE my story.

It is little more than a year since Agatha L'Estrange, as shy and blushing as any maiden—much more shy than Phillis—laid her hand in Gilead's, with the confession, half sobbed out, "And it isn't a mistake you are making, because I am not ruined at all. It is only you and these poor children and Lawrence."

We are back again to Empire City. It is the early fall, September. The yellow leaves clothe all the forests with brown and gold; the sunlight strikes upon the peaks and ridges of the great Sierra, lights up the broad belt of wood making shadows blacker than night, and lies along the grass grown streets of the deserted Empire City. Two men in hunting-dress are making their way slowly through the grass and weeds that choke the pathway.

"Don't like it, Colquhoun," says one; "more ghostly than ever."

They push on, and presently the foremost, Ladds, starts back with a cry.

"What is it?" asks Colquhoun.

They push aside the brambles, and behold a skeleton. The body has been on its knees, but now only the bones are left. They are clothed in the garb of the celestial, and one side of the skull is broken in, as if with a shot.

"It must be my old friend Achow," said Colquhoun calmly. "See, he's been murdered."

In the dead of night Ladds awakened Colquhoun.

"Can't help it," he said; "very sorry. Ghosts walking about the stairs. Says the ghost of Achow to the shade Leeching, 'No your piecy pidgin makee shootee me.' Don't like ghosts, Colquhoun."

Next morning they left Empire City. Ladds was firm in the conviction that he had heard and seen a Chinaman's ghost, and was resolute against stopping another night in the place.

Just outside the town they made another discovery.

"Good Lord!" cried Ladds, frightened out of sobriety of speech. "It rains skeletons. Look there; he's beckoning!"

And, to be sure, before them was raised, with finger as of invitation, a skeleton hand.

This, too, belonged to a complete assortment of human bones clad in Chinese dress. By its side lay a rusty pistol. Lawrence picked it up.

"By Gad!" he said, "it's the same pistol I gave to Leeching. How do you read this story, Ladds?"

Ladds sat down and replied slowly. He said that he never did like reading ghost stories, and since the apparition of the murdered Achow, the night before, he should like them still less. Ghost stories, he said, are all very well until you come to see and hear a ghost. Now that he had a ghost story of his own—an original one in pigeon English—he did not intend ever to read another. Therefore Colquhoun must excuse him if he gave up the story of Leeching's skeleton entirely to his own reading. He then went on to say that he never had liked skeletons, and that he believed Empire City was nothing but a mouldy old churchyard without the church, while, as a cemetery, it wasn't a patch upon Highgate. And the mention of Highgate, he said, reminded him of Phillis; and he proposed they should both get to Virginia, and call upon Jack and his wife.

All this took time to explain; and meanwhile Lawrence was poking the butt end of his gun about in the grass to see if there was anything more. There was something more. It was a bag of coarse yellow canvas, tied by a string round what had been the waist of a man. Lawrence cut the string, and opened the bag.

"We're in luck, Tommy. Look at this."

It was the gold so laboriously scraped together by the two Chinamen, which had caused, in a manner, the death of both.

"Lift it, Tommy." Colquhoun grew excited at his find. "Lift it—there must be a hundred and fifty ounces, I should think. It will be worth four or five hundred pounds. Here's a find!"

To this pair, who had only a year ago chucked away their thousands, the luck of picking up a bag of gold appeared something wonderful.

"Tommy," said Colquhoun, "I tell you what we will do. We will add this little windfall to what Beck would call your little pile and my little pile. And we'll go and buy a little farm in Virginia, too; and we will live there close to Jack and Phillis. Agatha will like it too. And there's capital shooting."

GABRIEL CASSILIS AND HIS WIFE reside at Brighton. The whole of the great fortune being lost, they have nothing but Victoria's settlement. That gives them a small income. "Enough to subsist upon," Victoria tells her friends. The old man—he looks very old and fragile now—is wheeled about in a chair on sunny days. When he is not being wheeled about he plays with his child, to whom he talks; that is, pours out a stream of meaningless words, because he will never again talk coherently. Victoria is exactly the same as ever—cold, calm, and proud. Nor is there anything whatever in her manner to her husband, if she accidentally meets him, to show that she has the slightest sorrow, shame, or repentance for the catastrophe she brought about. Joseph Jagenal is working the great Dyson will case for them, and is confident that he will get the testator's intentions, which can now be only imperfectly understood, set aside, when Gabriel Cassilis will once more become comparatively wealthy.

On a verandah in sunny Virginia, Agatha Beck sits quietly working, and crooning some old song in sheer content and peace of heart. Presently she lifts her head as she hears a step. That smile with which she greets her husband shows that she is happy in her new life. Gilead Beck is in white, with a broad straw hat, because it is in hot September. In his hand he has a letter.

"Good news, wife; good news," he says. "Jack and Phillis are coming here today, and will stay till Monday. Will be here almost as soon as the note. Baby coming, too."

"Of course, Gilead," says Agatha, smiling superior. "As if the dear girl would go anywhere without her little Philip. And six weeks old tomorrow."

(Everybody who has appreciated how very far from clever Jack Dunquerque was will be prepared to hear that he committed an enormous etymological blunder in the baptism of his boy, whom he named Philip, in the firm belief that Philip was the masculine form of Phillis.)

"Here they come! Here they are!"

Jack comes rattling up to the house in his American trap, jumps out, throws the reins to the boy, and hands out his wife with the child. Kisses and greetings.

Phillis seems at first, unchanged, except perhaps that the air of Virginia has made her sweet delicacy of features more delicate. Yet look again, and you find that she is changed. She was a child when we saw her first; then we saw her grow into a maiden; she is a wife and a mother now.

She whispers her husband.

"All right, Phil, dear.—Beck, you've got to shut your eyes for just one minute. No, turn your back so. Now you may look."

Phillis has hung round the neck of her unconscious baby, by a golden chain, the Golden Butterfly. It seems as strong and vigorous as ever;

and as it lies upon the child's white dress, it looks as if it were poised for a moment's rest, but ready for flight.

"That Inseck!" said Gilead sentimentally. "Wal, it's given me the best thing that a man can get"—he took the hand of his wife—"love and friendship. You are welcome, Phillis, to all the rest, provided that all the rest does not take away these."

"Nay," she said, her eyes filling with the gentle dew of happiness and content; "I have all that I want for myself. I have my husband and my boy—my little, little Philip! I am more than happy; and so I give to tiny Phil all the remaining Luck of the Golden Butterfly."

THE END

A Note About the Authors

Walter Besant (1836–1901) was an English novelist and historian. Born at Portsmouth, Hampshire, Besant was the son of a wine merchant, whose other children included William, a prominent mathematician, and Frank, the husband of renowned theosophist, socialist, and activist Annie Besant. After attending King's College London, he enrolled at Christ's College, Cambridge to study mathematics, graduating with first class honors in 1859. Besant worked for six years as professor of mathematics at Royal College, Mauritius, returning to London in 1867 after a period of ill-health. In 1868, he published his work *Studies in French Poetry* and was appointed to the Palestine Exploration Fund as Secretary. Three years later, Besant was called to the bar at Lincoln's Inn and began his literary collaboration with novelist James Rice. Together, they wrote such successful works of fiction as *Ready-money Mortiboy* (1872) and *The Golden Butterfly* (1876).

James Rice (1843–1882) was an English novelist. Born in Northampton and educated at Cambridge University, he became a lawyer at Lincoln's Inn in 1871. There, he befriended Walter Besant, with whom he would collaborate on over a dozen popular novels and short story collections, included *The Golden Butterfly* (1876). Their prolific working relationship ended in tragedy in 1882 with Rice's untimely death I Redhill, Surrey.

A Note from the Publisher

Spanning many genres, from non-fiction essays to literature classics to children's books and lyric poetry, Mint Edition books showcase the master works of our time in a modern new package. The text is freshly typeset, is clean and easy to read, and features a new note about the author in each volume. Many books also include exclusive new introductory material. Every book boasts a striking new cover, which makes it as appropriate for collecting as it is for gift giving. Mint Edition books are only printed when a reader orders them, so natural resources are not wasted. We're proud that our books are never manufactured in excess and exist only in the exact quantity they need to be read and enjoyed.

bookfinity™

Discover more of your favorite classics with Bookfinity™.

- Track your reading with custom book lists.
- Get great book recommendations for your personalized Reader Type.
- Add reviews for your favorite books.
- AND MUCH MORE!

Visit **bookfinity.com** and take the fun Reader Type quiz to get started.

Enjoy our classic and modern companion pairings!